Alex Brook

Alex Brook likes writing books that make her laugh as well as cry, drinks too much coffee and is fascinated with the petty evil that lurks beneath the surface of small English towns.

The Dog Day Murder

BY ALEX BROOK

A Katy Bennett Mystery

The Katy Bennett series:

The Dog Day Murder

The Laughing Minotaur

The Dog Day Murder is the first in a series of sassy-girl
crime mysteries set in the West Country featuring Katy
Bennett, journalist, romance novelist and trouble magnet.

IN THE BEGINNING...

I first met Patrick Underhill in the playground the day I started school. He pulled my pigtails. I kicked him up the bum. And I knew that I would hate him forever.

We grew up a mile apart in Sands End, a small seaside town on the Somerset coast. By the age of five-and-a-half, everyone already found his constant fibbing annoying. By six, he was well on his way to becoming a compulsive but not very accomplished liar.

The first big lie I remember him telling was when our class guinea pig – Formerly Known as Prince – disappeared: "It wasn't me who left the cage open, Miss. A man came into the classroom at break time and did it, Miss."

Liar, liar, pants on fire, Patrick. I saw you do it.

He was a weird looking kid with a pale face, sticky-out ears and jet-black hair that looked as if it was cut at home. He wasn't clean. Something unpleasant was always smeared on the lapels of his polyester school blazer, snot perhaps, or some other unidentifiable biological grease.

Patrick's family wasn't poor. His parents owned a big caravan park right on the beach. He told us he was allowed to stay up all night watching slasher horror films and he'd then inflict the gory details on us at school the next day.

As time went by Patrick's lies became more elaborate. In our last year of primary school, the police were called when he claimed a man had tried to drag him into a Vauxhall Corsa in the teachers' car park. The officers lost interest when Patrick told them the man had been the ghost of a Mexican bandit, with a knife between his teeth, a patch over one eye and wearing a sombrero.

When we went on to Sands End Comprehensive I tried to avoid him as much as possible. But, in the same way that cats are drawn to the laps of cat haters, Patrick Underhill was drawn towards me. It wasn't that he liked me – quite the reverse – but he seemed to take a perverse pleasure in winding me up. He might have been rubbish at everything else at school, but he was very good at that.

By the time I was fourteen I hated him with a passion. After he framed me for a rude limerick that he wrote on the wall of the boys' toilets, I wanted him dead. Not only was I suspended, but during the ensuing period of parental house arrest, my first boyfriend dumped me for Jo Rossiter.

A few months later, Patrick told us his mother had died of cancer when in fact she'd run off with a bathroom fittings salesman from Manchester. When puberty struck, he told everyone in our class he'd lost his virginity to a Page Three model who was staying at his father's caravan park; that he'd been abducted by aliens; that Jo Rossiter had snogged my beloved drama teacher, Mr Kent; that I wet the bed at night.

The last time I saw Patrick Underhill was thirteen years ago outside a pub called the Fighting Cocks on Sands End seafront. We were eighteen. He told me he'd won the National Lottery and was going to live in Rio de Janeiro. Yeah. Right. Of course he was.

So there you have it. He was a vile, crude, irritating, dishonest, unhygienic, thoroughly unpleasant boy.

That said, I never had him down as a killer. A few hours after I last saw him, he beat his girlfriend to death with an ashtray.

CHAPTER ONE

In winter, Sands End is a ghost town. Icy gales whip off the muddy Bristol Channel and the soggy beach is deserted. On a fine January day, with the right sort of sky, the brown sea can almost look blue. From Easter onwards the town begins to come alive and those in the tourist trade watch the long-range weather forecast with trepidation, praying for a heatwave. This year it seemed their prayers had been answered. For almost two weeks now the August skies had been cloudless with temperatures nudging thirty and the beaches were packed.

While most sensible people had bunked off work to sit in the sun, I was on a baking-hot train on my way to Bristol. I was due to meet Martin Sadler, my old news editor on the *South West Gazette* and I was feeling jittery about the meeting. The last time I'd seen Martin was just after the incident that prompted my departure from the *Gazette*'s newsroom. Secret Santa-gate, they called it.

The train was stifling and smelt bad. I hid behind my Jackie-O sunglasses and tried to ignore the screaming toddlers and the sweaty man next to me whose clammy bare arm seemed deliberately pressed against mine. The zip on my white cotton skirt was pressing onto my sunburnt hip and my fuchsia camisole was something to wear to the beach not a business meeting. I wondered if I'd have time to nip into Monsoon and buy a cover-up cardigan. I glanced at my watch. Probably not, and anyway, I was up to the limit on all my credit cards. For the umpteenth time, I raked my hair off my forehead and fanned my face.

Part of me wondered why I was even making the effort. I still didn't feel I'd had any choice about telling the editor where he could shove my job. The way I saw it, I'd been put in an untenable position through no fault of my own and resigning had been my only option.

Okay, it might have been a little bit my fault but in my opinion the editor – known as the Chief – had completely overreacted to my harmless little joke and anyway, he was a sexist bully. He'd had it coming. Of course, once I'd calmed down I'd realised that resigning had been really stupid. But by then it was too late and I was far too proud to crawl back and beg for my job. It wouldn't have done any good anyhow. He'd never liked me much.

I tried to shift my weight away from Clammy Arm Man and stared at the carriage ceiling. It was now six months since I'd left the *Gazette* and with my bank account down to pennies, I'd realised what the Chief had always known, that I needed the *Gazette* far more than the *Gazette* had ever needed me. Then yesterday, something remarkable had happened. Out of the blue, Martin had sent me an email saying he had some freelance work he might be able to give me; we should meet up for a drink. I'd bitten his arm off, "Love to! When?" So now I was on my way to see him and force down a massive slice of humble pie. I hoped I wouldn't choke on it.

Even though my train got in early I was almost late for the meeting, partly because it was hard to walk quickly in flip-flops with sweaty feet, and partly because I couldn't find the pub. Our meeting place had been Martin's choice. It was called the Naughty Monkey. I trudged through the city heat, bombarded by memories and feeling increasingly nervous. When I finally spotted the pub's sign, I realised that six months ago it had been a NatWest.

I pushed open the glass door and took in my surroundings. Talk about pretentious. The pub was on two floors. Most of the roof had been removed to create a soaring glass-domed atrium containing the most enormous palm tree I'd ever seen. It must have been at least forty feet tall. It couldn't possibly be real. The far end of the pub had been decorated to resemble a library in a stately home. Towering bookshelves contained silver trophies, hockey sticks, sepia cricket team line-ups and antique tennis racquets. Having sated their Brideshead moment, the decorators had turned the other side of the pub into a replica grocer's shop from the 1950s, complete with a fake counter, shelves of Ajax powder and tins of Heinz baked beans.

It didn't seem like Martin's sort of place at all, but then I realised that the temperature inside was at least ten degrees cooler than outside. Clearly Martin was prepared to put up with ostentatious surroundings as long as they were air conditioned. On a day as hot as this, I couldn't blame him.

Behind the bar stood a tidy row of bored-looking staff, kitted out in identical white shirts, black trousers and bistro-style waiters' aprons. A life-size toy chimpanzee, wearing denim dungarees and a red top hat, sat halfway down the bar, clutching a magnum of *Moët* to its chest. The naughty monkey, I presumed.

The lunchtime rush was over and only a few customers remained. I spotted Martin sitting on a high metal stool at the library end. Martin Sadler and the Chief were in many ways not dissimilar. Both were short and podgy, prematurely bald, as pale. as vampires, and with unpredictable tempers. I'd always felt Martin might have been the prototype for which the Chief was the final product. In ten years they would look identical.

Martin waved. I waved back and trudged towards him. Squeak, squeak, squeak went my feet.

"Katy! Good to see you," he grinned. "The Chief sends his fond regards."

I forced a smile onto my face. "How is the odious little runt these days? Unwell, I hope." Martin had once told me that the chief didn't like me because I was taller than him. Classic short man syndrome. It explained a lot.

Martin made a mock pout. "Don't be like that. It was you who quit."

I swept my hair off my face, a defensive gesture I'd never been able to kick. "I didn't have any choice. He demoted me."

Martin held up his pint of lager. "Drink?"

I nodded towards the chimp. "Well, a glass of champers would be lovely."

"Or how about a very small glass of house white?"

Cheapskate, but even a glass of rubbish house wine would be extortionate here and I couldn't quite believe Martin would be allowed to claim this meeting on expenses. He stood and walked to the bar. The uniformed staff jumped to attention.

I sat on one of the chrome stools, my shoulders hunched, and found myself staring into a small nautical-themed corner of the pub, a tip of the hat to Bristol's seafaring past. Underneath a painting of a clipper in full flight was a mirror. I looked at my reflection. The sun had really brought out my freckles and my nose was peeling. My usually flyaway shoulder-length fair hair was pancake flat from the humidity. I quite liked the freckles but the pancake hair was a disaster.

To distract myself from such a distressing view, I turned around for another gawp at the strange décor. I stared at the chimp. The chimp stared at me. There was something about its tiny head and crumpled simian features that reminded me of the Chief.

Martin placed my wine on the table and sat opposite. The glass was enormous but the amount of wine it contained was miniscule. Four sips would empty it.

"So, how's the freelancing going?" he asked, taking a gulp of his lager.

"Steady."

He smirked. "That means slow." His pale face was ghostly in the sunlight streaming through the glass ceiling. Despite the air conditioning, beads of sweat still flecked his forehead as if he had a fever. His khaki button-down-collar shirt was patched with perspiration. He said, "Well, I don't think we'll be organising any more Secret Santas in a hurry."

I sipped my wine. It was so cold it didn't taste of anything. Go on Martin, I thought, get the gloating over with so we can move on.

He gave me a thin smile. "I still can't get my head around why you didn't engage a little bit of brain and exercise a tiny amount of caution when you drew the Chief's name. You know what he's like."

Rather typically I had done neither. Instead I'd bought him a twelve-inch bright pink loofah. My first choice had been a giant dildo or a pack of condoms for unusually small penises but I hadn't been able to track down the condoms and I'd gone for the loofah because it was cheaper than the dildo and the message was the same: shove it where the sun doesn't shine. The Chief's face as he'd unwrapped my anonymous gift that wintry afternoon in the *Gazette*'s newsroom had been a Christmas present all in itself. First he'd read the gift tag on which I had helpfully written: *Please insert sideways.* Then he'd examined the loofah from all angles, turning it slowly as a chilly silence descended on the staff. "How nice," he'd said at last. He'd returned to the gift tag. "I wonder who it's from?" In retrospect I should not have written the gift tag by hand. The Chief's revenge had been swift and brutal. When I'd returned to work the day after Boxing Day, he'd told me he was cutting five-grand off my wages and I would be writing advertising features for the foreseeable future. I hadn't spent ten years slogging my way in news journalism to write sales blurb about double-glazing firms or extolling the virtues of frothy bridal gowns. So I'd told the Chief that in no uncertain terms.

I shrugged at Martin across the table. "Oh come on. He had it coming. It's not my fault he has zero sense of humour…" I shook my head. "I should have sued him for constructive dismissal." Instead I'd been even more idiotic.

"Yeah?" Martin said. "I never heard the whole story."

I could tell Martin was feigning his ignorance. Journalists were the worst gossips in the world. Of course he knew. Even though I'd been an ass, I still felt I needed to justify my actions. "Right. Well, I'll tell you what he said, shall I?"

I put on a winy high-pitched voice, no idea why because the Chief had sounded more like a bear with a toad stuck in its throat, "But you're so well qualified to write the Wedding Belles supplements, Katy. You're still so sadly single, still chasing those tragically unfulfilled romantic dreams. With your literary sideline, I'd have thought this was right up your street."

So I'd told him he was a pathetic, vindictive little worm who wouldn't recognise a good reporter or a decent news story if they bit him on the bum and he could therefore shove my job in the same place as the loofah. And in those few small seconds before I'd stormed out of his office, I'd caught his triumphant smirk and realised with a sinking heart, that I'd played right into his hands.

Martin winced. "Ouch. Still sadly single. That's harsh."

I took another sip of wine but it wasn't any more flavourful. "And how did he know about my literary sideline?" I snapped. "I told you that in confidence."

Martin's phone rang. He glanced at the screen, frowned and answered. "What? Yeah... No.... Absolutely no. Hang on..." He ambled away from the table, stood a few feet away with his back to me. Although I couldn't hear much of what he was saying, I decided someone in the newsroom was getting a roasting. At least it wasn't me for once. I watched him walk further away, well out of earshot now, the phone pressed against his ear.

I returned to my drink. My 'literary sideline', as the Chief had called it, was a bit embarrassing which was why I didn't shout about it. I wrote cheesy romance novels, hiding behind the pen name *Lori du Val*. My books were the type that had large print and covers that showed beautiful women in ball gowns clinging to the bare chests of impossibly buff men with names like Kirk or Trey. I enjoyed writing them. During my recent exile from journalism they had been a financial Godsend.

Martin was back. "So how is the world of bodice-ripping purple prose?" He took a long, appreciative pull of his lager. I supposed he was glad for an excuse to get out of the office. Lunch breaks on the *Gazette* were not encouraged.

"Fine." I didn't want to talk about it. "So, what's the deal? You said you might have some freelance work for me?"

Martin paused and smiled, and in that exact moment I knew I wasn't going to like what he was about to

14

say,

"Well Katy, remember Patrick Underhill?"

I don't know what I'd been expecting, but not that I put down my glass. My chest felt tight and there was a panicky burning sensation behind my ribs. For several seconds I couldn't speak. Patrick Underhill. The name alone made me feel as if I was coming out in hives.

Martin seemed to mistake my silence for ignorance. "Come on Katy. Surely your memory's not that bad? Or has lovely Lori du Val taken you over completely these days?" He grinned at me over the top of his pint like a man who held all the cards, which of course, he did.

I felt my cheeks flush. "Of course I remember him, unfortunately." There was a hollowness in my stomach that felt an awful lot like dread. "Martin, what is this story about precisely?"

He rested his fingertips on his lips. His nails were bitten down to the quick. That was what working for the Chief did to people. "Underhill's finally out of prison and he'd like the *Gazette* to tell his story." Martin paused and tilted his head to one side. "You don't have a problem with that, do you Katy?"

I picked up my glass and took a quick sip.

"Because I gather you and he used to be friends," Martin persisted and I swear I saw him wink. "Quite close friends, in fact…"

Good grief. What on earth was he implying? That I'd actually dated Patrick Underhill?

"Martin. We were never, *ever* friends, close or otherwise." I made a chopping motion with my hand for emphasis. "We just went to the same school."

"But you knew him? Didn't you?" Martin grabbed his pint and took a hurried swig. "Whatever. He knows you and that's all that matters."

15

I picked up a beer mat and picked at its frayed edges, pulling off little bits of cardboard and rolling them between my damp thumb and index finger. After a while I glanced up and Martin was smirking at me again. This time I was sure he winked.

"It seems Mr Underhill still thinks very highly of you, Katy. He specifically wants you to tell the world how terribly, terribly sorry he is for murdering that girl."

We locked eyes. Silence stretched as I tried to think of something to say. Then Martin seemed to lose patience with my lack of enthusiasm. "Look, do you want the work or not?"

My instinctive answer was, not. I chewed at my lips. Problem was, if I turned down this assignment, it was very unlikely that Martin would offer me anything else in the future. And goodness knows, I needed the money. My overdraft had assumed epic proportions. I willed my mouth into motion. "Yes," I said through gritted teeth.

"Good." Martin flashed me a cocky grin as if he'd always known I'd do it. He slid a large brown envelope across the table.

"What's that?"

"Photocopies of the stories the *Gazette* ran about the murder, although you probably know all the grisly details off by heart."

The truth was, I'd spent most of the last thirteen years trying very hard not to think about Patrick Underhill at all.

Martin sat back in his seat. "So, Underhill did the crime, he's served his time and now he's out."

"Right. And he wants to give the paper..." I hesitated, struggling for the right words. "A public apology for the murder?" It sounded so strange.

Martin nodded. "Yep. He wants to give us – or

more specifically you – an exclusive interview in which he will apologise for bashing his girlfriend's head in."

I flinched and tried to disguise it as a shrug. "Do you know why he suddenly wants to say sorry? I mean, he's managed not to say sorry for the last thirteen years."

Martin toyed with his glass. "Guilt? Religion? New start? Who cares? The Kelly-Anne Davis murder is still the biggest thing that ever happened in Sands End and plenty of people will be interested to hear what Underhill has to say about it. Plus, the *Gazette*'s sales in your charming hometown have been going down the toilet for months so this'll cheer the Chief up no end."

Martin paused for a swig of lager. "He's thinking of using a regular freelancer to cover Sands End in an effort to increase sales. Do a good job on this story Katy and that freelancer could very well be you. Do a good job with that and he might even offer you your old job back."

Even though the thought of seeing the Chief's face again filled me with a special kind of dread, a vision of a healthy bank balance flashed into my mind. I'd be able to afford decent clothes again, nice wine, a foreign holiday. Perhaps even a new car…

Martin reached for his pint. "I want a balanced piece, mind. I don't want you going soft on him just because he was a school chum of yours."

"I already told you. He wasn't even close to being a chum. We hated each other's guts."

"Whatever. Of course I want his apology – his remorse for killing her, his wasted life behind bars. But I also want the other side – the victim's side. Try and get some suitably outraged quotes from her family." He frowned. "Actually I don't think she had any family. Friends then, neighbours, people she worked with."

Martin paused to take another swig of his lager.

"Underhill's still a young man. He's what – thirty-one? Thirty-two?"

"Thirty-one. Same age as me."

"Right. So he's got a decent chunk of life ahead of him. That's more than you can say for the poor girl he murdered so I don't want him coming out of this as some kind of bleeding martyr. Okay?"

By then I'd started scribbling in my shorthand notebook – I hadn't even noticed that I'd taken it out of my black Radley tote – nodding and shaking my head at intervals. "Yes, Martin. No, Martin." It was just like old times.

"But what we really want to know is why he did it?" Martin said. "What was the trigger? What pushed him over the edge? What turned him from just another dysfunctional teenager into a cold-blooded killer?"

I fixed my stare on my notebook. The odd burning sensation returned behind my ribs as Patrick Underhill's eighteen-year-old face outside the Fighting Cocks flashed into my head.

"Katy, are you going up to Glitz tonight? It's just—"

Martin's voice jolted me back. "Earth calling Katy Bennett?"

I looked up. "Yes. I'm listening."

"I said, the interview's been arranged for tomorrow."

"Tomorrow?" Thanks for the advance notice. "Where?"

"Some dodgy pub in Bristol." Martin waved a hand across the table. "The details are in the envelope." He smirked at my horrified expression. "What's the matter, Katy? Get a nose bleed when you go too far from sleepy Sands End these days?"

I ignored him. "Presumably you'll pay mileage?"

He hesitated then nodded.

I resumed scribbling again. "Copy deadline? Word count?"

"Nine-hundred words by end of play tomorrow. The Chief wants it on the centre pages."

"No problem. What about photos?"

"We've got file pictures of Underhill from the murder."

"But don't you want an up-to-date one of him?"

Martin looked away. "Yeah. Ideally. But he doesn't want people to know what he looks like now. He fears retribution. Once he's given us his apology he wants to get on with his life in anonymity. That's the deal."

Retribution? Oh please. Probably didn't want people to see he was even more pug-ugly now than he was at eighteen. I was surprised Martin had agreed to no new pictures. Readers in Sands End would be curious to see what Patrick looked like after thirteen years in a maximum-security prison. Oh well. Martin was news editor, not me. I suppose if it was either that or no story then he had no choice.

We spent a short while thrashing out my fee. I eventually talked him up on the basis that the *Gazette* was a big regional daily that covered four counties, not some piddly little local weekly read by three men and a dog.

Time was getting on and Martin kept glancing at his watch. It was probably time for his afternoon news conference with the Chief. I rummaged in my handbag, pulled out a few of my swanky new business cards and handed them over the table. "Just in case anyone else you know needs my superb freelance writing skills," I told him. Well, a little networking was essential in this day and age. Plus, my phone hadn't exactly been ringing off the hook with commissions during the last six months. To be honest, it hadn't rung much at all.

Martin glanced at my cards. "Garden Flat, Bluebell Meadow Court? How quaint."

I felt myself blush. The address was embarrassingly twee. A defensive edge crept into my voice, "Yeah, but it's half the price of the place I was renting in Bristol. And it's really nice. Sea view and everything." Well, I could sort of see the sea, if I stood on the sofa. "I really like living back in Sands End."

Liar.

"Mud view, more like. Right. I need to make a move. Remember, that story needs to be nestling safely in my inbox by six-pm tomorrow." He paused for dramatic effect, "Otherwise you really will be history."

I gave Martin a sarcastic smile and only just stopped myself from doing an idiotic salute and saying *aye-aye mon capitaine*. I put it down to nerves.

CHAPTER TWO

By the time I was on the train back to Sands End, the wine-buzz had worn off and I was having serious second thoughts about saying I'd do the story. Here I was on my way back to a town that not long ago I never thought I would live in again, about to write a story for a newspaper I never thought I'd work for again, and about to interview a man called Patrick Underhill who I hoped I'd never see again. Somehow those three things seemed ominously related, as if everything that had happened since I'd quit my job had been leading to this strange convergence. It bothered me. Patrick Underhill bothered me. Of all the stories in the world Martin could have asked me to write, why did it have to be about him?

The strange prickly panic was back in my chest. Suddenly I had a really bad feeling. I stared at the carriage ceiling and chewed at my lips. Maybe I should say I couldn't do the story after all.

But if I turned it down there was no way the Chief would offer me the job of freelance Sands End reporter, and regular freelance work – freelance work I could rely on, payment I could rely on – would be wonderful. Martin had also hinted it might only be a question of time before the Chief offered me a reporting job back on the staff and that would be even better as I could afford to rent in Bristol again. I missed living in a big city. I missed my old flat in Redland. I missed the still-warm olive focaccia from the artisan bakery around the corner. I missed the street food at

St Nicholas Market and the handsome man who worked at the juice bar there who had inspired one of my strapping fictional heroes. I missed the Prosecco bar in Clifton, the Gin Palace in Old Market, the tapas restaurant on the waterfront, the little place opposite the Tobacco Factory that did spicy shakshuka, the potted brown shrimp and sourdough from Salt & Malt. I missed going for a cheeky lunchtime cocktail with my work mates and bitching about the Chief. I missed weekend shopping at Cabot Circus, the endless choice of stores, coffee at Harvey Nichols. I missed being twenty-five miles further away from my parents and less at the beck-and-call of my overbearing mother. I missed everything about Bristol. Sands End seemed so dull in comparison. It only had one nightclub and four restaurants, three of which were Indian, no good shops and not one pub that sold a decent New Zealand Sauvignon Blanc.

I stared out of the train window at the parched yellow fields as they flickered past. Oh come on, get a grip, I told myself. It was thirteen years ago. He won't even remember seeing you that night. It's just a coincidence that he wants you to write the story. It's probably because he feels more comfortable talking to someone he already knows. By tomorrow afternoon this will all be over and you'll never have to set eyes on Patrick Underhill ever again. This time next week you could be doing regular freelance work for the *Gazette*. This time next month you could be back living in Bristol.

The carriage was half empty and stiflingly hot. A strange mildew smell reminded me of paddling pools in the garden when I was a child. I reached into my handbag and tugged out the envelope Martin had given me and shook out the sheets. These old stories about the murder would provide the background for the new story. It wouldn't be complicated to write. Most of it would consist of reproducing Patrick's apologetic quotes verbatim, with a bit of gory background about the murder bolted on to the beginning and some angry quotes from those who knew the victim to balance it at the end.

My eyes fixed on the empty seat opposite. The fabric was hideous. Royal blue fuzz flecked with tiny red and gold oblongs. What sort of crazed, sensory-deprived people were employed to choose soft furnishings for public transport?

I slumped back in my seat. Stop stalling and get on with it. It's just a story, like the hundreds of stories you've written over the last ten years. Write it up, bash it out and forget about it.

With reluctance, I turned to the photocopied stories, staring at the sheets of paper; my portals into the past. I didn't really need to read them. Martin had been right. Every tiny little detail was etched into my mind. Always had been and probably always would be.

He'd killed her in August, the same day my A-Level results came out. That evening I'd been on a pub-crawl, celebrating my grades with my best friends from school, Susie Clifford and Becky Thomas. The weather had been sweltering back then too. That whole summer had been one long heatwave. The day after the murder, I'd gone on a Eurocamp holiday with Mum, Dad and my older brother Richard. By the time we'd got back from Frejus three weeks later, Kelly-Anne Davis had been buried, Patrick Underhill had confessed to the murder and everyone in Sands End was trying to forget all about it.

I took a deep breath and started to read. I went through the stories in no particular order, underlining certain facts and scribbling potential questions into my notebook. One of the first things I read was that Kelly-

Anne Davis had lived in the top-floor flat at Sea View Heights, an ugly block of flats on Sands End seafront. I wondered who lived in her old flat these days and whether the occupants knew a young woman had been murdered in their kitchen. I carried on reading. Kelly-Anne had been a bar manager at Glitz nightclub. She had only moved to Sands End three months before she was murdered. She had been Underhill's on-off girlfriend and was seven years older than him.

I put down the sheet of paper and my gaze returned to the train window. Wow, bit of an age gap. But the fact Patrick had duped someone into going out with him was more astonishing. She must have been weird too. I flicked through the stories until I found a head-and-shoulders photo of Kelly-Anne. To my surprise, she looked really normal and pretty, with long dark-brown curly hair. How on earth had Patrick Underhill persuaded such an attractive woman to be his girlfriend? I remembered a boy with a face like a ferret and the intellect of a woodlouse. Maybe he'd had hidden talents? Yuck. I blinked that image away fast.

I carried on flicking through the stories. The motive for the murder had been as pointless as Patrick: Kelly-Anne had dumped him, the hot weather had made him "irritable", so he'd killed her. He'd lain in wait inside her flat and when she'd come back from work that night he'd, "attacked her in the kitchen with a marble ashtray", a phrase that didn't do justice to the violent reality of smashing someone repeatedly in the head with a heavy blunt object until they were dead.

I winced, my mind recoiling from the picture sketching itself in my mind. What had he felt when he'd seen what he'd done? Or had he felt nothing? These were all things I'd need to ask him tomorrow.

Tomorrow... The burning sensation returned

behind my ribs.

Once again I stared through the train window. My memories of the murder weapon were especially vivid. Back when my mother still smoked we'd had an identical ashtray at home. It was made of onyx marble, large and square, pale green streaked with brown, and incredibly heavy. My idiot brother had once dropped it on his foot and broken all five toes. When Mum gave up smoking it was filled with Pot Pourri and kept on the coffee table in the lounge. Not long after the murder she gave it away to a charity shop.

I took a deep breath and forced my eyes back to the stories. Underhill had been arrested in the car park outside Kelly-Anne's home, trying to flee the scene and covered in her blood. A neighbour had dialled 999 when she'd heard shouts and screams from Kelly-Anne's flat. I turned to a new page. Underhill had been charged with murder the same night.

Of course, being Patrick Underhill, there were the usual surreal aspects to the story. Even in the aftermath of murder he'd not been able to resist telling stupid lies. During questioning after his arrest he'd told officers he'd prophesised Kelly-Anne's murder after finding a photograph that showed her already dead. He initially pleaded not guilty but within days of being remanded in custody, he changed his plea to guilty, telling police he'd decided to confess after having a bad dream about a Mexican ghost bandit.

I gave a snort. Good grief, even that lie wasn't original. He'd used it at school. I shook my head. Had Patrick been trying to convince the police he was insane in the hope he'd get away with manslaughter? If so, it hadn't worked. He was sentenced to life with the recommendation he serve a minimum of thirteen years. Within weeks of the crime his father had sold the caravan park and moved away from Sands End. His mother had already started a new life some years earlier with a new husband in Manchester.

I pulled another sheet of paper towards me and continued to read. Kelly-Anne's former boss at Glitz, Nick Padovani, had clearly been itching to put the boot in. After Patrick was sentenced, Padovani had given the press chapter and verse about how Kelly-Anne had been living in fear of Underhill for weeks. The night she died, Padovani told the *Gazette*, she'd quit her job and told him she was moving away. One of the more poignant aspects of the case was that police had found her suitcases packed and ready in her bedroom.

After the sentencing hearing Avon and Somerset Police had trotted out the usual clichés to the media: it was a "harrowing and tragic murder... justice had been done... it was an open-and-shut case... with overwhelming circumstantial and forensic evidence". Underhill already had a criminal record for theft and public order offences. The underlying message from the police was that it had simply been a matter of time before he committed a much more serious offence.

All the stories I'd looked at so far had been dry news reports. But there was a tragic sadness to the story covering the funeral. Usually funerals for murder victims attract huge crowds, but, for some reason, that hadn't happened for Kelly-Anne Davis. The top-half of the page showed a photograph of the graveyard at St Cuthbert's Church. It was pouring with rain and the wet weather leant even more misery to the picture. I counted only four mourners. Three women and one tall man with dark, slicked-back hair were following the white-frocked vicar and the coffin out of the church as the undertakers carried it towards a fresh grave. A very small bunch of white roses rested on top of the casket. All I could see of the female mourners were the tops of their colourful umbrellas and their bare legs. Beyond the graveyard wall, shoppers were scurrying along wet pavements, heads bent, eyes down, as if they were only too aware of the sad drama playing out a few yards away but were determined to ignore it. Only one curious passer-by had stopped to stare, a fair-haired man in jeans and t-shirt, standing on the path that led through the churchyard.

So few mourners... I remembered my mother telling me that local business people had resented the murder. They'd thought the crime would tarnish Sands End's carefully cultivated happy-holiday image. It was a bit like the hotels along the seafront. From the front their paintwork gleamed and exotic potted palm-trees framed the entrances. But if you walked around the back you would see rusty fire escapes, mildewed walls and over-stuffed wheelie bins. Perhaps, by avoiding the funeral, the good people of Sands End were in denial about the murder; trying to pretend it had never happened. Even so, I'd have thought some locals would have wanted to show their sympathy for Kelly-Anne's grieving family.

But as I read through the rest of the funeral story I realised Martin had been right. Kelly-Anne hadn't had any family: Nick Padovani had paid for her funeral because no one came forward to claim her body. Nor it seemed, had she any friends outside work. The caption on the photograph simply read: *Colleagues from Glitz nightclub pay their final respects at the funeral of Kelly-Anne Davis.*

Poor, poor woman. Murdered by her boyfriend, no family to grieve for her or pay for her funeral, and the only people who'd bothered to go and see her buried were from her place of work. Tragic.

I was pretty sure the man with the dark, slicked-back hair was Nick Padovani. I had a feeling he still owned

Glitz so maybe he'd give me some suitably outraged quotes about Underhill's release. Martin would like that.

The last story I read about the murder was printed in the *Gazette* in November of that same year, by which time I was as far away from Sands End as I could get, doing a BA in Media Studies at Lancaster University:

Memorial plan for Underhill murder victim: A memorial for the murder victim of killer Patrick Underhill could be located in a park in Sands End. Councillors are looking into plans to plant a tree in memory of 25-year-old Kelly-Anne Davis who was found dead at her flat in the town in August. Nick Padovani, owner of Glitz nightclub where Miss Davis worked, has offered to donate the money to pay for the memorial. Underhill is currently serving a life sentence for murder.

After that, the story, like its victim, was dead. Didn't seem as if Kelly-Anne had ever got her tree after all.

The train rumbled to a halt at Sands End station. I gathered up my things, stuffed the envelope back into my handbag and headed for the door.

*

It wasn't far from the train station to my flat so I walked home rather than getting the bus. The High Street was jam-packed with holidaymakers and my progress was infuriatingly slow. I made a detour to an off licence and bought a bottle of wine then took a shortcut to the seafront through the churchyard of St Cuthbert's. Inside the gate, I looked around, superimposing the funeral photograph onto what I could see now. Somewhere here was Kelly-Anne's grave. I wondered if anyone ever bothered to put flowers on it or kept it tidy. I thought about going to take a look then changed my mind. I was hot, tired and needed a coffee.

The seafront was also packed. I much preferred Sands End in winter when the crowds were gone, the beach had a raw, delicate loneliness and the roads were driveable at more than ten miles-an-hour. I stared down at the golden sand, the sun glinting silver off the mudflats and a sea the colour of hot chocolate. The donkey rides had finished for the day and the animals were being herded back into lorries. Beach cafés were closing their shutters. Polystyrene chip trays bulged out of overflowing rubbish bins. A few remaining holidaymakers shook sand out of towels and rounded up their sunburnt, mud-splattered children.

It was still incredibly hot as I walked up the steep road away from the promenade. My flat was in a quiet side street on the hillside. All the other properties in my road were large elegant Victorian townhouses. Bluebell Meadow Court was a modern three-storey yellow-brick monstrosity built a year ago. With its dinky blue balconies, it looked as if it had been beamed down from Legoland. I lived in the ground floor flat. Shaun, an Australian website designer a few years older than me, lived on the first floor and Davina, a gym-mad forty-something serial divorcee who threw swingers parties, lived on the top floor. I had never been invited to one of Davina's parties, but Shaun had. Once. He'd told me that it was full of very drunk women and very frightened men. He'd left when guests started throwing their car keys into a white cowboy hat. I liked Shaun. On the day I'd moved in he'd padded down to scrounge some bread and find out if I looked anything like Elle McPherson. Sadly for him I didn't, and since he didn't look like anyone I fancied either we'd decided to become friends instead. He made me laugh, even if he did take liberties with my spare key and the contents of my breadbin. I knew he'd come to England from Australia to forget some sadness in his past. A relationship hadn't worked out the way he'd hoped. I'd had experience in that department too so we'd bonded over broken hearts, turkey stir-fries and bottles of Barossa Valley white wine.

As I walked into the small residents' car park in front of the flats, I could see Shaun's long legs and bare feet sticking out of the driver's door of my ancient racing green Mazda MX-5. A few days ago, Shaun had very kindly fitted a new car stereo for me but the CD he had put in to test it – his bizarrely loved Whipped Cream and Other Delights by Herb Alpert and the Tijuana Brass – had refused to come out again, and wouldn't stop playing at full volume unless the ignition was turned off. Since then, whenever I'd driven the car it had been to an ear-splitting accompaniment of Mexican trumpets and showy vibraphone solos set to a jaunty Bossa Nova beat. The embarrassment alone had nearly killed me. Shaun had offered to try and fix the stereo while I was meeting Martin today.

Shaun sat up as I walked over. His face was bright red and dripping with sweat.

I felt a stab of guilt. "Oh Shaun, you haven't been doing this all day have you?"

He pulled himself out of the car, stuffed his feet into a pair of scuffed Dunlop Volley tennis shoes and shook the sweat out of his hair. He wore long surf shorts decorated with orange and lime palm trees and a baggy red vest, which was also wringing wet with sweat. He said, "Okay, I don't know how I've done it, but the good news is this."

He reached inside the car and turned the ignition key. All I could hear was the gentle purr of a ten-year-old 1.8-litre, fuel-injected 133-brake-horsepower engine, which

I knew on a good day could go from nought to sixty-two in six seconds despite having 89,000 miles under its belt. So far so good.

"And the bad news?"

"Well the bad news is I still can't get the flaming CD out, and I'm fairly sure if you switch the stereo on, it won't switch off again."

"Why?" I wailed.

Shaun wiped his palms on the front of his shorts. "Beats me. I've tried everything. Even drove it down to Halford's earlier to see if they could fix it." He looked a bit sheepish. "Actually, the bloke there did say he wasn't a hundred per cent convinced the stereo was legit. It could be a rip off."

Rats. I knew I shouldn't have got it from the Sunday market. But the price had been brilliant. The stallholder had told me the stereos were cheap because they were last year's colour.

Shaun shook his head and looked glum. "I'm really sorry Katy, but I think it'll be fine as long as you remember not to switch the stereo on." He paused. "Or I can just take the whole unit out and bin it?"

"But if you do that you'll lose your CD. No, I'll take it to Mike at the garage to see if he can do anything." I handed Shaun the bottle of wine. "This is to say thanks for trying. It's your favourite."

Shaun blushed and looked at his feet. "Aw Katy. That's an expensive wine. You didn't have to do that."

"It's the very least I can do to make up for your wasted day. Right. I need a coffee. You want one?"

Shaun slammed the car door shut. "Nah. Just had one thanks."

I picked up my handbag and headed towards the lobby door. My plan now was to read the background

31

stories one more time and decide which questions to ask Patrick. Once I'd finished preparing for the interview, I wanted a relaxing evening sketching out the plot of my next romance novel in my black Moleskine notebook. I already had some good ideas for my next hero. He was going to knock the socks off all the others I'd written. He would be blond and ripped and impossibly good-looking. His job would be something heroic, secret and dangerous, his character deep, dark and complex. My heroine would be putty in his hands. A few hours masquerading as Lori du Val would take away the vile taste of Patrick Underhill.

"Oh, by the way," Shaun called after me. "One of your mates came round earlier."

I turned around. "Susie?"

He shook his head. "Nah. The one with the purple hair."

For a second I had no idea who he meant then I said, "Oh. You mean Becky. Her hair's not purple, it's burgundy."

"Looked purple to me. Anyway she gave me a message for you. She said, don't forget you're seeing her and Susie tonight, but it's not the Raj anymore because their kitchen caught fire. You're meeting at the Italian instead now."

I put my hands up to my face. "Oh no!"

"You don't like Mario's? They do a great lasagne."

"It's not that. I'd forgotten all about it."

Susie Clifford and Becky Thomas were still my two best girl friends. I'd known them since before primary school. Both were married with children. Susie worked part-time as PA to the boss of a local building firm and Becky owned a fancy dress shop in the town centre. I loved them dearly but tonight I really didn't feel in the mood for their company. Mainly because I didn't want to have to tell them I was meeting Patrick Underhill the next day.

As I pushed open my front door and walked down my hall, I inhaled the unmistakable aroma of Shake 'n' Vac. This could only mean one thing: Shaun had been in my flat while I was out. He had raided my breadbin to make a sandwich, dropped crumbs all over the place then vacuumed them up. Shaun was obsessed with Shake 'n' Vac. His flat reeked of the stuff. The smell made me sneeze but I didn't have the heart to tell him. My nose began to tickle as I walked into the sitting room.

Despite my misgivings about moving back to Sands End, I quite liked my flat. Okay, the address was tacky but the landlord worked in Dubai and the muted Martha Stewart-on-valium-style décor might be boring but it was also inoffensive. The flat had two decent-sized bedrooms, one of which I'd turned into my office, a spacious kitchen with classy black marble worktops, and a bathroom with an excellent power shower. The sitting room had a stripped pine floor and a sliding door that led into the front garden. It wasn't a huge garden but it was nice and private, shielded from the road and the residents' car park by a high wooden fence. Cheery rose bushes surrounded a rectangle of sun-bleached lawn. A squat Torbay palm added a tropical touch in the middle of the grass and the fence at the far end of the garden was disguised with a man-height evergreen hedge. Henry my nervous tabby rescue cat was fascinated by the garden as we hadn't had one in Bristol. I liked it too. When the weather was fine I could write outside.

I kicked off my flip-flops, padded into the kitchen, fed Henry and clicked on the coffee machine. The flat was like an oven so I took my coffee out to the garden and sat at the patio table, worrying about the next day. Although it was a beautiful summer's evening, I couldn't shake off the feeling of unease. A cloud of tiny gold mosquitoes danced in the yellow sunlight as if being jerked upwards on strings held by invisible hands. The shadow from the palm suddenly looked like thin black fingers creeping across the grass. A plastic watering can lay on its side, its mouth making a shape like a screaming ghoul. A seagull swooping overhead shrieked like a car alarm, making me jump.

Patrick Underhill... Not looking forward to this at all. Not one bit.

CHAPTER THREE

I pushed open the door to Mario's and inhaled the smell of warm pizza dough and garlic. Framed photos of the Tuscan countryside had been hung on the yellow stucco walls. The tables were wooden, solid and rustic, the lighting subdued, the music Pavarotti.

The girls were sitting at a round table at the rear of the empty restaurant, their heads so close they looked like mismatched conjoined twins. Susie was pale and lanky, her ginger hair cut into a chin-length bob. Becky was tanned and curvy with very long curly hair, which this week was burgundy.

As I walked towards the table, I sensed something was wrong. Becky's hands were making anxious shapes in the air as she spoke. Her fingers were rigid, her shoulders hunched and tense. Susie rested a consoling hand on her arm while Becky took a gulp from a large glass of red wine.

"Sorry I'm late," I said, plonking my bag on the floor. It was a couple of seconds before the girls lifted their heads to look at me, and several more before their faces relaxed into rather forced smiles of welcome.

I sat. "What's up?"

Susie picked up a glass of orange juice almost the same colour as her hair. "Becky's had a terrible shock."

"Oh no. What?" I asked, imagining a child in A&E or a grandparent in the morgue, although it probably couldn't be anything too serious otherwise Becky would have cancelled. A waiter materialised at my side and handed me a laminated menu. "Can I get you something to drink?" he asked.

I nodded. "Just a glass of house white, please."

"Large or small?"

"I think you'll need a large one," Susie advised.

"Okay. Large. Thanks. So what's happened?" I asked Becky when the waiter had gone.

Becky sniffed as if she'd been crying although her eyes were dry and her make-up was intact which made me doubt that anything too dreadful had happened. I loved Becky to bits, but even when we were age three at Mrs Tiggywinkle's day nursery in Technical Street she had been a bit of a drama queen. She reached for her red wine and her hand trembled as she raised the glass to her lips.

Susie turned to her, "Start at the beginning, Becks," she said in a gentle voice. "Tell Katy everything you just told me."

Oh dear. Maybe something serious had happened on Planet Becky.

The waiter returned with my wine. Susie and Becky watched him leave and when he was out of earshot, Becky fanned her face with both hands. "God, I've gone all shaky talking about this." She lowered her voice, "Okay. Just before I came out I was on Facebook and I received a really horrible message." Her eyes darted around the restaurant. "From *him*," she hissed.

My brow puckered. "Who's him?"

Becky put her mouth against my ear. "Patrick Underhill."

"Ha! That's really weird–" I began, but something told me to shut up. Actually that was a really strange coincidence. I tried to ignore the unease creeping up my chest. I took a sip of my white wine. It was tepid.

Becky pulled away as the waiter returned to take our

food orders. I hadn't had a chance to look at the menu so I just asked for a lasagne.

Once again, the girls remained silent until the waiter was out of earshot.

"So you see, Becky's had quite a shock," Susie said at last.

I turned to Becky and tried to make my voice sound casual. "So, what did Patrick's message say?"

Becky looked as if she was about to burst into tears, "It was really, really horrible, all sorts of weird stuff about wanting to come to our school reunion."

My heart sank at the mention of the reunion. Becky had been organising it for almost a year, and I'd been dreading it for almost a year. It was now four days away. Four days for me to come up with a bombproof excuse that would get me out of going.

"How odd," I managed at last. "How on earth did he find you. I mean, surely you're not Facebook friends?"

Becky look horrified. "God no! Don't be stupid!"

Susie shook her head. "It was via the Facebook page Becky set up to publicise the reunion. Unbelievable, isn't it? By the way, Becks, did you remember to bring Katy's ticket?"

Rats. No escape.

Becky pulled her handbag up onto her lap, rummaged inside and pushed a small rectangle of cardboard across the table. "That's £15 you owe me, Katy. You can give me the money when we settle the bill."

Brilliant. Fifteen-pounds to stand around listening to a group of people I hadn't seen since school bragging about all the fabulous things they'd achieved in their lives – good jobs, happy marriages, Mensa-level kids. Maybe I could fake a migraine. I shoved the ticket into my handbag.

Becky shook her head. "I feel totally violated, and

I'm very surprised they even let Category A prisoners use social media."

"What was his profile picture like?" I asked her.

"Oh it was just some photo of a church. It looked like St Cuthbert's."

That was a sick. Kelly-Anne was buried in St Cuthbert's.

Susie rested a consoling hand on Becky's arm. "Well, at least we know he's just bullshitting about going to the reunion. I mean, he can't. He's in prison. But it's horrible that he's been able to message you. Maybe you should block him and update all your privacy settings."

Becky nodded miserably. "When I looked on Facebook a bit later, he'd deleted his account, but I think I will update everything and change my password, just in case he tries to contact me again. And you're right he can't come because he's in jail, which is a relief."

I fiddled with the stem of my glass. If I mentioned Patrick's release from prison, we'd probably end up spending the rest of the meal talking about him. But as we were, regrettably, already on the subject maybe I should just get it over with. The minute my story went in the *Gazette* they'd find out anyway.

I took a deep breath. "Actually, Patrick Underhill is out of jail."

The silence that followed was so loud it seemed to drown out the piped accordion music now playing above our heads. Becky broke it first.

"What?" She wailed. "You're joking? When?"

I shrugged. "Just a few days ago I think."

Becky rubbed at her temples. "He... he can't be... How do you know he's out?"

I gave another loose shrug. "He's offered the *Gazette* an interview. He's going to apologise for what he did." I deliberately didn't mention my involvement in the story.

"Oh my God!" Becky squealed. "Oh my God!" Her voice dropped, "Oh my God... Just think Katy. If you were still working for that paper, it might be you writing it."

I kept my eyes fixed on the raffia tablemat and pretended I hadn't heard her. I fiddled with the cutlery, picked up my fork and pressed its prongs against a finger. When I eventually glanced up, Susie and Becky were staring at me.

Becky's eyes narrowed. "Oh... my... God. You are writing it."

I felt my cheeks grow warm. "Well, I've been asked to write it—"

Becky snatched up her glass. "I hope you said no."

I took another gulp of wine, "I desperately need the money actually so I said yes."

"You're joking!" both girls exclaimed.

I shrugged. "It's just a story. I need the cash."

Susie's blue eyes creased into a frown. "But why have they asked you to write it? I mean, you don't work for the *Gazette* any more."

The odd prickly heat was back in my chest. I reached for my glass and took a hasty gulp.

Becky's eyes widened, "Is it because you knew him? Is it because the night it happened you and him—"

"Look, it's just a small freelance story," I interrupted, wishing I'd kept my mouth shut. "He just wants to say sorry. That's the angle. He's had a long think while he's been in prison and he wants to apologise." Good grief, now it sounded as if I was sticking up for him.

Becky swished her head, making her burgundy curls bounce. Her expression was incredulous. "I really don't think people like that should be encouraged. I mean, he's bound to be lying about being sorry. You know you can't believe anything he says. Don't you agree Suze?"

"Well..." Susie gave an uncomfortable shrug. "I do agree that you can't believe anything he says. Whatever he tells you in the interview, it won't be true."

Becky picked up her drink, "I'm just really surprised you'd be happy to sit down with him, Katy, write up his lies for other people to read and believe."

I tried dampen down my irritation, "Look, it'll be a balanced piece. And I'm not thrilled about meeting him either. But this is the first freelance work the *Gazette*'s offered me since I left. If I do a good job on this story, then I'll be offered more work and possibly my old job back. And I do seriously need the money." I was pretty surprised by the girls' reaction. I wasn't meeting Patrick because I wanted to. It was work. I was a journalist. I needed the money. It wasn't all happy golden wedding reports.

"I'd be terrified to meet him again," said Susie. "I wonder what he looks like now? I'm really surprised he's out though. I was sure he got life."

I nodded. "He did. It was life with the recommendation he serve a minimum of thirteen years." I grabbed the menu and fixed my eyes on the puddings section. "Wow, I hope I have room for a dessert. Death by Chocolate, that sounds amazing–"

"He should have died in prison," Becky sniffed, dabbing her nose on her paper napkin. They should never have let him out after what he did. Lock him up and throw away the key. Or bring back the death penalty."

I always tried to avoid talking politics with Becky. Her views were a little to the right of Genghis Khan and no way was I getting drawn in to an argument about capital punishment next. I swivelled around in my chair, "I hope our food doesn't take long. I'm famished."

Susie's voice dragged me back, "Katy, when you interview Patrick, will you ask him whether he really is planning to go to the school reunion? Because if he does go, you know he'll just ruin it for everyone."

I shook my head. "I'm sure he's not being serious—"

"But I still think you should ask him," Susie repeated. "Then at least we'll know for sure what he's planning."

Becky nodded and narrowed her eyes. "Exactly. Because he's obviously planning something."

Oh, for heaven's sake. I snatched up my glass. Patrick Underhill had already ruined my day and now he was ruining my evening. "Look, it's very simple. If you don't want him to go to the reunion, don't sell him a ticket."

But Becky seemed unwilling to relinquish the role of tragic heroine just yet. "What if he asks someone else to buy his ticket for him?" she wailed.

I shook my head. "But who would do that? No one liked him at school. He didn't have any friends plus he's been in prison for thirteen years. What did his message say exactly?"

Becky reached into her handbag. "I'll show you." She pulled out her phone. "I took a screen shot of it just in case. I probably need to show it to the police, now I know he's out."

"Police?" This was getting ridiculous. "Why on earth would you show it to the police?"

"Because it's threatening." Becky handed me her phone. The message said:

Hi Becky. Remember me? Just found out about the school reunion — sounds like a right laugh. I'll be coming home soon and I'd love to catch up with everyone at the party. Let me know how I can get a ticket. Patrick Underhill.

"Um. In what way is this threatening?" I asked her.

"Just generally it's threatening." Becky snatched back her phone. "The way he says, 'I'll be coming home soon'. It's like he's saying: *I'm coming to get you.*"

What utter rubbish. This was so obviously Patrick winding Becky up. No way was he really planning to go to the reunion. Martin had said that after my interview Patrick Underhill wanted to get on with his life in anonymity; that he so feared retribution he didn't even want his photo in the paper. A big school reunion back in Sands End would be the last thing he'd want.

"Let me read it again?" Susie asked, reaching across the table. "Gosh. It is a bit creepy, isn't it?" She gave a heavy sigh. "What a weirdo. I remember after the murder, the paper ran a picture of his girlfriend and I was really surprised because she was actually quite pretty."

Becky made a retching sound, "Pretty desperate, more like. I mean, can you imagine what it would be like going out with someone like Patrick Underhill?"

And then being murdered by him, I thought shaking my head.

Susie shook hers too. "Poor woman. How awful. So sad…"

I nodded. "I was looking at some of the old press stories today and the funeral photo was really sad. Hardly anyone went, just a handful of people from the club where she worked." Thinking about the other quotes I'd need to get for the story, I added, "Nick Padovani still owns Glitz, doesn't he?"

Susie nodded. "Certainly does–"

"Yuck. Padovani's a total slimeball too," Becky interrupted. "I really didn't want to book Glitz for our school reunion. But where else is there in Sands End?"

42

Susie said, "I reckon he only owns a nightclub so he has a constant supply of women to eye-up."

Becky nodded. "Oh yeah. Definitely. Well, you know he tried it on with me when I was only just eighteen. It was the night of our A-Level results. He grabbed my bum as we were leaving Glitz and–"

The waiter was back beside the table and Becky clammed up fast.

"Can I get you any more drinks?" he asked.

We shook our heads. Becky seemed to will a polite smile onto her face, "We're fine for the moment, thanks."

Once the waiter had drifted away, Susie picked up her glass of juice. "Goodness only knows what must have been going through Patrick's mind that night."

Becky turned to me, nodding, "Yes, that's what you seem to have forgotten, Katy. He killed someone in cold blood. Can you imagine what sort of person is able to do that to another human being? Just remember that when you're having your cosy little chat with him. Okay?"

She swished back her hair and adopted Becky Sulking Pose: arms folded, bum slouched back in her seat. As usual, it didn't last long. She turned to Susie. "Actually, I was always really surprised the police didn't want to interview us after the murder."

I frowned, trying to keep up with Becky's logic. "Why on earth would the police have wanted to talk to us?"

"Because we saw him the night he did it. We were probably the last known people in the world to speak to him before–"

Susie interrupted her, "Except you and me didn't actually speak to him. Katy did, but we didn't."

Becky whispered across the table, "We looked into the eyes of a killer."

Oh please. I glanced towards the bar, thinking

maybe I did need another glass of wine.

Becky picked up her spoon and stared at her reflection as if she was seeing back into the past. "It seems like yesterday. I remember exactly where we last saw him. That night is seared into my brain forever. And yours too Katy, it must be."

I felt a blush creep up my neck. "I hardly remember it at all."

Becky frowned in disbelief, "Oh Katy. You must do. We were outside the Fighting Cocks. It was the first time we'd seen him since leaving school. He was wearing a really naff shell-suit." She sneered. "It must have been the hottest night of the year and he was wearing a nylon shell-suit. What a div."

Susie sipped her juice. Her pale eyes met mine. "Becky and I had nipped to the loo and when we came back Katy, you were outside talking to Patrick and–"

I put out my hand in a stop gesture. "And the first thing he told me was a pack of lies about winning the National Lottery and going to live in Rio de Janeiro." I swivelled in my seat and looked towards the bar but once again, the waiter had vanished.

"But he didn't go to Rio, did he?" Becky whispered. "Instead, he committed cold blooded murder." She paused as if waiting for a thunderclap.

Susie's worried eyes again met mine. "And you really never got any impression from him that night about what he was going to do?"

I felt my cheeks grow warm. "No of course not."

The waiter reappeared behind the bar. I tried to attract his attention but he ignored me and began fiddling with the coffee machine.

Becky picked up her empty glass and twiddled the stem. "So that's really all he said? Just the rubbish about

Rio?"

I gulped more wine. "I honestly can't remember–"

"Because just now you said winning-the-lottery and-going-to-Rio was the first thing he told you. So what was the second thing?"

Katy, are you going up to Glitz tonight? It's just–

My face grew hot and my stomach clenched. The tips of my fingers tingled. "There... there wasn't a second thing." I fixed my eyes on the tablemat. "That was just a... a figure of speech... He didn't say anything else. Not one word. Nothing."

CHAPTER FOUR

The Barley Mow was a red-brick eyesore on Fishponds Road. A chalkboard on the wall by the door promised, *Debbi D Live Here Tonite.* I took the next right and turned into the car park. The MX-5 had behaved impeccably on the drive up to Bristol. I'd almost accidentally switched on the stereo a couple of times but had stopped myself just in time.

I pulled up in the scant shade of a mangy buddleia bush and stared through the windscreen at the high brick wall surrounding the pub's beer garden, drumming my fingers against the steering wheel and trying to ignore my churning stomach. Somewhere behind that wall was Patrick Underhill. It took all my self-control not to whack the gear stick into reverse and drive away. Instead, I fixed my mind on money in my bank account and my landlord off my back. After a while my breathing calmed. I pushed open the car door and got out.

I'd driven up to Bristol with the air conditioning going full blast so I wasn't prepared for the ferocious wave of heat. The air was suffocating and the sickly scent from the buddleia cones was like breathing through a perfumed sock. Perspiration trickled down my stomach.

I had dressed with care for the interview, hoping to exude a professional no-nonsense – and if I was honest, a let's get this over with – appearance: a smart black calf-length skirt, black sling-backs and a white sleeveless cotton blouse. Back when I worked at the *Gazette,* I used to buy these blouses in bulk because they could go straight from tumble dryer to wardrobe. My hair was tied back in a neat French plait. My make-up was minimal: just a bit of mascara and clear lip-gloss.

I locked the car and walked across the baking grey concrete towards a wooden gate set in the wall. The temperature must have been thirty-degrees, but it was the humidity that made it unbearable.

My throat clenched as if I was about to retch. Come on get a grip, I told myself for the umpteenth time since I'd left the flat. He's not going to do anything weird in a packed pub garden is he? He wouldn't have been released from prison if he was still dangerous. And anyway, he's here to say sorry.

The metal handle on the gate was almost too hot to touch and a small part of me hoped he wouldn't be on the other side. I glanced at my watch. It was bang-on three thirty. Putting my hip against the warm wood, I shoved the gate open and stepped through.

The beer garden was long and narrow, a rectangle of bleached yellow grass, on which were half-a-dozen tatty picnic benches, some shaded by threadbare parasols that had faded from red to an insipid pink. Tables bore the remains of long-departed customers. Screwed-up crisp packets were wedged between the slats, plates of half-eaten chips, globs of congealed ketchup, and empty froth-smeared pint glasses sat uncollected, attracting flies and wasps. In the distance, out of sight, a dog barked and a child's high-pitched voice shouted, "Mum-*eee*. Mum-*eee*. Mum-*eee*."

There was only one person in the garden. He sat with his back to me, facing the brick wall at the far end of the lawn. His hair was short and dark and he was dressed all in black. My chest tightened: Patrick Underhill.

Hitching my handbag further up my shoulder, I set off across the grass. The spiky blades pricked inside my shoes. I was halfway across the lawn when he turned and stared at me, shielding his eyes from the sunshine with his hand. He gave no gesture of welcome or recognition, just sat there, his small eyes squinting, his mouth turned down in a sneer, watching me approach.

I recognised him immediately. He looked older but he was still ugly and skinny. His hair was flat, as if he'd just got out of bed. I stopped a couple of feet away from the table, waiting for him to say something, wondering if perhaps he didn't recognise me. Then he slowly lowered his hand from his eyes.

"Katy." He didn't smile and his stare didn't waver. His eyes were the palest blue, the colour of sea ice. I tried to look away but I couldn't. I felt fascinated and repulsed. He looked ill. Yellowy-purple shadows under his eyes looked like bruises. Deep furrows ran down either side of his mouth. Spindly black bristles protruded from his chin and I could tell he would struggle to grow a decent beard. His face looked closer to forty than thirty but his body still had an adolescent gangly-ness. His arms and legs seemed too long, knees bent in, elbows sticking out like chicken wings. He wore black jeans, black trainers and, despite the punishing heat, a black nylon tracksuit top zipped up to his chin.

So this is what a murderer looks like, I thought.

"Want a drink?" he asked with no enthusiasm. His voice surprised me. It had a crafty Cockney accent and was nothing like I remembered from school. What a fake. Even his voice was dishonest.

I shook my head. "I'm fine."

He picked up a half-pint of lager and took a quick swig. The beer looked flat as if he'd been sitting here in the sun for some time, trying to string out his drink for as long as possible. He pointed to the wooden bench on the opposite side of the table, and I manoeuvred myself awkwardly onto the seat. A new iPhone sat on the tabletop beside him. Good grief, he'd only been out of prison for a few days and already he had the latest iPhone. I didn't have an iPhone. I had a rubbish phone. The injustice rankled. Maybe he'd nicked it.

"So. Long time no see." Again his voice was flat, inflectionless, bored almost. "Thirteen years to be precise."

I sat and stared at the tabletop, scrutinised the faded brown varnish, paper-thin and peeling in the heat. Despite the hot sun on my back, I shivered. When I looked up he was still staring at me.

His eyes drifted down and settled on my chest for a second too long. "Like your blouse," he said. "Very pretty. Like you."

I folded my arms in self-defence and leaned back, fighting the urge to get up and walk away.

He slowly stroked his cheek with his grubby, nicotine-stained fingers and made a creepy humming sound as if it felt nice. "You used to have short hair at school. You were pretty then too."

I stared at his fingers, thinking, was that the hand you used to beat her to death? Or did you use both hands? The breeze changed direction and brought his smell across the table, a sour biscuity odour of unwashed skin, dirty clothes and stale cigarette smoke. My throat tightened and I swallowed to stop myself gagging. Under the pretence of pulling my handbag onto my lap, I shifted along the bench so that we were sitting diagonally rather than opposite. I took out my phone and placed it on the table next to me, just in case I did need to call 999, then took out my digital voice recorder and angled it so that it was pointing across the table at him.

He scowled at it. "Nah. Don't want you taping me. Not comfortable with that."

My anger rose. I wanted to say, *hey, you asked me for this interview, not the other way around. Okay? The Dictaphone stays.* But when I looked up, his eyes were glassy like a dead fish. They held no expression at all. Becky's words from the restaurant came back to me and I thought, yes, I am looking into the eyes of a killer. A shiver danced across my shoulders. I turned it into a shrug and said, "Suit yourself."

Shoving the machine back in my handbag, I took out my pen and turned to a new page in my shorthand notebook. I dumped my bag under the table, and looked at him, my biro poised above the paper. I willed my voice to be civil. "Let's get started, shall we?"

He picked up his drink and sneered into the glass. "And there was me thinking we'd have a bit of a chat first. Talk about old times." He paused. "Just now before you turned up, I was sat here thinking about the last time we saw each other."

His eyes met mine. He dropped his voice and without thinking I leaned forwards to catch his words. "Do you remember that, Katy?" he whispered. "The last time we met? I remember it. Like it was yesterday."

Fear trickled into my chest and I jerked back, staring down at the tabletop until my eyes began to water. When I looked up he was staring at my notebook's blank page, his lips moving silently, as if he was reading words that were not there. I pulled it away.

He ran a hand through his greasy hair. Tiny flakes of dandruff fluttered onto the shoulders of his black tracksuit top. "Oh well. I guess I'd better make my pitch."

I started writing. "Pitch?" That seemed a strange choice of word.

"Yeah." He paused and ran a sickly tongue across his yellow teeth. "The thing is, I didn't do it."

For an insane moment I thought he was talking about the disappearance of the class guinea pig, Formerly Known as Prince. "What?"

"It wasn't me. I didn't do it."

"Didn't do what?"

"I didn't kill her."

I stopped writing and stared at him across the table. Stupidly I waited for the punch line to his very sick joke, for him to point and say, Gotcha! But he didn't. For a couple of heartbeats, he just stared at me, a funny little half-smile playing on his lips then he shrugged and swigged his beer.

My mouth had gone dry. "You're talking about the murder of Kelly-Anne Davis, right? The murder you confessed to. Or are you talking about another murder you've accidentally forgotten to mention?"

My sarcasm seemed to go over his head. He scowled. "Yeah. Kelly-Anne. Who else would we be talking about? Anyway, it wasn't me. I didn't do it."

Oh boy. I don't know what I'd been expecting him to say, but not in a million years had it been that. He squinted across the table. His pupils were tiny black dots in the ice. I wondered if he had taken something.

"Yeah," he continued, "the Mexican came to me when I was asleep. In prison. Told me to confess."

I don't know how I kept myself from laughing out loud. I turned back to my notebook as if I was about to resume writing.

"Oh yes," I said in a sarcastic voice. "That would be the bad dream you had about the Mexican ghost bandit that made you decide to confess." His lies were so pathetic.

But Patrick seemed oblivious to my mockery, or perhaps he'd told so many lies in his life he had simply forgotten that one. His eyes remained dazed and empty.

"He had a Mexican moustache. Like this." He ran his thumb and index finger down either side of his mouth then sat back on the bench, thighs splayed, and looked at me as if I was the cretin.

I put my pen down on the table to show him I had no intention of writing anything else down. "Patrick–"

He started to sing in a loud, high-pitched voice, "*Stool pigeon, ha-cha-cha-cha.*" He gnashed his teeth together on the cha-cha-cha bit.

Definitely on something. I wondered if he would try to stop me if I said I was leaving. I tried to keep my voice calm even though my whole body was tingling with nerves. "Patrick, I thought today's interview was about you saying sorry for murdering your girlfriend thirteen years ago."

He shrugged. "Nah."

"Right. So, you're not here to apologise?"

He picked up his glass and shook his head slowly from side to side. "Katy, Katy, Katy," his voice was frustrated. "Don't you see? I'm giving you a much better story. I'm giving you the opportunity to help me clear my name. This is your chance to make amends."

My lips suddenly felt numb. "Make… amends?"

He nodded. "I think we understand each other. Don't we?"

My face flushed and I looked away.

He continued speaking, "So, you'll need this." He leaned back, stuffed a hand in the pocket of his jeans, pulled out a scrap of paper and waved it at me, his eyes wild and unfocussed. "Ta-dah! This man knows the truth. He can prove I didn't do it."

Patrick's head wobbled from side to side as if his neck suddenly wasn't strong enough to support it. He reached across the table, grabbed my biro out of my hand and scribbled on a beer mat. As I caught the full impact of his smell, he put the beer mat down on the table, facing me. I stared at what he'd written but made no move to pick it up: *JACK DALE 0208 111 7777.*

He put my pen back on the table and I snatched it back. "Okay, Patrick, so why are you telling me all this? Why don't you just get a lawyer? Or talk to your parole officer, or the police?"

He flashed me a manic grin. "Because that's exactly what *they* want me to do." He shook his head. "You find me Jack Dale and all will be revealed."

Patrick swigged down the rest of his lager and pointed at the beer mat. "Course, that probably isn't his real name. He's probably called Mickey Mouse or Donald Duck now. And the other thing you need to know is, that number's already been disconnected." He grinned, "Sneaky, sneaky, sneaky. So, your first task is?" he cocked his head.

When I didn't say anything he spoke very deliberately, as if addressing a young child. "Your first task is… to find… his new… phone number. Right?"

I'd had enough. I went to stand but he beat me to it. "Bursting for a slash. Watch this space, as they say."

I watched him walk away across the stubby grass, into the long shadows created by the pub's back wall. He disappeared through the bar door, letting it slam shut behind him. But why was I even surprised by what I'd just heard? It was exactly as if we were back at school again:

Patrick opens his mouth, out comes a load of complete and utter rubbish.

I eyed the gate from the beer garden to the car park. By the time he returned I could be long gone. I picked up the beer mat. This was so obviously a made up phone number, the first random figures to pop into his pathetic head. I had a sudden, rather violent, urge to rip it into little pieces and leave them in a pile for him to find after I'd gone. Instead I folded the beer mat in half, pushed it between the wooden slats and heard it land on the grass.

As I grabbed my bag from under the table and shoved my notebook inside, my phone beeped to say I had a text message. It was from Martin: *Did you get the interview?*

My finger darted over the keypad: *Forget apology feature. Underhill now claiming innocence. He is certifiable. Total waste of time.*

Bees buzzed and the hot sun prickled on my bare arms. A motorbike whined down the road past the pub. Patrick seemed to have been gone for ages. My patience snapped. I hoisted my bag up my shoulder, and went into the pub to tell him I was leaving. But as I pushed the door open and my eyes adjusted to the gloom, I saw that the room was empty apart from a yellow-haired woman, eating crisps behind the bar. He couldn't still be in the loo, surely?

"Can I help you, love?" she asked.

I frowned around. "I was just looking for someone…"

"Tall, thin bloke with black hair?" She picked up a small towel and used it to mop something off the bar. "Left about five minutes ago." She wiped her greasy hands on the towel and grinned. "You two have a lovers' tiff?"

I hitched my handbag further up my shoulder. "Certainly not." Did she seriously think I looked like the sort of desperado who'd go out with someone as unappetising as Patrick Underhill?

She shrugged and sat back on her stool. "Looked like he was crying when he walked out. That's all."

Crying with laughter I expect. What a waste of space.

CHAPTER FIVE

The traffic heading out of Bristol was dreadful. "I hate you Patrick Underhill," I howled at the windscreen. A white Transit cut me up at a roundabout and I hurled the window down.

"Learn to drive, knobhead!"

I felt very much like punching someone, and top of the list was Patrick Underhill. Every time I thought back to the pub, I felt myself flinch in disgust. As I left the city behind and headed out into the countryside, I had the strangest urge to stop the car and roll on the verge, in case particles of his skin or flakes from his hair had settled on my clothes. But what I really wanted was to scrub my mind clean, to eradicate the memory of the last hour. I kept seeing the creepy way he had stroked his fingers against his cheek, his glibness when talking about the murder. His sheer audacity in now claiming he hadn't done it. Sick. Utterly sick.

Revulsion once again rolled over me. I imagined him chasing Kelly-Anne down her hall, grabbing her by her hair, yanking her back into the kitchen, forcing her down, screaming at her, telling her that he was going to kill her, picking up the heavy onyx ashtray, her eyes bulging, mouth stammering to formulate words – trying to plead with him – as her brain shut down in terror. And then he had brought the weight crashing down onto her skull. Probably not once or twice but many, many times, not stopping until he was sure, absolutely sure, she was dead.

A big truck thundered past making me jump. My heart thudded and my fingers tingled. Why had I ever agreed to take on this story? The moment Martin had said Patrick's name I should have made up an excuse and walked away.

Without thinking I reached out and switched on the car stereo and insanely loud wailing trumpets instantly blotted out everything.

"Oh no!" I yelled.

I yanked at the volume control but, as Shaun had said, it made no difference. I pressed the off button. Nothing happened so I pressed it again. Still nothing happened. Music continued to blast out at a migraine-inducing level. I gave the stereo a good hard thump with my fist but Mexican trumpets continued to squeal.

Four miles later I spotted a garage by the side of the road. Music blaring, I screeched to a halt on the forecourt.

Inside the gloomy workshop I saw heads turn in my direction. A man in overalls walked out into the sunlight, frowning at the noise and wiping his hands on an oily rag.

I jumped out of the car, leaving the engine running, and trotted towards him. "Make. It. Stop," I shouted over the noise. "I'll pay anything, but please-make-it-stop."

As I sat in the shabby waiting room next to the workshop, my phone rang. It was Martin.

"Katy. Are you still with Underhill?"

Even though he couldn't see me I shook my head. "No, I'm stuck in a garage because—"

He cut me off. "Okay. Just had afternoon conference with the Chief. We'd like a lead-length news story on Underhill's innocence claims for tomorrow. Can you still file by end of play?"

I held my phone away from my ear, trying to process what I'd heard. I fought to keep the incredulity out of my voice, "Sorry, you still want the story? You did get my text saying he wasn't apologising any more?"

Martin's voice was testy. "Ye-es. I got it. And of course I still want the story."

"Martin, this is all rubbish. Nothing Underhill told me was in any way shape or form the truth. He isn't innocent he's a lunatic–"

"So? If he's saying he's innocent, then it's still a story." Martin paused. "Can you do it or not? If not, email your quotes to Amanda and she'll take over."

I stared at my phone. The idea of dippy Amanda writing up Patrick's lies was even worse than me writing it. I thought back to the insane rubbish that he had told me in the pub. "Martin, the thing is, he was so weird I don't think I have any usable quotes–"

He cut me off again, his voice irritable. "You must have something, for God's sake. He's just told you he's innocent, hasn't he?"

"Ye-es. But I am one hundred and fifty per cent sure he wasn't telling the truth." I paused and wriggled my toes inside my shoes. "I'm not comfortable writing up something I don't believe."

Martin gave a derisive snort. "Oh grow up, Katy. Patrick Underhill has just told you he didn't murder his girlfriend thirteen years ago. Whether he is telling the truth is not your concern. You are simply reporting what he has said and you will balance the piece with a response from the police and something suitably disbelieving from someone who used to know her." He paused. "Are you still trying to get out of this story because you're his friend?"

I felt colour shoot up my neck to my face. "Certainly not. And I already told you, he is *not* my friend."

Martin sighed. "Will you do it or not?"

I chewed at my lips as my indecision stretched. This was getting worse and worse. But I needed the money, plus if I wrote the story I could at least retain some control over what went in the paper.

"Katy? Are you still there?"

I had no choice. I nodded. "Okay. I'll do it. But I don't want my by-line going anywhere near it."

Martin chuckled. "I'll tell the subs."

"I'm serious. This is going to come back and bite us on the bum, Martin. I just know it. So keep my name off it."

"Duly noted." He might as well have added, now stop whining and get on with it. Then the line went dead.

I pulled my notebook out of my bag and stared at my notes, what there were of them because I'd stopped writing down Patrick's idiotic quotes almost immediately. My shorthand scrawl stared back:

I guess I'd better make my pitch.
The thing is, I didn't do it.
It wasn't me. I didn't do it.
I didn't kill her.
The Mexican came to me when I was asleep in prison. Told me to confess.

Grief… What a total nightmare. I grabbed my phone and called the police press office.

A young-sounding woman answered.

I said, "Hi, this is Katy Bennett from the *Gazette*. We're running a story tomorrow about the Kelly-Anne Davis murder. Patrick Underhill is now claiming he didn't commit the murder, so do the police have a view on this?"

Of course the press officer wouldn't have a clue what I was talking about. The murder had been thirteen years ago, and thirteen years ago she was probably still at primary school. But I also knew she'd be writing down everything I said in order to consult with her colleagues.

The woman took my phone number and told me she'd get back to me. Because all press offices are hopeless at getting back with quotes on time, I added, "I am right on deadline with this so I need a response by half-five latest otherwise we'll have to go with a 'no one from the police was available for comment' quote."

Next I Googled Glitz nightclub on my phone and called the number. I wasn't hopeful there would be anyone there at this time in the afternoon, but so far Nick Padovani was the only person I knew who had known Kelly-Anne. The phone rang twice then a man answered.

"Yes?"

"Can I speak to Nick Padovani please?"

"Speaking." He had a deep, confident voice. I punched the air and mouthed a silent *ye-ess!* I tried to imagine him thirteen years on, probably in his fifties now, more conservatively dressed – no more shiny shirts or too-tight trousers – but still a bit flash, maybe a mauve polo shirt and tasselled slip-on loafers. His dark hair would probably be greying, but I bet he still wore it slicked back with oil. He'd probably have a gold pinky ring set with a ruby on the fleshy little finger of the hand that was holding the phone; still trying way too hard to look like some kind of Mafia *Capo*.

In the workshop someone started using a drill and I raised my voice over the din. "Hello Mr Padovani. My name is Katy Bennett, a reporter for the *South West Gazette*."

"Yes?" His voice was wary now.

"I know this is a bolt out of the blue after all these years, but I'm doing a story about the murder of Kelly-Anne Davis. Patrick Underhill, the man convicted of her murder, has now been released from prison. He has told us that he didn't kill Kelly-Anne and he wants to clear his name. How you feel about that?"

Silence. For several heartbeats I thought we'd been cut off. Then he said, "The line's terrible. I can hardly hear you."

"I said, I'm doing a—" From the workshop, Herb's trumpet began to blare.

"What?"

I glanced at my watch and bellowed, "Can I come and have a chat with you about the story? In about twenty minutes?"

Again there was a long pause.

"I know you're busy so I promise it won't take very long."

He made a noise as if he was blowing out all his breath. "Okay. I can give you ten minutes. No more."

"Great. I'll see you at the club."

As soon as I'd hung up, the young police press officer I'd spoken to earlier rang me back. That was a first, a press office coming back before deadline. The quote she gave me from the police was predictably bland and roughly translated it meant, look, we knew he did it then and we still believe that now: *"There are no plans to re-open the case and we are not looking for anyone else in connection with the murder."*

As I hung up, I realised I could no longer hear sporadic bursts of loud Mexican music. The mechanic came into the waiting room. He looked a bit frazzled. Moons of sweat darkened the armpits of his overalls.

"Brilliant! Is it fixed?" I asked.

He held up what remained of my stereo. A tangle of wires dangled out of the back. It looked as if he'd wrenched it out with his bare hands. He pointed towards the door. "And we're closing now."

I offered to pay but the mechanic said there was no charge. He couldn't get me out of the garage fast enough. Back in the car the silence was blissful. I nudged the gearstick into first, pulled back on to the road and headed towards Sands End.

*

Twenty minutes later I turned off Sands End seafront into Grenville Row, a neglected side street that led from the promenade into a rabbit warren of narrow roads at the cheap end of town. The buildings were tall and painted in faded pastel shades. On the ground floors were various down-at-heel businesses. Grimy net curtains obscured the windows above. Opposite Glitz was a kebab takeaway, its metal grille pulled down to the pavement, and next to that was a shop that sold shabby second-hand furniture.

Glitz was a narrow pink and cream building over three floors with blacked-out windows. It had a flat roof surrounded by a low crenelated wall making it look like a scruffy Disney castle. As my car approached the club, a lone seagull swooped low over the bonnet, making a demented screech.

I couldn't park outside Glitz because there were double yellow lines so I drove on past the entrance and took the next left, pulling up in the shadows of a narrow alleyway that ran between the high walls of the club and the taxi firm next door. When we were eighteen, Becky used to insist her father parked here when he picked us up from the club. Becky's parents had been terribly over-protective of their only daughter so we always had to leave at midnight and always got a lift home with her dad. It suited me fine. Becky's dad had a fancy car so going home in a brand new BMW convertible was a bit of a treat.

I got out of my old wreck, locked it and wandered back out onto Grenville Row. The late afternoon sun was even more punishing than earlier and the heat felt like a weight pressing down from the sky. The front door of the club was wedged open with a fire extinguisher. I walked inside, my eyes taking a moment to adjust to the gloomy foyer. There was no one around. I plodded up the stairs to the first floor. The walls of the staircase were black and the sticky carpet was maroon. As I reached the landing, I saw a pair of matt-black swing doors that led into the main bar. The stairs continued upwards to a smaller bar on the second floor.

For a moment I stood staring at the swing doors as distant memories bombarded me. Even the smell was the same, a mixture of spilled beer and citrus air freshener. Beyond the doors I heard the sound of a vacuum cleaner.

I hitched my bag higher up my shoulder, took a deep breath, pushed open the doors and stepped inside.

Glitz looked different to how I remembered it, but perhaps that was simply because the lights were on. My memories were of a dark cave of a club with two huge bars at either end of one massive dancefloor. Now the club looked more like a cocktail lounge but it still had the same seedy feel. The walls were a strange shade of mottled purple that reminded me of rancid steak. The dance area was much smaller and surrounded by black leatherette armchairs and low black tables. The DJ booth was where it had always been but now there was a raised seating area next to it: a cluster of cane tables, lime green sofas and armchairs, separated from the rest of the club by a low fence made of thick bamboo poles. A young lad wearing headphones was grooving away to silent music in the DJ booth while a plump, grey-haired woman in a blue tabard was vacuuming by the loos. Behind the bar at the far end of the room, a man in a white t-shirt and black jeans restocked the upside-down bottles of spirits.

It took a moment for me to realise a man was motioning to me from behind the low bamboo fence. He had dark slicked-back hair and wore grey trousers and a fine-knit black pullover. I was almost sure he clicked his fingers as he gestured for me to come over. I walked across the dancefloor and up the steps towards him.

He extended his hand. "Nick Padovani."

"Katy Bennett, *South West Gazette*. Thanks for taking the time to see me."

I sat on one of the armchairs. Mr Padovani sat on a sofa opposite, a glass-topped table between us. As he crossed his legs, I noticed he wore grey patent slip-on loafers with no socks.

"You want a drink?" he asked. His voice had the trace of a foreign accent. The name Padovani sounded Italian but I knew he was originally from Malta. He added, "Coffee? Glass of wine?"

"Coffee would be great. Thank you."

Even though I was planning to tape the interview, I also pulled my notebook out of my bag and took the top off my pen. Belt and braces, as Martin would say.

Padovani turned in his seat and yelled over to the barman, "Two cappuccinos. Bring them over. Okay?"

He turned back to me. He didn't look too dissimilar to how I had imagined him thirteen years on. He was in his early fifties, his coal-black hair flecked at the temples with grey. He was tall with slim hips and thin fingers. His nose was long and his small eyes such a light shade of brown, they looked gold. As he stared across at me, he reminded me of a hawk.

I put my Dictaphone on the table. "Do you mind?"

He picked it up and looked at it, turning it over in his hand. "Nice bit of kit," he said at last. "What is it, voice activated?"

I nodded, "It can be."

He replaced it on the table so the microphone pointed towards himself. "So, Underhill is out, huh? Jesus, it doesn't feel like thirteen years."

"What's your reaction to Patrick Underhill's claims of being innocent?"

Padovani cracked a thin smile. "Lies? Usual lies."

I smiled back, thinking yes you knew him well enough.

He spread his hands, "I mean, he was…" Padovani shook his head as if struggling for the right words, "like two bananas short of a whole bunch. Yeah?" He put a finger up to the side of his head and made a corkscrew shape in the air.

I nodded, scribbling my shorthand. "Did you ever doubt he was guilty?"

He gave me a look that seemed to say, are you stupid? "Not for a second. He confessed to killing her."

"Do you have any idea why he's claiming to be innocent now?"

Again his fingers made the corkscrew shape beside his head. "Loony tunes."

He sat back in his seat as if he had nothing further to say and the interview was already over. His gaze drifted over to the bar and I felt he was regretting offering me the coffee.

Loony tunes was not exactly the killer quote I'd been hoping for. I decided to get him talking again by asking about Kelly-Anne Davis. Reaching into my bag I pulled out one of the old news stories with her photo on it. As I handed it to him, the barman put two cups of coffee on the table. The smell of freshly ground coffee beans made my mouth water.

Padovani stared at the photo long after the barman had gone.

"Oh yes. Yes... yes..." he sighed. "So pretty... So young..."

I gave him a moment then I said, "Do you remember much about Kelly-Anne Davis, much of what took place in the days leading up to her death?"

He gave a hollow laugh. "Do I remember?" He shook his head slowly from side-to-side, as if stunned by my question. "You're asking me if I remember? Listen, I remember it all... everything..." His voice turned hard and angry, "And I wish to God I didn't. Okay?"

Once again, I gave him time, hoping his anger would simmer down. His Adam's apple jerked.

He jabbed a finger at the piece of paper. "I took this picture. It was me who gave it to the *Gazette*. The bar staff were celebrating a win on the horses. I'd given them a sure tip." His shoulders heaved. "See, she is smiling in this photo because it was before she met *him*."

He put the piece of paper on the table and sat back in his seat, arms folded.

I thought back to the old press stories I'd read. "Kelly-Anne hadn't been living in Sands End for very long before she died. Do you know where she was from originally?"

Padovani scowled. "Hey, I thought you wanted to ask me about Underhill, not Kelly-Anne."

I nodded. "Yes. I do. But this story is about Kelly-Anne Davis as well as Patrick Underhill. Just now you told me you have clear memories of Kelly-Anne and the murder. I'd like to hear what you remember. It's just for background. That's all."

Padovani seemed to relax slightly. "Oh. I see. Okay. No, I have no idea where she was from."

"Perhaps you could tell me how she came to work at Glitz?"

He gave a curt nod. "Okay. But it will be just the same stuff I told the police."

"That's fine," I nodded, thinking please get on with it. Time was ticking by and I needed to file the story to Martin.

He puffed out his cheeks and rolled his neck like a boxer limbering up before a fight.

"Okay. It was the middle of May and she just walked in, this sort of time, late afternoon, asking for work. She had a little suitcase on wheels with her, looked like she'd just got off the train." He shrugged and his eyes returned to her photo. "I said, sure. I always needed bar staff."

"Had she worked behind a bar before?"

He gave another little shrug, "She said she had. To be honest, they all say that, not that it matters. It isn't rocket science. But actually she was very good. Very capable. After a couple of weeks, I made her my bar manager."

"So, that first day, you got the impression she'd literally just arrived in Sands End?"

He nodded. "She didn't even have anywhere to live. She asked me if I knew of any flats for rent. I owned a holiday-let in Sea View Heights but the agent had let me down and it was empty. I said she could stay there until she found somewhere permanent." As if realising that sounded an over-forward thing to offer someone you'd only just met, he added, "She had no money, nowhere to stay, not even for that night. I felt sorry for her. She looked like she hadn't slept for days. I could tell – immediately – she'd run away from someone." He gave a loose shrug, "In my business, you know these things."

"Do you know who from?"

Padovani shook his head. "She never spoke about her past."

I turned to a fresh page in my notebook. "When did she start seeing Patrick Underhill?"

"About a month later. When I heard she was dating him, I asked her, what the hell do you see in that loser? But he'd told her some rubbish about his parents dying in a car crash so he'd inherited a fortune. She said she felt sorry for him. I tried to tell her it was bullshit but she believed him. God knows why." Padovani rolled his eyes. "Anyway, when she found out the car crash story wasn't true, she dumped him." Once again he clicked his neck.

"Because he'd lied to her? Or because he wasn't rich?"

Padovani shot me one of his, are you stupid, stares. "You like it when boyfriends lie to you?"

"Did they go out for long?"

"No. The papers said they were together for two months but it wasn't anything like that long. It was a couple of dates. Nothing more. But after she dumped him he wouldn't take no for an answer, kept pestering her, making a nuisance of himself. He was obsessed. Totally obsessed. I kept saying to her, go to the police but she wouldn't. She said the police wouldn't do anything until he hurt her."

I looked up. "So she thought he was going to turn violent?"

Padovani nodded. He picked up his coffee cup and I did the same.

"She was terrified of him," he continued. "I had to ban him in the end, just a few days before she died. He was freaking her out, staring at her all night. Every time any man looked at her, Underhill was onto her, who's he? Why's he looking at you? Are you seeing him now?" Padovani shook his head. "After that, he used to wait outside the takeaway opposite, watching her when she left work, calling out her name, trying to get her to talk to him. He wasn't right, you know, in the head. She told me he'd got into her flat, one night while she was at work, gone through her things. Probably trying on her panties."

I blinked away that image fast.

He reached for his coffee and took a sip. "After the break-in I told her, now you have to report this to the police. But still she wouldn't. No idea why. So, I decided to take action. I made up my mind to go the police myself and tell them what was going on."

He shrugged. "But something came up that day. I can't remember what – some problem with a delivery I think – and in the end I didn't go. It was that night she told me she was leaving. She came into work, normal time, eight o'clock, and just told me straight. She apologised for not giving more notice but she wanted to get away from Sands End that night. I tried to talk her out of it. I was short-staffed, apart from anything else. I said, look, Underhill can't get away with hounding you out of your job, your home. Let's go to the police right now, get some kind of restraining order put on him."

Padovani's shoulders sagged. "But she said she'd made her decision. Her mind was made up. She had to get away. She was crying… you know…"

I turned to a new page. "Where was she going to go?"

He shook his head. "She wouldn't tell me. She didn't want anyone to know. I think she was terrified he'd go after her." He tilted his hand one way then the other. "But, the police, they found holiday brochures in her suitcase, so perhaps she'd planned to go abroad. I don't know." He broke off for another sip of his coffee.

"What happened after she told you she was leaving? Did she leave straight away?"

Again, Padovani shook his head. "No, we were very busy so she worked on for a few hours, left just before midnight. She was worried Underhill might see her leaving the club, follow her home, so I arranged for a taxi to pick her up outside the fire exit in the alleyway."

Padovani's shoulders sagged, "What nobody realised, he was already waiting for her inside her flat. I remember watching her leave the bar. She didn't even look back. That was the last time I ever saw her and even now, all these years later, I still get angry with myself."

I turned to a new page. "Why angry with yourself?"

Once again, he looked at me as if I was stupid. "Because I should have made her go to the police that night. Or I should have phoned them myself. And I should have given her a lift home instead of calling her a cab. I should have gone in with her, made sure she was safe. If I'd done that, she would be alive today. Underhill wouldn't have attacked her if I'd been with her." His eyes dropped. "But I was too busy. I couldn't leave the club. And for that – yes – I still feel anger with myself. It will stay with me until the day I die that I could have prevented her murder."

Heat fizzed in my chest.

Prevented her murder...

...this is your chance to make amends...

Katy, are you going up to Glitz tonight? It's just–

All I could hear was the sound of my heart thudding, the blood pulsing across my temples. I kept my eyes fixed on my notebook.

Oh for heaven's sake, I told myself furiously, he wasn't going to say anything important to you that night. It was just going to be more of his stupid, idiotic lies.

After a long pause I cleared my throat. "I... I understand you paid for her funeral? That was very generous—"

His anger flashed. "Generous? Don't patronise me." His voice had a hard, defensive edge. "It was the least I could do. Okay? She had no one. No family. No friends. Okay?"

I remembered the scant number of mourners in the photo. "I'd have thought more people would have gone to her funeral. And more of the people who worked here, perhaps."

He spread his hands. "Awful to say, but she wasn't popular. The other girls didn't like her, thought she was aloof. And also, I think there was jealousy involved because she was so pretty." He gave a sad shake of his head. "I'll be honest with you, those girls who did go to the service, I had to make them go."

Poor, poor woman. "And you also wanted a memorial in the park?"

He waved a dismissive hand. "It was nothing; a small gesture, just a tree and a little plaque. But, I wanted to... Like I said... I should have done more...." He stopped talking and I waited. I was used to giving people thinking time in interviews. I felt a tug of sympathy towards the man and tried to ignore the image of him groping Becky's bum. "What did you think when you heard Patrick had been charged with her murder?"

"What did I think?" His voice rose. "What sort of a question is that?"

I shrugged, "Presumably you weren't surprised, given what you've just told me."

He shook his head. "No. I wasn't surprised. I felt sick. And after he pleaded not guilty…" His voice trailed off, as if he'd decided against what he was going to say.

"After he pleaded not guilty?" I prompted.

Padovani looked away. "Nothing." He rolled his neck and I heard the bones pop. He reached for his coffee cup, picked it up then put it back on the glass tabletop. His breathing was hard. I got the feeling he was fighting to keep his emotions under control.

"So, you met Underhill face-to-face for your interview? Or was it over the phone?"

"No, I met him."

"Where?"

"Bristol."

Padovani gave a hollow laugh. "Bristol? That close? Jesus… What else did he say?"

I reached for my coffee cup, wondering how much of Patrick's crazy claims to repeat. I kept my face professionally blank, made my voice neutral, "He said that a Mexican came to him when he was asleep in prison and told him to confess."

"God Almighty…" Padovani muttered in a disgusted voice. He looked away, his eyes blinking rapidly, his mouth set in a hard thin line. "And your paper is actually going to print that rubbish?"

"Well, it'll be a balanced piece–"

"*Balanced?* He gets to say, 'hey, I'm innocent; I'm the good guy really' and you print it and every one believes it?"

"Well, not exactly–"

Padovani jabbed an index finger across the table. "No one knows how hard I tried to put things right afterwards. No one knows–" He broke off abruptly.

He folded his arms and sat back on the green sofa, his fingers twitching restlessly as if he was trying to decide whether he should continue. I kept quiet and let him reach his own decision.

He shifted his weight on the sofa, leaned forward. "Listen to me. I didn't shout about this at the time because I didn't want to make myself sound a hero. And I don't want to now either. Okay? So don't put it in your story. This is just for you. So you can understand—" Once again he broke off, took a deep breath and seemed to steady himself. "I went to see Underhill while he was on remand, okay? Drove all the way up to where he was in prison, Long Lartin. You know where that is?"

I nodded. "Worcestershire."

He nodded back. "Worcestershire. I said to him: tell the truth for once in your miserable life, huh?"

I frowned. My pen paused above the page. "So, it was you who told Patrick to confess?"

Padovani's anger erupted. "Listen to me. I didn't tell him to do anything. I asked him. I begged him to tell the truth. I pleaded with him to do the right thing, to man-up to what he'd done." His mouth turned down in a petulant scowl, "I don't know if that made a difference – if he listened to what I said – but a few days later he did confess. So…" His voice trailed off.

I chewed at my lips then shrugged; nothing ventured, nothing gained. "Does the name Jack Dale mean anything to you?"

His eyes were still angry, "Jack Dale? No. Why?"

Again I shrugged, "Patrick told me a man called Jack Dale can prove he's innocent."

Padovani raised his coffee cup to his lips. "Unbelievable…" He shook his head. "Incredible…. Listen, you want to be very careful what you report." He stabbed a finger down at the sheet of paper on the table. "Read the news stories: the crazy things he said; fairytales of ghosts telling him what to do, pictures of Kelly-Anne already dead that didn't exist." He finished his coffee with two quick gulps. "He's sending you on a chase after wild geese."

I had more than enough for the story but I decided to try and tease out a couple more really meaty quotes to satisfy Martin. "Do you think it's wrong Patrick's moved back to Bristol, so close to where he committed the crime?"

"Wrong? Of course I think it's wrong. And if he has any sense, he will stay in Bristol. Listen to me. If he comes within ten feet of my club, I will call the police. You understand?"

"If Patrick was here now, what would you say to him?"

Padovani's voice rose in incredulity, "Say to him? I would say, stop talking all this crazy rubbish and stay far away from Sands End. You are not wanted here."

Great. That would do. I closed my notebook, replaced the lid on my pen and picked up the Dictaphone. "Thank you for your time, Mr Padovani. I really appreciate it."

"Pleasure." It didn't sound as if it had been a pleasure at all. He paused, "What did you say was your name?"

"Katy Bennett."

"Katy Bennett..." he repeated. *"South West Gazette..."* I got the feeling he was committing it to memory. "Okay, Katy. And if you get any trouble from Underhill or he makes any threats to you, or you spot him anywhere in Sands End, you tell me. Okay? That man is not safe." He stood and extended his hand. "Nice to have met you. Goodbye."

CHAPTER SIX

It was gone seven o'clock by the time I got home. Shaun was sitting on his balcony, wearing his favourite palm-tree surf shorts and a baggy orange vest, his bare feet resting on the railings. He waved and yelled down, "Fancy cheesy chips and a beer down the Crite?"

I shook my head, "I can't. I have to write something up and email it to the *Gazette*."

Shaun's face fell so I quickly added, "I'll only be half an hour."

Shaun came down and sat out on my patio while I wrote up the Patrick 'I am innocent' rubbish on my laptop at the breakfast bar in my kitchen. In the end I didn't include half the stuff Nick Padovani had told me because there wasn't room. I certainly didn't believe any of Patrick's crazy claims about the mysterious and clearly made-up Jack Dale so I left all that out and tamed down Patrick's ludicrous quotes, what there were of them. I honoured Mr Padovani's request for me not to mention he'd gone to see Patrick at Long Lartin to plead with him to confess, but I did include Patrick's quote that a Mexican had come to him when he was asleep in prison and told him to confess. Hopefully people would be able to read between the lines and realise the paper was giving absolutely no credence to Patrick's ridiculous claims. In a nutshell, the story said Underhill was out of prison, claiming innocence, and the police and Nick Padovani thought that was fiction. I fervently hoped Martin would bury the story right at the back or – even better – spike it.

I read it through one last time, changed the odd word or two then attached it with my invoice to an email and pressed send. Job done. Goodbye forever Patrick, you weirdo.

*

The Criterion was our closest local pub. It was a total dive but less than five minutes walk away. As we ambled down the hill, the evening sun was still punishing. Inside, the pub was packed and like an oven so we sat outside at one of the scruffy tables set on a baking slab of grey concrete surrounded by a high breezeblock wall. I felt exhausted.

"I'll buy the drinks if you go and get them," I told Shaun, pulling my handbag onto my lap. Wine was always a voyage into the unknown at the Criterion so I usually took the safer option of bottled beer. "I'll have a Bud."

As I yanked my purse out of my bag, a folded piece of cardboard flew up in the air.

Shaun caught it. "Sharkie one hander," he grinned and I assumed this was some obscure reference to Australian beach cricket, his current late night TV obsession. Shaun unfolded the piece of card and handed it to me.

I stared at it in disbelief. Impossible. It was the beer mat on which Patrick had written the made-up phone number. It must have dropped into my handbag when I'd pushed it through the table slats.

"So what's that?" Shaun asked.

"Get the beers and I'll tell you," I sighed, handing him a ten-pound note.

A bottle of beer later, I'd told Shaun all about my strange trip to Bristol. He managed to keep a straight face until I got to the bit about the Mexican ghost bandit and Patrick's singing, at which point he burst out laughing, spraying beer across the table. "Excellent!" He wiped his mouth with the hem of his vest.

"It's not funny," I told him. "And the worst bit was, even though I told Martin it was all rubbish, I still had to write it up for tomorrow's paper." I shook my head, "Everything that comes out of Patrick Underhill's mouth is fiction. He is physically incapable of telling the truth. Always has been. I just hope Martin doesn't want a follow-up story." I rubbed my eyes. Suddenly I didn't want to talk about it any more.

Shaun picked up the beer mat. "Well, if the paper does want a follow-up, at least you've got a phone number for this Jack Dale character."

I snatched the beer mat out of his hand. "This is also total rubbish. It's a made-up number. Jack Dale is made up."

Shaun grabbed it back. "You tried calling it?"

I took a gulp of beer and shook my head. "Of course not. And anyway, Patrick says it's been conveniently disconnected."

Before I could stop Shaun, he'd picked up my phone from the tabletop. "Well, let's find out, shall we? What's your passcode?"

"It doesn't need one."

Shaun grinned and shook his head. "Katy, you seriously need a better phone." He spoke out loud as he pressed the keys. "0-2-0-8-1-1-1-7-7-7-7." He held the phone away from his ear so I could hear too. After a short pause I heard a woman's recorded voice say: "*I'm sorry. The number you have called is no longer recognised. Please try again.*"

"See?" I said. "I told you. It's a made up number. Just like Jack Dale is a made up name."

Shaun picked up his beer and with his other hand rubbed at a mosquito bite on his bare shoulder.

"Or it could mean the number's been changed." He shrugged. "Just call directory enquiries and ask them for the new number."

He didn't seem to get that the number had never been real. I felt my irritation rise, "Shaun, it's all lies. Even the lie about the Mexican ghost bandit he's used before." I took an angry swig of beer. "The thing is, I think Patrick tells these lies so many times, he actually thinks they're real."

Shaun sat back on the bench and angled his face to catch the evening sunshine. "Yeah, that's called confabulation, apparently." He closed his eyes and reached down for his beer. His fingers fumbled blindly across the table until I picked up the bottle and placed it in his hand. He raised the bottle to his mouth. "Thanks. So, do you think he believes what he told you today?"

"I don't know. I seriously doubt it's what he told his parole board." I wondered how his parole officer would react when he or she read my story in the *Gazette*. Patrick's stupid claims could mean he'd broken the terms of his release. Straight back to jail, Patrick. Do not pass Go. Do not collect £200. Slam.

The barmaid came out onto the patio with two red plastic baskets of cheesy chips. For several minutes there was silence as Shaun and I stuffed food into our mouths, then he said. "See, I know someone who could find that guy's new phone number."

I picked up a chip. "Shaun, Patrick Underhill invented that number today–"

"Weird Will," Shaun continued as if he hadn't heard me. "He could hack into BT's records in about a zillionth of a second." Shaun nodded, "I'll ask him."

Weird Will was one of the stranger characters Shaun had met through his work as a website designer. When Will was a teenager he'd been a talented hacker, using the not very imaginative pseudonym, Hacker. These days, companies paid him to break into their systems to find and fix their security vulnerabilities. I'd only met Will once at a meal to celebrate Shaun's birthday back in March, and once had been more than enough. He'd told me his favourite song was the Dr Who theme.

"Oh please don't bother Will with this," I said, thinking the one thing I didn't need right now was another nutter in my life. "I'm not planning to spend another second thinking about Patrick Underhill or his ridiculous claims. And anyway, wouldn't hacking the number be illegal?"

Shaun shrugged. "Well, depends on how you look at it. I mean, technically, the software Will would be hacking, is his. Sort of." His voice turned serious, "Look Katy, you're skint. You need paid freelance work. If this is a story—"

"Shaun, the only way this would be a story is if Patrick is telling the truth which – and please, please believe me when I say this – he isn't." I folded my arms across my chest. "End of subject."

I could tell Shaun was only trying to help so I willed gratitude into my voice and added, "But thanks for taking an interest."

Two women with a clutch of noisy and bratty young children arrived so we finished eating and left. Shaun said he needed to get back to Skype someone and I was desperate for a shower to wash away any remnants of my time with Patrick.

As we walked home up the hill Shaun seemed a bit subdued.

"You okay?" I asked him.

He seemed to force a smile onto his face. "Yeah. Absolutely."

"You sure?"

"Absolutely. Tip top."

But when we got inside the lobby, he seemed reluctant to leave. He ran a hand through his wiry sandy hair, "Um… um… Katy…" His voice trailed off.

I turned to face him and to my surprise he was blushing, his cheeks so pink it looked as if he had sunburn. I grinned, "What?"

He stared down at his feet, "Um…" He gave a heavy sigh and his blush deepened.

"Shaun, is something wrong?"

Again his big hand raked at his hair. He seemed to shake himself. "Nah…" He managed a grin. "Nah… nothing's wrong. Nothing at all…" He turned away. "Turkey stir-fry on the menu tomorrow evening if you fancy it." Then he walked up the stairs to his flat.

As I pushed open my front door, I smelled something strange. I sniffed the air a couple of times. Yes, there it was again, an unpleasantly sweet smell; definitely not Shake 'n' Vac, more like a rather sickly perfume. How odd. The back of my neck prickled.

I walked down the hall, across the sitting room and into the kitchen. And then I smelt it again: the same pungent pong. I picked up my laptop to put it back in my office and to my surprise it was warm. I yanked up the screen and pressed a random key. The machine whirred and flickered in to life. Strange. I was sure I'd switched it off before I went to the pub. The back of my neck prickled again.

I went back into the hall, and sniffed but the smell had vanished. Maybe I'd imagined it. It was probably all this weird Patrick Underhill rubbish messing with my mind.

CHAPTER SEVEN

The next morning, I woke to the sound of my mobile ringing. I opened my eyes and glanced at the bedside clock: seven-fifteen. Way too early. I reached out a hand, fumbled my phone off the bedside table and peered at the screen. It was my mother calling.

I tried to shake the sleep from my voice, "Hello, Mum."

As usual she dispensed with any social preamble. "Katy. It's your mother."

I frowned and lay back on the pillow. "Yes. I know."

"So, what time are we expecting you today?"

"Hmm?"

"For lunch."

"Lunch?"

Mum's voice steamrollered over my sleep-befuddled brain. "Richard and Corenza are coming over at twelve. They don't want to eat late because they're off to Center Parcs this afternoon."

I slapped a hand up to my forehead. Lunch at my parents' house with my annoying older brother, his perfect wife and their noisy children. It had completely slipped my mind. Rats. I'd planned to start writing my next romance novel today.

"Oh, Katy... I knew you'd forget." Mum's voice was thick with disapproval.

I sat up, "No, I haven't."

"You've a memory like a sieve. I don't know how you ever manage to write your silly stories on time. And please don't be late because I need to talk to you about something before the others arrive."

"Oh? What about–?" But she'd already gone. I flung my phone onto the duvet and lay back on the bed. "Crap," I shouted. "Balls."

I made a half-hearted attempt to go back to sleep but it was impossible so I got up, made a coffee, put my laptop on the breakfast bar and switched it on. Half an hour of Google research later, I cracked my knuckles, created a new Word document called Sweet Little Lies/MS, and started to type:

Petronella Mainwaring stood on the quayside and stared at the sleek, white – impossibly huge – yacht moored in the bay. Sunbeams danced down on azure, white-tipped waves making them sparkle like a million priceless diamonds. She found herself thinking that Cap Ferrat was quite possibly the most beautiful place she had ever seen.

I consulted the image of Cap Ferrat I'd found on the Internet. Yep. Pretty stunning.

Petronella had dressed carefully for her first meeting with her new boss. She wore white linen palazzo trousers that emphasised her long legs and tiny derrière, and a black halter-neck top that showed off her golden, gym-toned arms. She knew she looked good yet her stomach was a-flutter with butterflies because the man she was about to meet was none other than Yuri Aristov, the world-famous Russian cosmonaut, oligarch and eighth richest man on the planet. He was also, according to the press, a ruthless and irresistible womaniser. Although she had yet to meet him, Petronella was already half in love with the man....

At eleven-thirty I took a break and walked down the hill to the newsagent to pick up a copy of the day's *Gazette*. The sun was scorching. Every day now seemed hotter than the last. The heat rose off the pavement in waves. It seemed to make the world move in slow motion. After only a few minutes my fringe was damp and plastered to my forehead, and the soles of my feet were slipping out of my flip-flops. I tried to remember the last time it had rained or when the temperature hadn't been in the thirties. I'd actually had enough of the heatwave. It was making me irritable, probably because it was too hot to sleep deeply.

After I'd bought the *Gazette*, I flicked through it as I walked home until I spotted the headline for the Underhill story:

Seaside killer claims innocence

It was, as I'd anticipated, a story on the very last news page. Then I stopped dead in my tracks because underneath the headline were the words:

EXCLUSIVE by Katy Bennett

Bloody hell! What part of "leave my by-line off this story" had Martin failed to understand? As I stomped up the hill, my mind composing the furious email I would send him, my phone rang. I glanced at the screen. Martin. Perfect timing.

I injected an icy tone into my voice, "Ah. I was just about to ring you. I thought we'd agreed not to put my name on the story?"

"Oops." Martin's voice had a mocking smugness that made me think he wasn't in the slightest bit sorry. Not long before I'd left the *Gazette*, one of my stories had appeared under the by-line Katy du Val. A slip of the sub's keypad, Martin had assured me in the same mocking tone. Yeah. Right. I hadn't believed him then either.

84

"Anyway," he continued, "about your Underhill story." He paused. "That was a sodding pile of crap. We would have sodding binned it if we hadn't been short on news today." Martin always used the word sodding when he would much rather use a stronger swear word.

I stared at my phone in disbelief. What a total ingrate. He'd be sitting in typical berating the reporter pose, the phone wedged under his left ear, legs bent, brogues braced against the edge of his desk, making his black chair swivel from side to side by shifting his weight from left bum cheek to right bum cheek, with a dozen smiling reporters pretending to be engrossed in their work, while straining to hear every word.

"Actually Martin, you were lucky to get that much—"

"Come on, Katy. It was shit. I mean, the stuff from Nick Padovani is all very nice, but the story wasn't about him. It was supposed to be about Patrick sodding Underhill's reasons why he's saying he's innocent of murder after thirteen sodding years."

"Well I told you I had hardly any useable quotes—"

Martin read them back to me, "*I didn't do it. It wasn't me.*" His voice rose in disbelief, "And what the hell is all that crazy crap about the Mexican? Didn't you read the sodding file stories? Underhill was spouting all that stupid stuff after he was first arrested."

Yes, and he's still spouting it now. I rolled my eyes, willing myself to remain calm. "That's my point, Martin. It is not true. He is making it up." Good grief. I'd told him that yesterday.

"But he must have said something else that was worth quoting for Christ sake."

My anger ignited, "Yeah, he started singing a song by Kid Creole and the Coconuts: *Stool Pigeon, ha-cha-cha-cha—*"

Once again, Martin cut me off. "Set up another chat with him immediately. Ask him what new sodding evidence he's offering that will clear his name." He paused, "Are you deliberately trying to make us look like a sodding laughing stock over this?"

I shook my head. "No! And anyway, I'm not sure I can set up another chat."

"Why?"

"Because after he told me all that rubbish, he vanished."

"Well, if you ever want any more work out of the *Gazette* I strongly urge you to sodding go and sodding find him. Ring me after lunch so I can update the Chief."

"Martin, this is fiction–" But he'd gone. I felt like hurling my phone against a wall.

"Ahhrr!" I yelled and an elderly man walking a Chihuahua shot me a startled glance.

Back at home I went through the envelope Martin had given me ahead of the interview and to my surprise found an email address for Patrick scribbled on a Post-It note.

I rattled off an email giving him my mobile number and asking him to phone me ASAP. Once I'd done that it was time to leave for lunch at my parents' house. I toyed with the idea of changing then decided it was far too hot for anything other than cut-offs and a camisole.

Soon I was in the car and making slow progress along Sands End seafront as day-trippers, lured to the coast by yet another hot and cloudless day desperately searched for somewhere to park. To make up for forgetting about lunch, I stopped off at a garage and bought a peace-offering bottle of over-priced white wine.

Back in the car, I rejoined the nose-to-tail traffic and worried about our family get-together. It might sound strange but my family was unaware of why I really left the *South West Gazette*. As far as my mother, father and older brother Rich were concerned I was cruelly made redundant in the first week of January, just another hapless victim in the latest round of swingeing cuts designed to keep the newspaper from going bust.

I don't make a habit of lying but in this instance, it was definitely kinder to tweak the truth: kinder to others and – if I was honest – kinder to me. If I'd told my parents that I had walked out of my job, I would have received never-ending lectures about irresponsibility, impulsiveness and the need for controlling my big mouth. My mother would have gone into stress overdrive, foreseeing a daughter forever on the employment scrapheap or worse, penniless and needing to move back into the family home. She couldn't have stood the shame. In her world children were born, grew up, left home, went into good jobs and married wisely, and all that was a direct reflection on parenting skills. Children who were still single at thirty-one then deliberately screwed up their careers were not what she wanted to talk about at her U3A meetings.

Thanks to my tweak of reality, I'd got a month's worth of sympathy and moral outrage during which my mother briefly cancelled her delivery of the *Gazette*, Richard suggested, in all seriousness, that I retrain in IT and my father said very little as usual and blamed the Government.

In the end I was only five minutes late getting to Mum and Dad's. My parents had a large, non-descript detached house on the south side of Sands End. They'd lived there since I was born. The house had mullioned windows, a big back garden, a small front garden, and rather ostentatious white colonial pillars on either side of the porch.

Dad was in the lounge watching the cricket. Mum was in the kitchen cooking, so I went to ask her if she needed a hand. Richard, Corenza and the twin brats, Macsen and Berin, hadn't yet arrived.

Even though the temperature in the kitchen was tropical, Mum looked immaculate as usual. Her blonde bob didn't have a hair out of place. She was wearing a novelty plastic apron over a pale pink blouse, smart black trousers she'd call slacks, and pale pink ballet pumps. The apron had a picture of a Marmite jar on the front. It had been a Christmas present from Richard, my brother's idea of a joke because, like Marmite, people tended to either love my mother or dislike her intensely.

"At last!" she said, shooting me an exasperated glance. Her eyes lingered on my cut-off denim shorts and then drifted down to my flip-flops. "I see you've made an effort with your appearance as usual."

I tried not to rise to the bait. "Can I do anything?"

"No thank you. I can manage."

I handed her the bottle of wine.

She glanced at the label. "Pinot Grigio. You know that always gives your father heartburn."

"I didn't know that actually. So, where are Richard and Corenza?"

"Running late. One of the children had a funny tummy this morning."

I sat down and flicked through a cookery book lying open on the kitchen table. "Traffic was awful."

"Well you should have left earlier."

Mum opened the oven door and poked at something inside with a wooden spoon. "I'm doing salmon. It's too hot for a roast."

"So, what did you want to talk to me about?" Might as well get the lecture over with.

"Ah. Yes. Becky Thomas's mother tells me you're back in touch with Patrick Underhill." Mum turned to face me, her eyes challenging a denial.

Wow, that had got around fast. I flicked through a few more pages of the cookery book, lingering on a glossy photograph of a roast chicken.

Mum pointed her wooden spoon at me. "I'm surprised at you, Katy. But then, you always were drawn to that sort of thing." She turned back to the stove.

I was baffled. "Drawn to what sort of thing?"

"Patrick Underhill. You always had an unhealthy interest in him at school."

Her statement was so outrageous I was briefly stunned. "Where on earth did you get that idea from?"

Mum opened a plastic tub of watercress sauce, poured it into a pan and lit the gas. "And I saw your story in the *Gazette* today – '*I didn't do it!*' Honestly Katy, I'm ashamed of you, giving that horrible man the opportunity to spout such rubbish. Totally irresponsible. And you didn't tell me you'd got your old job back."

I shook my head. "I haven't. It was just some freelance work. Look, I told the news editor I didn't believe Patrick but–"

"It only seems five minutes since he went to prison," mum interrupted. "The Dog Day Murder, that's what the *Daily Mail* called it."

I frowned. "What on earth is a dog day?"

"Dog days are when the weather is so hot people claim it makes them do terrible things. That's what Patrick

89

Underhill told the police." She paused for sarcastic emphasis, "He claimed it was the hot weather that made him kill her. What a ridiculous excuse. It was hot for all of us that summer but no one else resorted to murder." She gave a heavy sigh, "I simply don't understand why you've always been so keen to defend him."

I knew I should just shut up or change the subject but it was impossible not to respond to such a preposterous allegation. "When have I *ever* defended him?"

"I remember you saying, when he was arrested, that he didn't do it."

My voice rose, "Mum, that is simply not true! I suppose, before all the facts came out, I might have briefly suggested that maybe he didn't do it." I closed the cookery book with a snap. "I mean, innocent until proven guilty and all that–"

"There you are then. You were defending him."

I felt my irritation move towards anger. "I was *not* defending him, but I suppose we were all a bit surprised when he was arrested for murder–"

"Well, I wasn't surprised." Mum ground some black pepper into the saucepan. "He was always loitering around town wearing those nasty camouflage trousers or nylon tracksuits."

"So that meant he was bound to be guilty of murder did it?" It came out more sarcastically than I'd planned.

"There you go again. Defending him."

"No! I'm really not. Of course he did it. I'm just saying you can't judge someone because of the way they dress."

Mum stirred the sauce to within an inch of its life. "Don't be facetious, Katy. Anyway, he *was* guilty. He confessed to killing that poor girl. So you shouldn't be saying he didn't."

I wanted to scream. I couldn't believe we were even having this conversation but it was impossible to escape. "Look, I wasn't planning to do a story saying he's innocent. It was supposed to be him apologising for killing her so he could move on with his life. But when I met him to do the interview..." No, I couldn't be bothered to explain. "Anyway, the *Gazette* wants a follow up but I'm not going to write it—"

Mum shook her head. "Well, I for one won't be reading it."

"Like I said, I'm not writing any more stories about him."

Mum caught up with the conversation. Her voice rose an octave, "What do you mean, you're not writing any more stories about him? I don't think that's very sensible, given you're unemployed. Beggars can't be choosers."

Good grief, I couldn't win.

Mum poked a knife into a pan of new potatoes. "And I never liked you going to that nightclub where that poor girl worked. Ritz or Glitter or whatever it was called. It wasn't safe."

That was the first I'd heard. "Glitz. Why wasn't it safe?"

She wrinkled her nose. "That Maltese man who owned it was an unsavoury character. Always turned a blind eye to underage drinkers. And he was on the verge of going bankrupt."

I frowned. "Nick Padovani? He still owns the club actually—"

"We all hoped the wretched place would finally close down that summer after the murder. Instead he gave

91

it a refit and started calling it a cocktail lounge, can you believe."

She gave a derisive snort. "A cocktail lounge in Sands End?" She pointed the spoon at me again. "Honestly Katy, I really hoped you'd left this sort of smut-grubbing behind when you lost your job."

Smut-grubbing? "It was just a story, mum." I felt exhausted already and I'd only been here for a few minutes.

"You should write a report about Corenza's new jewellery business instead. People would much rather read that sort of thing."

As if on cue, I heard loud voices in the hall. My brother bellowing his hellos, the sound of two small boys making engine noises, then the kitchen door opened and Corenza, tall and slim with wavy auburn hair, wafted in. She was wearing a long pink sundress with one of her homemade Celtic pendants around her neck. She handed mum a bottle of fizzy rosé.

Mum glanced at the label, "Ah! Perfect! Lovely to see you, Corenza. What a super dress. I wish Katy would wear pretty things like that." She clicked off the gas under the sauce and rammed a lid on the pan. She turned around and frowned at me. "Why do you always have to dress like a homeless person? I can't remember the last time I saw you in a skirt. It's not like you haven't got the figure to wear feminine clothes. In fact, I'd say you're looking a bit thin at the moment."

I glanced at Corenza, hoping for some kind of sister-in-law solidarity but she was admiring her reflection in the mirror by the kitchen door.

Mum threw open a cupboard. "I don't expect you're eating properly." She waved a jar of multi vitamins at me. "Got them on three-for-two at Boots," and when I hesitated, "Oh, for goodness sake, take them. So, how's Shaun?"

"He's… fine…" I took the jar and shoved it in my handbag, struggling to keep up with the wild twists and turns of the conversation. Mum took a foil parcel on a tray out of the oven. Huge clouds of steam billowed into the kitchen. Corenza closed the oven door for her.

"Thank you, dear." Mum put the tray on the kitchen table and turned to Corenza. "I do wish Katy and Shaun would stop messing around and get together. He's such a nice young man. Always so polite to me on the phone."

I frowned. "When do you ever speak to Shaun on the phone?"

Mum turned to Corenza again. "I'm always calling Katy and finding Shaun in her flat. Poor lamb, he's obviously smitten." She giggled as if she couldn't imagine why.

I gritted my teeth, trying to remain calm. "It's very simple, Mum. Shaun's flat has a tiny balcony, mine has a garden. When the weather's nice I let him work on my patio. Anyway, he's only interested in women who look like Elle McPherson," I added, wondering how much time Shaun did spend in my flat when I wasn't there and why the cheeky sod was answering my phone. I resolved to have a stern word with him later.

Corenza took warm plates out of the hostess trolley. "Well, I suppose you could grow your hair longer like hers."

And presumably also get leg extensions. "Please, take it from me. Shaun and I are not, and are never going to be, an item. He's a really good friend but I don't fancy him and he doesn't fancy me. Full stop."

Mum began to dish up the food. She put a salmon fillet on each plate and poured over the sauce. "It's just sex, sex, sex with you young people. And if that's all you're looking for, Katy Bennett, you're going to die a lonely old woman." Mum took the new potatoes off the stove and hurled them into a colander. Her head disappeared into the cloud of steam. "Anyway, how's the job hunting going?"

I turned away. "Oh. Not bad."

She picked up a broccoli floret with a pair of serving tongs and waved it at me. "If I were you I'd be having a good, long think about your future. It's not natural to be single *and* unemployed at your age."

I took a deep breath and tried to remain calm, hoping I didn't kill her before the dessert arrived.

She handed me two plates to carry through to the dining room. "And don't write off poor Shaun just because he likes Australian women. Your father had a thing about Charlie's Angels when I first met him, so I went straight to the hairdressers and told them, I want to look exactly like Cheryl Ladd, thank you very much."

I rolled my eyes and followed her through, thinking only another hour. Only another hour…

CHAPTER EIGHT

Two hours later I managed to extricate myself from my family's clutches. Richard had bored us all into oblivion about the planned trip to Center Parcs, and the twins had destroyed two rose bushes in the back garden. But at least it had distracted Mum from her self-appointed role as life coach from hell. I'd had no response to my email from Patrick Underhill but Becky had phoned my mobile twice. Each time she had left the same message, asking if I'd told Patrick not to go anywhere near the school reunion when I met him. As I joined the main road back into town, the traffic slowed to a crawl because of a shunt between an undertaker's hearse and a Toyota Prius.

I rested my elbows on the steering wheel and stared miserably into the heat waves as they shimmered over the tarmac, easing the car forward on the clutch. The trouble was, when it came to my love life, my mother did have a point. It was over a year since my last steady boyfriend and before him there had only been two others, one of whom had turned out to be married, and I didn't do married men.

The car inched forward another few feet. Part of the problem was that my basic romantic requirements hadn't changed much since I was fifteen: I wanted a drop-dead gorgeous man who would sweep me off my feet, ruin me sexually for all other men and be madly and passionately in love with me forever. So far that hadn't happened.

I moved the car forward another few feet. That was the real problem here. It wasn't, as my mother said, unhealthy to still be single at thirty-one, but it was perhaps unhealthy to have never been in love at thirty-one. Not properly in love. Not the way the heroines in my novels fell in love, madly and passionately, dizzyingly and irrevocably. Besotted. Dazzled. Obsessed.

By the time I drove into my car park, I felt exhausted. Over lunch, my mother had told me that Sands End's pier was still advertising for summer staff. To get her off my back, I'd invented some freelance work, which I said would tie me up until September. More white lies, but I needed to protect my sanity.

Back inside the flat, I turned on my laptop and checked my emails. The first six were all from Becky. Each had the same subject line: *Re. School Reunion arrangements*. Nope. I'd look at those later. I scrolled on down. Still nothing from Patrick. No surprise there. The last email from Becky had as its subject line: *KATY OPEN THIS EMAIL RIGHT NOW!!!!!* I sighed and clicked on it:

Hi Katy. When you interviewed Patrick, you did make it clear that he is to stay away from the reunion. Didn't you?

I puffed out my cheeks. Becky was every bit as tenacious as my mother and would pursue me terrier-like until she got an acceptable answer. Okay, I hadn't asked Patrick about the reunion, but if I told Becky that she'd have another meltdown. So instead I wrote, *Hi Becky, 100% convinced he isn't coming. K x*. Well, that was true.

Then I remembered that I was supposed to have phoned Martin back by now about the Patrick Underhill follow-up. I chewed at my lips for a while then decided to email him instead:

Hi Martin, I emailed Patrick earlier asking him to call me so we can arrange another meeting but he hasn't come back to me. Just thinking, if I don't manage to find him before deadline, I've got loads of great unused quotes from the Nick Padovani interview so could easily knock you out something along lines of: Murder victim's boss warns Underhill, 'stay away from Sands End'. What do you think?

Almost immediately Martin sent his reply. Even by his usual standards, it was blunt: *No thanks. We'll handle this story in-house from here.*

A strange hollow feeling opened up in the pit of my stomach. I was off the hook with the Underhill story. Wasn't that what I wanted? So why did it feel as if I'd just been sacked? Did the Chief and Martin think I wasn't up to the job because my story in that day's *Gazette* hadn't been up to par? Did they think I was only fit for writing gooey romance stories? What was it Martin had asked me in the pub, if Lori du Val had taken over? I felt my cheeks flush in anger. Well if that was the case, maybe I'd had enough of news journalism too. Maybe I should try something else. I scrolled through my inbox and found the email alert I'd received a few days ago for a PR job:

This award-winning corporate communications and public affairs consultancy, based in Lincoln, is recruiting for a PR Executive to join their team…. this role will see you raise external awareness through a range of activities….

Yawn.

You will also promulgate the ethos and reputation of our client throughout the region; develop and…

Promulgate? Did I really see myself 'promulgating' and taking it seriously? I glanced at the salary. Hmm. Okay. I could promulgate. And Lincoln might be lovely.

I picked up my laptop and took it out to the patio table. Working outside was trickier – too many distractions – but wasting all this nice weather seemed sacrilegious.

An hour later, I sent off my application for the PR job and returned to *Sweet Little Lies.*

Where was I? Oh yes, beautiful blonde Petronella had flown to the Bahamas in a private jet to try and mend her broken heart over Yuri the Russian Cosmonaut-slash-Oligarch, but there was a violent tropical storm and...

...Petronella kicked the flimsy cotton sheets off her legs. Sweat trickled between her breasts. The humidity was suffocating. Just as she thought she would expire from the heat, the sky was torn apart by the loudest clap of thunder she had ever heard and white lightning daggered into her hotel room...

Daggered as a verb. Classy.

...Another ear-splitting clap of thunder reverberated around Paradise Beach. It was both terrifying and exhilarating. Her heart beat faster. Suddenly she felt warm breath on her neck and a man's soft voice in her ear. "Don't be scared, Petronella. I will keep you safe..."

I stared around the garden, as a trickle of perspiration ran down my chest too. I wished the weather would break in real life. A thunderstorm was exactly what we needed to stop this oppressive heat. I resumed typing.

"Yuri! It's you!" she exclaimed, hardly daring to believe he had followed her there. His masculine scent invaded her nostrils. Her head swam. She couldn't concentrate. All she wanted was to feel his warm, strong arms encircling her, to surrender to her pent-up desires...

My fingers were a blur on the keyboard.

I'd been writing for about twenty minutes when my laptop pinged to say I'd received an email. I frowned at the interruption. It was a typically terse one-liner from Martin: *Katy, did you did actually meet Patrick Underhill yesterday?*

What a bizarre question. Was he implying I hadn't? I wasn't the pathological liar around here. I clicked reply and typed: *Yes of course I did. Why?*

I tried to return to my writing, but I couldn't concentrate. Twenty minutes went by. Still no reply from

Martin so I sent him a text: *Why are you asking if I really met Underhill?*

More minutes ticked by but still Martin didn't respond.

In the end, I forced myself back in to the pink-tinged world of Petronella. There at least, everything would, ultimately, have a happy ending.

A short while later, Shaun ambled out into my garden, scratching at his arm. Another mosquito bite probably. Shaun seemed irresistible to them.

"Fancy a latte?" he asked, looking very pleased with himself.

I nodded and followed him into my kitchen.

"Weird Will came up trumps," he said, pouring us mugs of frothy coffee as I perched on one of the stools facing the breakfast bar. Shaun drank his slouched up against the sink.

"Sorry?"

"That new number for Jack Dale you wanted."

"Actually, I never said I wanted it."

"Will found it in about three seconds."

I was still smarting about Martin so I snapped back, "Good for Will."

Shaun sipped his coffee and seemed oblivious to my bad mood. "Six months ago that phone number Patrick gave you was registered to a company called S P International." He pulled a yellow Post-It note out of the pocket of his shorts and waved it at me looking smug. "And this is their new number."

I gave a sulky shrug. "Well, I'm not calling it."

"Aw Katy! Aren't you even a tiny bit intrigued about this Jack Dale character?"

"Not even slightly. And anyway, I'm off the story. Martin thinks I've lost the plot." Grief… Why did that sting so much?

I pointed at the Post-It, "That number proves nothing. It's a coincidence. Patrick thought up a fictitious phone number that just happens to have once been registered to someone. So what? It doesn't prove 'Jack' exists." My fingers made inverted commas in the air.

Shaun grinned. "But what if he does? What if Patrick is telling the truth?"

"He never tells the truth!" I howled. I took a deep breath. "Look, I appreciate that you're trying to help and please give Will my thanks but the *Gazette* doesn't want me to write anything else about this story. They've dumped me."

"Well, this would be the way to get the story back again." Shaun paused and looked down at his fingernails. "Look, if you don't mind me saying, you're behaving a bit weirdly about all this."

I felt a blush on my neck. "Meaning?"

"Meaning: you're a journalist, you chase stories." He ran his hand through his sandy hair. "But it's like you're deliberately trying to avoid this one. Like you're in denial it could even be a story." He paused. "It's almost as if you're afraid of what you might find out."

Katy, are you going up to Glitz tonight? It's just I need–

The blush reached my cheeks. I fixed my eyes on my phone. "That's… that's rubbish. I'm not interested in this story because it's a load of bull. Patrick is a load of bull." I took a defensive gulp of coffee.

Shaun shrugged. "Yeah, but it's gotta be worth a phone call, hasn't it? I mean, if I was a journo, I'd want to know if Jacko really existed."

Martin's strange email from earlier came back to me. *Did you actually meet Patrick Underhill yesterday?* I gave a huffy shrug, "Okay. Have it your own way."

I tapped in the number. The phone at the other end rang twice then the answer machine cut in, a woman's voice, friendly, well-spoken: *"Thank you for calling S P International. Please leave your message after the tone."*

As I was no longer officially doing the story for the *Gazette*, I decided not to mention the paper. I cleared my throat. "Hello, my name is Katy Bennett. I'm a freelance journalist. This message is for Jack Dale. I'd like to speak to him in connection with the murder of Kelly-Anne Davis." Out of force of habit I added my usual sign-off, "I am right on deadline with this story, so if Jack could call me back before end-of-play today I'd very much appreciate it." Then I left my mobile number and hung up.

Shaun grinned. "There. That wasn't too traumatic was it?"

I tossed my phone down on the breakfast bar. "In about five minutes, some poor receptionist is going to check the answer machine and be totally and completely baffled."

Shaun shrugged. "So what?" He collected our mugs and put them in my sink. "Right. That's enough hard graft for today. I'm off for a game of squash."

After Shaun had gone, I stared at the phone number for S P International. Was there any possibility that Patrick was telling the truth? That Jack Dale did exist?

I put the name into Google: 96,000,000 hits. I scrolled down the first half-dozen: Jack Dale Building Supplies, Jack Dale school football coach, Jack Dale estate agency... I tried again, this time adding S P International and the phone number. But all I found were random numbers in what looked like datasheet entries. Just looking at them gave me a headache. Pointless, utterly pointless. I shook my head. No, I was well out of it. I was off the story, and Patrick had vanished. Martin could deal with it now.

When I went back out into the garden, the sun had moved around and the patio table was no longer in the shade. It was far too hot so I relocated to the breakfast bar and distracted myself with Petronella. She had now been lured to Florida by a mysterious text. Little did she know it was from Yuri...

Movement caught her eye at the top of the gangplank and a man began to walk towards her. She felt her heart race. His hair was the colour of sun-ripened corn, he had high cheekbones and a jutting, square jaw. His black tailored trousers hugged strong, muscular thighs and his solid shoulder muscles clenched under his peacock blue shirt. As he grew closer she saw that his brooding eyes were the colour of dark chocolate. Then he smiled and spoke in a voice softly accented from his impoverished Muscovite childhood. "Petronella... I'm so glad you came."

*

An hour later, Shaun's return from the squash club interrupted my writing. His feet thudded up the stairs to his flat then thumped across my ceiling. Less than a minute later they thumped back across my ceiling and down the stairs. I closed my eyes in resignation and counted under my breath. "Three, two, one..."

On cue, Shaun's head poked around my kitchen door, his sandy hair wet with sweat. "Don't suppose you've got any spare bread?"

"Good grief, did I leave my front door wide open again?"

He at least had the decency to blush. "Ah. Well, I used my key actually."

"That key is for emergencies only."

"Well, it seemed a shame to disturb you. I'd guessed you'd be in full flow." He helped himself to bread and shoved it in the toaster.

I turned around in my seat. "Shaun, this isn't an episode of *Neighbours*. In this country, people don't just wander unannounced into other people's homes. If my front door is locked it's locked for a reason." I saved and closed *Sweet Little Lies/MS* as a precaution because Shaun could be rather clumsy. He'd once spilt a cup of tea over my laptop and there had been a very tense few hours while we'd waited outside the airing cupboard to see if it would still work when it dried out. "And that reminds me, stop answering my phone when I'm out."

He looked mystified. "When do I do that?"

"All the time, according to my mother."

He looked a bit sheepish. "Ah."

The toast popped up. Shaun plonked it on a plate, shoved in two more slices and set about slathering the first lot with butter. He shoved almost a whole slice of toast in his mouth. "Hey, did that Jack bloke call you back?" Crumbs sprayed everywhere.

What with Petronella's steamy exploits I'd forgotten about my stupid message for S P International. "No, of course not."

The toast popped up and Shaun began buttering the next batch of slices. "Ah well. Never mind. And anyway, you're off the story."

Yes, that still stung. I poured us coffee and felt guilty about being so snappy to him earlier. "Look, I know you're just trying to help and I really appreciate it but..."

I clicked on my inbox in case I'd any more emails from Martin. I hadn't, but there was one from Patrick Underhill. In the subject line it said: *Have you found Jack?*

I clicked on the email but all it said was, *Got your message. We need to meet.* Underneath it said: *Sent from my iPhone.*

At that same moment, my phone beeped to say I'd had a text. It was from a mobile number I didn't recognise: *Meet me in the bar of the Bay View Hotel at 6pm.*

"Hmm…"

Shaun looked over. "Problem?"

"Patrick Underhill has sent me an email asking if I've found Jack and now he's asking to meet me at the Bay View Hotel this evening."

Shaun shrugged. "Just ignore him. Like you said, you're off the story."

I got up, paced over to the sink and stared out through the kitchen window. "Hmm."

"Hmm?" Shaun echoed.

"See, Martin made me feel really useless earlier when he yanked me off the story." To my horror, I felt tears stinging behind my eyes. "It's… it's like he thinks I'm all washed-up as a reporter and that… that really hurts."

Shaun gave a solemn nod. "All washed up like a greasy spoon." He clicked on my coffee machine. "Well, like I said earlier, get the story back. Talk to Underhill, see what he has to say."

I frowned out into the garden. Shaun was right. I did need to get this story back, prove to Martin and the Chief that I had what it took to write a decent news report, even if Patrick was spouting rubbish.

A fat woodpigeon was sitting on the fence under the watchful stare of my cat Henry. I nodded. "Maybe I will go and meet him tonight."

Behind me, Shaun's voice turned anxious, "Can't you just speak to him over the phone, given he's such a nut-job?"

Quite frankly, meeting Patrick face-to-face again was the very last thing I wanted to do. But a face-to-face interview would be a lot easier than one over the phone especially if he started getting weird again, spouting nonsense about Mexican ghost bandits and singing bad eighties pop songs. I turned to face Shaun. "Look, say no by all means, but would you come with me?"

Shaun did a strongman pose. "You want me to sort him out for ya?"

I smiled. "Well, I was thinking more along the lines of you loitering in the background while Patrick and I have our little chat."

Shaun's face lit up. "Hey, like your bodyguard? Yeah! Count me in!"

My fingers hovered over my phone. I typed. *OK. I'll be there,* then pressed send.

Shaun wiped his buttery fingers on his sweaty t-shirt. "So what time's def-com one?"

"Six." I glanced at the kitchen clock. "Hell... It's half-five now."

He grinned. "Better go and change into my Superman outfit."

*

I didn't bother getting changed out of my denim shorts and yellow camisole. I supposed I should have made some effort towards a professional appearance, but to be brutally honest I couldn't be bothered. Shaun didn't look any smarter. He wore jeans with a rip in one knee and a baggy orange t-shirt advertising the Richmond Tigers, an Australian Rules football club.

At ten-to-six I followed him across the baking car park to his massive silver Toyota Land Cruiser. We drove to the hotel without speaking, listening to an old Elton John CD at full volume. I had hoped the music might take my mind off meeting Patrick again, but the track playing was *Saturday Night's All Right for Fighting*.

As we joined the seafront traffic, my phone rang. I glanced at the screen. Martin. Good grief. What now?

I gestured for Shaun to turn the music down a tad. "Hi, Martin."

His voice was blunt, "Katy, did you actually meet Patrick Underhill at that pub yesterday?"

I rolled my eyes. "I already told you I did." What the hell was Martin playing at? A bad feeling crept over me. "Why?"

There was a heartbeat's pause from Martin's end of the line then he said in a tart voice, "Because I've had what feels like endless phone calls today from a woman called Heather Sanderson at the Probation Trust press office complaining about your story in today's paper." Even though I couldn't see him, I could tell he was livid. "Sanderson says Underhill categorically denies giving you those quotes about being innocent and wanting to clear his name."

Panic jolted into my heart. "What?"

"Underhill is furious about your story because it could jeopardise his parole." Martin paused for dramatic effect, "He says he waited two hours for you at the pub to give you his apology story but you never showed."

The sheer audacity of Patrick's lie took my breath away. My whole body sagged. For a moment I was lost for words. "Martin... that's... insane–"

"Did you go to that sodding pub or not?"

"Yes!"

"Did he give you those sodding quotes or not?"

"Of course he did! I have it in shorthand–"

"Did you record the interview?"

"No, he didn't want to be taped…" Oh bloody hell. Legally, it was the shorthand that was crucial, but a recorded interview would bring about a swifter conclusion to clear things up with Martin. I should have insisted on the Dictaphone.

For several long seconds there was silence from Martin. Then he said, "If I can't smooth things over with Sanderson I'm going to want to see your shorthand notes. Right now she's threatening all sorts of trouble."

I felt physically weak, as if someone had punched me in the stomach. I said, "Martin, I swear to God, everything in that story was exactly what he told me–"

But he'd already gone.

"Arsehole," I shouted at the screen. "Dickhead."

Shaun glanced over. "Problem?"

I could barely control my anger. My hands were shaking. "I am going to kill him," I howled, thumping my hands down on the dashboard.

"Who?"

"Patrick Underhill!" What the hell was going on? Why was he doing this to me? Why was he denying what he'd said? How could he deny it?

Shaun's voice jolted me back. "Bay View Hotel," he announced, reading a sign by the side of the road. "Here we are then." He turned off the seafront, manoeuvred the huge car through the narrow white-pillared entrance and accelerated up its steep drive.

My hands were still shaking so I pressed my palms between my knees and concentrated on composing myself. Sod the story. Martin could have it with my blessing. And sod the money too. I'd rather flip burgers on the pier than put myself through another second of this.

I glanced up the drive. Somewhere inside the hotel was Patrick Underhill smugly sitting at the bar, waiting for me to turn up so he could have some more jolly japes at my expense. I felt my anger come to the boil. Well, two could play at that game. The only question I was going to put to the scheming little scumbag was why the hell had he retracted his quotes. And then I'd tell him to phone Martin – right then and there – to tell him the truth; that he did meet me and he did say those things. I shook my head and gave a bitter smile. The truth... Patrick Underhill wouldn't know the truth if his life depended on it.

The hotel was Victorian, its whitewashed frontage dazzling in the evening sunshine but it wasn't exactly humming with customers, judging by the car park. There was only one car, apart from Shaun's.

"Wow, would you look at that," Shaun said, his voice dripping with envy as he pulled into the space next to it. "That is the best car in the world."

Despite my simmering anger, I had to admit it was sex on wheels. It was gunmetal-grey, very low and very sleek with twin exhausts. It looked muscular and tough, like it wouldn't take any crap from anyone. It also looked very fast. I peered at the badge on the grille. "Is it a Merc?"

Shaun nodded. "It is. It's a Mercedes-Benz AMG GT. Oh yes. Yes please. That baby's got a mighty V8 under its bonnet. It'll do nought to sixty-two in three seconds. Top speed 193 miles per hour."

"Oh, not that dissimilar to mine then," I quipped. "It looks expensive."

"It is expensive."

"How expensive?"

"That model? A hundred-and-fifty-grand, give or take."

"Wow." Imagine being able to afford to spend that much on a car.

Shaun seemed unable to wrench his eyes away.

"Yeah, I think we can safely assume it doesn't belong to Patrick Underhill," I said at last. If I owned that car, I'd gun the engine and run him over.

Shaun seemed to remember our mission. "Yeah. Right." He was all business again as we got out of the car.

"Here's the plan," he said, slamming the door with more force than I felt was necessary. "We walk in together. You make contact with Underhill and I'll wait at the bar. If he starts getting weird, just wave your hand and I'll be right over to provide back up. Okay?"

Even though I was still fuming about Patrick's latest stunt, I couldn't suppress a smile. "My hero," I said in a high-pitched American accent.

But Shaun didn't smile back. "I'm being serious, Katy. Come on. Let's get this over with." Without another word he strode towards the hotel entrance.

Revolving glass doors led into a wide conservatory. White wicker armchairs faced matching tables strewn with glossy magazines. Palm trees in terracotta pots reached towards the glass ceiling. A receptionist behind a beech-wood counter glanced at us and I saw her give my scruffy appearance a disapproving up-and-down. A sign on the wall pointed left to the restaurant, right to the bar.

We turned right. As I followed Shaun along the corridor I felt a mixture of fury and anxiety: fury because I wanted to punch Patrick hard in the face, anxiety because the last person who'd crossed him had got her head beaten to pulp. Part of me wanted to turn around and go home. But a bigger part wanted Patrick to make the call to Martin. Yes, I had Patrick's quotes in shorthand, but what if Martin still believed Patrick over me? Technically, I could have made them up, scribbled them down at any point. I remembered the blonde woman who'd been behind the bar. She'd vouch for me, surely? And surely she'd remember Patrick? Or perhaps Martin wouldn't even try to find out if I'd really been to the pub, that he'd simply print a swift apology to pacify the parole officer and leave it at that. My name would be mud. I'd never work for another newspaper. I shook my head. My reputation as a journalist was at stake. Patrick needed to make that call to the news-desk right now.

I followed Shaun through the frosted glass door at the end of the corridor and stepped into the bar. The last time I'd been to the Bay View Hotel had been as a bridesmaid at Becky's wedding reception almost eight years ago. I had hazy memories of a large room with insipid blue walls that reminded me of a nursing home lounge. At some point during the celebrations I remembered dozens of silver balloons had drifted down over the guests and some rowdy friends of Becky's older brother, Jason, had great fun popping them with their cigarette lighters until Becky threw a tantrum and made them stop.

These days the bar looked as if it was trying to emulate a stuffy gentleman's club. Gilt-framed pictures of boxing hares hung on olive-green walls. Distressed brown leather armchairs clustered around low tables dotted with bowls of peanuts. A huge crystal chandelier, which I definitely didn't remember being here on my last visit, dripped down from the ceiling. My flip-flops almost disappeared into the deep rust-coloured shag-pile. Dark green velvet curtains were drawn back from huge sash windows. Evening sunshine streamed onto the carpet. A white baby grand piano sat at the far end of the room and twilight jazz played from speakers I couldn't see.

"This has changed a bit since my last visit," I whispered to Shaun, trying to ease the tension, but he didn't reply. My eyes followed his as he looked around, but I could already feel the anti-climax. The room was empty.

Shaun strode up to the bar and slapped his big palms down on the polished wood. A skinny barman dressed in a black shirt and trousers popped up behind the bar like a jack-in-the-box, a big smile of welcome on his face. "Hello! And what can I get you lovely people on this beautiful evening?"

Shaun shook his head. "We're meeting someone." He gave the room another pointless sweep. "Doesn't look like he's here yet though. Is this the only bar in the hotel?"

I glanced at my watch. It was three minutes past six.

The barman placed a bowl of peanuts on the polished wood. "Might I suggest that your friend is enjoying the splendid views from our sun terrace?" He nodded towards a set of white French doors.

Yes. The terrace made more sense. He was probably smoking for England out there.

I remembered the terrace too, an expanse of chipped grey concrete, bordered on three sides by a low whitewashed wall, overlooking the car park and a soggy expanse of lawn that sloped down to the seafront. I didn't remember any lovely views but that may have been because the weather had been awful for Becky's wedding. The after effects of Hurricane Charlie had brought brutal gusts of wind and random drizzly squalls. From what I could remember, grey sky had joined grey sea in a seamless bank of grey. More bad memories crept up on me as I remembered Becky's Moulin Rouge themed ceremony. She'd worn a show-stopping scarlet bridal gown. Susie and I had been her bridesmaids. We had been dressed in very short mini-dresses which had red and black striped bodices that made us look like Wild West hookers. An image popped into my mind of the two of us, tipsy and huddled underneath a patio umbrella on the hotel's terrace, laughing like idiots, trying to light sneaky fags away from disapproving parental eyes while my cigarette lighter clicked impotently in the wind.

I glanced towards the French doors and felt my heart beat faster. Shaun's eyes met mine. I chewed at my lips and felt a sharp pinprick of pain as a small piece of skin came away in my teeth.

"Okay. Let's get it over with," Shaun said, his voice gruff with tension. "Do you want me to wait in here or shall I come out with you?"

I shifted my weight onto my other foot as my indecision stretched. What was I going to do? Go in guns blazing and yell at him for landing me in it with Martin? Or try to remain calm and just get him to make the call to the news-desk. My anger rose just thinking about it. No, if I was going to lose my temper I didn't want Shaun standing there behind me. "Maybe just come out with me so Patrick sees I'm with someone then go back and wait at the bar while I talk to him?"

Shaun nodded. His wide shoulders tensed. "Okay. Like I said, if he gets tricky give me a wave and I'll be right out." He put on a strong Aussie accent and shook his fist, "And I'll say, back off you creepo. Or else."

Shaun's bravado wasn't fooling me. I could tell he was nervous. I felt a rush of affection for the big man.

"Yep. That should do the trick," I said, my bravado working overtime too.

Shaun held the door open for me. I pulled my sunglasses down from my forehead, rammed them over my eyes, balled my hands into fists and stepped out into the fierce evening sunshine.

CHAPTER NINE

The chipped, grey concrete had been replaced with sandy-yellow paving slabs. Instead of the scruffy white wall surrounding the hotel's terrace, there was now a chest-high glass barrier so guests would not be inconvenienced by the often bracing Sands End sea breeze. Below, a golf course-standard lawn sloped down behind the car park towards a row of tall palm trees. Beyond the promenade, the muddy sea sparkled – almost beautifully – in the evening sunlight.

There was only one person on the hotel terrace. He sat with his back to the hotel, shaded beneath a cream patio umbrella. My first glimpse was of a sun-tanned hand resting on a white metal table. A sprinkling of fair hairs led up from his knuckles to the chunky diver's watch on his left wrist. His fingers drummed gently on the tabletop. His fair hair was short and neat. I hadn't taken more than two steps onto the terrace when he stood and turned to face me.

My breath caught in my chest. He was perhaps ten years older than me – tall with an athletic build, and gob-smackingly handsome. At first, I thought his eyes were blue but on closer inspection I decided they were grey flecked with hazel. He wore a dark suit, the jacket of which was undone to reveal a cobalt-blue shirt but no tie. The cut of his jacket emphasised his broad shoulders and from the way his shirt was tucked into his trousers I could tell there wasn't an ounce of fat on his stomach.

"Katy. Glad you could come." He smiled and extended a hand towards me. His voice was quiet and had no accent. I could tell he never had to raise it to get things done. His skin felt warm and his grip was firm.

"I'm Jack."

My heart seemed to skip a beat.

"Jack…?" It was as lucid as I could manage. Oh. My. God. Jack Dale was real?

I rolled my eyes. "It was you… you sent me that text."

He frowned. "You look as if you were expecting someone else?"

I shook my head, feeling my cheeks flush. "Sorry, I thought the text was from someone not very nice. Um. I mean…."

Jack's eyes flicked over my shoulder towards Shaun. "Which is presumably why you brought your henchman with you?" He smiled.

My blush deepened. I wished I'd worn something smarter, or even just put on a tiny bit of make-up. I felt the blush spread down my neck as I turned around. "Oh. This is my friend Shaun. Shaun, this is Jack…"

Shaun walked over. He didn't look happy. He and Jack shook hands with no apparent enthusiasm on either side.

"So, I'll just be in the bar then," Shaun muttered, his eyes not quite meeting mine. "Unless you'd prefer me to stay?"

I shook my head. "I'll be fine. Thanks."

"So I'll just be in the bar then," Shaun repeated. After an awkward pause, he turned around and trudged back through the French doors.

Jack smiled his heart-stopping smile again. "What did you do, ring round all your friends until you found the tallest?" He indicated the seat opposite him. "Please."

I sat. My handbag was clutched hard against my chest. I dumped it on the ground next to my chair and gazed across the table. He was so unbelievably good-looking. His face was lightly tanned as if he spent a lot of time outside. It was a healthy face, a face that looked as if it belonged to a man who got up at six and went for a run along the beach with a black Labrador bouncing at his heels. The sort of face I dreamt about waking-up next to, especially the way his was looking at me, lips curving upwards in an easy smile which created pleasant creases at the corners of his eyes. The sort of face that provoked a strange fizzing sensation in my chest and made my stomach feel as if it was full of fluttering butterflies. *Hmm, I should write that down.*

The barman materialised beside the table and asked us what we'd like to drink. He looked to me first.

"I'd like a glass of dry white wine please," I said, praying my face had returned to its normal colour. "I don't suppose you have any Cloudy Bay Sauvignon Blanc?" I added, unable to keep the hope out of my voice.

The barman nodded. "We certainly do."

Wow. Somewhere in Sands End that actually stocked a decent wine. I would need to come back here again sometime.

The barman turned to Jack. "And for you, sir?"

"I'll have an Americano."

"Very good." The barman nodded and retreated back to the shadows of the bar.

Jack gave me another slow-burn smile. His eyes fixed on mine. I blushed and looked away. I needed to do something with my hands. A cigarette would have been perfect. If there'd been a beer mat on the table, I'd have started pulling it to pieces. I shifted on the metal seat trying to find a more comfortable position. I leaned back, then sat upright, crossed my ankles, uncrossed them and crossed them again, ran a hand through my hair, floundering for something intelligent to say. All the while Jack watched me, an amused smile on his lips.

So Jack, why did you want us to meet this evening?

He sat back in his seat and his shoulder muscles shifted under his suit jacket.

So Jack...

His grey eyes met mine. Goodness, he had fabulous eyes. And fabulous cheekbones.

So...

"Lovely weather, isn't it?" I said, my brain registering surprise as the words escaped my lips. *For pity's sake Katy*, I screamed silently, feeling my cheeks blush scarlet.

Jack smiled. "Spectacular."

"Phew! Almost too hot really." I fanned my face with my hand.

"Yes."

"I mean, it's usually quite nice here during the summer, which is useful, this being a holiday resort," *Shut up!* "But, I think it's been even hotter because Sands End has a microclimate." My voice burbled away, yet I felt powerless to halt it. "Like they have in San Francisco. I've heard the temperature there can vary by as much as five degrees, block to block." *Stop!*

"Really?"

No! Stop! "Oh yes." I heard my enthusiasm rise. "Quite often it's a lovely sunny day here in Sands End, but pouring with rain in the rest of the West Country. I think it's something to do with being this side of the Mendip Hills." I tried to point in their direction, but somehow my finger ended up wedged under the arm of my sunglasses and they flipped clean off my face. Horrified, I watched as they somersaulted twice in the air then landed with a loud clatter on the paving slabs and skittered away like some strange black creature.

Before I could react in any sane way, the barman reappeared on the terrace, a silver tray balanced on the palm of one hand. Without breaking his stride, he swooped down, scooped up the sunglasses and placed them, without a word, on the table in front of me, as if nothing had happened and anything we thought we'd just seen, we hadn't.

"Thanks," I muttered, my eyes fixed on my lap. My face felt as if it was on fire. My cheeks were actually throbbing. A heavy silence settled over the table.

After what felt like several years, the waiter spoke. "One glass of Cloudy Bay Sauvignon Blanc and one Americano."

He placed my wine on a square terracotta coaster. The glass of wine was huge and, judging by the droplets of condensation, icy cold. I picked it up and rolled it casually against my blushing cheeks as if this was something I always did when presented with a drink. *For God's sake, put it down*, my mind howled. *Just put it down and ignore it.*

The barman placed the coffee in front of Jack. "Is there anything else I can get for you?"

Yes. A very big hole so I can throw myself into it.

Jack shook his head. "No. Thanks."

I watched the waiter stride back across the terrace, the silver tray held loose at his side. He pulled open the French doors and dissolved into the shadows. I wondered how much Shaun could see from the bar and imagined him doubled over with laughter. I'd never hear the end of it.

Somehow the wine was back on the coaster. I stared at it.

117

"That's very interesting, about the microclimate," Jack said at last.

I squinted at him through my fringe, trying to gauge whether he was taking the piss. He smiled and took a sip of his coffee. There was no ring on the third finger of his left hand, I noticed. My hand snaked out and picked up my sunglasses. In a quick movement, I shoved them back on my face.

Jack reached forward for his coffee. The breeze changed direction and his aftershave wafted across the table. I closed my eyes and inhaled. He smelled amazing, sort of spicy and woody. Then he was speaking again. "Sands End seems a nice place. Have you lived here long?"

I risked a gulp of wine. It was delicious. I felt it roll, icy-cold across my tongue, on past my tonsils, down my throat and hit my stomach. Some of the tension eased from my shoulders. "Well, I grew up here but then I moved away, obviously."

He frowned. "Why obviously?"

I shrugged. "Well, it's not the most exciting place in the world."

"No? So why did you come back?"

Wow, his voice really was amazing. "Oh, I just fancied a change," I waved a dismissive hand, as if that was the sort of thing I did all the time; that I was such a free spirit, always doing mad, wild things on a whim. The phrase, *I've got fewer ties than a nudist* popped into my head, but thank goodness it stayed there.

I picked up my wine. It felt heavier than before. Puzzled, I glanced down and saw that the terracotta coaster had stuck itself to the bottom of my glass. I made a clumsy grab for it then watched in horror as it bounced off my thigh and landed flat on the ground, splitting clean in half.

"Shit," I breathed. My nuclear blush returned. I bent down, picked up the two halves and pressed them together on the table as if they would magically fuse. I glanced up to check Jack's reaction and he was staring deep into my eyes. Was he actually flirting with me? He smiled and took another sip. I did the same.

"So, you're a journalist?" he said, his amazing eyes still locked on mine.

I nodded and swallowed. "Yes." *Do not mention Lori du Val*, my brain warned.

"Who for?" he asked.

"Oh anyone who pays me. I'm a freelance." Hopefully that made me sound suitably mercenary and in demand. I gulped some more wine, almost emptying the glass. *Slow down! He's going to think you're an alcoholic.*

Jack glanced across the terrace and raised a hand. Following his gaze, I noticed the barman was hovering outside the French doors, as if he was wondering if he'd get away with a crafty fag. He scurried over.

"Same again?" Jack asked me.

I hesitated. Well, one more glass couldn't hurt. I nodded. "Thanks."

Jack granted me another heart-stopping smile. Oh my word. This wasn't my overactive imagination. This man was definitely flirting with me.

"So let's talk about this story you're writing," he murmured.

I sat up. Rats. I'd pretty much forgotten why I was here. Okay. This was going to be tricky. Obviously I didn't want Jack to think I actually believed any of Patrick's stupid lies, or have to admit that the newspaper had already yanked me off the story.

But then again, Jack was real. Jack was here. He must know something, otherwise why had he asked to meet? Was there any remote possibility that Patrick *was* telling the truth for once in his miserable life?

Silence stretched. Up in the blue sky, white gulls keened and drifted on the warm evening air. The salty smell of mud and chip fat drifted up from the beach. "Well, it's sort of a long story," I began.

Jack's lips curved up in a slow smile. He murmured, "That's okay. We've got all night."

I had a sudden image of tousled white cotton sheets, a tanned chest, broad shoulders, entwined limbs. The heat crept back on my cheeks. For heaven's sake, Katy – get a grip. He's not Petronella's Russian Cosmonaut-slash-Oligarch. Although, now I came to think about it, Jack did bear an uncanny resemblance to the picture my writer's mind had already formed of the physically perfect Yuri.

I reached for my glass. "It's also a bit of a bizarre story."

Jack leaned back in his seat. The same heart-stopping smile flashed across the table. "I like bizarre."

Wow. Me too. Kindred spirits. Okay, Katy. Keep it simple. "There was a murder here thirteen years ago. A man called Patrick Underhill killed his girlfriend. Her name was Kelly-Anne Davis." I paused, checking Jack's reaction, but he made no response. In fact, he suddenly looked rather bored. I soldiered on, "Patrick killed her because she'd dumped him, and also because he claimed the hot weather had made him..." I paused trying to remember the suitably disparaging word that had been used in the old news reports, "...irritable." The wine had done its trick. Words were coming more easily now, and they were even making a vague sort of sense.

Jack's face remained expressionless.

"I met with Patrick yesterday. At that meeting he told me he didn't murder Kelly-Anne Davis and he now wants to clear his name."

A frown creased Jack's brow. "So this is what your story is about? Helping this man, Patrick, clear his name?"

"Well that's what he wants it to be about."

Jack's grey eyes found mine.

"And what do you want it to be about, Katy?"

My face flushed and I looked away. In my stomach, a hundred more butterflies emerged from their cocoons and fluttered their wings.

The waiter was back with another glass of wine on his silver tray. Jack had not ordered another coffee, I noticed. As the waiter went to put the glass on the broken coaster, I snatched the wine out of his hand and took a quick, grateful gulp.

Jack waited until we were alone again. "So where do I fit into this?"

"Well, Patrick claimed a man called Jack Dale could prove his innocence. I assume you're who he was talking about because Patrick gave me this phone number." I reached down and pulled my handbag up on my lap. After groping inside I found the beer mat and passed it across the table. Jack stared at it for what felt like a long time.

I decided to make myself sound a little more investigative. "Obviously, that number's now been disconnected but I discovered it was registered to a company called S P International. It was then quite simple to find S P International's new phone number, which I rang earlier today to see if I could find Jack Dale. You."

So far so good. All that was true, even if I hadn't expected to get any response to my call. I grabbed my glass and took another gulp of wine, reminding myself that there was a fine line between alcohol-induced lucidity and

121

alcohol-induced incoherence. I felt I might be teetering on the brink right now.

Jack handed back the phone number. The tips of our fingers touched and electricity seemed to jolt through me.

He spread his hands, palms up. "Well, I'm afraid I don't know anyone called Patrick Underhill." He seemed to have no more to say on the subject. His gaze drifted away across the terrace.

I frowned. "And yet Patrick had your name and phone number?"

Could this be just a huge, strange coincidence? That Patrick had made up a number that had once actually existed, and was now registered to a company that employed a man called Jack Dale? I firmly believed in coincidences but that was stretching it even for me. And, if Jack knew nothing, then why was he here? It would have been the easiest thing in the world for him to ring me back that afternoon and say, sorry – don't know what you're talking about – I've never heard of Kelly-Anne Davis.

I took a punt. "So, as you didn't know Patrick, presumably you knew Kelly-Anne, or else you wouldn't be here."

For what felt like a long time Jack said nothing. Although his expression hadn't changed, I had the oddest feeling I'd touched a nerve, almost as if this was something he'd hoped I wouldn't mention.

He gave a curt nod. "Yes. I knew Kelly-Anne." His voice dropped as he said her name.

I choked on my wine. Some of it went up my nose. I coughed then sneezed. I hadn't seriously been expecting him to say that. Not really. Cheeks roasting, I reached into my bag, pulled out a tissue and dabbed at the wine on my face.

Jack's gaze drifted towards the sea and his eyes became sad. He was even more gorgeous when he looked troubled.

"So, how did you know her?" I asked.

He seemed to wrench his eyes back to me. I held his gaze but, despite my best efforts, my nerve broke and I looked away first, fixing my eyes on the damp tissue screwed up in my palm.

He gave a sharp sigh. "I only knew her briefly. It was a long time ago." His eyes remained fixed on the horizon. His shoulders seemed tense under his suit jacket. I could feel his discomfort. It came off him in waves. They'd been lovers, of course. That was obvious. It was the way he'd said her name. Perhaps their relationship had been illicit and that's why he hadn't volunteered their connection earlier. I rolled the idea around. Okay, it didn't look as if he was married now, but maybe he had been then? An uncomfortable silence settled across the table.

I said, "I'm sorry. It must be difficult talking about her."

His eyes returned to mine and he attempted a smile. "Not at all. Like I said, we only knew each other briefly."

I was about to ask when exactly, and if it had been while she'd been living in Sands End, but his voice cut through my thoughts.

"So how far advanced are you with your story?"

I blushed again. "Oh. You know. Early days."

Not at all advanced would be more accurate.

"Oh? Your message sounded as if you were about to file."

"Well, not exactly about to file. But you know, working on it…" I was such a rotten liar.

Jack spread his hands. "When you left your message today mentioning Kelly-Anne," again his voice dropped as he said her name, "I thought we should meet. And what you've told me is certainly intriguing. But Patrick Underhill is mistaken. I can't help him clear his name."

What a surprise.

Jack sat back as if, once again, he had nothing more to say.

Silence reclaimed us. I tried to think of a plausible explanation why Patrick had Jack's phone number. Maybe Patrick, suspecting Kelly-Anne had dumped him for another man, had gone through her address book. Maybe he had found Jack's name and a phone number, assumed he was the man she was now seeing and… And then what? Waited thirteen years then decided the man he thought had been shagging Kelly-Anne could prove he hadn't killed her? That was insane. It made no sense. And anyway, Patrick had confessed to the murder. I thought back to our strange meeting in the pub garden. No, Patrick had to be lying, lying about everything as usual. The only question was why? My daft ideas ran out. I twiddled the stem of my glass. What a disaster.

Jack's voice jolted me back, "So, Katy, did Patrick Underhill tell you who he thinks really murdered Kelly-Anne?" His voice was casual, teasing almost. Once again it dropped as he said her name.

I shook my head. "No… He um… he disappeared half-way through the interview."

Jack frowned. "Disappeared?"

"Well, he went to the Gents and never came back." I gave a shrug as if this sort of thing was an occupational hazard in the hard-knock world of press journalism.

"I see. And presumably that's who you thought you were meeting here this evening."

I paused, my wine glass halfway to my mouth. "Sorry?"

"Patrick Underhill. You thought you were meeting him not me at this hotel."

Good grief, Jack must think I was a right idiot. I felt a blush creep onto my cheeks. "It did... Uh, it did cross my mind. I was expecting to hear from Patrick, so when I got a text from a number I didn't recognise..." My words ran out.

Jack nodded in a reassuring way. "You thought it was from him not me."

My blush deepened.

He said, "I'm really sorry I can't help you with your story. Looks like I've wasted your time this evening." He stared at the sea.

"Oh no. Not at all," I said hurriedly. "If anything I've wasted yours by dragging you all the way to Sands End for nothing."

Jack shrugged as if it was no big deal. "I was due to be in the area on business anyway." His shoulders appeared to relax a little. "So, what else did Patrick tell you when you met?"

I certainly wasn't going to repeat any of Patrick's insane behaviour. It would make me look like an even bigger fool for meeting him. In the end I just said vaguely, "Oh... Nothing much. He said... um... he said he was... told to confess to the murder..." My tone of voice implied my scepticism.

Jack smiled back, as if he too found that unlikely. My heart did the funny missing-the-beat thing again.

"And did he mention who told him to do that?" he murmured.

No way was I mentioning the Mexican ghost bandit. I was about to tell him about Nick Padovani asking Patrick to do the right thing by admitting his crime, then remembered Padovani had asked me to keep that quiet.

125

I twiddled a strand of my hair between my fingers. Seconds ticked by. "Um. No. He didn't."

Jack again leaned back in his chair. The tension in him seemed to have disappeared. Maybe I'd imagined his discomfort.

I could hear the traffic on the main road, the thud-thud of bass music on someone's car stereo. The smell of roasting meat wafted from somewhere, the hotel restaurant perhaps. I looked at Jack's suit. It was beautifully tailored and his watch did not look like a knock-off from the Sunday market. Maybe that was his Mercedes AMG GT in the car park. "So, what is S P International?" I asked, hoping to string out our meeting a little longer. "What do the S and P stand for?"

"Specialist Protection."

Disappointing images of burglar alarm systems popped into my head. "Oh. Okay. Specialist protection of what? Buildings?"

"People."

I frowned. "You mean like... like a bodyguard?" I grabbed my glass. "So, you're a bodyguard?" I tried to ignore the high-pitched excitement in my voice. "What sort of people do you bodyguard? Famous people? Politicians? Celebrities?"

He shrugged. "Anyone who feels they need protection."

Sexy. I wondered if I could change Yuri from Oligarch to bodyguard without too much re-writing. Maybe I'd use Jack for a little impromptu research. I took a gulp of wine. "You know, there's something I've always wondered about bodyguards. I mean, why would you risk your life for someone you don't even know?"

Jack shrugged again. "Because they pay me to."

"But aren't you scared you'll get killed?"

126

He smiled. "No."

"Why?"

"Because I'm quite good."

Wow. "So can you protect your clients against anything... anyone?" The film *The Day of the Jackal* popped into my mind. "Like even against a... a professional assassin?"

Jack glanced down at the table. "Well, I guess if someone is absolutely determined to get through all the security measures I put in place, then he will."

I felt oddly disappointed by that. "Oh. So, then what happens?"

He looked up. "He gets me instead."

Double wow, it must be amazing having a bodyguard, knowing he'd protect you with his life, put his body between you and an assassin's bullet. Talk about heroic. I gulped down the last of my wine. "And you work for S P International?"

"S P International is my company."

The barman walked out through the French doors and I glanced down at my almost empty wine glass but Jack did not offer me another refill. The barman sauntered to the far end of the terrace and turned his back on us. A second later I saw a puff of blue smoke drift above his head.

Jack ran a hand through his hair. His fingernails were cut neat and short. "I expect your friend Shaun is getting bored."

My heart sank but I took the hint. "Yes, I should be going I suppose..." I left the sentence dangling but Jack did not take the bait. I stood and pushed back my chair. "Well, thank you so much for meeting me this evening." My voice had a forced cheeriness.

Jack stood too. "No problem. I'm sorry I couldn't be more help with your story. I guess Patrick just got confused."

That was a nice way of describing his delusions. I reached down and picked up my handbag. My fingers shook slightly as I pulled one of my business cards from the inside pocket and handed it across the table. "Just in case you think of anything else... you know... just in case..."

"Thanks," Jack took the card from my outstretched fingers.

I hitched my handbag up on my shoulder, aware I was shamelessly trying to delay leaving. "Actually you've been a lot of help. You've simply confirmed what I was thinking anyway."

Jack frowned. "Which was?"

I smiled. "Well, that as usual, Patrick Underhill was feeding me a complete pack of lies."

Jack smiled back. His eyes suddenly seemed darker, softer. "It was nice to meet you, Katy," his voice was low and husky. "I enjoyed it. I wish it could have been for longer but..." He tilted his hand, as if to say that he had other less pleasurable demands on his time.

My blush was radioactive again. "Absolutely. I really enjoyed meeting you too."

He extended his hand across the table. "Goodbye, Katy."

My stomach fizzed at the feel of his firm grip and his warm skin. The mating butterflies returned for another tryst.

I turned and walked towards the French doors, on legs that did not feel as if they belonged to me. *Don't look back, do not look back*, my brain implored.

Of course I did. As I pulled open the door, I risked a swift glance over my shoulder. But Jack wasn't looking anywhere near me. His head was turned towards the sea and his fingers had resumed their slow drumming on the table. I tried to ignore the hot flash of disappointment, then I stepped out of the sunshine into shade.

CHAPTER TEN

Shaun was leaning against the bar, reading the *Gazette*, an empty half-pint glass by his side. He looked up as I came in. I gave him a friendly wave and walked into a leather footstool. "Whoops."

He rolled his eyes and put down the paper. "How much have you had to drink?"

"Only two glasses."

"Are you done?"

I nodded.

"Great. Let's go. I'm starved."

I followed him down the corridor and out through the hotel reception.

"So, how did it go?" he asked, letting me go through the revolving door ahead of him.

The fabulous Mercedes was still parked next to Shaun's Toyota. I'd bet my last fifty pence it was Jack's. "Patrick Underhill is so full of rubbish. Jack had never even heard of him, let alone being able to 'prove his innocence'." My index fingers made sarcastic speech marks.

Shaun opened the Land Cruiser's door. I noticed he hadn't locked it, as usual. "So a bit of a waste of time then?"

I grinned. "Well, not entirely. I had two glasses of fabulous Cloudy Bay Sauvignon Blanc." I sighed theatrically, "and I may have met my future husband."

Before I got in the car, I glanced up to the terrace, hoping for a last glimpse of Jack, maybe even a goodbye wave from him. But all I could see were the tops of the cream parasols.

Shaun turned the ignition key and the engine expelled its usual fog of blue diesel fumes. I cringed, hoping Jack wasn't still on the terrace.

"Your future husband?" Shaun attempted a laugh as he reversed the huge car out of the space, clearing the front of the Mercedes by millimetres.

I put my hands up to my face. "Oh. My. God. He was so gorgeous!"

"Yeah?" Shaun aimed the big car down the steep drive. "Was he?"

"Well, you saw him too!"

He shrugged. "Yeah. He was okay looking I suppose."

"Okay looking? He was amazing looking. I mean, did you see that suit? I don't think I've ever seen anyone look that good in a suit. And his eyes. His eyes were incredible. And that's not even the best thing." I paused but Shaun didn't take the bait. "Want to know the best thing?"

He shrugged.

"Well, you'll never guess what he does for a job?"

"Nope."

"Go on. Take a guess."

Shaun opened the car window and the muggy evening air flooded in. "He works at B&Q?"

"Don't be silly. Guess again. Be serious this time."

"Aw, I'm no good at guessing games." He ran a hand through his wiry hair.

"Okay. I'll tell you. He's a bodyguard. He's here in Sands End on business."

Shaun rolled the car to a stop at the end of the hotel's long drive and waited for a gap in the seafront traffic.

I poked his shoulder. "Don't you think that's amazing?"

"What's amazing?"

"That Jack's a bodyguard! He bodyguards people! I bet he's got a gun and everything."

Shaun pulled out on to the seafront and rested his elbow on the open window as he drove. "Shouldn't think so. He'll have to obey the law like everyone else in this country, which means he can't carry firearms."

The smell of chips from the fish bars along the seafront wafted in through the open car window. I stared at the crowds of tourists ambling along the prom in the evening sunshine. They were easy to spot: third-degree sunburn and mountains of bare flesh. I wondered what Jack would look like shirtless. My heart did a little back flip in response.

"I bet Jack carries a gun," I said. "I bet he's one of those special bodyguards who have permission to carry firearms. You know, like if they're protecting foreign dignitaries or really important businessmen. Or when he's protecting people abroad. I bet he carries a gun then." I nodded. "Yeah. He has a gun."

Shaun grinned. "How much did you really have to drink?"

"I told you. Only two glasses. Why? Do I sound drunk?"

"Just a bit. I'll rustle-up that turkey stir-fry when we get back. That'll sort you out."

I was far too wired to eat. On the prom, an elderly man on a mobility scooter zoomed up behind a family, tooting his horn and scattering them like starlings on a lawn. As he shot past, he shook his fist at their startled faces and yelled something I couldn't hear.

Shaun turned off the seafront and we headed up the hill towards home. He said, "Well, I guess that really is the end of your Patrick Underhill story."

And the end of Jack too. The wine buzz was wearing off.

"So everything Patrick Underhill told you in that pub was rubbish then?"

I shrugged "Well, ninety-nine-point-nine per cent was rubbish. The only part that was true was that Kelly-Anne Davis and Jack Dale did know each other briefly a long time ago. I think they might have had a short affair. But, like I said, Jack had never even heard of Patrick."

Shaun pulled into his parking space outside our flats. "So I wonder why Patrick thinks that Jack can clear his name?"

I released my seat belt and got out of the car. "Because Patrick is certifiable."

As Shaun slammed the driver's side door, I heard his stomach gurgle. He blushed and patted his tum. "Reckon I need refuelling pronto. How about I make us both a quick sandwich now then get the stir-fry going in half-an-hour or so?" Shaun's appetite was so enormous. "Have you got any more bread?"

I had a secret emergency loaf in the freezer. "A bit."

A few minutes later I was sitting at the patio table in the garden with a small glass of wine, my phone and my laptop next to me while Shaun assembled ham sandwiches in my kitchen. I could hear him humming cheerfully through the open window. Food made him happy. Making food, doubly so.

I felt restless. I wanted to do something, go somewhere, listen to loud music, dance; smoke. Maybe I should've suggested to Shaun that we stay for another drink at the hotel. That way, Jack could have joined us. I stood, paced down the lawn and poked at the leaves of the thick hedge at the far end of the garden. A large emerald dragonfly rose off a twig and shot up into the cloudless sky, its wings whirring like some kind of crazy wind-up toy. But in my mind all I could see was Jack's perfect face, his grey eyes staring deep into mine. I smiled and took a swig of wine while my heart gave a little dance of delight. He had been flirting with me, no doubt about it.

Henry trotted down the garden towards me.

"Hello chap." I bent down and rubbed him under his chin. He flopped onto the grass, stretching himself out in the heat, making himself as long as possible.

I returned to the patio, took another sip of wine and winced. Compared with the Cloudy Bay I'd had at the hotel, this was like drinking vinegar.

My phone beeped to say I'd received a text. I grabbed it, thinking, please let it be Jack. But it was from Becky: *Katy can you phone me ASAP about the arrangements for the reunion?* I scowled and ignored it. Only two days to go until the school reunion and I still hadn't come up with a fireproof excuse that would get me out of going.

Shaun stuck his head out of the kitchen window. "See, what's weird is that Patrick must have known that once you tracked down Jack Dale and Jack denied knowing Patrick, you'd discover Patrick was lying." He shook his head. "It doesn't make any sense."

I went to take another sip of wine then pushed the glass away. "Nope. But that's Patrick for you." Behind me I heard the sound of Shaun using a spoon to scrape every last bit of something from a jar. I hoped it wasn't the mayonnaise from my fridge because that had been festering ever since the weekend I'd moved in.

The scraping noise stopped. "Unless…"

I turned around. "Unless what?"

Shaun grinned back at me. "Unless it's Jack who's lying and Patrick who's telling the truth."

"That's not even a remote possibility." I picked up my glass and swirled the wine around, wondering if I should nip to the off licence and pick up something decent. The sensible voice in my head, the one I didn't listen to very often, said I'd had more than enough alcohol for one evening.

Shaun waved the spoon at me. A blob of mayonnaise dropped off the end and landed on the grass under the window instantly attracting a huge bluebottle. "I'm just saying, what if Jack can prove that Patrick didn't kill that girl? Jack would hardly say, 'oh sure, I've been hoping someone would ask me that question for the last thirteen years – sorry, should've mentioned something at the time'."

Shaun turned back to his sandwich-making duties then his head reappeared out of the kitchen window. "And doesn't it strike you as a bit fishy, the way Jack just happened to be in Sands End on business tonight? What possible business could there be for a professional bodyguard down here? Protecting the donkeys on the beach?"

I knew Shaun was deliberately trying to needle me, probably because he was annoyed that Jack had been so astonishingly good looking, but I couldn't stop myself rising to the bait. "I don't know," I snapped.

Shaun gave a smug chuckle. "I've got it. He must have seen his name in your story in the *Gazette*."

I shook my head. "No. I didn't mention anything about Jack Dale in that story…"

But now I thought about it, Jack's story didn't make much sense. If all he'd been planning to tell me at the hotel was that he and Kelly-Anne Davis had once had a fling, then why hadn't he just told me that on the phone? Why had he bothered to meet me?

I rolled the stem of my wine glass between my palms and tried to think of any celebrities or VIPs who lived locally and might need the services of a professional bodyguard. I couldn't think of any, although there had been an unfounded rumour many years ago that the Crankies were moving here. I shook my head. People who had enough money to need a bodyguard also had enough money to live somewhere nicer than Sands End.

And that was another odd thing. Jack had sent his text only half-an-hour before we were due to meet. That meant he was already in Sands End – possibly even sitting on the terrace of the Bay View Hotel – when he'd sent it. Maybe he had been at a loose end after his business meeting and just fancied a chat in the sunshine with a journalist. Hmm. Not very convincing. My chest fizzed as his face popped back into my mind.

I took a very small sip of wine. I was missing something. I could feel it. I pulled my laptop towards me and switched it on. So, what did I have here? I had a totally implausible story from a man I knew was a compulsive liar. And yet, one thing Patrick had told me in the pub that afternoon turned out to be true: Jack Dale did exist. And he had known Kelly-Anne Davis. I thought about the strange moment on the terrace when I'd asked Jack if he'd known Kelly-Anne, the feeling that I'd touched a nerve.

A funny thought occurred to me. What if Jack had been Kelly-Anne's secret lover at the time of her death? Was it possible he could have somehow provided Patrick with an alibi but hadn't?

Reaching down, I pulled up a long stem of grass and waved it at Henry. He ignored me. It was far too hot for games. Shaun came out through the patio doors carrying two plates. He plonked them on the table, but I still wasn't hungry.

"There you go, get your chops around that beauty." He picked up his sandwich and winked. "Or maybe, Jack thought the personal touch would be the best way to put you off the scent of a good story." I could tell Shaun was still relishing winding me up over Jack.

"There is no good story. And what do you mean, the personal touch?"

Shaun picked up his glass and tilted it so the sun glinted into my eyes. "Well, you were massively smarmed tonight if you don't mind me saying."

I felt my cheeks roast. "That's utter rubbish Shaun, and you know it. Jack wasn't smarming me." I nibbled a small corner of my sandwich then put it down again. He'd been flirting with me, and that was quite different.

Shaun poured himself a huge glass of wine from my bargain wine box and gulped about half of it down in one go. "Yeah. You're right. The fact Jack knew Kelly-Anne is just a big unhappy coincidence." He eyed my barely touched sandwich. "You going to eat that?"

I shook my head and he grabbed it off my plate.

A big unhappy coincidence…

My eyes strayed towards my laptop. Now I thought about it, Jack had seemed rather passive during our meeting, almost as if he'd been waiting to see how much I knew before volunteering any information. Maybe he had been hiding something. Maybe his flirty behaviour had been designed to soften me up. And it did seem weird that Jack just happened to be in Sands End on business on the same day I'd phoned him saying I was doing a story about the Kelly-Anne Davis murder.

"*When you left your message today mentioning Kelly-Anne, I thought we should meet…*"

I stared down at my empty plate. I saw my sunglasses tumbling through the air and felt heat rush up to my cheeks. I must have come over as such an idiot. A bit of flirting, a couple of glasses of nice wine and I'd been putty in his hands. I saw Martin's smug smile, "*Or has Lori du Val taken over completely now?*" I thought back to my conversation with Patrick in he pub, "*Course Jack Dale probably isn't his real name…. Stool pigeon, ha, cha, cha, cha…*"

I yanked my laptop towards me. My fingers hovered over the keys. Okay, if the name Jack Dale wasn't real, that meant it was an alias or a pseudonym. I had a feeling that stool pigeon was slang for a police informant. A quick Google-search confirmed I was right. Without really thinking about what I hoped to achieve I put *pseudonym, alias, police informant, Jack Dale* into Google, and hit return.

Twenty-eight thousand results. I slowly scrolled down the first dozen or so. I found a review of a political thriller called *The Police Informant*, the phone number for a man called Jack White in the staff directory of the City of Fort Lauderdale Police Department, a story about a police informant called William Dale on a dodgy-looking website called Mafia Rats. I added UK to the search: more reviews of the political thriller, articles on why authors write under pseudonyms, an intriguing-looking story about the South African Apartheid Secret Police. I was about to give up when a hit on Wikipedia caught my eye:

Using the **pseudonym...** the real name of the undercover **police** officer from SO10 was **Jack Dale**...

I clicked on the story. It was titled *The Lucas Brennan Murder*. I read the first few paragraphs then frowned. "That's weird…"

Shaun shoved the last of my sandwich into his mouth. He made appreciative humming sounds then reached down and stroked Henry under the chin. "What's weird?"

"There's an article here on Wikipedia about an undercover police operation that went wrong – a honey trap – and the real name of the undercover officer who set the trap was Jack Dale…."

Shaun gave a disparaging snort, "Wikipedia?"

I shook my head. "Not everything on Wikipedia is made up, Shaun. Not any more."

I read quickly through the rest of the story looking for any mention of Patrick Underhill or Kelly-Anne Davis but there was nothing. I scrolled back up. "It says Jack Dale's name was accidentally released by the police after the operation was over and he had to change it… Hmm, just a bit of a balls-up."

"So what's he called now?" Shaun asked.

"Well, it doesn't say, obviously. I bet he was furious…" I continued reading. "Jack Dale's undercover name during the honey-trap was Giles Mailer."

I read through the article again. I had to admit, it was a peach of a story. The Metropolitan Police had received a hefty rap on the knuckles following the underhand methods they'd employed to trap a man called Ray Butcher, a suspect in the murder of police officer, Lucas Brennan. During Operation Sweetheart, Jack Dale, a colleague of the murdered officer had gone undercover as Giles Mailer, seduced the suspect's girlfriend, had surveillance photos taken showing the two of them in "compromising positions" and taped their pillow talk, during which she'd appeared to incriminate Butcher in Brennan's murder.

I winced. Nice.

Butcher had been convicted of the murder then freed on appeal less than a year later when the evidence at his original trial was dismissed as entrapment. In his summing-up, the appeal court judge had strongly criticised the Met for its "excessive zeal", describing the honey-pot trap as "grossly deceptive" and the undercover police officer as "morally bankrupt".

Underneath the story were four small photographs. The first showed Lucas Brennan, a pleasant-looking young man with dark brown hair. The second showed Ray Butcher, his hair styled into a ridiculous bleached mullet. The third photo showed Butcher's girlfriend, a statuesque blonde wearing a sparkly blue mini dress. The fourth showed a tall man with fair hair and broad shoulders, looking impossibly good in a dark suit as he walked towards the imposing entrance of the Old Bailey. To disguise his identity, his eyes had been blacked out. Underneath the photo it said: *The undercover police officer known by the alias Giles Mailer arrives at court to give evidence at Butcher's trial.*

I stared at the photo. I stared at the suit. Then I grabbed my phone.

Shaun reached for the wine box. "What are you doing?"

"You lying sod," I muttered, scrolling down my texts.

"Who's a lying sod? Patrick Underhill?"

I shook my head. "Jack Dale. I think he's an undercover police officer not a bodyguard…"

I found what I was looking for. The text message I'd received from Jack earlier in the day. Above the message was the sender's phone number.

"Gotcha," I breathed. I created a new contact saved the number as JACK DALE and pressed call. "I do not like being lied to, Shaun. Nor do I like being made to feel stupid."

"Aw, Katy, leave it. I was only yanking your chain earlier–"

I waved him quiet and leaned back in my chair. Jack's phone purred twice then his recorded voice said, *"Leave a message."*

"Hello Jack. This is Katy Bennett. I do not believe you were entirely honest with me this evening. I have some follow-up questions I'd like to put to you, specifically why you told me you were a bodyguard when you are actually a police officer."

I ended the call and tossed the phone over my shoulder. It sailed through the open patio door and landed on the sofa with a soft thump. Such a smooth move.

Shaun chuckled at me across the patio table. "You daft wombat." He picked up the wine box. "Reckon I'll pop the Chateau Cardboard back in the fridge for a bit. It's warmer than a sheep shearer's armpit."

As he walked into the sitting room, my mobile rang. Shaun stopped and turned to face me. For several long seconds we stared at each other then I jumped up and grabbed the phone from the sofa.

"Hello?"

"Katy. It's Jack. I'm coming over now." Then he hung up.

I blinked. "Wow."

"What now?"

"That was Jack." I chewed at my lips. "How long do you think it'll take him to drive here from the Bay View Hotel?"

Shaun grinned. "In a Mercedes AMG GT? About thirty seconds."

"Rats. I need to sober up fast."

I ran to the kitchen, flung open the breadbin, grabbed a slice of bread, folded it in half and shoved almost all of it in my mouth. I filled the percolator jug with water and dumped a load of coffee in the filter. Caffeine, in industrial quantities, was required.

As I rammed the rest of the bread in my mouth, chewing madly, my teeth chomped down on the side of my tongue. White agony exploded in my head. The pain was so extreme I couldn't even think. I dropped the coffee bag on the work surface. "Ughrr," I spluttered.

"What's up?" Shaun asked.

I coughed the half-chewed bread chunks into the sink. They were scarlet with blood. "It i ung."

"What?"

"I *it* i ung." I coughed and spat. Globules of crimson streaked the basin. "Uck."

I ran to the lounge and over to the mirror above the mantle piece. About halfway down my tongue was a dark red cut. "O ucking ell."

My jaw felt as if it was on fire. I ran back to the kitchen, grabbed a glass and filled it with water. I took a swig and sloshed the water around my mouth, hoping the cold would numb the pain. It didn't. Instead it stung like hell. I spat red water into the sink. I could really taste the blood now. The back of my neck went icy cold and I felt sick. Could you bleed to death from a tongue cut? It wasn't like you could put a plaster on it.

"Want me to take a peek?" Shaun said in a helpful voice.

I shook my head and trotted back to the lounge mirror. "Ugging ell." This was just what I didn't need. Jack was going to arrive any second, for my interrogation about things I'd been distracted from asking him at the hotel, and I couldn't even speak properly. I poked out my tongue. The

142

blood seemed to have stopped but when I prodded the cut, the pain made me flinch.

Shaun handed me a mug of coffee. "This'll sort you out. Right, I'd better scarper before Jacko turns up." He winked as he ambled towards the hall. "Don't forget to give him a proper grilling this time. Hey, maybe you could give him a Chinese burn? That would do the trick."

I'd be lucky if I could say hello. I'd probably start drooling blood the second I opened my mouth.

Shaun added, "Keep your phone close by and if he gets weird, call me and I'll be straight down on my white charger."

"Ess. Ess." *Just go.* I definitely didn't want Shaun here when Jack turned up. I herded him down the hall and out of the front door.

I dashed to the bedroom, wondering if I had time to change in to something more alluring. I charged over to the wardrobe and pawed through the hangers. My hand hovered over my default little black dress then I shook my head. It would look as if I'd gone to way too much trouble. This was an interrogation, not a date.

Okay, maybe I could do something impressive with my face instead. I slicked some bright pink gloss on my lips, dusted some glittery bronzer across my cheeks and brushed my hair upside down. It crackled with static and when I looked in the mirror, I was horrified to see it was sticking out in a triangle. Crisis. Time for an emergency ponytail with a few coquettish spirals. I scraped it back. Crapping hell. What a mess. I cupped a hand under my jaw and my tongue throbbed.

Darting back to the wardrobe I grabbed a silky rose-patterned camisole and held it up in front of the mirror. Yeah, that would dress up the shorts. As I pulled my t-shirt off, yanked on the cami and squirted some perfume on my wrists, someone tapped at my front door. *Oh my God...* I ran out of the bedroom, across the lounge, skidded down the hall and pulled the door open. Shaun stared back at me.

Aghhrr. "Ot ow?"

"Just thought of something else you might want to ask Jacko," he said with a helpful smile.

"Ess?"

"How did he know you live in Sands End?"

I willed my mouth in to action. My tongue felt about three times its normal size and I didn't seem to have complete control over its movements.

"Gave him biz card at hotel," I managed. I couldn't believe how painful it was to speak. My voice sounded really weird and low. Jack was going to think I'd had a stroke or something.

Shaun shook his head. "Not then. Earlier. When Jack sent you that text this afternoon, how did he know you'd know the Bay View Hotel was in Sands End?"

Alcohol and pain clouded my brain. I couldn't understand what he meant. "Um–"

"What I mean is, if you lived anywhere but Sands End, him saying, 'meet me at the Bay View Hotel' would have meant nothing to you." Shaun winked. "So that means he already knew you lived in Sands End before he sent you that text." He turned away and plodded up the stairs. "Don't forget. Ring me if he gets weird." The door clicked shut.

The space between my shoulder blades prickled. I put my hands up to my face and slumped back against the hall wall. Stupid, stupid, stupid. Shaun was right. How the hell had Jack known I lived in Sands End?

Then someone rang the doorbell to my flat and my heart nearly stopped.

CHAPTER ELEVEN

The doorbell rang again, the chimes echoed down the hall. I picked up the entry phone. "It's Jack," came his incredibly sexy voice.

Fingers trembling, I pressed the release button. Quick, solid footsteps crossed the lobby and stopped outside my door. I took a deep breath, wiped my palms on my shorts, and reached for the Chubb lock. The muscles in my legs quivered. My stomach churned. I took another deep breath, turned the latch and pulled the door open.

We stared at each other. Neither of us moved. Oh my word. He looked even more devastating. He'd changed out of his amazing suit into faded Levis and a short-sleeved black t-shirt. His upper arms were muscular without looking freakish. He looked tougher than earlier.

Right. Come on Katy, time for some tough questions. A bizarre image of myself as a Dalek popped into my mind. *Interrogate, interrogate, interrogate.*

I stepped backwards, inviting him in with a nod of my head. I didn't want to speak just yet in case the cut on my tongue started bleeding again. Dribbling blood-streaked saliva would be neither professional nor alluring. And I wanted to be professional and alluring. Well, as professional and alluring as it was possible to be in scruffy denim shorts and a top that looked a bit like bed-wear. Good grief, what if he thought I'd been so drunk earlier that I'd been on my way to bed when he called?

Jack's bare arm brushed against mine as he walked past. He strode down the hall into the lounge, and looked around. He wandered over to the open patio doors, looked outside then slid them shut with a thud. He crossed the room and looked into the kitchen, as if he was making sure we were alone. Maybe I should phone Shaun... But then again, if Jack was a police officer then he was just casing the joint, making sure it was secure and I was safe. Wow. Sexy.

Silence stretched. I wondered if I'd be able to ask if he wanted a drink without sounding like I had a sock in my mouth. "Wine?" I managed, wrenching my tongue into the correct movements.

"Thanks."

It was impossible to judge his mood from his voice, but I imagined he was pretty pissed off, having been dragged out of his comfy hotel. I walked into the kitchen, took the wine box out of the fridge and decided to risk a small glass too. The alcohol would hopefully numb the pain in my tongue. My hands shook as I filled the glasses. I took a gulp and sloshed the wine around my mouth. It stung like crazy. I spat the mouthful in the sink then gulped some more, this time swallowing, and winced. It tasted terrible. The wine was not going to impress Jack one bit. But then again, this was not a social occasion. This was going to be an interrogation. The wine was just to soften him up.

Taking a deep breath, I walked back to the lounge. Jack was scrutinising the books on my bookcase. A rivulet of perspiration trickled down my ribs. With the patio door closed, the room already felt like an oven.

He picked up my last romance novel and read aloud from the cover, "Night of the Dark Secrets."

I felt a blush creep up my neck. He flicked through the pages, appearing to stop at random, halfway through.

My books always seemed to fall open at the cringingly graphic sex scenes.

He snapped the book shut and put it back. "Lori du Val," he said in a dry voice. "I don't think I've read anything by her." He examined the spines of the other books. Thank goodness I had some weightier tomes on the shelf: a pristine and obviously unread copy of War and Peace, Tom Wolfe's The New Journalism, looking impressively well-thumbed, and a massive hardback entitled Greece and the Hellenistic World, which a very hard of hearing aunt had given to me one Christmas in the mistaken belief that I was working in Athens not St Albans.

Jack's eyes returned to what I called the pink-tinged end of the bookshelf.

"You certainly have an eclectic taste in literature," he said after a while.

Wow. Eclectic. Good word. I tried a quick calculation: what was worse, him thinking I actually enjoyed reading romance novels or admitting I wrote them? Okay, they were drivel but they were still published books. That was an achievement in itself. The blush reached my cheeks. "Actually that's me. Lori is me," I managed.

"Is that so?" He smiled and I could tell he'd known that already. But how?

The wine seemed to have done the trick and the throbbing in my mouth was just about tolerable, but my tongue still felt as if it belonged to someone else. "It's just… it's just a sideline. I mean, primarily I'm a news reporter." Well, I used to be. I remembered Martin's earlier roasting about Patrick's 'I am innocent' story and felt a stab of panic. Maybe I had lost the plot. Maybe I'd never had it. Maybe I had turned into Lori du Val.

As I handed Jack the glass of wine, my fingers brushed against his and my skin tingled.

Jack took a sip and walked over to the mantelpiece. He picked up my ticket for the school reunion, looked at it and put it back. I could read nothing in his face.

Start the interrogation: interrogate, interrogate.

He walked across the room and sat on the armchair.

Interrogate…

I perched myself on the edge of the sofa facing him. I fiddled with the stem of my wine glass, rolling it between my damp palms. *Say something,* my mind screamed.

I took a deep breath. "Why did you lie about being a bodyguard?"

Jack took a tiny sip of wine. Fair play, he managed not to wince.

"I didn't lie."

I frowned, "So you are a bodyguard?"

His eyes were fixed on mine, his shoulders seemed rigid under his t-shirt. He nodded. "Yes."

"Right... But you were the undercover police officer accidentally named in the honey-pot trap; the case about the Lucas Brennan murder: Jack Dale?"

He gave a curt nod. "Yes."

I cast my mind back to the article I'd just read. "So, you were SO10?"

Another nod. "After that I transferred to Specialist Protection SO1. Then I left the police and went into private close personal protection."

"Oh." I felt oddly disappointed that he hadn't lied to me. So why had he come haring back to my flat? Why hadn't he just told me that over the phone?

"So, after the honey-trap, how was your real name released?"

He shifted back in his seat. "I can't talk about that."

"Is that why you left the police?"

He didn't answer.

I felt my irritation rise. "Okay, so you used to be Jack Dale and you were Giles Mailer in the honey-pot trap. I'm not interested in finding out what name you go by now, if that's what's bothering you. I'm just trying to figure out why Patrick Underhill thinks you can clear his name."

Jack shrugged. "I thought we'd been through all that earlier."

Funnily enough the name Jack suited him perfectly. "Yes, we did, but there were some things I forgot to – I mean – didn't ask you. Okay?"

He nodded. "Okay."

No, he didn't look anything like a Giles. "Let me just get a couple of things straight. You had a brief relationship with Kelly-Anne Davis?"

For a fraction of a second, Jack seemed to hesitate then he said, "Yes."

"And, obviously, she knew you as Jack Dale."

Jack frowned as if he couldn't see where this might be leading. "Yes…"

"So, that relationship must have taken place before you were forced to change your name following Operation Sweetheart?"

Jack seemed to be eyeing me a little warily. I felt a stab of doubt. Maybe I was talking complete rubbish. "What I'm trying to say is, was your relationship with Kelly-Anne while she was living here in Sands End?"

For a couple of seconds Jack simply stared at me. Then he gave me one of his slow-burn smiles. "You're being very smart."

I felt a brief stab of surprise followed a fizz of pride.

He placed his wine glass on the carpet, put his hands on his thighs and for a heart-stopping moment I thought he was going to get up and leave. Right. I'd try a

150

brief change of tactic to get him talking. I'd play him at his own game with a bit of flirting. Distract him with small talk. Lure him into a false sense of security. Then I'd go back to the tough questions.

I leaned back on the sofa and tucked my feet under me. I smiled and tried to make my voice silky but because of my cut tongue it sounded like I had a bit of a lisp, "You know Jack – oh, I hope you don't mind me still calling you Jack – I'm fascinated about you being a bodyguard. I mean, have you ever, you know, had to save someone? Save their life, I mean?"

He shrugged making his shoulder muscles shift under his t-shirt. "On occasion."

"Wow. How brave!" I sipped my wine, wondering if he would have a second glass? Or a third? A third would mean that he couldn't drive back to his hotel…. "So, when you saved that person, did you have to…? Did you have to–"

"Kill someone?"

His bluntness startled me and I felt heat rush up to my cheeks. I glaned away, fixed my eyes on my drink swirled the wine around the glass. When I looked up, his eyes were staring into mine and my heart went into freefall. I wondered what his body looked like under his t-shirt.

Jack leaned forward. "Are these questions about my career relevant to your story?"

I felt my cheeks blush scarlet. "No, not at all. I'm just… just curious. I've never met a bodyguard before."

His shoulders seemed to relax a little. He picked up his glass and ran his middle finger slowly around the rim. "Katy, I appreciate you're just doing your job here – trying to chase down a story."

My chest fizzed with pride. "Absolutely."

"It's just–" He glanced up and his eyes met mine. "It's just we need to exercise some caution here."

My stare returned to his slowly circling finger. I couldn't seem to wrench my eyes away from it. "Oh absolutely. Caution. Absolutely."

"Can I ask you something, Katy?"

My blush intensified. I loved the way he said my name. "Absolutely." *Stop bloody saying absolutely.*

"Are you writing this story because you believe Patrick Underhill is telling you the truth? That he is innocent of murder?"

I opened my mouth but nothing came out.

Jack's finger resumed its gentle, hypnotic circles. "Because if you really believe him – and I mean truly believe him – then I will do everything I can to help you."

Wow. Noble.

"But before we go any further I need to know if you believe him and if so, why you believe him." Jack's finger stopped its movement around the glass and I realised I was holding my breath. "Because, Katy, you said earlier that you didn't believe Patrick. You didn't believe he was telling the truth about being innocent."

I felt my blush flare up again. I wanted to pace, walk around. I stood. "Can I top up your drink?"

Jack shook his head. "Not just yet, thank you."

I sat again.

He said, "Can I ask you something else?" His voice was barely above a murmur.

I leaned forward and nodded.

"Is there anything about this murder – perhaps something you'd rather keep private for now, or perhaps even something uncomfortable concerning Patrick Underhill – that you should tell me?"

Are you going up to Glitz tonight, Katy? It's just I need–

152

Jesus. It was as if he'd smacked me in the face. The whole room seemed to lurch to one side and my vision misted. I looked down at my glass. My voice was too high, "No…"

I stood. There was a clanging noise in my ears and the back of my neck felt icy cold.

"Excuse me," I muttered. "I need to get a glass of water."

I stumbled across the lounge to the kitchen and filled my wine glass from the cold tap. I placed my hands flat on the breakfast bar and hung my head. Oh no. I was going to cry. I bit my lip and stared up through my lashes at the ceiling but the tears were already there. They stung my eyes. Shame roasted my cheeks.

Behind me, I heard Jack's sharp footsteps on the floor tiles. As I picked my glass, it slipped from my grasp, hit the kitchen floor and shattered. The noise echoed around the room. "For heaven's sake…" I breathed.

Jack walked towards me. He stood very close. I could feel the warmth rising from his body and smell his amazing aftershave. I felt dizzy.

He brushed a strand of hair away from my face and my tears welled up again. Oh no, now my nose was going to run. He put his fingers under my chin and lifted my head.

Oh good grief. He was going to kiss me. Should I mention my cut tongue? What if he kissed me and tasted the cut and it put him off me forever? No. I couldn't kiss him with a sore tongue. I pulled back a little.

But what if he kissed me and it was the best kiss I'd ever had and one thing led to another? But I'd only met him a couple of hours ago. Was it slutty to sleep with a man you'd known for so little time? What sort of message would it send? I didn't want him to think I was that easy.

153

His fingers gently stroked my cheek, his eyes stared into mine and I felt a shot of adrenalin burn into my heart. *Oh shut up. You might be about to kiss the most gorgeously attractive man you have ever met and then have sex for the first time in over a year. Mess this up and I guarantee you'll regret it for the rest of your life.*

As I leaned towards him and closed my eyes, an awkward voice behind me said, "Ah. Sorry."

I sprang back and whirled around. Shaun was standing in the kitchen doorway holding a frying pan at shoulder height.

His shoulders sagged. "Sorry. I heard breaking glass. Thought you might need…" He turned and walked away. "My mistake. As you were." He flapped a big hand behind him. His bare feet padded across the lounge and down the hall, then I heard the sound of the front door closing.

I glanced towards Jack but the spell, if there was one, was broken. "I need to go," he said.

I looked away, knowing my face was scarlet with embarrassment. "Yes. I should be going too – I mean, going to bed not going out of my flat – because, of course, ha, ha, I live here…"

He nodded at the broken glass. "Do you need a hand clearing that–"

"No." I shook my head, my eyes fixed on the floor.

"I'll see myself out."

A moment later I heard the front door shut behind him.

I had to know if I was right about the car. I ran into the lounge, slid open the patio doors and sprinted across the darkening lawn to the fence that bordered the car park. I squinted through a gap in the wood. Jack was walking towards the same sleek and impossibly sexy Mercedes I'd seen outside the Bay View Hotel. He opened the drivers side door, took his phone out of his jeans back pocket and hurled it onto the passenger seat. Then he slid inside and the door slammed shut with a solid thud. The engine revved and the car accelerated away as he punched up through the gears. Then the noise gradually faded away and the night was silent again.

For a long time, I stood in the garden as my pulse returned to something approaching normal and the fizzing in my stomach went away. It was a good job Shaun arrived when he did, I told myself. A man like Jack will chew you up and spit you out and smash your heart into a thousand little pieces. Don't even go there.

I trudged back inside, locked the patio doors, swept up the broken glass and took myself off to bed. As sleep began to tug me under, snapshot memories of Jack's visit continued to explode like random fireworks in my brain. What kept coming back, over and over again, was the strongest feeling that I had missed something vital – an important clue – something he had said or maybe something I had said. But too much wine and not enough food made my thoughts slip away every time I reached for them. In the end I surrendered to a deep, alcohol induced unconsciousness. I'd think about it all again in the morning.

CHAPTER TWELVE

I woke squinting against bright sunlight. I must have been drunk if I'd forgotten to close the curtains last night. My mouth tasted as if I'd been chewing one of Shaun's squash socks. A hangover headache stabbed across my forehead. My tongue throbbed in unison. The clock radio was chattering away to itself and I realised I'd slept through my alarm.

I groaned and pressed a hand onto my forehead, as snippets of memory from last night filtered back into my mind. Too much to drink. Not enough food. Oh well, it was nothing a bacon sandwich wouldn't fix. *Sandwich... Ham sandwich. Garden...*

Throwing back the duvet, I sat bolt upright. It was all coming back now: Jack, the hotel, drinking. A phone call to Jack. *"I do not believe you were entirely honest with me this evening...."* Jack in my kitchen, standing very close. Tears. A glass breaking. *"Is there anything about this murder – perhaps something you'd rather keep private for now, or perhaps even something uncomfortable concerning Patrick Underhill – that you should tell me?"*

I jumped out of bed and pressed my fists against my eyes, pushing the memories away. My face flushed with embarrassment. "You stupid, stupid cow," I breathed.

Pulling on my dressing gown, I walked into the sitting room and stared through the sliding doors out into the sunny garden. Two empty plates were on the patio table, one of which was being pecked clean of crumbs by a sparrow.

"How's your head?" a loud Australian voice called from my kitchen and I nearly jumped out of my skin.

Shaun poked his head around the door. "Cup of coffee?"

I strode into the kitchen. "Did you just let yourself into my flat again?"

He switched on the percolator. "Well, I'd run out of milk so I thought I'd make a coffee down here and..." His voice trailed off. "You look a bit rough if you don't mind me saying."

I clenched my fists. "Your key is supposed to be for emergencies."

Shaun tried to look apologetic. "This is an emergency. I'm out of milk. Look, if it's a problem just say and I won't do it again." He slapped some bacon in a frying pan on the hob. As it began to sizzle, the smell made me feel dizzy.

"And anyway," he added, "I thought you might like a bacon sarnie for breakfast."

My head was pounding and my tongue throbbed. I dragged myself up onto one of the stools facing the breakfast bar and groaned.

Shaun prodded the rashers with a fork and looked a bit sheepish. "Look, sorry about the misunderstanding last night..."

I winced and put my head in my hands.

"I thought maybe he'd attacked you."

I wanted to say something sarcastic like, yeah thanks Shaun, you probably saved me from being ruined sexually for all other men, but don't worry about it. Instead I said, "That was very thoughtful of you. And thanks for making me a bacon sandwich."

He placed a mug of coffee in front of me and said, "See, I suppose if I'm brutally honest, I don't altogether trust this Jack character."

No shit, Sherlock.

"If you want my advice, I'd say you should stay well clear of him."

I took a sip of coffee. "Hmm." Probably wouldn't have much choice about that after last night.

Shaun slapped the bacon onto slices of bread. He put one sandwich in front of me and picked up his mug of coffee. "Well, I'd better get back to work. I was going to suggest I make paella this evening but I've got to go over to Bath later." He turned away, scratched at his chest and ambled out of the kitchen. "And stay away from Jacko, that's my advice."

For the next ten minutes I stared at the bacon sandwich. My insides were in knots. Last night's butterflies had turned into feral cats. Had Jack really been about to kiss me? If Shaun hadn't interrupted, would we have ended up in bed? Or had Jack been flirting to distract me from something he didn't want me to find out?

Honey-trap undercover police officer...

So why had Jack come to my flat? To "urge caution" with my story? He might not be a police officer anymore, but old habits died hard and the one thing that pissed the police off more than anything, was the press speculating about things that weren't true. I took a bite of my sandwich. It was dry. I wondered if I had any ketchup in the fridge.

On the other hand, Jack had offered to help me clear Patrick's name. But only if I truly, honestly, totally believed Patrick was telling the truth. And I didn't believe that, so end of story again.

I pulled a piece of crispy bacon out of the sandwich and nibbled at it. The ghost of Jack's fingers stroked my cheek and my heart went into freefall at the memory. I switched on my laptop and stared blankly at the screen for a few minutes, then I revisited the Wikipedia story I'd found the previous night. I scrolled down, reading it more carefully this time in case if I'd missed anything vital. But there was nothing, just the report of how the police had unwisely used a dodgy honey-trap to catch a suspected murderer.

I shoved the rest of the bacon in my mouth, wiped my hands on a tea towel and stood. Why was I even wasting time thinking about this? Martin had yanked me off the story and my name was dirt at the *Gazette* thanks to Patrick's retraction. I pictured myself in a swanky office in Lincoln, doing the cushy public relations job I'd applied for. Sod it. I didn't need this hassle. I sent Patrick an email. I didn't mince my words. I told him I was furious to hear he'd retracted his quotes and had denied meeting me at the pub in Bristol. I didn't want an explanation, I told him, because I didn't want him to contact me ever again; my involvement with him was over. Even someone as intellectually deficient as Patrick Underhill would be able to realise what I'd really wanted to write: *piss off and bother someone else with your insane lies from now on.* I jabbed a savage finger at the keyboard and hit send. Goodbye and good riddance Patrick, I thought. Have a nice life, loser.

I took my laptop out to the garden to write some more of my novel, but my mind kept drifting back to Jack. I gave myself a shake and started to type. Before long I was swept away into my imaginary world. Petronella was now in Nice, trying to forget Yuri, the steel-eyed, steel-thighed Russian oligarch-slash-cosmonaut with commitment issues.

159

I hadn't been writing for long when I heard my doorbell ring. Jack! It had to be! I jumped up, scooted across the lawn and peered through the gap in the fence. But it wasn't Jack. It was a young woman standing beside a florist's van. Wow. Flowers. Had Jack sent me flowers? I ran back inside the flat, skidded down the hall and flung open the front door.

Standing in the lobby was a teenage girl wearing a green tabard printed with the words Eloise Florists. A name badge announced her as Penelope, Trainee. She had shoulder-length blonde hair streaked with pink and was trying to look very serious. Her eyes were fixed on the floor.

"Eloise Florists send our heartfelt condolences for your loss," she mumbled and thrust a two-foot-long floral display towards me. She had one of those voices which rose at the end of every sentence as if everything was a question.

I stared at the display. The word RIP was spelled out in white chrysanthemums set on a background of purple satin. "Um. I think you've delivered this to the wrong address."

Penelope looked panic stricken. "Oh Christ?" She plonked the flowers on the floor, pulled a notebook out of her tabard pocket and flicked through the pages. "I've got this as as the delivery address?" She held her notebook up so I could see.

I frowned. The address was mine. "Ye-es…"

"And when I put the postcode into the van's sat-nav it brought me here."

Weird. "These are for a funeral," I said at last.

Penelope tried to look solemn again. She lowered her eyes. "They are," she intoned.

"I'm definitely not the right recipient. Sorry."

"Christ, not another one. I'm going to get crucified for this." Penelope put her hands up to her face as if she was going to cry.

"No harm done," I said, trying to reassure her. My eyes returned to the tribute. I could just about handle the idea that it was a delivery mix-up but it was still creepy.

Penelope bent down and picked up the display with both hands. "God, I'm so sorry."

"Just a mix up. Don't worry." I watched as she crossed the lobby and went back out into the car park.

I closed the door. The person who took the order must have messed up somehow, I told myself.

Half an hour later, I went to make a coffee then I realised I'd run out of milk. A quick check to the breadbin showed Shaun had cleaned me out of bread, and when I looked under the sink I'd run out of cat food too, plus my bargain box of wine had felt perilously close to empty last night. I couldn't put off a supermarket run any longer.

When I got back to the flat I took the carrier bags out of the boot and trudged across the car park. But as soon as I pushed open the lobby door I froze. Propped up against the door to my flat was the floral tribute.

"For heaven's sake…" I breathed.

After I'd put away the shopping, I phoned Eloise Florists. The woman who answered, Eloise herself for all I knew, was very apologetic, especially after I explained I'd already sent the flowers back once.

"I don't understand the mix up," she said, sounding worried. "The delivery note says it needed to get to your address before three this afternoon. Is there a sender's name on the card?"

Card, of course. I hadn't thought to look. I hurried into the kitchen and pulled a small white envelope off the back of the display. But when I opened it, all it said was: *I'm thinking of you.*

I felt a strange shiver between my shoulder blades. "So, you don't know who ordered it?" I asked.

"I'll check the order book. Bear with me. It's been chaos this week. The over nineties are not coping well with this heatwave."

There was the sound of pages flicking then the woman was back. "Hmm… for some reason there isn't a name with that order… I'm ever so sorry. Leave it outside and I'll send someone up to collect it. As soon as the person who ordered it realises they haven't been delivered to the right person, I'm sure he'll call us."

My shoulder blades prickled again. "He?"

"I'm fairly sure it was a man who ordered it but I couldn't say for sure."

After I'd hung up I took the creepy tribute out into the car park, propped it up against the wall for collection and went back to my writing.

Petronella stared at the brown-paper parcel the bellboy had handed to her. The label said: Special Delivery for Miss Petronella Mainwaring. Her fingers tore at the paper. Underneath was a square silver box, tied-up with a red silk bow.

Her heart thudded. Yuri. It had to be from Yuri. What was it, she wondered? A silk negligee? Swiss chocolates? A bottle of expensive perfume? She tugged at the bow and eased the box open. Her brow creased as she peered inside, her brain trying to make sense of what she was seeing.

Then she felt the box slip out of her hands and tumble onto the floor. Bile rose in her throat and her legs turned to jelly because it wasn't a negligee, or chocolates or perfume. It was a severed human hand…

I stopped writing and stared at the screen. Odd. I hadn't wanted to write that. What on earth was a severed hand doing in my romance novel? I highlighted the chunk of text and deleted it.

"Oh Yuri," she sighed, scooping up the beautiful red silk dress and crushing it against her heaving chest. A small note fluttered down onto the carpet. "I miss you," was all it said...

*

The next time I looked up from my writing, I was surprised to see the sun was slipping behind the houses opposite and the garden was dappled in shades of purple and blue. My stomach rumbled and I thought wistfully about romantic candlelit dinners with Jack at the Bay View Hotel.

I returned to my writing, re-read the last paragraph I'd written.

She felt his warm, strong arms envelope her. 'I want you,' Yuri groaned. 'And I mean to have you.' His breath was hot on her neck; his broad, manly chest, damp with perspiration. Their bodies moved together as one, frictionless in the heat—

My stomach rumbled again and I had a sudden desire for Chinese food. Visions of crispy lamb in chilli sauce from the Lotus Blossom takeaway drifted in front of my eyes. After wrestling with my financial conscience for a minute or two I phoned through my order. The man there was very apologetic. He said they were really busy. My food wouldn't be ready for an hour. I didn't care. A takeaway from the Lotus was well worth waiting for.

Not quite an hour later, I stopped writing, stuffed my feet into a pair of flip-flops and grabbed my handbag. As I walked out into the car park I noticed the funeral tribute was gone, thank goodness.

It was dark by the time I parked the car outside the Lotus Blossom. Inside the takeaway, the smell of sesame oil and garlic made my stomach rumble. After another ten minutes, a man appeared from the kitchen, apologising profusely for the wait and handed me a white carrier bag.

As I pulled away from the kerb, the takeaway bag rocked forward on the passenger seat and I pressed it back until it felt stable enough not to topple over.

My route home started with a labyrinth of quiet back roads that ran parallel to the seafront. The terraced houses were tall and Victorian. Most were painted white with basement gardens and ornate wrought iron balconies. Those that weren't cheap B&Bs had been converted into flats. Warm light glowed from behind their curtains. But as I went to make the turn back onto the seafront some idiot had doubled parked and I couldn't get through. Tutting irritably, I reversed back and headed towards what was locally known as Wasteland Road. That wasn't its real name. I don't think it actually had a name. Some years ago an old furniture factory had been demolished for a new housing estate but before building could begin the developer went bust and ever since the area had remained an unpopular local eyesore, a deserted stretch of road bordered on both sides by a wilderness of abandoned shopping trolleys, fly-tipped mattresses and rubbish. Becky wouldn't even walk along Wasteland Road in daylight. At night it really was creepy. I put my foot down and the takeaway bag swayed precariously. As I jerked out my hand to steady it, bright headlights flashed up behind me and a Transit overtook so close it clouted my wing mirror then screeched to a halt in front of me.

I slammed my foot on the brake and the takeaway bag shot off the front seat, cannoned into the foot-well, and landed upside down. My car stopped about a foot from the van's back bumper. My heart thudded and adrenaline tingled in my fingertips. What an idiot driver! Bet it was a man.

Reaching over, I pulled the takeaway bag upright but I could already see that the lid had come off the crispy lamb and most of the chilli sauce was now on the floor. Brilliant.

I pushed open the car door and got out to inspect the damage to the wing mirror. The glass was smashed. That would not be cheap to replace. No way was I ruining my no claims bonus. The van driver could pay for it. I slammed my car door behind me to indicate I was not best pleased and glared towards the van as I waited for the driver to get out, apologise and give me his insurance details or better still some cash. But he didn't appear. Maybe he was hurt. Maybe he'd had a heart attack. I hurried over and peered through the van's side window.

A big man was sitting in the driver's seat with his head turned away from me. He had a shaved head and massive fleshy shoulders spilled from underneath a grimy white vest. As he turned his head towards me, I saw a monkey's crumpled face. I flinched then realised it was a plastic mask, like a child's toy. How odd. I took a couple of steps backwards.

The man shoved open the van's door, jumped down onto the road and stared at me. He was still wearing the chimp mask and looked even bigger now he was out of the van. Tattoos covered his meaty forearms.

I took another hasty step backwards and one of my flip-flops slipped off. I jerked my thumb back towards my car and said, as politely as I could manage, "Um. You hit my wing mirror just then."

But the man said nothing. He began to walk towards me, his right hand behind his back. Then he suddenly jerked his arm out front and to my horror he was holding a baseball bat.

Oh shit.

My mind raced. Could I outrun him? Probably not in flip-flops. I could scream – there were no houses nearby so it wouldn't attract anyone's attention – but maybe it would scare him off. What did he want? Did he have the bat because he seriously thought the collision was my fault? Or was he going to rob me? I pictured the lone ten pound note in my purse. My phone was so old it wasn't worth anything. My mouth went dry.

I said, "I…. um… that wasn't my fault, you know…"

He paced towards me, the baseball bat swinging threateningly from side to side. I continued to back away as the muscles in my legs quivered as if I had palsy. I put up my hands, tried to make my voice sound braver than I felt, "If you don't stop and get back in your van right now, I'll scream."

He didn't stop.

I took a deep breath, sucking the air into my lungs, the muscles in my neck tensing so I could try to make the loudest scream on earth.

"HELP!"

My shout echoed out into the silent night. I tried again, louder this time, "HE-LLL-PP!"

I continued to take small steps backwards until I felt the broken wing mirror against my wrist. My heart was hammering so hard it felt as if it would crack my ribs.

As I turned to jump into my car, he lunged. One of his meaty hands slammed into my shoulder sending me sprawling sideways onto the road. As I glanced up through my fringe, he swung the bat upwards, aiming it straight at my head. *Oh my God…*

I flinched, shut my eyes and rolled away from the blow, heard the bat bounce off the tarmac inches from my face. I managed to scramble onto all fours as he raised the bat above his head for another go.

Then, from the road behind me, I heard a car. The engine slowed, purred and stopped. Oh dear God, please let that be the police. A car door slammed, footsteps came closer then a man's voice said, "What's going on?"

My heart seemed to stop mid-beat. I knew that voice.

Van man paused, the baseball bat still raised above his head. "None of your business." He had a hard Bristol accent. "Scram."

I turned my head and peered up. Jack was standing next to me. His arms hung loose at his sides. He said, "Looks like my business. Put the bat down."

Van man spat onto the road. "Clear off or I'll do you too."

Jack stepped in front of me.

"Get back in your car Katy," he said without looking round.

I managed to scramble to my feet but my legs no longer seemed connected to my brain. I couldn't remember how to walk. Something trickled down my arm. Blood.

Van man tossed the bat from one hand to the other. Then he gripped the handle with both hands and swung it sideways at Jack's head.

Jack ducked. He threw a fast punch into the man's face followed by a hard jab just below his ribs.

The man gave a muffled roar and spun away. He doubled over, moaning as he fought to catch his breath. Blood dripped from under his monkey mask. Then, surprisingly quickly for such a bulky man, he reared up,

167

swinging the bat wildly. Blood continued to stream down his chin.

Jack ducked and stepped backwards.

Van man spat out more blood then swung the bat at Jack's head again.

Jack effortlessly tugged the bat out of the man's hands and tossed it away. It landed with a heavy clatter on the road and rolled into the gutter. Grabbing the back of the man's neck with both hands, Jack yanked his head down and jerked his knee up into the man's face. There was a horrible crunching noise. The man howled. He grabbed at the plastic chimp mask with both hands. As he tried to straighten up, Jack punched him twice, hard in the face. The man staggered backwards. His legs buckled and he sank down onto the ground. As his head drooped onto his chest, he began to make a pathetic mewing sound.

Jack reached down, tore off the monkey mask and threw it on the road. "Do you know him?" he demanded.

"N…no…" I stammered.

Jack grabbed the front of the man's vest and hauled him back to his feet. The man's eyes were swollen over. His mouth was slack and hanging open. Blood poured from a deep cut on the bridge of his nose. Spit and blood spooled off his chin. His face was mushy and so swollen it was hard to see where one feature ended and another began. I wouldn't have thought bare hands could do that much damage to human flesh.

As Jack drew his fist back again I screamed, "No! Stop!"

He looked at me for a full second before he dropped the punch. The man collapsed and lay groaning on the ground.

Jack wiped a hand across his mouth. His breathing was heavy. He grabbed my arm and steered me to my car. "Are you okay?"

I was shaking all over. I felt tears welling up. My vision misted and my nose started to run.

"Are you hurt?" he asked.

I pointed to where I'd felt blood trickling down my arm.

Jack looked at my elbow. "Just grazed. Can you drive?"

I nodded.

"Get in. I'll follow you home."

I wiped at my nose with the back of my hand. "Do you think we should call an ambulance?"

"No."

He walked away from me, back to his car.

*

My hands were shaking so much I could hardly turn the ignition key. The muscles in my thighs had gone into convulsions. When I put my foot on the clutch it kept bouncing off. I stalled the car twice before I finally got moving. All the way home, I drove like a learner, hardly going over twenty, lurching up to junctions then waiting ages until I was sure there were no cars approaching. I could make out the headlights of Jack's car in my rear view mirror but my eyes were so full of tears I could hardly see the road ahead.

"Concentrate, you stupid cow," I told myself, wiping at my eyes with the back of my hand. The smell of chilli sauce was making me feel sick.

What felt like a lifetime later, I drove into my car park and pulled up in the first empty space. I took a deep breath and got out. Jack's car stopped next to mine. My hands were still shaking and I had a powerful craving for a cigarette.

Jack got out and frowned at me across the low roof of the Mercedes. "I can smell Chinese food."

"It spilled, when he cut me up," I managed, jerking a hand towards my car.

As I stared at Jack's face in the moonlight, I felt my breath catch in my chest. In the darkness his grey eyes looked black and his face seemed harder, tougher, more angular.

"Why are you still in Sands End?" I blurted and immediately felt really stupid. Maybe I was in shock. I pointed a shaky finger back towards town. "What... what the hell was that about? I mean, that really wasn't my fault.... He hit my wing mirror as he overtook me..." My teeth began to chatter. I desperately wanted to feel Jack's arms around me but he didn't move, almost as if he didn't want to come any closer. My eyes filled with tears. Good grief. He must think I was such a cry-baby, what with this and my tears in the kitchen last night. *Oh please suggest you'll come in with me.*

Jack seemed to reach a decision. He opened his car door. "Okay, Katy, have it your way. Drive carefully from now on." He sounded really angry.

"I... I was driving carefully..." I protested. But Jack had already disappeared inside his car. The door slammed shut. He reversed quickly out of the parking space and powered the Mercedes out to the road without another glance in my direction.

For at least a minute – maybe longer – I was rooted to the spot. So that was it? No wave goodbye? No comforting hug? Not even a peck on the cheek? Nothing, after what I'd just been through? It was like we were total strangers rather than two people who had come close to spending a night of passion together. Or had I imagined our near miss? My bottom lip began to tremble. I reached into the car, picked up the crushed takeaway bag and ran inside.

I plonked the bag on the breakfast bar. The lid had also come off the egg-fried rice and everything was sitting in a puddle of congealed chilli sauce at the bottom of the bag. I stared at globs of white fat coagulating on the spilled slices of lamb, but all I could see was Jack's expression in the car park, the hard look in his eyes. It was as if he'd been furious with me. As if he thought I'd deliberately provoked the van man's road rage. As if it had been my fault I'd been attacked and he'd had to rescue me. I shoved the takeaway in the bin and went into the lounge. The light was flashing on my answer phone. I pressed play.

For a moment there was silence. Then I heard a voice whisper, "*I hope you liked the flowers.*"

CHAPTER THIRTEEN

I spent the next hour lying on the bed worrying about the answer-phone message and trying to decide if I should report the baseball bat attack to the police. I should report it because a violent thug like that should be locked up. But if I did report the attack, I'd also have to mention that Jack had beaten the living daylights out of the man and left him in a bloody pulp in the road. Panic kept fluttering in my chest. What if the van man was seriously injured and was now in Intensive Care? What if he'd died?

Oh God... I wiped at the tears on my cheeks. To take my mind off the attack, I decided to worry about the weird answer-phone message instead. I got up and pressed 1471 but the recorded voice told me the caller had withheld their number. I made myself listen to the message over and over for some sort of clue. But it was impossible to tell anything from the creepy whispered voice. A possible explanation was that the person who'd rented the flat before me was the intended recipient of the flowers. The whispering voice could have been a confused grieving relative checking the flowers had arrived, not realising I lived here now.

But what if the tribute had been intended for me? Had it been sent by Patrick to scare me, to freak me out? Revenge because I'd told him never to contact me again? Was that his whispered voice on the message? I re-played it several more times but I simply couldn't tell if the voice was Patrick's. In the end I deleted the message, rubbed antiseptic cream on my grazed arm, put the security chain on the front door and went to bed.

*

The next morning, I decided I had to find out if van-man had reported the incident to the police. I phoned the Avon & Somerset Police press voicebank messaging service and listened to the recorded list of recently reported local crimes. But there was just a burglary and a stolen car set on fire in a lay-by. Even so, late morning I drove down to Wasteland Road, worrying that I'd see police tape and forensics people wandering around in paper suits.

But the only evidence of what had happened was a smudge of black rubber from my emergency stop and some rusty splodges of what looked like dried blood on the tarmac. Once again, I thought about reporting what had happened. But it was too late now. The police would want to know why I hadn't called it in at the time. And they'd want to know why I'd left the scene without phoning for an ambulance.

I consoled my prickling conscience by telling myself that the van man couldn't have been badly hurt because he'd obviously managed to drive away after the attack. Maybe Jack's beating would make him think twice next time he wanted to have a go at a defenceless motorist.

I drove back home, the smell of chilli sauce still making me gag. To take my mind off everything, I spent an hour scrubbing the chilli sauce out of the MX-5's floor mats but I couldn't get rid of the smell. In the end I pulled down the soft top to air the car. The graze on my arm was sore and kept catching on things. I didn't have any plasters big enough to completely cover it so I decided to go to

Boots and buy some larger ones. As I walked down the hill to the shops, Becky texted me.

Katy – please ring me ASAP about the arrangements for the reunion.

And then it hit me. The reunion was that night. My heart sank. Maybe I could use the horrible road-rage incident as an excuse to get out of going? I could tell Becky I was in shock. Or maybe I should just go to the sodding thing. Get it over with. Gritting my teeth, I continued on down the hill towards town.

The weather was still sweltering. The slightest exertion raised a sweat. The Boots store in the High Street had its air-con on full blast. People were coming in just to cool down before going back outside. I took my time with my shopping to take my mind off Jack, the weird flowers, the baseball bat man and the creepy phone message. At the cosmetics display I caught my reflection in one of the mirrors. A shiny, make-up-free face stared back. Beads of perspiration ran over my top lip, freckles covered the bridge of my nose. A new wrinkle creased my forehead. I tugged my fringe down and sighed. It was not a face that would have captivated someone like Jack for very long.

The queue for the till snaked almost to the back of the shop. I counted eleven people ahead of me, all tourists buying things they'd forgotten to bring on holiday, such as toothbrushes or shower gel. My patience stretched like a piece of frayed elastic.

Eventually it was my turn, but as I walked towards the cashier, a tiny elderly man in a Galvin Green golf hat doddered straight past me and plonked his almost-full basket on the counter. I was fairly sure he'd been the driver of a mobility scooter that had nearly mown me down on the High Street a few weeks ago. The dozy sales assistant didn't seem to care he had pushed in.

I walked up and tapped the man on the shoulder. "Excuse me, I was next."

He cupped a hand to his ear and shouted, "Eh?"

"I was next," I repeated, a little louder.

"Eh?"

The sales assistant glared at me. "You're holding up the queue."

Someone behind me gave an irritable tut that seemed to be aimed at me. "Oh forget it," I snapped, stepping back. The canny elderly of Sands End knew just how to play the system. If I'd been feeling less fragile, I might have protested longer. Instead I felt defeated and fumed silently while keeping a sharp look out for any more pensioners planning to pull the same stunt.

After I'd eventually paid for my shopping, I slapped the biggest size plaster on my arm and trudged back through town. Once again, the High Street was packed with holidaymakers, dawdling along as if they had all the time in the world. Eventually my patience ran out so I took a shortcut through an alleyway to the seafront, planning to walk back home that way instead.

I walked along the prom, staring over the sea wall at the packed beach and the heat haze shimmering above the mud flats. I could be wearing a bikini and I'd still be sweltering. This relentless heat – day after day – was beginning to get me down. I felt crabby. I thought about Jack and his mysterious link to Kelly-Anne. I thought about the fight. I thought about the flowers. I thought about the phone message. I thought about Patrick denying his quotes in my story. From the moment Martin had said Patrick's name my life seemed to have gone haywire.

I glanced up. I had been so deep in thought that I'd walked too far along the seafront and missed the turning that led up to my flat. As I crossed over the road to double back, I realised I was outside the Fighting Cocks.

For a while I stood on the pavement staring at the pub's grimy whitewashed walls. The smell of stale beer drifted out through the open door. It looked and smelled exactly the same as it had when I'd stood here nursing my half of lager thirteen years ago, the night celebrating my A-Level results. The night Kelly-Anne Davis was murdered. In my mind I saw crowds of people standing outside the pub in the late evening sunshine, laughing and drinking. Susie's ginger hair had been much longer back then. Becky's long dark curls had been bleached blonde. I remembered there had been a group of lads, watching us. They were dressed up like spoof day-trippers with Kiss Me Quick hats and tops that said, *My Mum Went to Sands End and All I Got Was This Crappy T-shirt*. Susie and Becky had gone to the loo, leaving me outside while I finished my drink.

And that was when I'd seen Patrick Underhill.

From inside the pub, the thunk-thunk sound of a fruit machine disgorging a pile of winnings jolted me back. I needed to get home.

The space between my shoulder blades prickled. I spun around. A man was staring at me from the other side of the seafront.

My hand jerked up to my chest.

Patrick Underhill.

He wore the same black jeans and black tracksuit top that he'd worn when we'd met in the pub in Bristol. Something about his posture, arms folded, back resting against the sea wall, made me think he had been watching me for some time. My anger ignited. I stormed across the road towards him.

"Why did you deny your quotes, Patrick?" I yelled. "How the hell could you say I didn't turn up?" I had to use every shred of self-control not to hit him.

Patrick pushed himself away from the seawall. He sneered but said nothing.

"I mean, what is wrong with you? Why do you have to lie about *everything*?" I jabbed a finger against the side of my head, "You've got a screw loose, you weirdo, you loser, you—"

"Must be something about this pub," he said softly. "It always seems to bring out the worst in people."

I tried to step around him but he blocked my way. His gaze swept down the seafront towards the pier. "Yeah, I just popped down to Sands End for a quick visit. See how it's changed." His eyes scowled, but his tone of voice was casual, as if we were two old friends catching up in the sunshine. He glanced across the bay. "Just went to put some flowers on Kelly-Anne's grave. Looked fairly tidy, well maintained. Nice spot, actually. Under the yew trees at the far end."

I winced. Putting flowers on the grave of the woman he'd murdered, that was sick beyond belief. I took a step backwards and made my voice as threatening as possible, "Patrick, if you're trying to freak me out – guess what – it isn't working." *Liar.* "Just leave me alone. Okay? And if you send me any more weird flowers or do anything else to try and scare me, I'll go to the police. Okay?"

He rubbed at the spiky black bristles on his chin as if they were itchy. His lips curled up in a sneer. "I haven't a clue what you're talking about."

"I am off the story, Patrick. I am not going to help you 'clear your name'," my fingers made inverted commas in the air. "You know why? Because I don't believe you. No one ever believes you."

He stood facing me, scowling, his feet slightly apart, leaning back on his heels. "Yeah. I got your email. But this isn't about clearing my name."

My voice had an edge of hysteria to it, "No? Then what is it about?"

"I already told you. I didn't kill her."

"For heaven's sake Patrick! Stop talking in riddles! You confessed to killing her! You said you did it! You served thirteen years for it!"

"Yeah, well I had to," His voice sounded tired but there was no expression in his eyes. "He made me. I had no choice. He made it pretty clear that if I didn't fess-up..." He ran a finger across his throat and made a squelching noise.

"So, who was this mysterious *he*, Patrick?" My voice was heavy with sarcasm. "Nick Padovani? Because – guess what – I already know about that. And he didn't *make* you confess, he asked you, he begged you–"

"Nick Padovani?" Patrick frowned and stared at me as if I was a lunatic.

I glared back at him. "Yes. Nick Padovani. Kelly-Anne's old boss at Glitz. He went to visit you while you were on remand in prison and tried to persuade you to do the right thing: to plead guilty."

"Who told you that?"

"He did. Nick Padovani."

Patrick looked away and seemed to stifle a laugh. "Padovani told you that? Jesus... Let me tell you something, Katy. No one came to visit me in prison. Not when I was on remand, not after I'd been sentenced. Not even my own mother and father, and certainly not that shit Padovani."

"So who are you talking about?"

"The man with the Mexican–"

I waved my hands. "Stop! I've had enough of this Mexican. He does not exist! You made him up at school."

178

He carried on speaking as if he hadn't heard me, "See, I read her diary. And his name was in there. She'd written how he'd as good as killed her; that he might as well have smashed her head in and left her to die. It was like a prophecy, see? Everything in that diary came true: her murder, even the way he killed her in that photograph." He looked away. "You have no idea how much I wish I'd taken that diary with me – and the photograph. It had her name on the back – not the name I knew her by – her other name – and written next to it one word: dead."

I shook my head. What on earth was wrong with him? Maybe his constant lying was a medical condition, something he couldn't help, like a sort of Tourette's.

He licked at beads of perspiration above his top lip. "You really landed me in it with that story you wrote, Katy. You wrote it too soon. I should have known to never trust a journalist." He looked away. "They were going to put me back inside for saying those things, that's why I had to tell them you'd made it up. And I can't have that. Not yet." His voice dropped, "So, did you do what I asked? Did you find Jack Dale for me?"

I wanted to scream. "Patrick, can't you get it through your stupid bloody head–"

"Did you find him?" he repeated. His voice was a murmur.

Maybe I should just tell him the truth about Jack. Maybe that would make Patrick understand that no one was going to take him seriously and then he'd stop this madness once and for all. I hitched my handbag further up my shoulder. "Yes I did find Jack, as a matter of fact."

Patrick's eyes narrowed. "And?"

"And he made it completely – abundantly – plain that he couldn't prove your innocence. He can't clear your name. He'd never even heard of you. Okay?" I decided not to mention Jack's offer to help if he could. The proviso for that had been that I believed Patrick was telling the truth. And no way did I believe that. "I have to go now," I snapped.

As I tried to push past him, his hands grabbed my shoulders and he pulled me hard into his chest. I struggled against him. "Get off me–"

His voice was hoarse in my ear, "Just giving you a goodbye hug, Katy."

I tried to pull away but he'd pinned my arms to my sides. "Let go." My cheek was pressed against his tracksuit top. It smelled horrible, sour with body odour and stale cigarette smoke. A couple of feet away, holidaymakers sauntered along the prom. None of them paid us any attention. We were just a man and a woman enjoying an embrace in the sunshine.

"Get off me–" I tried to knee him in the groin but he was standing too close and I couldn't get the angle right. Instead I stamped down on his trainer with my flip-flop. He didn't seem to notice. Then something cold and solid jabbed against the base of my spine and I froze. My whole body went rigid.

His other hand moved up and clamped around the back of my neck. His voice murmured into my hair, "Katy, let me tell you the truth about what happened that night. I was watching her, see? She leaves work early, in a taxi. I follow her but by the time I get to where she lives she's already gone inside. I go up in the lift. And when I get to her floor, her front door is wide open. Right? So I go into her hallway. It's dark but I can see the kitchen light is on so I walk towards it. I'm calling her name, Kelly-Anne, Kelly-Anne. No answer."

His voice dropped to a whisper, "She's lying on the kitchen floor, Katy. Blood everywhere. All over the floor.

All up the wall. Next thing I know I'm lying next to her. In her blood. It's all over me. On my clothes. In my hair. On my face, my lips. I can smell it; taste it. It's everywhere. And there's a big green marble ashtray next to me on the floor, covered with her blood."

All I could hear was the pulse pounding across my temples. "Patrick–"

The hand around the back of my neck tightened. "Shut up. So, when I see her, dead lying in the blood, I actually think, 'Jesus, did I do this to her?' But then I realise. Of course I didn't. And now he's getting away. So I went after him."

My legs felt as if they were going into spasms and I couldn't catch my breath. "Let go of me now–" My voice was high with panic.

"Be quiet. From that moment all I cared about was finding him. And the funny thing is, later – much, much later – I realise I already know his name, from her diary. So, in prison, I'm asking around, seeing if anyone knows him; how I can find him when I come out. Then this new guy comes up to me and says he used to work with him and…" He gave a short laugh like a bark, "And then, Katy, guess what? I had a phone number to go with his name."

Abruptly he released his grip and I staggered backwards. I stared at his hands but he wasn't holding anything. He smiled and tilted his head to one side. "Oh Katy. Did you think it was a gun?" He made his fingers into a pistol shape then blew on them. "Pow. Pow."

My heart felt as if it was trying to bust through my ribs. "Patrick, if that really is all true, tell the police."

His voice dropped, "Katy, he *is* the police. Or rather, he used to be."

He turned and began to walk away.

My lips felt numb. "Wait a minute," I called after him. "Are… are you saying Jack Dale killed Kelly-Anne Davis?"

But Patrick didn't look back, he just continued walking down the seafront.

*

For a very long time I didn't move. I watched him walk away along the promenade, his black silhouette dwindling until he was just a small dark smudge in the distance. My breathing slowed and my heart rate gradually returned to normal. Was he really fit to return to society? Despite the heat, a shiver ran across my shoulders carrying with it the inkling of a thought. Was there any chance Patrick was telling the truth about Jack? I shook my head to help the shiver dissolve. However Patrick had arrived at the conclusion that Jack had murdered Kelly-Anne, it was just crazy. He had to be mistaken. Yet the unpleasant prickle of discomfort remained in the pit of my stomach.

As I turned and continued walking along the seafront towards home, I realised the flats where Kelly-Anne used to live were only about a hundred yards away. I don't know what I hoped to achieve by going there but a minute or so later I found myself walking through the pillared entrance and staring up at Sea View Heights.

It was a modern five-storey redbrick building, out of keeping with the rest of the Victorian seafront. Considering the number of balconies, I guessed there were four small flats to each floor. Each balcony was just big enough for a couple of chairs and a small patio table. To the front of the flats was a tarmac driveway flanked by well-maintained lawns.

The sun was ferocious and my bare arms prickled with sunburn. I walked up to the main doors and peered through the glass into a small lobby: magnolia walls, an artificial fig tree in a wicker pot, beige Hessian carpet, a row of black metal mail boxes along one wall, a staircase and two lifts. I wondered if this was the way Patrick had run out of the building that night, covered in her blood and straight into the arms of police officers who'd been summoned by the neighbour's 999 call. Leading off from the lobby was a door marked FIRE EXIT & GARAGE.

I continued walking around to the back of the building. A slope led down to an underground car park. I ducked around the barrier and waited for my eyes to adjust to the gloom. There was a door at the back of the garage with a sign on it saying *Stairs to Lobby*. I looked around. I couldn't see any CCTV cameras but, as I walked closer, I saw the door to the stairs had a security keypad.

If – and it was a very big 'if' – if Patrick had been telling the truth about being innocent of the murder, theoretically, the 'real killer' could have fled the building this way, unseen through the dark car park, well away from the main entrance.

I stared at the door and rubbed at my sunburn. But just because it was theoretically possible didn't make it true.

I walked out of the garage, retraced my steps to the front of the building and out through the pillared entrance. As I crossed back onto the seafront, a car's horn beeped behind me. I spun around and Shaun was leaning out of the window of his massive Toyota, grinning.

"Nearly got ya. You'd have been ten points." He leaned over and pushed opened the passenger door. "Hop in."

As I pulled the seat belt around me he said, "Glad I bumped into you. There's something I want to talk to you about."

"Look, if it's about Jack, you're wasting your breath."

"It's not about Jack." He glanced across at me. "You okay? You look like you've seen a ghost."

I sighed. "Just had a very weird encounter–" Suddenly I felt too weary to explain. I didn't want to think about Patrick Underhill or talk about him anymore.

Instead, I willed a smile onto my face. "So what do you want to talk about?"

"Linzi."

I frowned. "Ah."

Linzi was Shaun's Elle McPherson look-alike ex fiancée. She had jilted Shaun a few weeks before their wedding to run off with an insolvency lawyer called Larry who drove a lemon yellow Lotus. Shaun had been so *devo*, as he'd put it, he'd moved to the other side of the world to forget her. I'd nicknamed her Queen Bitch of Bitch World.

"So? What about Linzi?" I said as we set off back down the seafront. The traffic was awful, nose-to-tail and hardly moving.

Shaun raked a hand through his sandy hair. "It's ah… it's…. So have you heard from Jack?"

I looked away. I wondered if I should mention the baseball bat attack on the way home from the Chinese takeaway last night then decided against it. Every time I thought about the fight my blood ran cold. If I closed my eyes I could still see the fury on Jack's face, the precise, methodical – professional – way he'd beaten that man, then the chilling moment when he'd seemed to lose control and couldn't stop. On the other hand, if he hadn't beaten the living daylights out of chimp-mask man, I could be in hospital now undergoing reconstructive surgery to my face, or perhaps even dead. If I was brutally honest, seeing Jack fight had been a bit sexy, but it had also been very scary. Much like Jack in fact: sexy and scary. Probably for the best if I didn't see him again. I changed the subject. "So, what about Linzi?"

Shaun shrugged and looked a bit awkward. "Yeah. Look, it can wait."

"No, no I'm happy to talk about it." I paused, "If you want to that is." Shaun had always been wary of revealing too much about his break-up.

An old motorbike sped past us, backfiring and making me jump. Shaun glanced across at me, "You sure you're okay? You seem a bit on edge?"

"I'm fine. So, back to Linzi?"

Shaun shifted in his seat. "Well, the thing is, she broke up with Larry Lawyer."

"Oh? How do you know that?"

He looked away. "She told me. We've… we've been Skyping."

I put my hands up to my face. "Oh no. No. No."

Shaun scowled. "See, I knew you'd react like that."

"Like what?"

He mimicked my voice. "*Oh no. No. No.*"

My irritation sparked. "Listen, I don't remember you holding back your opinions about Jack the other day."

Shaun rolled the car forward a few feet. "No. Well, that's different."

"Oh? How is it different?"

"He's bad news."

"Really? How so?"

Shaun shifted in his seat again, fiddled with the air vent to make it point straight at him. "I could just tell. He's

185

not right for you. Try and imagine he's pug ugly. Maybe then you'll see him straight."

I felt my face flush. "Well, maybe Linzi isn't right for you either. She broke your heart. Remember?"

"Yeah." His gaze drifted away towards the sea. Further down the road I spotted the reason for the hold-up. It looked as if there had been crash at the traffic lights down by the pier. I could see the blue flashing lights of police cars in the distance.

"So, what did Linzi say?" I asked, thinking it would have been quicker to walk home at this rate.

Shaun shrugged. "Just that she and Larry broke up. She found out he was seeing another woman behind her back."

"Good. Now she knows how it feels." It came out a bit more violently than I'd intended. "So what else did she say?"

"Um… um… That's about it."

"Oh." A wasp flew in through the open window and I backhanded it away.

The traffic began to move again. Shaun flicked the indicator, turned off the seafront and headed up the hill. He grinned, "So, looking forward to your school reunion tonight?"

I took the hint. The Linzi *convo*, as Shaun would say, was over.

I sighed. "Oh yeah. Can't wait."

*

As soon as I was back in my flat I noticed there were five messages on the answering machine. Odd. I was lucky if I got one a week. The bad feeling crept back as I remembered the creepy, whispered voice. I took a deep breath and pressed play.

"*Hi Katy, it's Becky I've been calling you all day.*" She gave what sounded like an irritable tut. "*Anyway, can you call me back ASAP because I need to tell you about the arrangements for tonight. Bye.*"

I poked out my tongue at the machine. "One text at lunchtime, Becky, does not qualify as calling me all day."

I skipped to the next message.

"*Hi Katy. It's Becky again.*" This time there was a definite edge to her voice. She hated being ignored. "*Just checking you got the messages I left earlier? Can you call me please? Thanks.*"

Groan. No escape. I skipped to message three. "*Hi Katy, it's Susie. Becky's been trying to get hold of you urgently. Might be an idea to call her back because she's on the verge of reporting you missing to the police. See you tonight. Bye.*"

"I. Was. Out!" I shouted. There could never be an innocent explanation for anything in Becky's world. I went to the next message.

"*Katy — it's Becky again. Really worried about you now.*" She spoke very quickly, her voice tinged with panic. "*Can you call me as soon as you get this message?*"

I rolled my eyes and waited for the next message to play.

"*Katy. It's your mother. I've just had Becky Thomas on the phone. She says she's been trying to call you all day with no success. I told her you're more elusive than Lord Lucan. By the way, I found a super wrap-around dress of yours hidden away in the wardrobe in the spare room. It'll be perfect for your school reunion. It's the satin one with the orange and brown zigzags. I'll pop it in a carrier bag and leave it in the porch for you to pick up. Corenza has very kindly offered to lend you one of her lovely Celtic pendants.*" She paused.

"I'm assuming you're planning to look presentable for once at the party?"

I put my hands up to my face. "Leave. Me. Alone."

Then the phone rang. I snatched it up thinking, please let it be Jack. "Hi."

But it was Becky. "Oh. You *are* home." She sounded hurt.

"Yep. Just got in."

"I've been really, really worried about you–"

"I'm fine. Just popped into town."

"Oh. Right..." Her voice became brittle. "I thought you might be avoiding me..."

I felt a blush on my neck and gave a little high-pitched laugh. "Avoiding you? Why would I be avoiding you?"

"Well, avoiding the school reunion more like... Anyway, I need to tell you about the arrangements. I am so excited! It's going to be so brilliant. I can't believe it's here after all my hard work organising it."

I closed my eyes. There was no way I could pull out. The reunion meant everything to Becky.

"Okay," she said. "Do you have a pen and paper? I'll give you the running order."

"Running order?"

"The party kicks off at seven–"

"Seven? That's a bit early isn't it?"

"Katy, Glitz is only open until two and we've got to fit in an awful lot of socialising before that."

Good grief. Seven hours of saying the same thing to people I hadn't set eyes on since school. In a voyeuristic way I was a bit curious to find out how life had treated my former classmates, but it was the reciprocal part I wanted to avoid: having to tell them I wasn't married, didn't have kids, didn't have a job, didn't even have a boyfriend.

"Anyway," Becky continued, "we're meeting at six o'clock at mum and dad's holiday flat for drinks. Did I mention we're all staying the night there after the party?"

Becky's parents owned an apartment on the seafront which they let out during the summer. It was only a five-minute walk – if that – from Glitz but I still didn't want to stay there tonight. I wanted to go home after the party.

I winced. "Um…. Gosh, that's really kind but…"

Becky's voice turned petulant. "There's plenty of room, if that's what's bothering you. It sleeps eight but only four of us are staying."

I frowned. "Four? Who else is staying then?"

"Jo."

"Jo?"

"Jo Rossiter."

I closed my eyes. Jo Rossiter, Queen of the Undercover Bitches, stealer of my first boyfriend. This was just getting better and better.

"Jo. Great," I said with no enthusiasm.

"She's been living in New York for the last ten years," Becky continued. "She's a top TV producer over there, can you believe?"

Better and better. "Wow."

"Anyway, like I said, we'll meet at the flat first, down a few glasses of bubbly, then head over to Glitz for seven. And don't forget, it's first-come, first-served on the clothes. Bye." And she was gone.

I blinked. Clothes? What on earth was she talking about?

189

CHAPTER FOURTEEN

At ten to six I was ready to go. As I opened the front door to leave, Shaun was in the process of raising his hand to knock on it. He pointed at his fist, grinned and mimed a knocking motion. "See? I remembered!" Then his face fell. "Ah... You off out already?"

"Yeah... The party starts ridiculously early..." I tried to squeeze past him into the lobby.

"Oh. Well, I can give you a lift there if you want?"

Bless him. He was so thoughtful. "Thanks but I'm going to walk."

"Okay, but I don't like the idea of you walking back in the dark. I could pick you up afterwards if you like? Save you the taxi fare?"

Sweet man. "Thanks but it won't be dark. I'm only staying for an hour or so." One drink, two maximum, and I was planning to get out of there.

Shaun glanced down at my skinny black jeans. "Hey, I thought you'd be frocking-up for tonight. What's the dress code?"

I shrugged. "No idea."

"Doesn't it say on the ticket?"

I slapped a hand against my forehead. "Forgot the ticket."

I ran back into the flat, grabbed the ticket from the mantelpiece and shoved it in my handbag.

As I returned to the lobby, Shaun said, "Look Katy, there was something else I wanted to tell you earlier–"

I was never going to get away at this rate. Becky would kill me if I was late.

"Um, can we talk about it later? I'll bang on your door when I get home. Okay? It won't be late." I hurried across the lobby.

Shaun looked down at his bare feet. "Yeah, catch you later. Have fun."

It only took ten minutes to walk down to the holiday flat. Although I was still dreading the reunion, I was feeling pretty good – for once – with my appearance. I'd gone for casual smart – a pair of tight black jeans with a silky red vest, big hoop earrings and my high red wedge sandals. I'd let my hair dry naturally and coaxed it into waves with hot tongs. As I walked up the front path, I could hear loud music and excited female voices coming out of the open window of the ground floor flat. I knocked twice on the door then a very beautiful woman opened it. She had long, glossy black hair, olive skin, almond eyes and what looked like a 34DD bust. She wore a very short black dress with a lacy white collar and black fishnet tights. A lacy white apron was tied around her waist. Maybe she'd been helping Becky clean-up the flat.

I willed a smile onto my face "Hi Jo. Long time no see."

"Katy! We were just beginning to think you'd stood us up." Jo Rossiter now had a cool American accent. She pointed at her dress. "What d'ya think? Awesome, eh?"

I nodded thinking, a bit odd more like. She looked like a cross between waitress in a coffee shop and a hooker. My eyes drifted down. On her feet was a pair of incredibly high black shoes. I could just see their shiny red lacquered soles. Oh please. Not Louboutin.

She stepped back to let me in and Becky shot up from the sofa. "Bloody hell Katy! About bloody time."

191

Becky too was curiously dressed. Her curly burgundy hair was pulled up in a high ponytail and had been sprayed silver. She wore a silky yellow mini dress with what looked like the USS Enterprise logo embroidered on the chest and silver ankle boots. Her cheeks were sprinkled with glitter. The penny dropped and my heart plummeted with it. Of course. It was fancy dress. Becky had told me months ago but with all the crazy Patrick stuff I'd totally forgotten.

Susie waved and grinned as she joined us in the room. She was dressed as a female pirate. Her short ginger hair poked out from underneath a purple three-cornered hat and she wore a brown velvet tunic and over-the-knee, brown leather boots. "The outfits are all from Becky's fancy dress shop," she said. "Aren't they fabulous?"

Becky said, "Come on. Get changed. Chop-chop!"

"Um. Actually Becks, I think I'll pass on the fancy dress thing if you don't mind…"

But Becky was shaking her head. She grabbed her ticket and waved it at me. "You can't. No fancy dress, no *admissioni*. Come on. Let's get you into your outfit."

She grabbed my wrist and dragged me into one of the small bedrooms leading off the lounge. The air was heavy with perfume. She pulled a plastic suit carrier off the bed, unzipped the front and held it out to me. "Ta-dah!"

For a couple of seconds my brain couldn't make sense of what she was holding. I saw a pair of purple satin dungarees and a shiny blue blouse. Okay, Jo had blagged the sexy French maid, Becky was someone from Star Trek and Susie was a character from Pirates of the Caribbean. But what on earth was this?

Becky tossed a small purple cap at me. She put on a silly high-pitched voice, "Hi *ho*!"

Oh no. Oh no way. "I… I can't wear that…"

Becky scowled, "Oh stop being such a party pooper. It's your own fault for turning up late. And anyway, everyone's going to be in fancy dress so you'll be the weird one if you go in ordinary clothes."

I shook my head. "Doesn't bother me. I'm not staying for long and–"

Becky's lower lip began to tremble and her fake lashes blinked rapidly as if she was going to cry. "Oh Katy. Don't you dare ruin tonight for me. You have to dress up. I've told everyone that fancy dress is compulsory."

No one could induce guilt like Becky. She'd been practising since she was in nappies. I supposed there was one small advantage to going in fancy dress: it would make it less likely that anyone would recognise me. But one of the Seven Dwarves?

Jo and Susie appeared in the room behind me. Jo glanced at my horrified expression and said, "Guess you're not going as Happy, then?"

"She can be Grumpy," Becky replied and the two of them burst out laughing. When I didn't join in the joke, Becky snapped, "Oh for God's sake Katy. Stop making such a big deal. We all look silly."

Except they didn't. They looked really good. My cheeks roasted as I pulled off my jeans and top.

"So, Becky," Jo drawled, "any teachers going tonight?"

In the wardrobe mirror I saw Becky shake her head. "No. None of them have bought tickets and no ticket, no *admissioni.*"

"Shame," Jo said, taking a sip of Champagne.

Susie turned to her. "Who did you want to see?"

I buttoned the blouse, stepped into the dungarees, tugged the straps over my shoulders and pulled up the bib.

The trousers stopped just below my knees. Maybe the outfit was for a real dwarf...

Jo smiled. "Well, I wouldn't have minded seeing Mr Kent our drama teacher again. I seem to remember he was an excellent kisser."

I froze. My beloved Mr Kent. So, Patrick had actually been telling the truth about them snogging on the playing field. Amazing. A small part of my heart snapped off and broke all over again.

Becky rammed the purple cap on my head and Jo nodded at my reflection. "Aw you look *sooo* cute!" She paused, her head on one side, "Might I suggest a small finishing touch?" Becky might be Queen of the World, but Jo was still her Minister of Fashion.

Jo grabbed her make-up bag and before I could stop her, she had rubbed some scarlet lipstick on my cheeks.

I stared in the mirror and it was all I could do not to burst into tears. The purple satin dungarees had huge red clown buttons on the straps. The blue blouse had a round cutsie collar and looked like something I might have worn when I was six. The little purple pixie cap had a yellow pom-pom on the end. But the absolute *pièce de résistance*, was Jo's addition of two massive red rosy cheeks. I looked like a feverish child auditioning for panto. I blurted, "Listen, I'll go home and find something else—"

But the girls all shook their heads. "There isn't time," Becky wailed. Her eyes narrowed. "And anyway, once you go, you won't come back. I know you, Katy. You've been trying to weasel out of this school reunion since day one."

I felt a stab of guilt.

Susie made a brave attempt at sincerity, "You look really original. I bet no one else will go in the same outfit."

194

My eyes returned to my reflection, thinking Susie was spot on about that.

The girls left the bedroom to top up their glasses and change the music. Becky said, "Five minutes then we're going, Katy. Okay?" She pulled the door shut behind her. Through the wall I heard glasses chink and Becky's voice say, "Well ladies, here's to a party we'll never forget–" Then Michael Jackson's Burn This Disco Out drowned the rest of her words.

I went over to the mirror and made a half-hearted attempt to rub off the lipstick on my cheeks. But all I managed to do was smudge it even more.

Then the music abruptly stopped and Susie poked her head around the bedroom door. Her eyes looked worried. "Um, Katy. There's someone here to see you."

I frowned. "To see me? Who?"

She glanced over her shoulder. "I think you'd better come and see for yourself."

*

Susie held open the door. I tugged up the bib of the dungarees and stepped self-consciously into the lounge, wobbling a little on my wedge heels. Becky and Jo were sitting side-by-side on the sofa, Champagne flutes gripped in their hands. Both women's smiles were a little too bright.

And in the middle of the room stood Jack. He was wearing a black leather jacket and a black t-shirt over faded jeans. The leather jacket did absolutely nothing to disguise his killer body. Neither did the jeans.

Blood rushed up to my face. What the hell was he doing here? And, more importantly, how did he know I was here? I caught a glimpse of the droopy pixie hat in the mirror on wall opposite, and fought the urge to run back into the bedroom and barricade myself inside.

After what felt like several years Becky said, "Well, Katy. Aren't you going to introduce us?"

My cheeks felt as if they were on fire. "Oh. Yes. This is Jack—" I stopped because I suddenly realised I probably wasn't supposed to be calling him by that name in front of other people. Oh well. It wouldn't mean anything to the girls. "Um. Jack's been... he's been helping me with a story." A vision of him standing in my kitchen popped into my mind, his fingers gently stroking my face.

Becky smirked. "A Lori du Val story?"

My blush deepened. The two girls nodded their hellos from the sofa. Jo moistened her lips with her tongue. She extended her long legs and leant forward, giving Jack a grandstand view of her cleavage. She reached a slender, bare arm upwards as if she expected him to kiss her hand. My heart sank to somewhere around my knees. This was going to be Niall Sinclair all over again. I could just feel it.

I glanced at Jack to see if he was responding to her outrageous flirting, but he wasn't looking at Jo. He was staring at me. His eyes were hard and he wasn't smiling. The tension in the room was suddenly unbearable.

Becky willed a smile onto her face. "Okay. It's almost seven so we need to go. Katy, you'll have to come with us because I've only got one key to lock up."

On stiff legs I followed the girls outside. Jack's magnificent Mercedes was parked at the kerb and Becky's eyes nearly popped out of her head when she saw it. He clicked the key-fob, reached into the car, grabbed something from under the dashboard and shoved it inside his jacket.

Susie, Becky and Jo walked a little ahead of us along the seafront, their heads together, whispering. Every now and then Jo sneaked a glance back at Jack. I was about to break the stony silence by saying something witty like, *I'm beginning to think you can't stay away from me, Jack,* when he said, "So, what's the deal?"

I frowned. "Deal?"

"Has he threatened you? Made any kind of direct threat about tonight?"

I had no idea what he was talking about. "Sorry, has who threatened me?"

Jack stopped and turned to face me. "Your text."

"What text?"

He reached inside his jacket and pulled out his phone. His fingers stroked the screen then he held it out for me to read.

Jack. This is Katy. I need your help. Meet me at my school reunion tonight at Glitz. Please come. I am so scared. My life is in terrible danger. I know who really killed Kelly-Anne.

My head felt as if it was full of cotton wool. "That… that isn't from me…" I managed at last.

Jack's eyes were cold. "No?" I could tell he didn't believe me. He replaced his phone inside his jacket.

I managed a laugh. "That's got to be a joke. Right? Someone messing around?" My fingers tugged at the pom-pom on my hat. "Honestly, Jack. That text isn't from me." I reached into my handbag. "Look, I'll show you it isn't from me…"

My fingers went straight to the little phone pocket inside my bag, but my phone wasn't there. I reached deeper into the bag, my hands pawing through the contents, but they failed to close around anything that felt like my mobile. I put the bag on a garden wall and began dumping the contents next to it as Jack watched. There wasn't much: make-up bag, shorthand notebook, purse, sunglasses, seven biros, Dictaphone, pair of lime green leather gloves leftover from the winter and a small white plastic cube which was probably something techy belonging to Shaun, although how it had got into my handbag was anyone's guess. No phone. So where the hell was it?

Jack turned away and resumed walking. Susie, Becky and Jo had already disappeared around the corner.

I chewed at my lips, trying to remember when I'd last seen my phone. I recreated my day in my mind. I'd definitely had it when I'd walked into town earlier because Becky had sent me a text reminding me the school reunion was that evening. After that I'd gone into Boots... Could it have dropped out of my bag when I'd pulled out my purse?

Meet me at my school reunion tonight at Glitz.... I know who really killed Kelly-Anne....

Whoever sent that text not only had my phone but they also had Jack's phone number. They knew about Kelly-Anne. They knew about the school reunion....

My hand slapped up to my forehead. Patrick Underhill. The toe-rag had nicked my phone when he'd forced me into that strange hug on the seafront earlier.

So, did you find Jack for me?

"Jack. Wait," I called.

He stopped and turned to face me.

I caught him up. "I think Patrick Underhill sent you that text. I saw him this afternoon. I think he stole my phone." I tried to keep my voice neutral, "I think Patrick believes... I think he believes that you killed Kelly-Anne Davis."

Jack didn't respond. He turned and continued walking towards the club.

For a few seconds I watched him then I willed my feet into movement and followed.

*

The street outside Glitz was packed with people – all of them in fancy dress – laughing and chatting in the evening sun as if no one wanted to be the first to go inside. I turned to Jack intending to reiterate my innocence about sending him the text but he'd vanished.

My mind raced, trying to think things through: somehow Patrick Underhill had convinced himself that he hadn't murdered Kelly-Anne Davis, a lie he'd probably told himself so many times during his thirteen years in prison that he now believed it to be true; more strange confabulation, as Shaun had called it. But if Patrick truly believed his false memories of the murder, and he now truly believed that Kelly-Anne had been killed by Jack… Patrick had wanted me to find Jack. Patrick had used my phone to lure Jack to the reunion…. An icy thought sank through me. Patrick was going to do something at the party; he was going to hurt – maybe even kill – Jack.

My heart thumped, my eyes darted around the crowd. I saw a man in an Afro wig and running gear, a sexy Catwoman wearing black patent boots with skyscraper heels, a man in a chain-mail tabard with the words *Knight To Remember* written on his chest. There were lots of men in Captain Jack-type pirate outfits, a few silver-suited space aliens, and loads of stupid-looking Fat Elvis characters. Any one of them could be Patrick Underhill.

Becky appeared from the crowd and grabbed my hand. "Come on. It's about to start. We need to go inside."

Susie and Jo were nowhere in sight. A bouncer was checking tickets on the door. I pulled back. "I need to find Jack. I need to warn him—"

Becky turned to face me. "Oh yes. Jack." Her eyes narrowed. "Well, you certainly kept him quiet. He is spectacularly gorgeous." From her tone she might as well have added, and much too spectacularly gorgeous for you. "Well, I hope he's not expecting to be let in the club – no ticket, no *admissioni*."

I nodded to myself, trying to damp down the panic fluttering in my chest. *No ticket, no admissioni*. Patrick didn't have a ticket so he couldn't get in. As long as Jack was inside Glitz, he'd be safe.

"Becky, do you have any spare tickets?"

"For Jack, I assume?"

"Yes. Is that okay?"

She shrugged. "Guess so. Give me the money later." She rummaged inside her handbag, took out her wallet and handed me a ticket.

"That's the only one I have left," she snapped. "So don't lose it or he will not get in. The door staff are on strict instructions. I will not have Patrick Underhill ruin this party for me."

I hurried after Becky and in through the door of the club. Becky handed her ticket to the bouncer and so did I. Inside the lobby we joined the crush of crazily dressed people. There was no sign of Jack. Becky immediately headed up the stairs and I followed, trying to catch her up so I could explain I needed to go back to the lobby to wait for Jack but there were too many people between us. As she disappeared through the black swing doors, I felt a hand touch the small of my back. I heard the ghost of Patrick's voice say, "*Pow, pow.*"

I jumped a foot in the air and spun around. And there was Jack, standing behind me. I frowned. How had he managed to get in without a ticket? I managed to say, "Jack, listen. I think Patrick's planning to–" Then the doors swung open and the music drowned out my words.

Jack didn't reply but his hands remained, lightly touching my back. As we walked into the club, a woman dressed very skimpily, Arabian Nights-style, stopped in front of me. I staggered backwards, almost falling into Jack's arms. Something heavy nudged against my shoulder then Jack stepped in front of me. He grabbed my hand and, despite everything, my heart swooped at the touch of his skin.

He towed me across the crowded room. As I looked around, Glitz had been transformed back into the dark cave I remembered. A rig of coloured disco lights swirled over the dance-floor. The black leatherette sofas melted into the gloom. At the far end of the club was a long bar, illuminated in lime green and neon pink. A canopy of blue chiffon covered in twinkling white fairy lights billowed down from the ceiling. My eyes searched every face but it was impossible to tell if any of them belonged to Patrick. No, he wouldn't be able to get in. No way. And anyway, Nick Padovani had told me he'd call the police if Patrick came within ten feet of his club. Padovani was bound to be on the look out in case Patrick turned up to cause trouble at his school reunion. But despite my frantic attempts at reassurance, the fluttery panic was back in my chest.

Jack found a space in the crowd, stopped and turned to face me.

I started to say, "Jack, listen to me—" But he put his mouth against my ear. His breath was warm. My scalp tingled.

"Is there anyone here you don't recognise?" he asked.

I nearly laughed out loud. "Jack, it's a fancy dress party! I don't recognise anyone. And anyway, it's Patrick Underhill you need to be on the look out for not some stranger." I paused and took a deep breath, "Jack, I think Patrick is going to try to hurt you tonight. I'm sure he hasn't bought a ticket so I don't think he's going to be able to get into the club, but…" My voice trailed off as I realised Jack didn't seem to be listening to me. His eyes were scanning the room.

I pulled away and scanned the room too. There must have been more than fifty people already in the club. They stood in tight clusters and the queue for the bar was ten deep. A group of women dressed as The Spice Girls had hit the dance-floor, and were lip-synching along with the music. *"I'll tell you what I want, what I really, really want…"*

Jack didn't look happy. His eyes frowned. Then his mouth was back against my ear. "Has anything unusual happened to you during the last few days?"

You mean apart from being made to dress up as a dwarf? "Well, there was the thing with the… with the van man." I tried to disguise my discomfort about the fight by making light of it, "But I don't think he's going anywhere in a hurry."

"What about your flat, anything that made you think someone had been in it while you were out?"

I started to shake my head then stopped. "Well, funnily enough there was an evening a few days ago when I did sort of briefly think that maybe someone had, because my laptop was switched on when I came home. But I think, actually, I must have left it on and–"

He cut me off, "Anyone suspicious hanging around outside your flat?"

"No."

"Odd phone calls? The caller hanging up when you answer?"

"No, nothing like that. Oh, there was the weird phone message after the funeral flowers."

Jack frowned, "Funeral flowers?"

I was about to explain my theory about Patrick sending them when a group of drunken lads dressed as characters from the A-Team jostled past us.

Jack's upper arm pressed against my shoulder, his body was angled into mine. But it felt protective rather than seductive. I felt a surge of panic. Was he body-guarding me? But that made no sense. Jack was the one in danger tonight. Not me.

I turned to face him. My voice became high with alarm, "Jack, what do you think is going to happen here?"

He looked away and didn't answer.

Every time a woman walked past us she glanced at me but stared at Jack. A man, his face covered with a *Friday the 13th* Jason hockey mask, walked by. He made a hissing noise and I flinched away. A zombie, scarred with bloody sores, held my gaze. Fake blood oozed between his lips. One of his eyes was swollen shut. His lips turned up in a snarl, "Any idea where the little boys' room is in this place, sweetie?" The Penguin from the Batman movies appeared at my elbow. He wore a mauve top hat and matching bow tie. A cigarette holder was gripped between his teeth. "Hello Katy Bennett, *haw-haw-haw*." His tongue made an odd clicking noise against the roof of his mouth. "What have you been up to since school, *haw-haw-haw, click-click-click*? I work in PR in Swindon, *haw-haw-haw*. Three kids, two divorces, one dog. How about you? *Haw-haw-haw. Click-click-click*." He melted away into the crowd.

Over Jack's shoulder I could see Catwoman snogging the face off a dumpy Cardinal who I thought might have been in my biology class. Nearby, a Viking and Father Christmas seemed to be having a heated argument, which Snow White was trying to defuse by bopping a red balloon on their heads. Swirling disco lights made kaleidoscopes of people's faces. Strange shapes loomed out of shadowy corners.

Panic rose in my chest.

"I think we should go," I told Jack. *Yes. Leave.* I nodded and felt the pom-pom on my cap touch the back of my neck. My heart thudded underneath the bib of my dungarees. Jack's lips were inches away from mine. I had to use every shred of self-control not to kiss him. Instead, I found myself bursting into hysterical laughter.

Jack pressed his mouth against my ear. "I need to stay." He glanced away. "Katy, listen to me. I'm here to protect you tonight. Okay?"

My chest tingled. I shook my head, "No, you don't understand. It's you Patrick wants. Not me–"

But again, Jack didn't seem to be listening. He glanced across the room. "Let's go and stand with your friends."

I followed his glance. Jo, Susie and Becky were sitting at a table near the dance-floor.

I grabbed Jack's wrist with both hands and followed him. As he walked he made sure his body was never more than a few inches from mine. Under other circumstances I'd have been ecstatic at the proximity.

As we reached the girls, the disco lights dimmed and the music stopped. A spotlight pooled on the dance-floor. A short bald man in a white tuxedo skipped through a silver lamé curtain holding a microphone. He plonked the mic in a stand. "Good evening Sands End Comprehensive," he shouted.

People began to shuffle self-consciously off the dance-floor. Everyone in the club turned to look at him and their conversations gradually died.

"Hello and welcome. My name is Daniel and I'm your *compère* for this evening. Now, I'm sure you're all keen to get back to exchanging your scintillating life stories," he paused for a ripple of polite laughter, "But first we have some entertainment, which like the rest of this splendid school reunion, has been very kindly organised by Becky Thomas – or should I say," he consulted a small card in his hand, "Lieutenant Nyota Uhura." Becky stood and gave the room a curtsy, followed by several low bows as if she was expecting an encore.

Susie touched my arm, "He's going to do a spoof awards ceremony. You know, Biggest School Geek, Pupil Most Likely to Underachieve. We had to cast our votes on Facebook."

Oh great. My eyes gave the crowd another scan but Patrick's face still didn't jump out at me. I shook my head. I was letting the situation get to me. I needed to calm down. I pulled air in through my nose, held it for a second before I exhaled and felt my breathing slow a little.

The *compère* started going through his routine. Every now and then some poor fool had to do the walk of shame and collect a cheap silver trophy for such humiliations as Boy No One Fancied, or Girl With Biggest Boobs. Surprisingly, Jo Rossiter didn't win that one, although she did win Most Fanciable Girl. Becky feigned surprise when she was voted Most Popular Girl, and a podgy man wearing a kilt and a Tam o' Shanter looked mortified to find he had won Most Fanciable Boy. With a jolt, I realised it was Niall Sinclair. The years had not been kind to him.

Just as I thought the dreadful awards ceremony was over, the *compère* said my name. Susie pinched my arm and squealed.

"Katy Bennett?" the *compère* repeated. "Person Least Likely To Go To A School Reunion."

205

There was a small ripple of laughter. Susie, Becky and Jo broke into wild applause. Heads turned in our direction.

"Go on!" Jo hissed. She stood and pointed at me. "Here she is!" she shouted. "Grumpy the Dwarf!"

"But she's staying right here," I muttered, trying to make myself as small as possible.

"Oh get up there, Katy," Jo snapped, her eyes fixed on Jack.

The *compère* grinned. "Actually, someone else is going to present this award. Sand End's very own celebrity VIP, or so he tells me." He stood to one side. "Over to you, Mystery Celebrity Guest."

People peered at the dance-floor. They exchanged curious glances. Good grief. What now? I just wanted the night to be over so we could leave. The bad feeling was back in my stomach.

The house lights dimmed and the dance-floor turned into a fairy grotto surrounded with twinkling white lights. The crowd gave a collective, "Oooh." Dry ice floated across the floor. Then the silver lamé curtain rippled and the Grim Reaper appeared. I felt myself flinch. He wore a floor-length black cloak. A black hood covered his face and he was holding a very realistic looking scythe. He walked up to the microphone. "Hello?"

Lo, lo, lo, echoed around the room. Feedback screeched and people put their hands up to their ears. The man gave the mic a sharp tap and fiddled with a button on its side. His voice dropped an octave as he put the mic on some kind of echo mode, "Hello—*lo-lo-lo*?"

I glanced at Jack. His face was expressionless but his body language seemed every bit as tense as earlier. I forced my eyes back to the man on the dance-floor. People craned their necks as they tried to get a better look, their faces puzzled.

The man took the microphone off its stand. In a rumbling tombstone voice he boomed, "Hello! Is that better? All hear me at the back? Good. Hi! I'm Death. So, here we all are again." He paused. "And you're all still alive! Nobody's dead yet! Although some of you look so old, you might as well be dead!"

The crowd's laughter became more confident.

Susie touched my arm. "Becky said she'd arranged a comic. She wouldn't tell me who it was but do you remember that weird boy, Eric, in our chemistry class? He entertains the kids on the pier dressed as a chicken and does a bit of stand-up comedy. I reckon it's him."

A shiver rippled across my shoulders. Jack's arm pressed against mine. I snuck a glance at Becky but she seemed totally relaxed, laughing along with the comic. I felt some reassurance return.

The Grim Reaper took a few steps backwards and nodded. "Look at you all, in your fun little outfits. All the effort you've put into being the craziest, wackiest person at the party."

The crowd laughed a little self-consciously. I glanced down at my bare knees poking out from the bottom of the purple satin dungarees. My hand tugged miserably at the pom-pom on the end of the hat.

He took a couple of paces towards the edge of the dance-floor. "Anyway, I expect you're all wondering who I really am? Anyone guessed yet?"

"Elvis lives!" a man yelled from the back and was rewarded with much raucous laughter and jeering. Susie grinned and shouted, "Chicken Eric!"

The Grim Reaper waited for the laughter to fade. "Okay, I'll give you a few clues," he said in his deep, rumbling voice. "Well, like you I was a pupil at Sands End Comprehensive but I haven't seen most of you for a very long time."

He shifted his weight onto his other foot, rested a hand rather camply on his hip and I realised he was about to go into his comedy act. I snuck a glance at Jack but his face was still expressionless, his eyes still scanning the crowd.

The Grim Reaper rumbled, "Yeah, I was as thick as two short planks at school. Hated lessons. Didn't learn a thing. Anyone remember Mr Green the geography teacher?"

A few voices shouted, "Yes!"

"He asked me once, 'what's the capital of France?' I said, 'it's F isn't it?'" He paused for a smattering of laughter and a few groans. "So, did you all like reading at school?"

There was a small ripple of yes's and no's as the audience warmed up.

"I like those whodunit thrillers. Anyone else like those sort of books?"

I saw heads nodding in the audience. A couple of people yelled, "Yes!"

"See, what I love about them is the way you follow the clues, like a trail of crumbs through a forest." His fingers made a sprinkling gesture. "And if you're smart enough, you can sometimes work out who the bad guy is before you get to the end." He paused. "I was in a real-life whodunit thriller. No, seriously. I was. See, I was in a gingerbread forest and I was hoping someone would follow my little trail of crumbs..." His booming voice trailed off as if he'd lost his thread. "Um... I was in a forest hoping..." He waved down a ripple of laughter. An awkward silence stretched then he seemed to remember his act. His voice snapped back into his rumbling tombstone delivery, "But whodunits are rubbish really. Always end the same, don't they? Bad guy led off in handcuffs. Life sentence. Slam."

Again, a shiver raced across my shoulders. I glanced at Jack but his eyes were now fixed on the comic.

The Grim Reaper leaned on his scythe. "You know, when I first heard about this school reunion I was a bit lukewarm about it, to be honest." His hidden eyes seemed to peer at the crowd from under his hood. "And then I thought, hang on a minute. It's not like I haven't achieved anything since leaving school. I've done things. Seen things." He paused and his voice dropped to a murmur, "I've seen things you wouldn't believe, not in your worst nightmares." His hand waved down at his Grim Reaper cloak. "Occupational hazard as they say." He paused for the laugher. "But that's what I like about being Death. I'm the great leveller, aren't I? I'll make you all equal in the end."

He straightened up and his hooded face scanned the audience. "So, it's great to see so many familiar faces tonight. What a great turn out, eh? Becky Thomas should be very proud of herself."

The Grim Reaper panned his hood back the other way. "You know. I don't think Becky got enough praise earlier for all her hard work tonight. Do you?"

Jo and Susie yelled, "No!"

The Grim Reaper nodded. "That's what I reckon too. So, Becky Thomas, you want to come up here and get an extra special reward?"

I felt some of the tension ease from my shoulders. It definitely couldn't be Patrick under that costume. What would he want with Becky? It probably was Chicken Eric from the pier.

The Grim Reaper signalled off-stage and Daniel handed him a chair. He positioned it underneath the spotlight and sat down.

Becky was now doing an, oh-no-I-couldn't-possibly gesture, while at the same time scrambling to her feet. She trotted up to the dance-floor and made 'look at me' jazz hands.

The Grim Reaper patted his lap. Becky giggled and perched herself on his knee, beaming at the audience, clearly loving the attention.

He growled, "So, little girl. What do you want for Christmas? Whoops. Sorry. Wrong costume."

Becky made a playful attempt to tug off his hood but he jerked his head away and boomed, "Not just yet. Don't spoil the surprise for everyone." He paused and seemed to peer at Becky's outfit. "So, Becky, you've come as Lieutenant Uhura from Star Trek?"

Becky beamed and nodded.

"You do know that Uhura was a woman of colour?"

She giggled and shrugged.

"Not very convincing are you? Shouldn't you have blacked-up?" He offered Becky the microphone then snatched it away before she could say anything and tipped her off his lap. "That's enough attention, little girl. Back to your hutch."

Becky said something to him I couldn't hear.

The Grim Reaper nodded. "Oh yes. I promised you a special reward, didn't I? Well, we're a bit pushed for time now. But you'll get your reward in the Afterlife." He seemed to leer up at her. "Don't look so put out, Becky. You won't have long to wait."

Beside me, I felt the muscles in Jack's arm stiffen.

For a moment, Becky remained on the dance-floor as if hopeful of being included in the rest of the act, but the Grim Reaper leaned towards her and shouted, "Scram, Queen of the World."

Becky flinched and walked back towards us, a plastic smile fixed on her face, as if determined to show she'd been in on the joke. I heard her say to Jo, "Queen of the World! So funny! Really funny act."

Once she had sat down again, the Grim Reaper pushed back his chair and got to his feet. "So, anyone want to take a guess who I am yet?" The hood panned across the room. "No? Aw, come on. No one? Do you give up? Do you?"

The crowd seemed to have grown tired of the comedy act. Everyone wanted to get back to drinking, dancing and talking. A chorus of listless 'yes-es' rippled around the club.

The comic's hands reached up to his hood. "Are you ready for this?" he asked. "Are you ready – *really* ready – to look Death full in the face?" He flung the hood back from his face. "Ta-dah."

And suddenly Patrick Underhill was staring out at the crowd with dark, angry eyes.

My breath caught in my chest. Oh Jesus. Oh shit. Oh God. Jack put an arm across my chest and I heard him say, "Don't move."

Patrick said, "Anyone recognise me?" His voice was back to normal now. "No? Christ, I haven't changed that much, have I?"

I turned to look at Jack. His left arm was still slung over my chest; his right was tucked inside his jacket. Oh my God. Did he have a gun in there?

Patrick's black hair looked soaked with sweat. His hands shook as he held the microphone. He seemed barely

211

in control of his anger. "Thirteen years ago I was just another eighteen-year-old with the rest of my life ahead of me. Then everything changed and my life went down the shitter."

His eyes scanned the crowd, stopped and seemed to peer straight at me. "All I wanted from you that night Katy Bennett, was your help; I wanted you to take her a message – here, up in Glitz – asking her to meet me outside the club," his voice cracked, "so I could tell her I loved her, that I'd always love her, to beg her not to leave me... to never leave me...."

He took a deep breath. "But you wouldn't help me. You didn't even let me finish what I was going to say. You fixed me with that snooty, 'I'm so much better than you' look, and walked away. You didn't give a toss. I was shit on your shoe." He wagged a shaking finger, "And you could have stopped it, Katy. All of it. Right then and there, if you'd taken her that message. Instead, I had to go to her flat to talk to her and..." his voice trailed off. "And we all know what happened next."

Faces turned in my direction. I couldn't breathe. My legs began shaking so violently I thought I might collapse. Jack's arm was pressed hard against my chest. I heard him murmur, "Stay calm," but he said it so quietly it was as if his words were inside my head.

Patrick's eyes seemed glassy. "It was all in that diary... her secrets, her fears, how she couldn't handle it no more." He put on a weird high-pitched voice, '*Oh my God. I think he's found me!*' His head wobbled as if he was struggling to keep it upright. "How soon she'd be free and so rich she could leave this dump forever, leave me forever..." He shook his head again. "You think *I'm* mad? You should've read all that mad stuff *she'd* written then you'd..." His voice trailed off and he seemed to shiver.

"Where was I? Oh Yeah…" He peered at the audience. "Katy, don't be shy. Come on up and get your crappy award. I have to say though I think I should have won."

Jack put his hand on my arm. "Don't move."

Patrick's eyes drifted over to where I was standing. But he wasn't looking at me. He was looking at Jack.

"Well, well, well. You must be the famous Jack. I've read so much about you," Patrick's voice seemed to drip with hatred. "Why don't you come up here and collect Katy's award for her? I think she'd appreciate it. She looks so scared she might wet herself any second."

My heart felt as if it was trying to fight its way out of my chest. Jack didn't move.

Patrick shrugged. "Okay, Jack. If you won't come to me, I suppose I'll have to come to you. See, I've waited a long time to do this. Too long." His hand reached under his Grim Reaper cloak and he began to walk towards us.

As Patrick withdrew his hand everything seemed to go into slow motion. Becky screamed, "He's got a knife!" Niall Sinclair jumped up from his seat, punched something on the wall and the fire alarm went off. Above the wailing I heard a man's voice yelling, high and panicky over the PA system, "Monica, Monica, Monica…."

I had the weirdest feeling, as if I was falling forwards. Then Jack scooped me up and slung me over his shoulder like a sack of potatoes.

CHAPTER FIFTEEN

The next thing I knew, my head was resting on my knees and a woman's voice was saying, "That's it. Nice deep breaths." The back of my neck was icy and there was a clanging noise in my ears. My knee hurt and as my eyes focussed I could see a small purple bruise in the shape of a love heart.

I sat up and looked around. I was sitting on the kerb outside Glitz. Amber street lights glowed through the dusky gloom and the warm night air settled around my shoulders like a blanket. People in fancy dress were getting into taxis, some of them were on their phones. Two police cars pulled up on the kerb outside the club, blue lights strobing, creating crazy shadows on the walls of the buildings. The uniformed officers got out and hurried inside Glitz.

And then I remembered.

"Patrick… knife!" I managed to blurt.

"It's all right. You're safe now," a fairy told me in a matter of fact voice.

I stared at her freckled face. Her shoulder-length fair hair was the same shade as mine. My mouth was dry and my head felt spongy. I looked around but there was no sign of Jack. Panic clutched at me. "What… what happened?"

The fairy leaned back a little on the kerb as if making herself more comfortable. "Well, first Becky Thomas screamed that Patrick Underhill had a knife then

214

Niall Sinclair set the fire alarm off so we all had to leave. You went a bit faint when you got in the fresh air so the man who carried you out asked me to sit with you while he went back inside."

Fear grabbed my heart. "He… he went back inside? Where's Patrick?"

The fairy shrugged. "He ran away. But he didn't have a knife."

As I pulled myself up to my feet, I heard a woman's voice behind me. "Katy!"

I turned around and Susie enveloped me in a hug. "What a palaver. You feeling okay now?"

I pulled away. Becky and Jo were standing either side of her. Becky had a very small plaster above her left eyebrow. Jo was scowling and holding her Christian Louboutin shoes. One had its heel missing.

"What happened to your head?" I asked Becky.

Becky made a sniffing noise as if she was going to cry. "I must have gashed it when we were leaving the club."

I started to say, "Oh my God—" But Susie gave a quick shake of her head and mouthed the word, "Scratch."

Two fire engines pulled up in the road. Firemen started getting out, heading towards the entrance of the club.

"Where's Jack?" I asked Susie.

Susie shook her head. "No idea. I thought he was with you."

Becky made the sniffing noise again. "What a terrible evening. We could've died in there. I knew that bastard would ruin the reunion, but no one listened to me."

Jo's angry eyes snapped back to her. "Hey, if you hadn't started screaming about a non-existent knife, no one would have panicked and I wouldn't have fallen down the stairs." Jo held up her shoes and shook them in Becky's face.

Becky gave another defensive sniff. "Well, he was holding something in his hand…"

"Yeah – that stupid trophy thing for Katy," Jo yelled.

Susie leapt in as if to try to defuse things. "In fairness Jo, the only person who panicked was Niall Sinclair when he set off the fire alarm. I thought it was a very calm evacuation under the circumstances."

My stare darted around the road, "Susie, where is Patrick now?"

Susie shrugged. "No idea. What a shock, him turning out to be that comic. I suppose he just wanted to spoil the party." She turned to Becky, "So who was the real comedian?"

Becky wrapped her arms around herself as if she was cold. "Chicken Eric from the pier," she said gloomily. "When I was getting my First Aid just now, one of the bouncers told me they found him locked in a storeroom still in his cockerel outfit. He wasn't hurt but he's a bit shaken. He said Patrick did it. I suppose he's gone on the run now."

Susie and I exchanged glances.

Becky reached up and prodded the plaster on her forehead. "This cut's so painful. I hope I don't get a scar."

"It's just a scratch!" Jo snapped. "The bouncer only put a plaster on it to stop you howling."

I looked around. People were drifting away up Grenville Row towards the seafront. Becky had been right. No one was going to forget this school reunion in a hurry. A taxi pulled up nearby and Jo said, "That's my cab." Without another word she stalked off into the night.

Susie's eyes creased with worry. "Oh dear. Jo seems a bit peed off."

Well, who could blame her? She'd flown all the way from New York for this, plus she'd ruined a pair of $700 shoes. I looked around. Where *was* Jack? I heard Susie say to Becky, "Come on. Let's get you home."

In a shaky voice Becky replied, "Thanks Suze. I feel a bit wobbly now. I think it's from my cut head." She turned to me. "Katy, what did Patrick mean when he said you could've stopped things that night if you'd helped him?"

A shiver ran across my shoulders. I pretended I hadn't heard.

Susie touched my arm. "Are you coming with us, Katy–"

But at that moment there was an ear-splitting scream from above our heads followed by a loud thud in the alley at the side of the club.

For several heartbeats, Susie and I stared at each other then we turned and ran towards the noise. Two uniformed police officers beat us to it. As we rounded the corner Susie and I both stopped dead. Susie's hand grabbed mine. "Oh my God!" she whispered.

Lying on the ground was the Grim Reaper.

The police officers were already crouched beside him, one talking into the radio on his chest. I wrenched my hand from Susie's grip and ran over too. The other officer had eased the hood away from his face. His eyes were wide open, staring at nothing. Blood trickled from the edge of his open mouth. One of his hands was lying limp, palm-up.

"Oh no… Oh Jesus…" I whispered

Katy, are you going up to Glitz tonight? It's just I need your help–

Bile rose in my throat. I ran back towards Susie, screaming, "He's dead... he's dead..."

Two more uniformed police officers sprinted past us towards Patrick. Another officer took my arm and led me back out of the alley. He was a young constable with eyelashes so fair they looked white. "Did you see what happened?" he asked.

In a halting voice I said I hadn't seen him fall, just heard the scream from the roof and the thud, then Susie and I had followed the two police officers into the alleyway and saw him lying on the ground. The officer wrote down everything in his notebook.

"Do you know who he was?" he asked. His use of the past tense was chilling.

I nodded and tried to swallow the lump in my throat, "Patrick... Patrick Underhill."

The officer took my name and address. He said I might need to give a statement.

"Tonight?" I asked.

He told me to wait and he'd let me know.

I watched him walk across to Susie, heard her say, "No, we just heard the scream. It seemed to come from the roof of the club... I'm guessing he jumped or fell..."

Firemen were coming back out of the club. One of the fire engines revved its engine as if impatient to leave.

A plainclothes police officer came over to talk to me. He introduced himself as Detective Sergeant Harper. He was tall with dark hair and looked in his early forties. He asked me the same questions. I gave him the same answers. Another constable joined us and said to Harper, "Sorry to interrupt, Sir. Can I have a quick word?"

Harper turned his back while he spoke to the constable. I couldn't hear much of what was being said, just caught the words, "…spoken to a witness who saw him on the roof…"

Harper turned back to me. "Okay, Katy. You can go. I'll be in touch if we need you to give a statement." He went over to talk to Susie. Becky was with her now, looking shaken and cold.

I realised Nick Padovani was standing next to me, staring towards the body. "Dead?' he asked.

I managed a quick nod.

He shook his head. "Well, I can't pretend I'm upset." He gave a heavy sigh. "I should have called the police earlier. I saw him skulking around outside the club this afternoon. I went up to him, told him not to even try getting in tonight. He just laughed at me, said he was going to reveal the truth; blow things sky high." Padovani's shoulders sagged, "I just thought, you know, stupid lies as usual."

I stared at Padovani's lank black hair. The breeze changed direction and I could smell his lemon-scented hair oil. I shot him a cynical stare as if to say, you couldn't have been that worried about Patrick, otherwise you'd have stopped the show as soon as you realised it was him under that costume.

As if reading my thoughts, Padovani gave what looked like a defensive shrug, "I was working in my office… I knew a comedian had been booked as cabaret so… By the time I realised it was Underhill…" He spread his hands, palms-up, as if there was nothing he could have done to prevent the tragedy.

An ambulance stopped at the entrance to the alley, lights flashing. Two paramedics jumped out and ran past. But I already knew they were too late. More partygoers were getting into taxis; others formed a quiet, curious circle, staring at the ambulance, pretending they weren't trying to peer at the body.

Then a man's angry voice shouted, "Katy!"

I turned around. Jack's Mercedes was at the kerb, engine purring. He leaned across the front seat and pushed open the passenger door. "Katy, get in the car."

My mind froze.

His voice rose, "Get in the car!"

I couldn't move.

"For Christ Sake! Get in the car now. Please."

My legs began to walk towards him. I almost fell inside and slammed the door.

The last thing I saw, as the acceleration knocked me back into my seat, was Susie and Becky staring at me, eyes wide, mouths hanging open.

*

As the central locking clicked, I felt a surge of panic. Maybe getting into Jack's car hadn't been the smartest move. Maybe I should have stayed with Susie and Becky.

My heart was thudding against my ribs. I tucked my hands under my thighs so Jack wouldn't see they were shaking.

He turned to look at me. "You okay?"

I nodded and pressed my hands harder against my legs. "Patrick's... Patrick's dead," I told him, my voice dull with shock.

Jack nodded but kept his eyes on the road. He powered the Mercedes down Grenville Row, turned right, onto the seafront.

I cleared my throat and tried to make my voice sound authoritative, "Where are we going?"

Jack glanced in the rear-view mirror. "I'm taking you home."

He opened the window on his side of the car and the smell of candyfloss from the stall by the pier made me feel sick. The night sky above the Bristol Channel was lilac, fading up to purple. But all I could see was Patrick's broken body in the alley, his eyes wide but staring at nothing, his mouth open as if frozen mid-scream. I realised my mouth was open too. One of my tears found its way onto my tongue. My throat clenched as I tried not to retch. With the sleeve of my blouse, I gave a quick, surreptitious wipe across my cheeks, kept my head turned away from Jack and fixed my eyes through the side window. Oh God Patrick, I bloody hated you, but I never wanted you to die.

A directionless anger was building inside me. I tried to kick it away but fear kept it there. I was angry with Martin for offering me this story. I was angry with myself for taking it. I was angry with Patrick because, after all these years, he'd still been telling his crazy lies and now he was dead. But mostly I was angry because another part of me was seriously wondering if they had been lies; that maybe he'd been telling the truth all along.

Patrick, are you saying Jack Dale killed Kelly-Anne?

Jack turned the car off the seafront and headed up the hill. My muscles were so tense they felt like concrete. It wasn't until he drove the Mercedes into the parking area in front of my flat that I felt them relax a little. Shaun's lights were still on. I could hear the distant thud of bass music and the sound of laughter drifting down from Davina's flat on the top floor. She was having one of her parties. I looked up. Her balcony door was wide open. Yellow light spilled out. I glanced away. The sky was indigo now and a golden full moon was rising through the cherry trees in the road.

221

Jack parked next to a builder's skip full of broken tiles, a discarded sink and a white toilet bowl. Davina must have had a new bathroom fitted. As soon as I heard the central locking click off, I jumped out of the car and began striding towards the entrance of the flats. Jack's footsteps followed me across the car park.

I stopped at the lobby door and turned around. He had a small cut on his right cheekbone. Other than that he looked every bit as heartbreaking as he had earlier. Visions of him standing in my kitchen, stroking my face crowded my mind. I blinked them away.

Katy, he is the police or rather, he used to be…

My anger freed itself in a single pulse. "What the hell is going on?"

He gestured at the door. "Let's go inside."

I shook my head. "No. Not until I get some straight answers."

A woman's voice above my head said, "Katy? Is that you? Cute outfit!"

I looked up. Davina was standing on her balcony wearing tiny cut-off jeans, a pink bikini top and a white sequinned cowboy hat. "Come up for a drink," she called down. "And do bring your stunning friend with you. We're very short of attractive males tonight."

I waved a hand up at Davina. "Thanks. Maybe another time."

A strapping Nordic-looking man with long fair hair wearing nothing but a gold lamé posing pouch joined Davina on the balcony. They both lit cigarettes and started to chat.

My eyes returned to Jack. My voice was blunt, "Why did Patrick think you murdered Kelly-Anne Davis?"

Jack didn't reply.

"He told me she kept a diary, wrote about a man who'd as good as killed her. Was that you?"

"Katy, we need to go inside."

I didn't move. "Why did you really come to the party tonight?"

"I told you. To keep you safe."

My voice rose in disbelief, "From who? From Patrick? Why? In case he accidentally hurt me instead of you? Where did you go after you got me out of the club? How did you get that cut on your cheek? Did Patrick fall off that roof? Or was he pushed?"

I caught a glimpse of my reflection in the lobby door and my heart sank at my ridiculous appearance. One of the red clown buttons had dropped off the satin dungarees and underneath the pom-pom hat, my hair stuck out like a scarecrow's.

Jack took a step towards me. "Katy, we need to go inside—"

I put up my hand. "I think Patrick came to the reunion tonight to kill Kelly-Anne's murderer. Patrick believed that was you. And now, Patrick is dead. Explain."

"Katy, trust me. I had nothing to do with Patrick's death," Jack's voice was weary. "And I didn't kill Kelly-Anne either." His eyes held mine. "Please let's go inside."

I chewed at my lips, scrutinising his face, his body language, trying to gauge if he was telling me the truth. "Prove it then," I said at last. "You prove to me you didn't kill either of them. Then we can go inside." I felt tears welling up. Oh no. Not again. Why did I always end up in tears around Jack?

Jack ran a hand through his hair, glanced around the dark car park.

"I'm sorry, Katy," he said at last. "You're right. You deserve a proper explanation."

223

It was his voice that really did for me. I could listen to it forever, especially when he used it to say my name.

He nodded towards the Mercedes. "You look cold. If you don't want to go inside, let's talk in my car."

I didn't move. A solitary tear slid down my cheek.

Above my head I heard Davina laugh and say, "Oh Sven, you are so naughty…"

Jack walked towards me. He stood very close. I could feel the warmth rising from his body and smell his amazing aftershave. I felt dizzy. The muscles in my legs began to vibrate. I wiped at the tear with the back of my hand but more followed. "I… I just want you to tell me the truth."

Jack brushed a strand of hair away from my face. "Katy, we can talk all night, if that's what you want." His thumbs gently rubbed away my tears. "Or if you prefer we don't have to talk at all."

The vibrations in my legs turned to full-on trembling. I prayed he wouldn't notice. Why did I go to pieces every time I was with this man? Above me from Davina's flat I heard Tom Jones crooning, *you can leave your hat on.* Then the music faded, as her balcony doors were pulled shut.

Jack took out his car keys and turned towards his car. He reached back and took my hand in his. His grip was firm, his skin warm.

The yellow full moon had risen above the roofs of the houses opposite. Davina's party must have moved to the 'car keys in the cowboy hat' phase, because the music had stopped and the evening was silent and still.

Jack pressed the key fob. Across the car park I saw the hazard lights of the Mercedes flash twice. And then I heard a faint rapid beeping that I thought I recognised from somewhere. I glanced over at the cherry trees in the road, and their inky silhouettes were so perfectly round, they looked like a child's drawing against the indigo sky. Then a bright ball of blue white fire exploded and rushed towards me, all the time growing bigger and brighter, until there was no room for anything else in the world, and then everything went black.

CHAPTER SIXTEEN

White ceiling tiles came into focus. I was lying on my back in a bed, pale green curtains either side of me. The light was harsh and my face throbbed. As I turned my head I saw Shaun hunched forward on a plastic chair, peering at me with worried eyes.

He attempted a smile. "Hey. How're you feeling?"

I tried to shrug but I didn't seem able to move my neck. "Not sure. Depends. Am I in hospital?"

He nodded. "Yeah. But don't worry. You're fine."

"Which hospital?"

"Weston General." Weston General was our nearest hospital, seven miles away from Sands End.

I tried to clear away the fog in my head. "But, why... what's happened?" I wondered if I'd hurt myself at the school reunion. But I sort of remembered leaving the party. Panic jolted into me. My hand jerked up to my neck, "Oh my God... Do I still have both my legs?"

Shaun smiled. "Both legs, both arms. Nothing missing. The docs say you have a slight concussion, plus you've got some paper stitches above your left eyebrow. They're going to keep you in overnight for observation but it's just a precaution."

My fingers touched the stitches on my forehead. "But what happened? Did I fall over?"

I could hear people talking beyond the curtain and in the distance a man's drunken voice singing out of tune. I was wearing a pale blue cotton nightdress. I glanced at my wrist but a plastic nametag had replaced my watch. "What time is it?"

"Not quite midnight." Shaun's eyes glanced towards the curtain. "Actually Katy, the police are fairly keen to have a word, if you feel up to it."

"The police? Why?" My panic rose again. I tried to think but my head still felt full of fog. "Did I do something?"

Shaun scratched his shoulder. "No, you didn't do anything." He took a deep breath. "It seems a bomb exploded in that builder's skip in our car park."

"A bomb?" I tried to sit up. The green curtain rippled as if it was under water so I lay back again.

We can talk all night, if that's what you want. Or we don't have to talk at all…

Panic clutched at my chest. "Jack—"

Shaun ran a hand through his hair. "He's fine, apparently, although his car's a total write off. He discharged himself from hospital an hour ago."

A heavy weight seemed to drop through me. So, he hadn't even hung around to see if I was okay.

Shaun nodded towards the curtain. "Look, I'd better tell the police you're awake. I'll get a coffee and come back when they've finished."

As Shaun parted the curtain to leave, a man appeared, followed by a pale woman, whose eyebrows had been plucked into surprised arcs. I recognised the man. It was the plainclothes police officer I'd spoken to after the school reunion. For a second or two I grappled for his name then remembered: Sergeant Harper.

Harper's opening gambit was to place a plastic evidence bag on the bed. Inside was a mobile phone.

"Yours I believe," Harper said in the dull, inflectionless voice the police use when they're being careful not to apportion blame. It had the effect of making me feel as guilty as hell.

"It was found in Patrick Underhill's pocket," he added in the same dull voice. He gave me a look that seemed to say: Explain. Now.

I told the officers everything I knew: how Patrick had sent Becky the Facebook message saying he wanted to go to the school reunion, how he'd given me an interview for the *Gazette* claiming he hadn't murdered Kelly-Anne Davis, how I thought Patrick had stolen my phone to lure Jack to my school reunion; that Nick Padovani had told me he'd thought Patrick might try to cause trouble at the party.

He said he was going to blow everything sky high…

Fear prickled in my fingertips. "Do you think Patrick Underhill planted that bomb?"

Harper gave me his inscrutable policeman's face, told me it was one line of enquiry but he couldn't discus it further.

The female officer asked what Patrick had pulled from under his Grim Reaper costume at the party. I said I hadn't seen, but someone told me it was a silver trophy, and my friend Becky had mistakenly thought it was a knife. The two officers exchanged brief glances when I said that. More fear bubbled. *Had* he had a knife on him? Had he been carrying it when he'd hugged me on the seafront?

Harper gave me his business card and told me to call him if I remembered anything else. My head was pounding and all I wanted was to go back to sleep. It wasn't until after the officers had gone that I realised they hadn't asked me anything about Jack. He must have given his statement before he left hospital.

I closed my eyes and when I next opened them it was daylight. A plump blonde nurse and a very tall Asian doctor were standing beside the bed. The doctor told me I could go home.

On a chair beside the bed was a pair of grey jogging bottoms and a black t-shirt. Shaun must have bought them in for me. Bless him. My handbag was under the chair. It looked miraculously undamaged. There was no sign of the fancy dress outfit. Becky would go ballistic.

As I was getting dressed, my mother flung back the curtain and treated the passing doctors and nurses to the sight of me in my bra and pants.

"For heaven's sake, mum!" I yelled.

She pulled me into a brief hug then gave an exasperated sigh. "Oh Katy. I don't want to say I told you so about getting involved with Patrick Underhill again. But, I told you so. Shaun was good enough to phone to say you were in hospital. Goodness knows when you'd have got around to telling me." She stared at the stitches on my forehead and gave a disapproving tut. "Well, that's going to leave a nasty scar."

How did my mother always manage to make everything sound as if it was my fault? I shoved my legs into the joggers. Mum stared down at them. "Oh Katy. You didn't wear those to the party did you?"

"No, I went as one of the Seven Dwarves," I snapped, pulling the joggers up to my hips.

"Don't be facetious." Mum plonked herself down on the plastic chair. "Now, I've had Becky Thomas's mother on the phone this morning. Who was that man you were with at the school reunion?"

I assumed she meant Jack. "Just someone I know."

"I see. Because Cathy said he didn't go to your school."

"He's just someone who was…" Where to begin? "He was just someone who was helping me with a story. That's all." I pulled the t-shirt over my head.

"I see. Cathy says Becky told her he was very dishy."

Dishy? What a typical mother word. And how typical that she was much more interested in who I'd been seen with at the reunion than the fact that Patrick had perhaps planted a bomb outside my flat.

Mum's eyes met mine. "So, what was that man doing with you at your flat after the party? And where were you sneaking off to with him?"

"We weren't sneaking off anywhere." I winced with pain as I struggled to push my hands through the armholes in the t-shirt. I felt as if I'd been run over. Everything hurt. Little blue lights flashed in front of my eyes.

Mum dropped her voice, "I do hope there was nothing improper going on, Katy Bennett, because I assume you know he's a married man."

I froze.

"His wife came to collect him from hospital last night. She looked like one of those supermodels. Blonde hair down to here," mum gestured to her waist. "Legs up to here," she moved her hands up to her armpits. "And she drove a beautiful black Porsche. It was very touching seeing them together, actually."

My lips felt numb and the back of my neck had gone icy. My legs turned to jelly. I sat back down on the edge of the bed.

Wife.

Shaun popped his head around the curtain. "Hello Mrs Bennett. I'll give Katy a lift home, if that's okay?"

"Oh Shaun, that's so terribly kind. Katy is so lucky to have you." She patted his arm. "I was saying to Katy, just the other day, what a super son-in-law you'll make for someone." She shot me a meaningful glance. "Isn't that right Katy?"

As I followed Shaun out of the ward, Mum grabbed my arm and hissed, "Will you please take my advice for once in your adult life and do something about poor Shaun."

Wife.

*

Shaun and I were driving out of the hospital car park when I turned to him and said, "So, did you know about Jack's wife coming to collect him?" The inside of his car was so hot it was making me feel queasy. I opened the window.

Shaun kept his eyes fixed on the road. "Yeah. Sort of…"

"And you didn't think you should mention it?"

"Aw Katy, I just thought you had enough on your plate."

"So, did you see her last night?"

"Just a glimpse."

"And was she, as my mother so thoughtfully told me, stunning looking?"

Shaun shrugged. "I didn't really get a good look at her to be honest…"

"But long blond hair? Tall? Leggy? Supermodel pretty?"

He shrugged again. "Pretty much…. Listen, I've got something for you." He reached an arm onto the back seat and grabbed a box. He handed it to me. "There you go."

I stared open mouthed. The box contained the newest iPhone. "Is this for me? Oh wow…"

"The police told me last night that Patrick had nicked your mobile. I don't know when you'll get it back and I know you've always wanted an iPhone, and I was due an upgrade…" Shaun shrugged. "Anyway, they did me a cracking deal. One for you. One for me. You'll have to set up a contract though."

"Oh Shaun…. Are you sure? Listen, I'll give you the money–"

"No. It's my treat." He blushed. "I still feel bad I couldn't fix your flaming car stereo the other day."

That seemed like a lifetime ago.

Twenty minutes later, we were back in Sands End. Shaun pulled off the seafront and headed up the hill towards our flats. "Oh, and another thing, when we get home. I'm doing you lunch: roast chook with all the trimmings. Your favourite."

I heard myself sigh. He was such a sweet, thoughtful man.

*

I'd assumed the bomb must have been pathetic, given that Patrick had made it. But as soon as Shaun drove into the car park in front of the flats, I was astonished by the amount of damage it had caused. There was no sign of the wreckage of Jack's Mercedes or the builder's skip but where the skip been parked, there was a rectangle of melted tarmac roped off by yellow police tape. In the centre of the rectangle was a hole about a foot wide and a foot deep, presumably directly under the bomb. The cherry trees in the road looked as if a giant had reached down and snapped off all their lower branches. Bits of splintered wood and leaves were scattered all over the place.

A glazier's van was parked outside the entrance to the flats and a man in Davina's lounge was replacing her shattered balcony doors. Shaun's bedroom window and sitting room windows were boarded over with plywood.

"Oh wow…" I muttered.

Shaun pulled up next to the fence that bordered my garden. "Yeah, you missed all the excitement. Bomb squad, forensics people. They took every little bit of what was left of the skip and Jack's car away in bags."

My heart lurched. "Henry?"

"Fine. He's a bit jumpy. I shut him in your spare room with a litter tray over night."

I felt tears pricking. Shaun was such a good friend. "Thank you…"

While Shaun got the food going in my kitchen, I had an emotional reunion with Henry then cut off my name tag and took a shower to wash away the hospital smell. The warm water was agony. Apart from the cut on my forehead I also had little scrapes and scratches all over me. They stung like mad.

After my shower, I put on shorts and a t-shirt. Shaun pulled a sun-lounger onto the lawn for me. My head throbbed and every bone in my body ached. I felt as if a truck had run me over. Warm puffs of roasting chicken aroma wafted out from my kitchen.

Shaun walked across the grass, picked up small chunk of twisted, blackened metal and flung it in the border. "So, how're you feeling?"

"Okay." I stared at the piece of metal, thinking if we'd gone any closer to Jack's car both he and I would be dead. We'd have been right next to the skip when the bomb went off. All I could see was Jack's hand reaching back for mine outside the lobby doors then hearing the faint beeping noise. My eyes filled with tears.

Shaun strode over and knelt beside the sun-lounger. "Aw Katy. Don't cry. You're safe now. It's over. Patrick's dead."

"Could… have… died," I managed, wiping at my nose with the back of my hand.

Shaun pulled a piece of kitchen towel from his jeans pocket and handed it to me. "It's shock. The nurses told me it'd probably hit you later."

I blew my nose. "The police made it sound as if they thought Patrick planted the bomb."

Shaun nodded. "Reading between the lines I'd say he's their chief and only suspect. I told them I'd never met the bloke. But I did tell them some of the stuff you'd told me about him; the lies and weird stories he used to tell. How you'd thought he was making up his 'I am innocent' claims. That he was a nutter. But I also got the impression from the police that you weren't the target, which is reassuring. Sort of…"

I nodded and tried to clear my thoughts. "So the police think Patrick planted the bomb to kill Jack? Makes sense…"

I frowned over at the Torbay palm on the lawn. But actually, that didn't make a whole lot of sense. Patrick had stolen my phone and used it to lure Jack to the school reunion. He'd clearly been planning to try to kill Jack at the party. So why bother to plant a bomb? Belt and braces in case the club plan didn't work? I wasn't sure. And how had Patrick known Jack would give me a lift back to my flat after the party? How had he known Jack would park his car next to the skip? How had he known Jack would be anywhere near the skip when the bomb went off?

Shaun's voice jolted me back, "Nearly gave me a heart attack when it went off. Blew out my bedroom window. Luckily I was in bed so most of the glass landed

234

on the duvet. The toilet bowl in the skip was spectacular, apparently. It ended up two streets away."

"And no one else was hurt? Not you or Davina? None of Davina's guests?"

"Nah, they were all in her spare back bedroom by then. Luckily they'd all parked out on the road so there were a couple of broken windscreens but no serious damage. Most of the front windows of the flats were smashed though yours survived, probably because you're on the ground floor and the fence acted as a shield. And by another miracle your MX-5 and the mighty Land Cruiser escaped pretty much unscathed. A few dings and scratches, that's all. Yeah, if Jack hadn't…" Shaun stopped talking and looked away.

I frowned. "If Jack hadn't what?" Panic tingled in my fingers.

Shaun mustered a weak smile. "Well, much as it grieves me to admit this, if it hadn't been for Jack you probably wouldn't be here right now."

Shaun paused and looked down at his hands. I noticed they were shaking. "Jack took the brunt of the explosion. Threw himself over you."

I grabbed Shaun's arm. "But, at the hospital, you said he was okay–"

Shaun nodded. "He was okay. Just not as okay as you."

My voice was a whisper, "But they let him out. He couldn't have been that badly hurt."

Shaun's eyes didn't quite meet mine. "Yeah. It probably looked worse than it was. He walked to his wife's car, with a little help."

"Oh my God…. I should phone him. Check he's okay. Say thank you for saving my life." But then I remembered. I didn't have his mobile number any more. It was in the phone Patrick had stolen.

Shaun stood up. "Yeah, I'd maybe take a rain check on calling him. After all, he was on his way back to his hotel with another woman…"

I frowned. "What on earth makes you think we were going back to his hotel?" I'd thought we were just going to sit and talk in his car. "Is that what Jack told the police? That we were going to his hotel?"

We can talk all night if that's what you want. Or we don't have to talk at all…

Shaun snapped off a blade of grass, wound it around his finger but didn't reply. "Anyway, his wife is looking after him now."

It felt as if Shaun had plunged a dagger into my heart. I saw long blonde hair skimming Jack's face as her cool hands cupped his jaw and elegant fingers stroked his cut cheek. I bit my lip and looked away.

Shaun seemed to will a smile on his face. "Oh well, at least you're in one piece," his voice shook slightly. "Nobody… nobody… died."

To my surprise he reached over and took my hand. His thumb rubbed my knuckles. He stared up at the sky. "The thing is, Katy…" His voice cracked. "Ah shit… Look, when I saw you lying in the car park… I thought… I thought you were… dead."

I glanced up and to my astonishment he was crying. Big fat tears rolled down his sunburnt cheeks. He brushed at his face, swallowed hard and kept his blue eyes fixed on the sky. "Shit… I knew I'd cry… Anyway, it felt as if my world had… had… you know…."

I gave his hand a tight squeeze. "Oh Shaun…" I didn't know what else to say.

236

Tears rolled into his mouth. "You mean the world to me, Katy. And I just… If you'd died… I don't know if I could've…" His hand reached up and wiped at his wet cheeks. "I don't think I realised, not until that moment, just what you mean… The thing is, it made me realise I might be…"

Little alarm bells started going off in my head.

He closed his eyes, parted his lips and leaned towards me.

Oh my God. He's going to kiss me.

At the last moment I turned my face and his wet lips landed on my cheek.

For a couple of very long seconds we stayed that way, his lips welded to my cheekbone. Then he pulled back and hurried into the flat.

I stared after him. Oh dear…

By the time I'd mustered the courage to go in to the kitchen, Shaun was serving up. We ate at the breakfast bar. Neither of us referred to the incident in the garden. After a while I began to wonder if I'd imagined it.

Once we'd finished eating, I helped Shaun load the dishwasher. He seemed on edge and I suspected he might be feeling as embarrassed as I was about our maybe-kiss in the garden. Shaun wasn't the world's most effusive man so his outpouring of emotion had been entirely out of character. I didn't want to make him feel any more awkward about the incident so I decided not to mention it unless he did.

He made us coffees and we sat on opposite sides of my breakfast bar. Shaun took a couple of sips then pushed his mug away. "I feel really bad about this, but I need to be somewhere." He stared down at the black marble surface.

I shrugged, "That's okay."

"It's not okay. I don't want to leave you on your own today."

"I'll be fine."

"Look, I've got Susie and Becky on standby—"

I shook my head. I didn't want to see either of them. They'd want to talk about the bomb and Patrick.

"Or I could take you to your mum's—"

"No!" I nearly choked on my coffee. "Shaun. I'll be fine. I'll just have a lazy afternoon. Maybe watch a film. Read a book. Set up my new phone."

He stood. "Well, if you're sure."

"I'm sure. Go."

He stared at his fingernails. "Look, about earlier—"

I glanced up through my fringe.

He shook his head. "Ah… Nothing. We'll talk later. If you need me call me. The phone company says my number probably won't be transferred to my new phone until this evening so I'll leave you the new phone's number, but if that doesn't work, it means the transfer's gone through so call my usual number. You'll be able to get me on one or the other."

I smiled and rolled my eyes, Goodness. He was such a worry-wort.

Shaun scribbled the temporary number on the back of an old envelope and pinned it to my fridge door with a donkey-shaped magnet.

After Shaun had gone back to his flat, I set up the contract on my new phone. I didn't know which mobile network Shaun was on, but my phone company told me it could take up to five working days to transfer my number. I couldn't be out of touch for that length of time so I texted my temporary number to Becky and Susie and my brother Rich. Although I didn't have Jack's mobile number any more, I did have the number for S P International that

238

Weird Will had found. I keyed in the number, saved it and stared at the wall.

You're right Katy, you deserve a proper explanation…. We can talk all night…

I fidgeted in my chair, raked a hand through my hair, stared at my new iPhone. Jack had been about to tell me something before the bomb exploded. I needed to know what that was.

There was only one way to find out.

Obviously I didn't expect Jack to be in his office so soon after leaving hospital so I planned to leave a message asking him to call me when he was back at work. But when I dialled the number for S P International all I got was a recorded voice, *"I'm sorry. The number you have called is no longer recognised…"*

So, he'd changed the number again. I hung up and went onto Google, typed in *S P International, phone number, bodyguard, London.*

Nothing.

I spent half an hour searching the net but I found no trace of Jack's close personal protection business. Looked like I'd have to get Weird Will on the case again. I'd ask Shaun to call him later.

I made another coffee and sat out in the garden. The glazier was on Shaun's balcony, replacing the windows. Mid afternoon, the glazier left and not long after I heard the lobby door slam shut. Through the gap in the fence I saw Shaun hurry across the car park towards his Toyota. He looked pretty spruced up in a natty blue and red check shirt tucked into belted cream chinos. He must have a client meeting. Poor bloke. And he'd been up most of the night.

I returned to the patio and pulled my chair into the shade. To stop myself thinking about the bomb, I worried about the almost-kiss instead. Although Shaun and I had only known each other for six months he was easily my best male friend. I cared about him. He made me laugh. His happiness was important to me. But, I'd never, ever thought about him in a romantic way, by which I probably meant in a sexual way.

On the day I'd moved in, he'd tapped on my door to introduce himself and ask if I needed a hand and could he borrow some bread. I'd stared up at his tall frame, his chubby cheeks, his wiry sandy hair, his shapeless baggy t-shirt, through which I had seen the outline of his nipples, and it sounded awful, but I had experienced a brief pang of disappointment that my friendly new neighbour wasn't a sex-god. But then, Shaun hadn't seemed remotely interested in me in a romantic way either, wasting no time telling me how beautiful his ex girlfriend had been, that she was the spitting image of Elle McPherson, and how much he'd been in love with her. Since then our friendship had become something I hoped would last a lifetime but until today it had never come close to being anything other than platonic.

I ran a finger across the patio table and shrugged. Well, there was no reason why I couldn't think about Shaun in that way.

A vision of Jack popped into my head, standing in my hall wearing a tight black t-shirt and faded Levis. My heart did a crazy somersault. My heart didn't do that when I thought about Shaun, although if I was honest, I had felt a strange jealous lurch in the heart region when he'd told me he was back in touch with Linzi.

I stood and paced down the lawn. My fingers flicked at the palm fronds as I walked past. But Jack was irrelevant. He had a wife. He was a married man. I paused and stared down at the grass. But he had tried to seduce me in my kitchen. I was sure of that. Well, that didn't mean anything. Jack had also been a "morally bankrupt police officer" so maybe he didn't have a moral compass.

And yet, I remembered the gentle way he had rubbed away my tears outside my flat the previous evening.

"Get out of my head," I breathed. My bare feet paced back across the lawn. Stop using Jack as a benchmark. It's pointless. Irrelevant. Get him out of your stupid head. Maybe I should phone Susie and ask her advice. But I already knew what she'd say: "*Shaun is a lovely, sweet bloke and he thinks the world of you. You could do a lot, lot worse.*"

And I had done a lot, lot worse in the past. But could I love Shaun in that way? A physical way? Well, he'd once snared a woman who allegedly looked like Elle McPherson, so maybe he was ace in bed? My mother's words came back to me. "*It's just sex, sex, sex with you young people. And if that's all you're looking for, Katy Bennett, you're going to die a lonely old woman.*"

I didn't want to die a lonely old woman. I was sick of being single when all my friends were married. It made me feel inadequate; sometimes it made me feel lonely. I wanted to love and be loved in return. And sex wasn't everything. It was someone's character that was important, not the way they looked. To only like someone because they were good looking was shallow. In light of my near-death experience, maybe I should re-think things with Shaun. Maybe he was the man for me. Maybe I was the woman for him. Maybe we did have what it took to make each other happy. When Shaun got back from wherever he was this afternoon, we'd sit down on the sofa and have a proper heart-to-heart.

I went back inside and tried to watch TV to take my mind off things, but I couldn't concentrate. I felt dizzy and tired. My stitches hurt. I wanted Jack to kiss them better. In the end, even though it was only four in the afternoon, I went to bed.

*

The next time I opened my eyes, I was curled up on my side, hugging Henry like a teddy bear. The sun had moved around to the west and long shadows fell across my bedroom floor. When I looked at the bedside clock I was shocked to see it was half-past seven in the evening.

I got up, went into the sitting room and noticed I had one new email and two text messages on my new iPhone. The email was from Martin, left while I'd been asleep and asking me to phone him ASAP about the bomb outside my flat and the Patrick Underhill roof-fall death. I could tell from his smarmy tone of voice that he didn't want to commission me to write a story. He wanted to interview me for a follow-up story someone else was writing. I sent him an email back saying that until he gave me a heartfelt apology about my 'made up' Patrick Underhill quotes, he could get stuffed about any interview. Put that in your pipe and smoke it, Martin.

I clicked on the *Gazette*'s website. They'd already run a short story about what had happened. The police said they were not treating Patrick's death as suspicious, which meant they either thought it had been suicide or an accident. Two unnamed people had sustained minor injuries in a blast outside Bluebell Meadow Court – good, sounded as if Jack hadn't been badly injured – and the police had issued a statement ruling out terrorism, and confirming they were investigating a link between the bomb and the death of Patrick Underhill earlier that evening. The police said they were not looking for anyone else in connection with the explosion. The implication was clear:

the police were pretty damn sure Patrick Underhill had planted the bomb.

The text messages on my new phone were from Susie and Becky checking I was okay. I sent them quick replies saying I was fine and I'd see them soon.

Pacing back out into the garden, I took a deep breath of the warm, salty, evening air. In a funny sort of way, it reminded me of Jack's aftershave. Forget Jack. Concentrate on Shaun, I told myself.

Actually, it was odd that Shaun hadn't been down to see how I was. Maybe he wasn't back yet. I peered through the gap in the fence. But to my surprise his giant Toyota was parked in its usual place. My stomach rumbled. Perhaps I should make him something to eat for a change; show him I did have domestic goddess potential. I couldn't expect him to cook every meal. I went into the kitchen and opened the fridge. There was the half-eaten chicken carcass from lunchtime, a pack of bacon and four eggs.

I couldn't be bothered to walk up the stairs so I called his new mobile number. It rang three times then a generic voicemail message cut in.

I said, "Hi Shaun. It's Katy. If you've got some new potatoes, I could cook us bacon, eggs and sautés tonight, or if you have any mayonnaise I could do chicken sandwiches. Give me a call if either of those whets your appetite." I ended the call. Maybe he was in the shower.

Half an hour later, Shaun still hadn't returned my message. Again I called his new mobile number. Again I got the generic voicemail. I left another message. "Hi Shaun. Me again. Just checking you got my message about cooking for us tonight."

Maybe he was having a nap. Or perhaps his usual number had now been transferred to his new phone. I tried it but it just rang and rang, so I called his home phone. It rang twice then he answered with a rather breathless, "Yes?"

"Shaun. It's me. Did you get my messages?"

There was a pause, almost as if there was a delay on the line. "Messages?"

"I left you two messages about me cooking tonight–"

"Oh yeah. Got them, thanks."

I frowned. "So, do you want to share food? Or not?"

Another pause. "Um… Yeah. Thing is, I'm not that hungry."

I smiled. Shaun not hungry? That was a first. "Oh. Well, join me for a glass of wine instead. I feel quite a bit better now. Had a good sleep this afternoon."

Again there was a pause. "Yeah. Could do…"

I felt a stab of irritation. "Well, don't sound too keen."

"Sorry. I'm just a bit knackered. Been a long day. I'll be down in a minute."

Guilt flooded through me. Poor Shaun. Not only had he spent most of the previous night at the hospital, he'd also been working all afternoon not sleeping, like I had.

I darted into the bedroom and applied a fresh swish of pink lip-gloss and dusted some bronzer over my cheeks. I checked my face in the mirror – thankfully the stitches on my cut eyebrow didn't look too gruesome – then went into the kitchen, poured two glasses of wine and took a sip of mine. I smiled.

"You never know Katy, I said aloud, "this time tomorrow your life could be completely different. Completely different."

CHAPTER SEVENTEEN

Twenty minutes later my glass was half empty and Shaun's wine was sitting on the breakfast bar getting tepid. This was ridiculous. What was keeping the man? I grabbed my phone and called him again.

"Yes?" He answered with the same strange breathlessness.

"Hi. It's me. Your wine's getting warm."

Silence.

"Hello? Shaun?"

"Yep. Just coming now."

A few minutes later there was a tap at my front door.

I opened the door and did a double take. Shaun wore tan deck shoes, smart black jeans, and a lilac polo shirt. I squinted at the little horse and rider logo on his chest. Hmm. How very so not Shaun.

"Hey, you look nice," I told him. Maybe that was why he'd been so long. He'd been trying to decide what to wear. Encouraging.

I handed him his glass of wine. "Sorry. It's a bit warm. Do you want a fresh one?"

He shook his head and didn't move. For an odd couple of seconds, I wondered if he was planning to drink it in the lobby.

I smiled and stepped backwards. "Enter!"

He followed me down my hall and when we got to the sitting room I caught him glance down at his wrist. For the first time in living memory he was wearing a watch, a big chunky metal one, a bit like Jack's but not quite as fabulous.

"New watch?" I asked.

He blushed. "Yeah."

I indicated his polo shirt and jeans. "And they're new too aren't they?"

He looked down at his feet. "Popped to the shops in Bath today."

So he'd been to Bath again. But Shaun, posh clothes shopping? That was another first. I'd only ever seen him in Bondi Beach wear. I took a sip of wine. "How was your afternoon?"

"Yeah. Okay."

An awkward silence stretched. At exactly the same moment I said, "Listen about earlier–" and Shaun said, "Look, Katy about earlier–"

I laughed. "Sorry. You were saying."

Shaun shook his head. "No. You go first."

"No, seriously you first." We stared at each other.

His cheeks were flushed pink with embarrassment. "Look Katy, there's something I need to say…"

I nodded and took a sip of wine. "Okay."

I waited for him to say something like, "*I know you only think of me as a mate, but I think I might be falling in love with you.*"

But he didn't say anything, just stared into his wine glass. He took a gulp then nodded. "Okay. About earlier, in the garden… I'm really, really sorry."

I frowned. Sorry sounded like regret and regret didn't bode well for a fledgling romance.

He sat on the armchair, hunched over, cradling his wine glass in his hands. "Look, I've been meaning to tell you all this for a while…" he shrugged, "but it was difficult finding the right moment and also because…" he shrugged again. "Well, I suppose because I was a bit scared."

"Scared?"

"Well, worried more like. I was worried you'd try and talk me out of it." Shaun stood again. "You always talk such sense and I suppose in my heart there was a part of me that knew I might be doing the wrong thing." He paced across to the mantelpiece. "Not that I do think I'm doing the wrong thing. Not now. But maybe, in the beginning…" His voice trailed off.

I frowned. He wasn't making any sense. "What wrong thing?"

"See, I was planning to tell you before you went off to your school reunion but I lost my nerve again."

I felt a prickle of unease. "This isn't about Linzi, is it?"

Shaun nodded miserably. "I'd better start at the beginning."

My heart felt like a hot stone sinking to my stomach. It was too stuffy in the sitting room. I needed fresh air. I fanned my face with a hand. "Shall we sit outside?"

He shook his head. "I'm fine here."

He took a gulp of his wine. "Remember I said I'd been back in touch with Linzi? That she'd broken up with the lawyer?"

I nodded.

"Well, I wasn't exactly honest with you about that. I mean, I was honest in the sense that all that was true. It's just there was a bit more that I should've told you."

"I see."

"Look, there's something you don't know about Linzi. She's really–"

I couldn't help myself. "She's really a man!"

Shaun frowned. "No. She's not really a man. She's really British."

"British? I thought she was Australian? I thought you met in Melbourne?"

He nodded. "We did. Her parents moved to Australia from the UK about three years ago. Her father works there. They live next door to my parents. We met at a 'meet the new neighbours' barbecue."

"Right."

"Then, three months ago, when she and Larry broke up, she came back to live in England and we sort of got in touch again via Skype."

"Three months? You've been Skyping for three months?" *Without getting round to mentioning it? I thought we were best mates.*

Shaun nodded miserably. "Yeah. So we decided to meet up for the first time since we'd split. She'd been staying with her sister." He looked up and his eyes met mine. "Her sister lives in Bath."

Aha. So that explained his mysterious trips across the Mendip Hills recently.

"We'd thought we'd better see if we still had feelings for each other."

My lips felt numb. "Right."

"She'd booked a table at that posh hotel in the Royal Crescent as a surprise." He smiled. "I was rather under dressed, as you can imagine. We talked about a lot of personal stuff. Why we'd broken up."

Shaun shrugged. "It wasn't because we'd fallen out of love or anything but our wedding plans had just got totally out of control. I wanted a small ceremony. She wanted to invite everyone she'd ever known. Pink swans, purple doves, you know the sort of thing."

He stared down at the carpet. "I guess I felt it was all about the wedding and not really about us anymore. We started bickering, broke up and she started seeing Larry. I was pretty cut up about it so I decided to get away for a while."

I nodded. "So you came to Sands End, of all places." The legend, as Shaun told it, was he'd simply stuck a pin in a map of Great Britain and it had brought him here. But now I knew Linzi had a sister who lived less than forty miles away, I wasn't so sure it had been such a random choice.

Shaun rubbed at his temples, "We talked for hours at the restaurant and eventually we decided we might have made a mistake about breaking up."

My heart sank even further. "Right."

"Then we thought, probably we should get married after all."

For several seconds all I could hear was my heart thudding in my chest and the blood pulsing against my temples. "Married? You're getting *married?*"

Shaun shook his head. "I should've said something. I'm really sorry. But like I said, I was worried you'd have a go at me about it."

I stood and stomped across the room. "That's not fair. I wouldn't have had a go at you." I thought about that. "Well, maybe. But she broke your heart. I wouldn't have wanted you to get hurt again."

Shaun nodded. "Yeah. Well, you and me both.

He shrugged. "I don't kid myself. I'm not the best looking bloke in the world, whereas the world is full of flash-Larrys."

He stood and paced in the opposite direction. "But she told me that she loved me. That she had always loved me. That she would never love anyone but me. That she'd never loved Larry. That breaking up with me was the biggest mistake of her life."

I snorted. It was all I could do not to shout, Shaun! How can you be so stupid?

"She told me she wanted us to get married as soon as possible," he continued. "Here. In Sands End. It was her gesture. Putting right the wrongs from before: a really small wedding, not a church wedding, a Register Office do. Very simple. Just us."

I was stunned. Good grief, she had some gall.

Shaun stared down at the carpet. "I love her, Katy. It's as simple as that. I really love her."

I took a gulp of wine. Fantastic. All it takes to mend your broken heart, apparently, is a quick chat in a swanky hotel, and Bob's your uncle.

Shaun put his empty glass down on the rug. "But I am doing the right thing," he said quietly.

I nodded. "Well, yes. Of course you are." The words tumbled out, meaningless.

"So you're okay about it?" he said.

No not really. I took another gulp of wine. "Why shouldn't I be okay about it?"

Shaun looked over. A pink blush spread over his cheeks. "I don't know. I…" His blush intensified. "No reason," he said at last.

I felt a blush spreading up my neck too. If there'd been a brick wall handy I'd have banged my head against it. How could I have been so incredibly, utterly stupid? He hadn't been about to snog me in the garden earlier. It had just been a friendly peck on the cheek. I willed a smile onto my face. "Seriously, I'm fine about it. Thrilled. Really, really happy for you. Congratulations."

Shaun grinned. "Phew! Like I said earlier, you mean the world to me, Katy. You're my best mate." His faced turned serious, "But actually, there is something else I wanted to ask you."

I stared into the depths of my glass, swirled my drink, feeling utterly miserable.

He said, "You've no idea what your friendship has meant to me since you moved into this flat." He paused and his blush deepened making him look as if he had third-degree sunburn. "So, I was wondering if you'd do me the honour of being my Best Man?"

I nearly choked on my wine. "What?"

"I mean, you wouldn't need to dress up as a man," he added hastily. "It'd be a sort of metaphorical role, if you see what I mean. I've talked it over with Linzi and she thinks it's a great idea."

Quite frankly I would rather chew off a leg. But when I looked up into Shaun's face and saw the raw, hopeful expression in his eyes I couldn't bring myself to say no. I heard my voice say, "Well, that would be lovely. Next time you phone Linzi tell her I'd be delighted."

Shaun slapped his huge hands down onto his thighs and leapt up. "No need to phone her. We can go and tell her in person."

I tried to swallow my wine and speak at the same time, which resulted in a tense two-minute choking fit. When my coughs subsided and I'd drunk the glass of water Shaun brought me from the kitchen, I managed to whisper through burning lungs, "Tell her? Where the hell is she then?"

Shaun grinned. "Upstairs in my flat."

*

251

I followed Shaun up the stairs on wooden legs. "Listen, maybe I should meet her tomorrow instead? I mean, I haven't eaten yet this evening and it's getting on a bit now."

Shaun's wide shoulders shrugged. "No worries. We'll get a takeaway."

"But you said you weren't hungry."

Another shrug.

My feet felt like lumps of concrete. I didn't want to meet Linzi. Not now. Not ever. It wasn't that she had beaten me hands down in the fight for Shaun's affections. I wasn't sure I even wanted to be in a fight for them. It was more that everything I knew about Linzi made me eager to dislike her. Not long ago she had hurt Shaun. She'd broken his heart, ridden roughshod over his feelings, trading him in for a plonker with a yellow Lotus. Now, here she was, back on the scene, muscling back into his life as if nothing had happened. Please God, I've had a really crappy couple of days, so can you let her have a huge spot on the end of her nose?

Shaun pushed open the door to his flat and walked down the hall. I felt about thirteen again, awkward and self-conscious.

"Linzi honey?" Shaun called in a saccharine voice I'd never heard him use before. "Look who's here?"

I followed him into his sitting room trying not to sneeze from the Shake 'n' Vac. The balcony doors were open. Gauzy white curtains billowed into the room on the warm evening breeze and the setting sun made a copper fire bowl of the walls and ceiling. A long shape uncurled itself from the sofa. It extended a slender arm up towards me. "You must be Katy," it purred in a very cut-glass English accent. "I'm so pleased to meet you at last."

I felt like a tatty mongrel at a pedigree dog show. Of course she looked exactly like Elle McPherson. It wasn't just her height and perfect figure; it was the whole damn package. Her long caramel-blonde hair waved down over gym-toned bare arms. She had smoky dark brown eyes, the longest eyelashes I'd ever seen, and skin the colour of set honey. She didn't appear to be wearing any make-up and her teeth were so white they had to be veneers. She wore a pair of grey jogging bottoms and a sporty black vest. When I wore jogging bottoms I looked as if I was about to clean the loo, but Linzi looked amazing in hers.

She smiled and turned to Shaun. "Looks like I arrived in Sands End just in time. You didn't tell me that Katy from downstairs was such a pretty little thing."

Patronising cow. I felt myself blush and wished I could think of a smart retort. She pointed to the armchair opposite. "Do sit down."

My legs had no problems obeying Linzi so I sat, while Shaun beamed like a proud dad at a christening. He said, "I've filled in Katy about the plans and the good news is, she says yes about being Best Man."

Linzi's eyes widened. "Really? Oh that's great." She made her eyes look grave, "And so, so sorry to hear about what happened here last night. It must have been terrifying for you."

"So, have you set a date then?" I asked, more to change the subject from the bomb than because I really wanted to know.

Linzi glanced over to Shaun, a puzzled look on her face. "Shaun, I thought you said you'd–"

He blushed and looked down at his feet. "Yeah, but not that bit."

My eyes were going from his face to hers then back to his again. "What bit?"

Linzi said, "We did think about postponing the wedding because of what you've been through." She waved a hand in a rather dismissive way. "But then we realised it would be just too much hassle. So, the wedding, it's tomorrow."

"*Tomorrow?*"

Linzi nodded. "It can't come soon enough and then I'll be a very happily married woman."

I felt a tingling anger rise. This wedding must have been planned for ages yet I'd had absolutely no idea.

Linzi touched Shaun's arm. Her fingers were slender too and her nails were long and French manicured. I wondered if they were false. "Shaun, honey, why don't you get that takeaway ordered and open the Champagne in the fridge? I expect Katy would like a glass of fizz and something to eat."

I tried to make my voice enthusiastic, "Ooh. That's very kind but I don't want to intrude–"

Shaun said. "Consider it opened. Everyone okay with Mario's pizzas?"

Linzi said, "Good choice. I'm starved." She grinned and prodded Shaun in the leg. "We haven't even had time for a cup of tea since we got here, have we?" She giggled, "You horny lurve stallion."

Horny lurve stallion? Shaun? I stared at the carpet and counted the silent seconds. After a while I looked up. Shaun's face was crimson. He didn't seem able to look me in the eyes. And in that exact instant I realised his kiss in the garden had never been intended as just a peck on the cheek.

Linzi said, "Get me a pizza with a really thin base, just a sprinkling of shaved Pecorino, baby artichoke hearts, some Queen olives – but only if they do them in oil not canned, fresh basil and lots of really crisp rocket on the side."

She'll be lucky from Mario's, I thought. Shaun nodded and reached for his phone. "Katy?"

"Anything," I mumbled, as Shaun disappeared into the kitchen.

After he'd gone, Linzi said, "I can't believe Shaun didn't tell you the wedding's tomorrow. He hasn't given you much advance notice."

"No…" What on earth was I going to wear? I only had one dress and that was black. "I gather it's just going to be us three at the service then?" I asked, trying to be polite.

Linzi shook her head. "No, my parents are coming over from Australia." She glanced at an expensive-looking platinum wristwatch. "They should be landing in a few hours."

"Aren't they going to be a bit tired?" The last thing I'd feel like after a twenty-four-hour flight would be a long drive to Sands End followed by a wedding.

Linzi frowned. "Why would they be tired?"

"Well, it's such a long flight."

She waved a dismissive hand. "Oh they'll sleep most of the way. They always fly first class. And they'll have a car pick them up from Heathrow."

So, Linzi was not only beautiful but her family was also minted. Lucky old Shaun. I felt tired again and my headache was back.

Shaun returned with a bottle of *Moët* and three glasses. "Ladies, chilled Champagne, plus the pizzas are on their way."

*

The pizzas arrived. I ate mine fast enough to give me heartburn so I could make my excuses and leave. But before I had the chance, Linzi turned to Shaun and said,

255

"I've just realised, I'm not supposed to see you before the wedding, am I? It's bad luck."

"Well, you can get ready down in Katy's flat," he suggested.

Linzi frowned. "But isn't it tonight we're supposed to spend apart? Hey, maybe I should stay with Katy in her flat?"

I felt a prickle of fear. "Um. Could do, but I only have one bed, so one of us would have to sleep on the sofa." And I already knew which one.

Shaun shrugged. "Well, I could sleep in Katy's flat and Katy can sleep in the spare room up here."

Linzi swigged down the last of her Champagne. "Perfect."

I wanted to say, no it is not perfect; I want to sleep in my own bed tonight with Henry curled up on my feet. But Linzi's mind was clearly already made up and I got the feeling that whatever Linzi wanted, Linzi got. Poor Shaun. I was trying to be objective about their nuptials, but I already had a bad feeling about his future. Shaun took his wedding clothes and disappeared downstairs.

"See you tomorrow, husband-to-be," Linzi called after him.

Linzi poured us more Champagne then plonked herself down on Shaun's sofa in a way that made it seem as if she'd been living here for years. I remained perched on the edge of his blue-checked armchair while Linzi switched on the TV and channel hopped.

I wanted to go back to my flat. I wanted to sit on the patio, yakking with Shaun and cuddling Henry, sipping wine, watching the moon rise. The idea of sitting here until bedtime, making small talk with Linzi was torture. "You know, we could go and sit in my garden and keep Shaun company," I suggested.

"Could do," Linzi replied without enthusiasm, her eyes fixed on the TV screen.

"I mean, it's just overnight you need to avoid him," I continued.

She changed channels again. "Yeah..." Her face brightened, "Oh wow. A re-run of *Friends*. I just love that series. Don't you?" She tucked her long legs under her bum and I realised that was how the rest of the evening would be spent. Oh well. At least we wouldn't need to talk.

Within a couple of minutes Linzi was totally engrossed in the programme. I wondered if she'd notice if I nipped back to my flat for a while. I could probably invent an excuse. While I plucked up the courage, I flicked through a bridal magazine lying on the carpet.

From the sofa I heard Linzi giggle. "I love Monica. Monica's my favourite character. She rocks."

I blinked. *Monica.* Why did that name ring a bell? I thumbed through a few more pages of white-frothed Bridezillas.

Monica.

A tiny memory flickered bright blue for a split second then it was gone again. I shook my head, trying to clear my thoughts. Was it someone I'd seen at the school reunion? No, that wasn't it. But it *was* something to do with the reunion. I sipped my Champagne, closed my eyes and tried to nail down the memory.

On the TV I could hear Joey saying, "*Oh no-no-no, I wasn't waving at you, lady. Whoa, maybe I was! Hey, Monica, this totally hot girl in Ross's building is flirting with me.*"

Linzi giggled.

And then I got it. The man I'd heard shouting when the fire alarm went off at the reunion: "*Monica! Monica! Monica!*" The voice had been Patrick's.

"The photograph in her diary, it had her name on the back – not the name I knew her by – her other name…"

My spine tingled. "Um, Linzi?"

"Yeah?" Her eyes didn't leave the screen.

"Would you mind if I nipped down to get my laptop? I've just remembered something I need to do."

She flapped a hand at me. "No probs."

I ran down the stairs and unlocked my front door. "Only me," I yelled as I pelted down the hall and pushed open the sitting room door.

Shaun was lying on his stomach on the floor wearing just a pair of boxer shorts. He too was watching *Friends*. Perhaps they really were made for each other.

"Hey! We're watching that upstairs," I said, as I grabbed my laptop from the sofa and tried to pretend I hadn't noticed his semi-naked state.

Shaun looked a bit embarrassed. "Yeah?"

"Go up and watch it if you want."

Shaun shook his head. "I think Linzi wants me to stay here."

I nodded, wishing he would go so I could stay. "Okay. Well, see you tomorrow."

Back upstairs I Googled everything I'd already searched under – *Jack Dale, police informant, Patrick Underhill, murder* – but this time I added *Monica*.

As I started scrolling through the results, I heard music from the TV. One episode of *Friends* finished and another began. Linzi poured herself more Champagne and seemed to have forgotten I was even in the room.

The first dozen or so results were all about people who'd been murdered in Santa Monica. I felt my optimism slipping away. Then I noticed one of the results was something I'd looked at before. It was the Wikipedia story I'd found the night I'd first met Jack: the one about the

Lucas Brennan murder and the morally bankrupt undercover officer in the honey-pot trap:

Using the pseudonym... the real name of the undercover police officer from SO10 was Jack Dale... contacted **Monica** Fullegar, ...

A peculiar fizzing sensation spread up my chest. I clicked on the story. Ray Butcher's girlfriend, the woman tricked by Jack in the covert police honey-pot operation, had been called Monica. I puffed out my cheeks. "That's... very... odd..."

I read on down. Monica Fullegar had been the star witness for the prosecution in the Brennan murder. The man in the dock for that murder had been Ray Butcher. I put 'Ray Butcher' into Google.

Good grief... there was tonnes of stuff on him. For some inexplicable reason, the Wikipedia story had omitted to mention Butcher's impressive criminal pedigree, possibly because the author had assumed everyone would already know who he was.

I'd never heard of Ray Butcher, but back in his day, it seemed he'd been one of Britain's biggest – and most dangerous – gangland criminals. And Lucas Brennan hadn't just been any old police officer. He'd been an undercover officer in SO10, murdered while trying to infiltrate Butcher's criminal organisation. Monica Fullegar had been Butcher's girlfriend, until she'd grassed him up. After Butcher's conviction, he'd put an open contract on Monica's life believed to have been worth at least a million pounds. Once his trial was over, Monica had gone into hiding under police witness protection. Less than a year later, Butcher had had his conviction for Brennan's murder quashed on appeal. Butcher's defence had argued that Monica Fullegar only implicated Butcher in Brennan's murder because she'd fallen in love with undercover police officer Jack Dale and would have said anything to impress him. Her evidence had been declared unsafe.

Halfway down one of the Butcher stories was a larger version of the photograph of Monica Fullegar wearing the sparkly blue mini dress. A tall, slender woman with long blonde hair, she was being escorted by two unformed police officers. One of her hands was blurred, as if she was about to hide her face. She was smiling. Under the photograph it said:

Ray Butcher's girlfriend, Monica Fullegar, is led away by police from her apartment in London's Docklands following Butcher's arrest for the murder of undercover police officer Lucas Brennan. It is now known the real reason Monica agreed to testify against Butcher was because she had been tricked into an affair with an undercover SO10 police officer, then blackmailed by the police into giving evidence. Three months after entering police witness protection, Monica Fullegar vanished. Given the number of Metropolitan police officers allegedly in Butcher's pay at that time, Fullegar's disappearance was hardly surprising. Seven years after Monica Fullegar disappeared, she was officially declared dead.

At the bottom of the article were more links to old press stories about Butcher's trial. I clicked on the first one. He really had been an odd looking man. Sporting a holiday tan and his ridiculous mullet, he'd had a thin, jowly face, as if he'd once been very fat and had lost a lot of weight. He had sad, hooded eyes that made him look like a bit like a Bloodhound. I clicked on another story and found another picture. On the day Butcher had been freed on appeal for the murder of Lucas Brennan, he'd worn a pastel pink polo shirt with the collar rakishly turned up, looking as though he was saying, "Screw you, coppers."

I glanced at the dates in the story. To my surprise, Monica Fullegar had disappeared from under police protection three months before Patrick's arrest for the murder of Kelly-Anne Davis; right about the time Kelly-Anne had moved to Sands End, in fact. Ray Butcher had been freed on appeal six months after Patrick Underhill had been arrested for Kelly-Anne's murder.

I frowned. "That's… that's really weird…"

I remembered my words to Jack on the terrace at the Bay View Hotel, *"As you don't know Patrick, presumably you knew Kelly-Anne, or else you wouldn't be here."* His discomfort when he'd replied: *"Yes, I briefly knew Kelly-Anne. It was a long time ago."*

Then later that night when he'd come to my flat, *"What I'm trying to say is, was your relationship with Kelly-Anne while she was living here in Sands End?"*

Jack smiling as he'd replied: *"You're being very smart."* I realised now that he hadn't actually answered my question.

I scrolled on down through the article. Before being freed on appeal, Ray Butcher had served his brief time in prison for the murder of Brennan at Long Lartin jail in Worcestershire. My fingers tingled. Long Lartin was where Patrick had been sent on remand. Again I checked dates. Butcher had been in Long Lartin at exactly the same time as Patrick.

"That's… so… weird…"

From the sofa Linzi chuckled, "You all right over there, Katy? You're muttering away to yourself like an old woman."

My eyes didn't leave my laptop's screen. "Yes… fine… sorry…"

This was getting seriously, seriously strange. My hands shook as I picked up my glass from the floor. I returned to the photo of Monica Fullegar. Her hair was blonde and straight. Kelly-Anne's had been dark and curly.

But hair could easily be dyed and permed. Going onto the *Gazette*'s website, I found the story I'd written a few days ago and stared at the old photo of Kelly-Anne Davis that had been used to illustrate the piece. Using my fingers, I covered-up both women's hair, leaving just their faces exposed. There was something eerily similar about their secretive smiles.

I went back to the Wikipedia article about the Brennan murder. Monica Fullegar had been twenty-four years old when Butcher had been arrested. Kelly-Anne Davis had been twenty-five when she'd died. I checked dates and found that there had been a year between Butcher's arrest and Fullegar's testimony at his trial. Fullegar would have been twenty-five when she'd entered police witness protection, exactly the same age as Kelly-Anne had been when she'd died.

I realised I was holding my breath. My palms were moist. Could Kelly-Anne Davis and Monica Fullegar *really* have been the same woman?

I frowned up at the ceiling and shook my head. No, if that had been true, the police would have released Kelly-Anne's real name when she'd been murdered. If the press had discovered Kelly-Anne Davis had really been a supergrass called Monica Fullegar, they'd have been all over it. And I was absolutely sure Monica Fullegar's name hadn't been mentioned in any of the old *Gazette* stories Martin had given me. I went back onto Google, trawling the Internet for any newspaper or news agency that had made that connection. None of them had. I felt my enthusiasm slipping away. It was impossible they were the same woman.

Unless…

I took another sip of tepid Champagne.

Unless… the police had never known that Monica Fullegar had changed her name to Kelly-Anne Davis; that when Monica Fullegar disappeared from under police protection, she'd come up with the name Kelly-Anne Davis all by herself. And if Kelly-Anne Davis *had* been Monica Fullegar then all of a sudden it seemed much more likely that her murder had been a contract killing, ordered from jail by Ray Butcher and carried out by a professional hitman. I stared down at the carpet. And that meant Patrick really had been innocent, and that the man who Patrick claimed had told him to change his plea to guilty – or else – while he was on remand might well have been Ray Butcher.

"Oh… my… God…"

Linzi turned her head. "You sure everything's okay?"

"Sorry…"

But I still couldn't quite bring myself to believe it. Apart from anything, Patrick had always described the man who'd told him to plead guilty as a Mexican, and blond-haired, pale skinned Ray Butcher certainly didn't look Mexican.

I Googled more on Butcher, and discovered that at its height, his criminal empire had been worth more than £30million, and after he'd been cleared of the Brennan murder, he'd moved to Spain, bought a bar and had apparently gone straight. But that wasn't what I was looking for. I was looking for the final smoking gun.

And then, all of a sudden, there it was: in his police mug shot, taken the day he'd been arrested for the murder of Lucas Brennan, Ray Butcher had sported a long, droopy moustache. He'd looked exactly like a blond Mexican bandit in a cheap spaghetti western.

Oh Jesus.

Oh God.

Patrick had been telling the truth all along.

From the sofa I heard Linzi say, "Bedtime, I guess."

I looked up. The sky outside the window was inky black. But I didn't want to go to bed. I wanted to Google some more. Much more. "Um. I thought I might stay up for a bit," I said.

Linzi frowned. "Katy, we have a very busy day tomorrow."

Maybe I'd do a little surreptitious surfing from the spare room. But the battery on my laptop was down to five percent and my charger was downstairs. "Linzi, do you know where Shaun's Mac lead is?"

She shook her head. "Enough Katy! You've had your snout stuck in your computer for the last two hours. You're as bad as Shaun. Bed. Now."

As she pointed towards the spare room, my laptop died.

CHAPTER EIGHTEEN

Shaun had already gone to bed when I went down to my flat to retrieve my toothbrush. By the time I returned to his flat, Linzi had switched out all the lights and gone to bed too. I did the same. Lying in the dark in Shaun's spare room, my mind churned. My fingers itched to get back online. I was sure I wouldn't be able to sleep but the next thing I knew, it was daylight and I could hear raised voices. Someone was crying.

I got out of bed, pulled on my clothes and put an ear to the bedroom door: two voices, one was Shaun's low rumble, the other was high-pitched and verging on hysteria. Pulling the door open, I stepped into the sitting room. The smell of last night's pizzas mixed with alcohol lingered. As I pulled the balcony doors open to air the room, Shaun came out of his bedroom wearing stripy boxer shorts and a creased navy blue t-shirt. He looked awful.

"Hey, aren't you supposed to be in exile?" I asked him.

Shaun's hands raked at his sandy hair making it stand up in tufts. "Yeah, there's been a bit of a setback. The wedding's ah... the wedding's..."

My heart surged with something that felt an awful lot like hope. "Off?"

Shaun sagged onto the sofa. "Yeah."

Oh my goodness!

From his bedroom came the sound of sobbing. I lowered my voice to a whisper. "Did you call it off?"

Shaun shook his head. "Nah. It's nothing like that. But we're going to have to postpone it for a while, that's for sure."

I sat in the chair opposite. "Why? What's happened?"

He rubbed at his temples. "Linzi's mother was taken ill on the flight from Melbourne. She's been rushed to hospital in London. They think she might have had a heart attack."

"Oh no… That's terrible. Linzi must be in an awful state." I felt awful for my uncharitable thoughts earlier.

As if on cue I heard a yell and what sounded like something heavy being hurled across the bedroom. Shaun's eyes flicked towards the door. "Yeah. She's not best pleased." He slapped his hands down on his thighs and stood. "We're heading off to see her mum right away."

"Oh Shaun. I'm so sorry. Have you spoken to the hospital? How is she?"

"Yeah. Stable." He shrugged. "But no wedding." He turned towards the door. "Right, I'd better grab my glad-rags from your place."

I followed Shaun down the stairs and made us coffees. We drank them sat on opposite sides of the breakfast bar and I had the feeling he wasn't in a tearing hurry to go back to his flat. Every now and then footsteps pounded across my ceiling followed by more loud thuds, presumably the sound of Linzi packing. It sounded to me as if she was more angry than upset at the news about her mother.

Shaun finished his coffee, went to the sink and rinsed his mug, "Listen Katy, maybe you should go stay with your parents for a few days while I'm away."

I frowned. "Why?"

He looked away. "Just because of the bomb and everything."

I noticed my hands were shaking as I tried to put my coffee mug back on the breakfast bar. "I'm fine."

"I'd feel much happier if you stayed with them. Just in case—"

I shook my head. "Look, Shaun, it's already been in the paper that the police believe Patrick Underhill planted that bomb. And Patrick is dead. So—"

A shuffling noise made us both jump, but it was only Linzi. She looked very demure in a black linen trouser suit, but her voice was hard as steel. "Shaun, my mother is lying at death's door and you're down here chatting to Katy without a care in the world. We need to go *now*, and you're not even showered."

"Yeah. On my way," he said. But he didn't move.

Linzi turned and stormed out of the room. A moment later I heard my front door slam.

"She's a bit upset... You know..." Shaun mumbled. "Her mum isn't at death's door. She's stable and undergoing tests and—"

My eyes met his. "You need to go."

"Yeah. Okay." He padded barefoot across my sitting room and out of my front door. I sat and listened to the sound of his heavy feet plodding up the stairs to his flat.

Ten minutes later he banged on my door, his hair still wet from his shower, to say they were leaving.

As soon as Shaun and Linzi had gone, I decided to go and see Sergeant Harper immediately and tell him what I'd discovered. When I too was showered and dressed, I switched on my new phone to discover six texts from Becky, all asking if I was all right and telling me to call her ASAP. She sounded so anxious, I decided to pop into her fancy dress shop on my way back from the police station to

267

reassure her that I was fine. Actually I felt better than fine. I felt terrific. I didn't know whether it was because Shaun wasn't marrying Linzi today or because I might possibly have solved the mystery of who had really murdered poor Kelly-Anne Davis and could now do what Patrick had originally asked me to do that hot, suffocating afternoon at the Barley Mow in Bristol: help him clear his name.

*

Annoyingly, all the parking bays at the police station were taken so I left the car in a pay-and-display nearer the town centre. This part of Sands End hadn't changed at all since I was a teenager. Opposite the car park was a rough biker's pub, and next to that a small ten-pin bowling alley, the venue for my first date with Niall Sinclair when we'd been fourteen. I remembered being horrified by the blue and white bowling daps I'd had to wear; how ridiculous they'd looked with my lime green mini skirt. Patrick Underhill had also been at the bowling alley that night, not with anyone, as usual, but slouched in the little café area staring at all the girls, picking his nose and wiping the bogies on the Formica tabletop.

For as long as I could remember, Patrick had been an unpleasant part of my life. Even after he'd gone to prison, the memory of our strange encounter outside the Fighting Cocks the night of the murder had haunted me. Then, less than a week ago, he'd come out of prison, claiming innocence and again asking for my help. Again I hadn't believed him. Now, only a few days later, here I was on my way to tell the police that I believed Patrick had been innocent. But it was too late. Way too late. Patrick was dead.

Hot tears stung my eyes. I blinked them away, strode across to the ticket machine and distracted myself with dithering over how much time to put on the car. I had a feeling it might take ages to explain everything to Sergeant Harper. In the end, I bought three hours and shoved the ticket on the dashboard.

I walked through town, staring down at the pavement. In my mind I rehearsed what I would tell Harper about my discoveries the previous evening: that nightclub bar manager Kelly-Anne Davis was really the supergrass Monica Fullegar who'd fled police witness protection thirteen years ago and had gone to ground in Sands End in a desperate effort to evade the contract Ray Butcher had put on her life. Tragically, it hadn't worked.

Scenes began to play out in front of my eyes like a film: blonde Monica Fullegar arriving in Sands End as curly brunette Kelly-Anne Davis, sweet-talking her way into the job at Glitz, going out for a couple of dates with Patrick Underhill, perhaps because she felt sorry for him, or because she'd thought he was rich and going places, then realising that had simply been another of his stupid lies and he was a weirdo. So she'd dumped him, got on with her life, and after a few months had gone by, maybe she'd even begun to believe she was safe in Sands End; that Ray Butcher had lost her.

I glanced up as a bus rumbled past. A poster on its side advertised a zombie film, its cast of gruesome corpses so realistic they made me feel briefly queasy. My stare returned to the ground.

It was hard to believe it was only a few days ago that Martin had asked me to write the story about Patrick. I thought back to my train journey home from that meeting, reading through the old newspaper stories. I remembered one of the crazy claims Patrick had made to the police after

269

his arrest, that he had "prophesised" Kelly-Anne's murder because he'd found a photograph in her diary that showed her "already dead". He'd mentioned the photograph to me too, that afternoon before the school reunion when I'd spoken to him on the seafront. I'd written it off as more Patrick craziness but now I wasn't so sure. I frowned, trying to bring his exact words back into my mind:

"Everything in that diary came true... her murder, even the way he killed her in that photograph... You have no idea how much I wish I'd taken that diary with me – and the photograph... it had her name on the back – not the name I knew her by – her other name... and written next to it one word: 'dead'."

So, according to Patrick, before Kelly-Anne had been murdered, he'd found a photograph tucked inside her diary that showed her already dead from head injuries. Written on the back had been her real name: Monica. I shook my head. That made absolutely no sense. How could there have been a photo showing her corpse before she'd died?

I frowned as I tried to puzzle it through. The photo had to have been faked, that much was obvious. My fingers massaged my temples as I walked. Had it dated from the time Monica Fullegar had fled police witness protection? That she'd faked her death to the police using a stunted-up photograph of her 'corpse'?

I shook my head. No, that didn't work. As far as the police were concerned, Monica had simply vanished while under police protection. She'd only been officially declared dead after the mandatory seven years had gone by. And anyway, if the photo had shown her as blonde Monica Fullegar, dozy Patrick would have struggled to recognise her. The photo must have been of her as curly brunette Kelly-Anne Davis. It had to have been taken after she'd come to live in Sands End, not before.

270

My mind squinted back to the dates I'd found the previous night. Ray Butcher had still been in prison for the Brennan murder when Kelly-Anne died. But he would have already issued the open contract on her life. His henchmen, or anyone else who felt like earning a large pay cheque, were already hunting her down.

Kelly-Anne must have been scared stiff that they'd find her. I felt myself shrug. But if Ray Butcher believed she'd already been executed, then the contract had been fulfilled. Perhaps the strange photo had been stunted up by Kelly-Anne to convince Butcher she was dead. A fizz of excitement tingled in my chest. Could that really be what had happened?

I took a shortcut up an alleyway between two shops as I mulled it through. Patrick had mentioned her diary again, at the school reunion, not long before his own death. It wasn't difficult to call his words back into my mind: "*It was all in her diary... how one day soon she'd leave this dump... she'd be rich and free... Oh my God. I think they've found me...*"

I nodded to myself as I'd dodged around a dawdling group of shoppers. Sounded like she thought Butcher's men had found her

Rich and free...

I jerked my eyes up from the pavement, stopped so abruptly I felt someone stumble against my arm. My hand slapped up to my forehead. I heard a man's voice exclaim, "Look where you're going, love," as he pushed past me.

Rich and free...

Suddenly everything seemed to fall into place. Yes, the photo had been intended to make Ray Butcher believe she was dead, and yes, it had been taken after she'd fled to Sands End. But there had been more to it than that. Much more. A small disbelieving laugh escaped my lips. "No... way...." I muttered. "No... way...?"

271

If I was right, Kelly-Anne hadn't just wanted Butcher to believe she was dead, she'd also tried to sting him for the bounty he'd put on her life. Those were the 'riches' she'd boasted about in her diary. But something had gone wrong with her plan and she really had been murdered.

I continued to stare blank-eyed down the road, shaking my head in astonishment. On one hand, it was a great story. On the other, it was extremely far-fetched. I forced my feet back into movement telling myself, hang-on Katy, think it through from the start; is it really possible?

Maybe it had been Patrick, always on the alert for potential love rivals, who'd unwittingly alerted her to the danger. Poor Patrick, still smitten with this beautiful older woman, still hopeful of getting her back, watching her while she worked behind the bar. And one night he'd seen a man watching her with the same keen interest as his own, and he'd asked her – or demanded, more likely – "Who's that bloke over there staring at you?" She'd followed Patrick's eyes, through the smoke and the gloom, the strobing disco lights making masks of people's faces. She'd looked at the man; he'd looked back at her, and there had been something about him that had frightened the crap out of her. Perhaps it had been the way he was watching her; a bold curiosity bordering on rudeness, as if he was trying to decide if she was who he thought she was, and whether he should contact his boss, Ray Butcher. I imagined her terror as panic leapt up her throat, only one thought in her mind: *Oh my God. I think he's found me.*

A horn, a loud screech of brakes. Looking up I realised I'd stepped out into the road in front of a courier van. The driver glared at me through the windscreen. But I barely registered him.

If I were Kelly-Anne, that would have been the moment I'd have known I needed to run. But I'd have also known that running was useless; Butcher wasn't ever going to give up trying to hunt her down. So she'd needed to think of a way to stop him, once and for all. And the only way he'd stop was if he thought she was dead.

Maybe it was later that night, after work, when she'd come up with her plan: if Butcher was shown a photo that appeared to show her dead body that might just be enough. But perhaps then, another idea had opened up; she'd thought, why stop *there*? Butcher wanted her dead; he would pay to have her dead. All she had to do was prove she *was* dead and *she* could collect the million-pound bounty.

I imagined her, lying in bed, smiling up at the dark ceiling of her flat, revelling in the brilliance of her idea, the simplicity of it; the way it would solve two problems in one fell swoop: she'd be free of Butcher. And she'd also be rich.

But Kelly-Anne couldn't have done it alone. She'd have needed someone to help her stunt up the photograph, maybe help her with the make-up and fake blood so she looked convincingly dead. And she couldn't have just popped the photo in the post to Ray Bucher and expected him to send a cheque for the bounty by return. Her accomplice must have delivered the photo to Butcher in jail, calmly told him Monica Fullegar was dead and claimed the reward. Whoever he was, he must have had balls of steel to waltz into that prison, knowing who he was dealing with, that one false move would mean a death sentence for him too.

I nipped up a side street, away from the shopping crowds, aware that my pace was accelerating along with my thoughts. She couldn't have entrusted that to an idiot like Patrick, and anyway, they weren't seeing each other by then.

She hadn't had any friends or family to ask either, judging by the old newspaper reports and the scant mourners at her funeral.

But someone had helped her, and something had gone wrong.

I ran up the steps of Sands End police station and pushed open the glass door.

*

I asked to see Sergeant Harper but was told he was out. He was expected back in an hour.

The officer on the front desk said I could wait, but the reception area smelt revolting, as if something unpleasant had been cleaned away with a very strong disinfectant. And anyway, I felt too restless to sit. I needed movement, something to distract me until Harper returned. The time was ticking down on my parking ticket so I decided to kill the hour by getting the visit to Becky out of the way.

Becky's fancy dress shop was in a narrow side road off the High Street. As I pushed open the door, a bell above my head made a loud ting-ting noise. Becky was slouched over the counter doing something fiddly with a pair of tweezers. She looked up. "Katy!"

I managed a cheerful smile, "Hi Becky, thanks for all your texts. Just popped in to let you know I'm fine."

Becky popped a pair of ornate false eyelashes into a small plastic bag. She was wearing a pink t-shirt with an appliqué of Zippy from Rainbow on the front. He even had a real zipper for his mouth.

"Oh my God," she said. "Tell me about that bomb. Is it true Patrick planted it?" She stared at the stitches above my eyebrow. "Oh my God! Is that from the explosion? Oh my God! You could have been killed!" She touched a finger to a barely visible scratch above her left eyebrow. "Looks like we'll have identical scars, thanks to that vicious bastard. See, I did say he was going to do something terrible. Didn't I?"

Even though there was no one else in the shop Becky lowered her voice, "I heard he was trying to escape from Glitz by jumping from the roof of the club to the roof of the taxi firm next door but he fell and broke his neck."

A shiver rippled across my shoulders.

Becky picked up her phone. "Hey, want to see the photos I took at the reunion? Before Patrick ruined it, obviously."

No, not really. I managed another smile. "Sure."

As I flicked through the pictures, Becky came and stood at my side, talking me through them. "That's Kimberly from our English class. She came as Anne Boleyn…. That's Niall Sinclair… he's really packed on the weight since school. Wouldn't have recognised him in a million years… That's Amy Stevens as Snow White. Apparently that's not a wig. Her hair really is like that."

The reunion photos were making me think about Patrick again. I wanted to leave.

As I glanced at the door, planning my swift exit, Nick Padovani walked past the window, black shirt, black trousers, fast paced, head down. A pretty, young woman was on his arm. Padovani and the woman paused at the kerb then turned to face each other as if saying goodbye.

Becky followed my stare. "Him. Yuck. I swear to God he's got a different one every week. Still, it's amazing how money can make a pervy old man seem irresistible," she added bitchily.

I frowned, "Since when has Padovani had money? I thought Glitz was always on the brink of going bust?"

Becky gave a dry laugh and shook her head. "Nick Padovani is absolutely minted. As well as Glitz he also owns the big amusement arcade on the seafront, and he owns Mario's. He'll be on his way there now to strut around looking important."

She gave a disparaging snort. "Oh yes, he's quite the wealthy, respectable businessman these days." She jerked a thumb towards the young woman. "Pound to a penny she works up at Glitz. According to my brother Jason, Padovani tries it on with all his barmaids. Always has done."

She plonked her phone back in her handbag. "You must have heard he was shagging Kelly-Anne Davis?"

I felt my eyebrows jerk upwards. "Seriously?"

Becky nodded. "It was supposed to be very hush-hush because Padovani was still married back then. But Jason had a mate who DJ-ed up at Glitz and he said it was an open secret that there was something going on between Padovani and Kelly-Anne; you know, cosy after-work – hem-hem – drinks in his office. According to Jase, his DJ mate walked in on them one night and caught Padovani in a pair of red satin boxer shorts snogging her face off."

I winced at the image.

Outside the shop, Padovani pulled the young woman into an embrace. As she turned to walk away he patted her bum.

Becky made a retching sound. "Dirty old perve. You know, at the reunion the other night, Amy Stevens said Padovani used to grope her bum at Glitz too exactly like he groped mine, and bum groping is actually sexual assault isn't it? I'd have pressed charges after the night of our A-Level results but I thought the police would be much too busy investigating the murder."

I frowned as I tried to gather my thoughts. "Are you sure it was that night, Becks?"

Becky gave an emphatic nod. "Certainly was. I told you, that whole night is etched in my mind forever. We were standing outside the swing doors on the first floor, waiting to go down the stairs and I felt someone grab a right handful." She mimed the action with her hands. "So I turned around to give them an earful, and Nick Padovani was stood right behind me, leering, so I gave him an evil stare instead. When we got outside, Dad was parked up in the alley as usual, then Padovani came into the alley too and I thought Jesus, he's going to have another go right in front of my dad, but instead he jumped into his car and sped off, thank God."

My mouth had gone dry. "Becks, I don't suppose you remember what time that was?"

She shrugged. "Midnight, of course. We always had to leave at midnight, didn't we? Thanks to my pathetic curfew."

"And you're absolutely, one hundred per cent sure it was the night of the murder?"

Becky nodded. "Absolutely sure. I'd swear my life on it."

"Oh my God…"

She frowned. "Katy? What's the matter?"

I turned to Becky. "I… I have to go…."

CHAPTER NINETEEN

The whole time I was walking to Mario's restaurant, I tried to convince myself there might be an innocent explanation why Nick Padovani had lied about not leaving the club that night.

As I neared the restaurant's door, I saw a silver Maserati parked at the kerb. The number plate read A1 NIC.

I stared at the car. I stared at the restaurant. I stared at Padovani standing inside. I saw Patrick reading Kelly-Anne's diary thirteen years ago, seeing the stunted-up death photo, realising something odd was going on but not understanding what, only that she was planning to leave Sands End and disappear from his life forever. I saw him in the August evening sunshine outside the Fighting Cocks, telling me the nonsense about winning the lottery and moving to Rio, and then he'd said:

"Katy, are you going up to Glitz tonight? It's just I need your help—"

But I'd cut him off after he'd said just those few words. *"Oh, you need my help? What for, Patrick? Because space aliens are going to invade? Because the Mexican ghost bandit is coming to get you? Listen, I have had enough – more than enough – of your stupid pathetic lies. Have a nice life, loser."*

And I'd turned on my heel and walked away.

But now I heard him saying the rest of the words I hadn't given him the chance to say that night:

278

"I need you to take a message to Kelly-Anne Davis. She works behind the bar. I need you to ask her to meet me outside the club on her next break. It's really important, I really need to talk to her."

But I hadn't let him say any of that, so he'd had no choice but to go to her flat instead, planning to plead with her to stay, not realising the killer was already there and she was already dead. Next thing he knew, he was lying on her kitchen floor, covered in her blood, the murder weapon by his side; the cold realisation, when he'd run outside and seen the police car, that he was going to be blamed for her murder; the diary and the photo that could have cleared him, already destroyed because her killer had keys to her flat. He owned her flat.

I heard mum's voice inside my head, *"Padovani was on the verge of going bankrupt that summer… next thing we know, he's given the club a refit and he's calling it a cocktail lounge…"*

I stared through the restaurant windows. My fists were clenching and unclenching at my sides. I felt my face flush scarlet, my anger rise. How could I have been so incredibly, totally stupid?

I took a deep breath. What I was about to do was risky. The sensible voice in my head told me I should go straight to the police. But I wasn't going to. Partly it was because I still thought I could be wrong. Mostly it was because I knew I was right, and at that precise moment I had never hated anyone so much in my life.

*

He was behind the bar, his black hair, greying at the temples, slicked back with oil like a wannabe Mafia *Capo*. A thin waiter tried to intercept me at the door but I sidestepped him and marched up to the bar.

279

I flashed Padovani a big smile, pulled my Dictaphone out of my handbag and pointed it at him. "Mr Padovani? Remember me? Katy Bennett, *South West Gazette*. I wonder if I could have a few minutes of your time?"

"I'm busy." He walked away to the other end of the bar.

I followed him. "This really won't take a moment. I just want to double check a couple of things for my story." Out of the corner of my eye I saw curious diners pause in their eating and turn in my direction.

He turned to face me, mouth set in a scowl. "What story?"

I made my voice sound surprised, "The story proving Patrick Underhill didn't murder Kelly-Anne Davis." I adjusted the Dictaphone. "Mr Padovani, were you and Kelly-Anne having an affair?"

He snatched his eyes away. "None of your business."

I raised my voice, "A few days ago, you told me you went to see Patrick while he was on remand at Long Lartin prison. But when I spoke to Patrick before his tragic death at your club he told me you didn't visit him. No one did. What's your response to that?"

Padovani opened the wooden flap at the end of the bar and tried to push past me. "You must leave now. As you can see I'm very busy–"

I stood my ground. "Sorry, but could I just check one more fact? You told me – and presumably also the police – that the night Kelly-Anne Davis was murdered, you were at your club all night. But I've since spoken to someone who saw you leaving Glitz at midnight," I paused. "That was shortly before Kelly-Anne was murdered. I just wondered if you have a response to that too?"

280

His palm jerked up towards my face and for a horrible moment I thought he was going to slap me. Then he seemed to regain control, but his index finger shook as he wagged it in my face. He hissed, "Miss Bennett. I don't know who you think you are, storming in to my business making your slanderous allegations, but one thing I can guarantee. If you print one word – one word – of what you have just said, I will sue you and your newspaper out of existence. Now, get out."

He tried to push me out of the way, but I braced my arms against the side of the bar and the top of the nearest table. I could tell he was torn between hurling me against a wall and not doing anything violent in front of his customers. I wanted to say: You went to Long Lartin but you didn't go to see Patrick Underhill. You went to see Ray Butcher. And you didn't show him the faked photo as Kelly-Anne had asked you to. You told him you'd found Monica and offered to kill her for a price. You betrayed her; sold her out. When you thought I might have worked that out, you tried to scare me off the story by sending me funeral flowers and arranging to have me attacked by a thug with a baseball bat. You planted the bomb too, either another scare tactic or to convince me Patrick really was a murdering nut-job. And you lied about seeing Patrick outside Glitz before the school reunion. What you said about him planning to blow things 'sky high', you made that up so he'd get the blame for the bomb. Exactly like you lied to the police thirteen years ago about Patrick's violent threats against Kelly-Anne. Smart, but not smart enough, Mr Padovani. If you'd been really smart you'd have killed Patrick in Kelly-Anne's kitchen instead of knocking him unconscious, meaning you wouldn't have had to throw him off the roof of your shitty little nightclub thirteen years later.

281

But I didn't say any of that. Instead, our eyes locked and I said, "This will be printed, Mr Padovani, but I think that's the least of your worries. We both know what really happened that night and as soon as I'm finished here, I'm going straight to the police."

He lowered his head so his face was almost touching mine. His lemon hair oil smelled sickly, like perfume, and in that exact second I realised where I'd smelled it before. It had been him in my flat the night I thought I'd left my laptop switched on, hunting around trying to establish how much I already knew.

In a low voice he said, "Katy, let me give you some advice. You want to play games with me? Huh? You like playing games? Well, you go ahead. Because you picked totally the wrong person to mess with, you silly, little bitch." He snatched the Dictaphone out of my hand, hurled it to the floor and stamped on it with his grey slip-on loafers until it was just a mess of flattened metal.

I held his gaze as I fought to control my temper. Then I snatched up the remains of the Dictaphone and walked out of his restaurant.

.   *

Once outside, I ran across the narrow road to a coffee shop opposite. My legs felt like jelly. Now all I had to do was wait. One of two things was going to happen. If I was wrong about all this, a furious Nick Padovani would already be on the phone to Martin lodging an official complaint, and an equally furious Martin wouldn't hesitate to pass that roasting on to me.

But if I was right, then Padovani was going to run.

One of those two things was about to happen.

I chose a window table that gave me an unobstructed view of Mario's. My heart was thudding so violently I thought it might crack a rib. The windows of the coffee shop were wide open and a hot breeze wafted in from outside. When the barista caught my eye, I asked him for an espresso. Minutes inched by. At one point I was sure my watch had stopped. The second hand seemed frozen between the ten and the five. My phone lay silent on the table.

The barista brought my coffee over. I made a point of paying him for it right away in case I had to make a swift exit.

Through Mario's windows, I could see occasional movement as waiters brought bills and collected empty plates. I checked the time and reckoned that it was thirteen minutes since I'd left the restaurant. By now Padovani would have had ample time to do what I hoped he was going to do.

A bus drove by and for a couple of seconds I lost sight of the restaurant's frontage. I took a sip of coffee, picked up my phone and checked for the umpteenth time that it hadn't magically switched itself off. No call or email from Martin so far.

And then it happened. A young waiter dashed out of the restaurant, got into the Maserati, drove away at high speed and a taxi pulled up in its place. The restaurant door opened and Nick Padovani hurried out. He wore a tan sports blazer over his black shirt and trousers, and towed a small silver suitcase on wheels. His phone was clamped to his ear and he was talking quickly. He broke off to shout through the taxi window, "Bristol airport. Fast." Then he threw himself into the back and slouched down in his seat. For the briefest second, I thought I saw someone sitting

283

next to him. Then the taxi pulled away and disappeared, leaving a blue fog of exhaust.

Bingo.

I had him.

I swigged down my coffee and took the business card Sergeant Harper had given to me out of my purse, then I hurried out of the café and phoned him as I ran back to my car. To my relief he answered.

"It's Katy Bennett. From the school reunion at Glitz. I came to see you earlier but you were out."

"Hello. Yes. I got the message. How are you?"

I didn't have time for small talk. "Listen, I know who really murdered Kelly-Anne Davis."

Harper's voice rose slightly. "Oh?"

"It wasn't Patrick Underhill. It was Nick Padovani. He killed her for money. I also think it was Padovani who planted that bomb and I'm sure he murdered Patrick."

I yanked my car keys out of my bag. "Google the name Monica Fullegar: it's spelt F U L L E G A R. That's Kelly-Anne's real name. Then you'll see where I'm coming from. Padovani's just taken a taxi from his restaurant. He's on his way to Bristol airport, and I'd bet my last fifty pence he's planning to catch the next flight to Malta." I paused as I crossed the road towards the car park. "Meet me at the airport and I'll explain everything. But you have got to stop Padovani getting on that flight." Then I hung up.

*

The quickest route to the airport from Sands End was up Cheddar Gorge and across the Mendip Hills.

As soon as I was on the main road out of town, I could tell the weather was going to break. The air became much more humid and the sky was covered with a thin white haze. Even with the top down and doing a steady sixty, I was sweltering. My black camisole was damp and stuck to my back, my jeans dug into my hips.

I nudged the accelerator up to seventy, my mind buzzing, continuing to rehearse what I would tell Sergeant Harper when I met him at the airport. I didn't think Nick Padovani had always intended to frame Patrick for the murder. For a start, Padovani couldn't have known Patrick would go to Kelly-Anne's flat that night. The choice of murder weapon now made me think Padovani had initially wanted to make it look as if she'd been the victim of a botched burglary – Kelly-Anne disturbing the intruder, the intruder grabbing the nearest heavy object.

I overtook a tractor so fast it seemed stationary. When Patrick had unexpectedly arrived at Kelly-Anne's flat, Padovani realised he could take advantage of the situation. He'd crept up behind Patrick, knocked him unconscious then, once Padovani was cleaned up and safely back at Glitz, he'd immediately started inventing Patrick's harassment of Kelly-Anne – perhaps crossly telling other employees they would be short-staffed for the rest of the night because a terrified Kelly-Anne had fled Sands End to escape Patrick's obsessive stalking. The following day when the news broke of Patrick's arrest Padovani had already laid the groundwork, painting him as a violent, deranged teenager capable of murder. Poor Patrick never had a clue it was Nick Padovani who killed her.

My anger came to the boil again. I pressed the accelerator, wondering how many police Harper had sent to the airport, whether they were already ahead of me or still behind me. Ahead of me, I decided, blue-lighting it all the way. I had to hurry if I wanted to see Nick Padovani's arrest. For all sorts of reasons, I needed to see that. The speedo briefly touched eighty, then I turned off the main road and headed towards Cheddar.

When I got up to the top of the Gorge and out onto the Mendips, the road levelled and in my rear mirror I could see all the way back across the Bristol Channel. Huge purple, flat-topped clouds that looked like islands towered into a sky the colour of blood. Within minutes it was so gloomy I had to flick on the headlights.

The first drops of rain were the size of pound coins and I only just managed to pull over and yank-up the soft-top before the deluge began. As I set off again, the rain was so heavy I could barely see through the windscreen even though the wipers were going full pelt.

I turned the car into a narrow hedge-lined lane signposted to Priddy. After a while the hedge changed to a dense row of trees that arched overhead, further exaggerating the false twilight. There was no one else on the road but the terrible weather made it slow going. The miles inched by and the deluge continued. The lane was beginning to flood quite badly in places which slowed me down even more. My anxiety began to rise. I didn't want to miss seeing Padovani being arrested. For Patrick's sake – and mine – I really needed to see him in handcuffs being shoved into the back of a police car.

The MX-5 sat low to the ground so I had to power through the floodwater, revving the engine as the front wheels created arcs of rust-brown tsunamis. But the next patch of flooding I encountered was more of a challenge, a vast lake thirty or forty feet across. The lane was much wider here and the flood stretched the full width of the road. I stopped and tried to assess my chances of getting through. Problem was, I had to try. If I turned around and went another way to the airport, I'd lose too much valuable time.

Just take it fast, I told myself. I patted the steering wheel. "Come on little car. You can do it."

But as I gunned the car into the water, the engine faltered, coughed then died.

"Oh no! Don't you even think about it!" I shouted. I tried turning the ignition key gently then turned it hard, frantically pumping the accelerator and praying the engine would catch. But it wouldn't. The water had flooded the engine.

"Crapping hell!"

I slammed my hands down on the steering wheel.

In my rear mirror I saw the headlights of a car some distance behind me. Great. Maybe the driver could help me jump-start the engine, but when I glanced back the lights had vanished. The driver must have turned off when they'd seen the flood ahead. Wish I'd done the same.

I stared gloomily through the windscreen. Actually jump-starting my car would probably have been impossible. We'd have had to somehow turn the MX-5 around first so it was facing dry ground. It might just be simpler to phone Mike at the garage and ask him to tow me home or maybe he could get my car going again. Either way, I'd miss seeing Padovani arrested, which was a shame. But I'd get to see him in court. And if asked I would gladly testify against him.

I grabbed my handbag off the passenger seat and found Mike's garage card in my purse but when I tried to make the call nothing happened. I tried four more times then realised I had no signal.

"No!" I yelled at the windscreen.

Even though I tried and re-tried until my fingers went numb, I couldn't make the call. I pushed my jeans up to my knees and got out of the car. My flip-flops disappeared into the floodwater. It was surprisingly cold and most likely churning with farm slurry. I winced at the thought of the filthy water swirling around my toes. Within seconds my clothes were soaked with rain. I paced around waving the phone, studying the screen. Still no signal.

Raking my sopping hair out of my eyes, I got back in the car. My only option was to wait for another motorist to come along and pray they had a phone on a network that did work up here. Or perhaps the engine would dry out before then and I could get moving again.

The rain was torrential, coming down like a curtain of nails. I stared miserably through the wet windscreen, continuing my efforts to re-start the car, trying to remain calm. Someone would come along soon. I tried my phone again. Nothing. Tried the engine. Nothing.

Over the sound of the rain I heard a crash of thunder followed by a blue-white flash of lightning. I tried to remember what would happen if a car was struck by lightning. I had a vague idea that the rubber tyres would safely earth the electricity. Or was it the other way around and everything metal on the vehicle would become live? Maybe I should get out of the car. But I was surrounded by trees, and trees were definitely bad news during thunderstorms.

Precious minutes ticked by. My anxiety ratcheted up. What if the police hadn't taken my claims seriously? What if they hadn't sent anyone to the airport? In my mind, I saw Nick Padovani get out of the taxi and calmly trundle his suitcase up to the Air Malta check-in desk. I clenched my jaw, drummed my fingers on the steering wheel, my eyes fixed through the windscreen as if by sheer force of thought I could will a passing motorist into existence. "Come on… come on…" I muttered. The next crash of thunder was so close the car rocked.

Then, in the distance ahead, two shimmering white lights cut through the artificial dusk. My heart leapt. I wiped at the misty windscreen. Headlights were coming along the lane towards me. Oh thank goodness. I clicked on my hazards and flashed my headlights several times to indicate I had broken down. The car ahead slowed then stopped about thirty or forty feet away on the far side of the flood. It was a massive white 4x4, the sort of car that should relish the conditions but the driver seemed reluctant to come any closer to the floodwater.

For a while we just stared at each other. Well, presumably the driver was staring at me because I couldn't see anything through the gloom and the rain. Then the headlights of the 4x4 flashed onto high beam for a second.

I frowned. What did that mean? Pull over so I can get past? Or 'I can't drive through this either'? Maybe the driver really was unsure about driving through the flood. There might be anything lurking under the water – rusty nails, broken glass – and tyres on a 4x4 probably weren't cheap. Looked like I was going to have to wade through the water to them if I wanted their help. I hoped it wasn't too deep.

I shoved open the car door and got out, cupped my hands around my mouth and just in case they could hear me, shouted, "I've broken down. Can I borrow your phone?" I pointed at my submerged feet and bellowed, "I'm only wearing flip-flops," to explain why I was reluctant to walk through the flood water. The lights of the 4x4 flashed again as if to say, okay, I hear you.

The driver's door opened and someone got out. Great. Looked like they might be bringing the phone to me. I squinted through the slanting rain, trying to see if it was a man or a woman. From their height and build I was more inclined to think it was a man wearing a chunky black anorak and Wellington boots. A farmer perhaps. Another clap of thunder seemed to split the sky and lightning strobed down through the trees turning the floodwater briefly silver.

The rain was so heavy it was painful against my face. I wiped the drops out of my eyes and waited for him to start walking through the flood but he continued to stand beside his car, staring at me, a tall, dark figure against the dark trees. Then he reached back inside the 4x4 and took out an umbrella. Good. He was going to come to me. My feet felt freezing in the floodwater so I walked back out of the water to a dry area of road.

I didn't hear the car coming up behind me until it screeched to a halt in what sounded like a panicky emergency stop.

I glanced back, wondering if the driver hadn't seen my hazard lights because their car had stopped parallel to mine, presumably to avoid crashing into the back of it. The car was a brand new black Porsche. The driver flung the car door open and I heard a man's voice shout my name.

"Katy!"

I blinked rain out of my eyes. I knew that voice. I'd know it anywhere.

"Jack?" I called back a little uncertainly.

And that's when everything went into slow motion, or at least that's how it seemed.

Jack jumped out of the car and sprinted towards me, splashing through the puddles, raindrops scattering, one hand reached inside a black leather jacket, the other stretched out towards me as he yelled, "Get down! Get down!"

I looked back towards the man standing beside the 4x4. He had raised the umbrella up to his face so it was pointing straight at me. And somewhere inside my brain, synapses sparked, connected, whirred, and flashed-up their assessment of the situation: *It's not an umbrella. It's a rifle.*

Then Jack slammed into me. The impact knocked the breath from my lungs and we both went flying. As my feet left the ground, I heard a crack and Jack seemed to shudder into my side.

I landed flat on my face. Jack landed on top of me, pinning me to the road, my mind screaming, *rifle, rifle.* I gulped air uselessly like a landed fish. Bits of wet grit were stuck to my lips and my cheeks.

"Jesus Christ!" I screamed. My voice was hysterical. It didn't even sound like me. I kicked my legs in panic, somehow managed to turn onto my side so I was almost facing Jack. He wasn't even blinking, just staring up the lane through the rain. "Stay still," he whispered.

My arm was trapped awkwardly underneath my chest so I wriggled onto my front again, freed a hand and clawed my soaking hair out of my eyes. The man was walking towards us, wading easily through the floodwater in an unhurried sort of way. One hand was behind his back, the other flicked up the collar of his anorak. He had sad hooded eyes, a loose jowly face. My breath froze.

It was Ray Butcher.

And then from behind his back he drew the rifle.

"Jesus! Jack!" I yelled, kicking my legs. My head was screaming, *Get out of here! Run!* But I couldn't move.

Wellington boots scrunched to a halt on the tarmac in front of us.

A toneless Cockney voice said, "Happy days, Jack. I always say, if you want something doing properly, do it yourself."

He lifted the rifle. My heart felt as if it was about to explode through my ribs and there was a whooshing noise in my ears. "Jack!" I screamed. "Oh God! Jack!"

I felt a small movement behind my head. Underneath my wet hair, something cold and heavy rested against the side of my neck, and Jack's voice, so quiet it was as if it was inside my head, said very calmly, "Don't move."

But before my brain could even process his words, I heard two incredibly loud shots, right next to my ear.

Butcher's legs swayed then his knees buckled and he crumpled, quite gently it seemed, hitting the road face first. A crimson pool flowed from beneath his forehead.

I was too terrified to move. Jack's body seemed even heavier than before. I struggled to force air into my lungs. "Jack?" I whispered. I tried to turn my head. Butcher's body remained face down, immobile.

"Jack? I can't move…. Are you okay?"

Thunder growled again but further off this time. Abruptly, the rain eased. It dripped from the trees above my head. Water gurgled somewhere close by. The sun came out from behind the clouds and steam began to rise like mist from the tarmac.

I tried to wriggle out from under him but he was too heavy.

"Jack?" It was almost a shout. He still didn't answer.

My panic surged. It started raining heavily again. Water ran down my face. I wiped it away and saw my hand was covered with blood. More blood dripped off my chin onto the tarmac.

"*Jack!*" This time it was a scream.

I went rigid, anticipating unbearable pain but I felt nothing. Jack's weight seemed to press harder onto me. My vision darkened and my whole body went numb. In the distance I heard the wail of police sirens.

Jack's voice was against my ear. It rasped as if he had a heavy cold, "It's not you."

"What? *What?*" My voice was verging on hysteria.

"It's me."

"*What?*"

The whooping sirens were coming closer. Blue lights flickered on the puddles. I heard the screech of tyres and running footsteps behind me. Jack's weight was suddenly lifted away. I managed to scramble up onto all fours, my eyes still fixed on Ray Butcher.

"Are you hurt?" asked a deep male voice.

Police officers wearing baseball caps and stab vests ran over to Butcher. One of them, a woman, her dark hair tied back in a stubby ponytail kicked the rifle out of his reach.

I turned to look at Jack. They'd got him lying on his back, raindrops pattered onto his face. His eyes were closed and his lips were slightly parted. In the distance I could hear the sound of a helicopter.

And then I saw the scarlet puddle pooling from beneath his back. His torso was completely soaked with blood.

There was a dull clanging in my ears. Once again my vision darkened. I had the strangest feeling I was falling forwards, then everything went black.

CHAPTER TWENTY

Hours later, after I'd given my statement at the station, the police dropped me back at my flat. Shaun wasn't home. Presumably he was still in London with Linzi.

Once I was alone, I couldn't stop shaking. I poured a massive glass of wine, necked it and immediately threw up in the kitchen sink. Then I peeled off my clothes and stood under the shower, turning up the heat until it was almost too hot to bear, watching through the steam as the blood in my hair – Jack's blood – ran rusty around my feet. I stayed in the shower, unable to move until the hot water turned tepid then cold.

I wrapped myself in a towel, put my dressing gown over the top and lay on the sofa listening to the rain lash against the patio door, Henry perched protectively on my chest, sniffing at my damp hair. Every time I closed my eyes, all I saw was Jack, the raindrops pitter-pattering on his lips, and the blood soaking across his chest.

I forced myself to watch the evening news. The police hadn't named him yet. The report simply said that a man had been airlifted to Bath's Royal United Hospital with chest injuries following a shooting near Priddy. There was no mention of me at all.

I immediately phoned the RUH to find out how he was, but the woman I spoke to on the main switchboard told me no-one called Jack Dale had been admitted. I didn't know his new name, so I hung up then rang back saying I was press, following up the shooting on the Mendips earlier; I wanted a to do a condition check on the victim. I was transferred to another woman who told me she couldn't comment as the patient had already been transferred to another hospital. She wouldn't say which one. Nor would she tell me his name.

As the rain continued to pour and the murky twilight outside the patio doors turned into inky blackness, I couldn't shake off a panicky feeling that I was never going to see Jack again; that he had vanished from my life as mysteriously as he'd entered it. And without Jack I would never know the whole story. Almost everyone who knew the truth now was dead: Kelly-Anne Davis was dead, Patrick Underhill was dead, Ray Butcher was dead and, in a final sordid twist, Nick Padovani was also dead.

The story about Padovani's death hadn't been on the news. Sergeant Harper had told me at the police station. He'd wanted to know what I knew about it, which was nothing. It seemed I'd been right about Padovani fleeing to Bristol airport. He had booked a seat on an Air Malta flight that afternoon. But instead of the taxi taking him to the airport it had apparently dropped him in the countryside up near Priddy, coincidentally not more than a couple of miles from where I'd been ambushed by Butcher. A man walking his dog had found the body. Padovani had hung himself from a tree with his Gucci belt. He hadn't left a suicide note.

It was awful to admit, but I felt nothing about Padovani's death except frustration that he was no longer alive to confirm the truth about Kelly-Anne's murder. Under tough police interrogation I was absolutely sure Padovani would have cracked and confessed everything. One of the many questions I'd have liked to ask him was why he'd stuck around in Sands End after the murder. Butcher had paid Padovani a lot of money for Monica's execution. Padovani could have used that money to go anywhere, do anything. He could have bought a really decent club abroad – perhaps back in his native Malta – lived out the rest of his life in luxury under sunny skies. Instead, he'd stayed in Sands End, ploughed the blood money into making Glitz profitable again then reinvested his fortune in a tacky amusement arcade and a mediocre Italian restaurant. There was a pettiness about what he'd done with the money. Or perhaps, deep down, he'd known he was always destined to be a small fish in an even smaller pond.

But it also made me wonder if killing her hadn't just been about the money; that maybe Monica Fullegar had got under Nick Padovani's skin in the same way she'd got under Ray Butcher's skin, and Patrick Underhill's skin, and when she'd announced she would be taking her share of the bounty and leaving Sands End, maybe Padovani hadn't been able to stand the thought of her with anyone else either. I wondered if she'd got under Jack's skin too, not to begin with, but perhaps right at the end of the honey-trap operation.

With a sigh I pulled my laptop onto my legs and continued to write the story that would appear in the next day's *Gazette*. Of course I was writing it. It was my story. Always had been.

I added the quote given to me by the police press office and gave the intro a quick re-read:

The murder of Kelly-Anne Davis in Sands End thirteen years ago will be reinvestigated, police have confirmed...

Then I attached the story to an email to Martin and hit send.

*

The next morning, I sat in the sunshine at my patio table listening to the sound of Shaun making toast in my kitchen. He'd arrived home after I'd gone to bed the previous night. The noise of his footsteps pounding across my ceiling had briefly – but only briefly – woken me. To my secret joy, he'd come back from London alone. Linzi had flown back to Australia with her parents. Her mother hadn't had a heart attack, Shaun told me. It had been a panic attack. The wedding was on hold. He wouldn't go into any more detail.

In return, I'd told him about my near-death experience, playing it down as much as I could, and in a funny sort of way the less I made of it, the more the fear inside me retreated. And anyway, I was safe now. Everyone who had apparently wanted to hurt me was dead.

Shaun appeared on the patio stuffing toast into his mouth, wearing grotty surf shorts, his Dunlop Volleys and a baggy orange t-shirt with a hole under one armpit. In Linzi's absence he had immediately reverted to his old ways, and that also included letting himself into my flat whenever he felt like it.

A tiny pale blue butterfly fluttered down and sunned itself on the rim of my mug. I gently shooed it away. Henry ambled out into the garden and gave a long, contented stretch in the sunshine. I picked up my phone and re-read the curt email Martin had sent me earlier in response to the story I'd filed the previous night. *Good work*, was all it said, which in Martin-speak was the equivalent of high-praise and gushing congratulations.

I should have felt relief mixed with a certain amount of pride. Because of me, Kelly-Anne's murder was being reinvestigated. Patrick Underhill's name would be cleared. I was back in the *Gazette*'s good books. I'd proved to Martin and the Chief I still had what it took to chase down a decent news story. But I didn't feel any of that. I felt edgy and restless. Something had been bothering me ever since I'd got home the previous evening. But it wasn't something I could put into words and certainly not something I could discuss with Shaun. And anyway, I could be wrong. With all my heart, I hoped I was wrong.

Shaun took a swig of his coffee. "I've got a surprise for you later. Something I think will cheer you right up after your recent ordeals."

I wondered if he was including his engagement to Linzi in that list. "Oh? What?"

Shaun tapped a finger against his nose. "Well, if I tell you then it won't be a surprise, will it? Fancy another coffee?"

"Yes please."

He stood, walked into my sitting room then paused. I saw him reach into the pocket of his shorts and pull out his phone. His fingers tapped at the screen and a second later my phone pinged to say I'd received a text message. No Caller ID. The message said: *Be at the Bay View Hotel tonight at 6pm.*

I had to stop myself from laughing out loud. Oh Shaun. You are so transparent. I grabbed my phone and replied: *Gosh. How mysterious. I'll be the one wearing a yellow gerbera in my top hat.*

As I pressed send, I watched Shaun. A second or two later his phone pinged and I heard him chuckle.

So, that was my surprise. Drinks – or perhaps even a meal – at the Bay View Hotel. Bless him. As Shaun continued to walk towards my kitchen, I felt a hot rush of affection for the man. He might be as subtle as a flying brick, but his heart was in the right place. Once again I felt a strange twinge in the heart region. Ever since Linzi's comment about Shaun being a horny lurve stallion, I'd been experiencing disconcerting flashes of Shaun ripping off his t-shirt. The only problem was, as soon as he'd tugged said t-shirt over his head, he always turned into Jack. I slapped both thoughts firmly away. Jack was married – yes that still hurt – and Shaun would soon be married. Just be grateful you'll still have Shaun as a friend and a neighbour, I told myself. But even so, I knew Shaun and I were on borrowed time. Soon, Linzi would come back here and things would never be the same again. Maybe it was time for me to move on too. Any day now I'd hopefully get an email inviting me to an interview for that PR job in Lincoln.

Shaun brought out my coffee and took his back up to his flat. Giving a heavy sigh I pulled my laptop towards me. I couldn't put it off any longer; I needed to attempt the ending to *Sweet Little Lies*. Taking a swig of coffee, I forced myself back into the world of Petronella and Yuri.

Petronella grasped Yuri's hand across the hospital bed as she fought back her tears. "I'm so glad you're alive," she sobbed. "You should never have gone up in that experimental jet. Your days as a test pilot are behind you now."

Yuri squeezed her hand. His pale eyes found hers. "I needed to prove to you that I still had the right stuff."

Petronella wiped at the tears rolling down her cheeks. "You don't have to prove anything to me, Yuri. You know I love you. That I'll always love you."

Yuri turned his head away. His hand jabbed up to the bandages covering his face. "Even now?" he asked in a bitter voice. "Now that I'm scarred and disfigured forever?"

Petronella's tears were flowing faster now. They tasted salty on her lips. "Oh Yuri. I'll love you however you look. You're beautiful on the inside. That's what's important."

Yuri nodded. He smiled. "Ah... Sweet little lies." He shook his head as laughter rippled through him. His smile became a grin as wide as the Moskva River. "You keep telling me those sweet little lies."

299

Through her tears, Petronella found herself laughing too. "I will Yuri. I will. Forever, and forever and forever."

At midday I stopped reading through the finished manuscript and walked down the hill to the newsagent to buy a copy of the *Gazette*. My report was the front page lead. I felt a fizz of pride. But my good humour was short-lived because underneath the headline, all it said was:

EXCLUSIVE

Where the hell was my name?

"Bloody Martin, I breathed." My fingers shook as I dialled his number. It rang twice then he answered with a curt, "Katy."

I cut straight to the chase. "Martin, where's my effing by-line?"

I heard him chuckle. "But Katy, I thought you didn't want your by-line going anywhere near any Patrick Underhill stories? That's what you told me."

I felt colour shoot up to my face. "But not this story, Martin. Not this one."

"Oops," Martin said.

My voice rose with my fury, "Oops? Is that all you've got to say?"

Martin made a sound as if he was puffing out his cheeks. "What do you want me to say? We'll have the paper reprinted just to satisfy your ego? Look, the Chief knows it was your story and that's what's important. Isn't it?"

Even though Martin couldn't see me I shook my head. "No, it's more than that. Much more. It's–"

"Listen I've got another call coming through."

"Martin–" But he'd already gone.

"Jerk," I muttered. "Double-crossing, double-dealing… bald-headed, total jerk…."

300

At a quarter to six I was sitting at my patio table, sipping a coffee, when I heard the rhythmic tick of a diesel engine in the car park. I hadn't gone totally over-the-top with my appearance, but I had made an effort partly because the Bay View Hotel was posh but mostly because this was Shaun's treat and I wanted to show him I appreciated it. I wore a short denim shirt-dress and high gold stilettos. I'd let my hair dry naturally then coaxed it into waves with hot tongs. My make-up was more glittery than usual.

I walked over to the fence and peered through the crack in the wood just in time to see Shaun bound out through the lobby door towards a taxi. Crumbs, he was actually going to be early. He looked very smart. I squinted closer. Was he wearing a suit? Yes, he was. Goodness.

I glanced at my watch. My taxi should arrive soon too. Silly really to fork out for two fares when we could easily have gone together, but never mind. If that's what it took to maintain Shaun's rather ham-fisted subterfuge for my surprise night out at the Bay View Hotel, then so be it. I rehearsed the look of fake astonishment I'd have ready on my face when I saw him. *"It was you who sent that text? Gosh. How clever! I had no idea! What a lovely surprise!"* Shaun would beam with pleasure that his plan had worked.

As I sat back down, wondering how many days we'd have left before Linzi returned, my phone rang. I didn't recognise the number. "Hello?"

"Katy. It's Linzi," said an icy voice. "Put Shaun on please. I'm guessing he's with you. As usual."

Shaun must have given her my number so we could liaise about the rescheduled wedding. I picked up my mug and took a sip of coffee. "You've just missed him I'm afraid. So, how's your mum–"

She cut me off, "Katy, why isn't Shaun answering his mobile? It just rings and rings and doesn't even go to voicemail."

I frowned. "No idea. Are you still calling his new phone number? Because I think his usual number should have been transferred by now."

For several heartbeats there was silence then Linzi said, "What new phone number?"

I felt a strange, prickly alertness. I sat up in my chair and put down my mug. I did a quick calculation and worked out it was about three-thirty in the morning her time. She couldn't have been back in Australia very long. "Linzi, are you okay?"

"Of course I'm okay. Why shouldn't I be okay?" Her voice had a brittle, panicky edge. "Anyway, I need to speak to Shaun right away because we've had the offer accepted on the house we're buying over here."

My lips suddenly felt numb. "House?"

There was another long pause from her end. "Shaun's told you of course? That we're moving back to Melbourne?"

I felt my stomach clench. I suppose I'd always known, deep down, that despite Linzi's assurances about living wherever Shaun wanted to live, a move back to Australia wouldn't be off the cards. I just hadn't expected it to be so soon. I couldn't imagine Shaun not living upstairs, not hearing his huge feet as they pounded across my ceiling, not having him raid my breadbin and steal my coffee whenever he felt like it, or popping down for an inane chat when he was bored.

"So is this move imminent?" I asked, as casually as I dared.

"Very imminent."

There was another awkward pause, or maybe just a delay on the line then Linzi snapped, "Katy, I need to ask you something and I would appreciate a totally honest answer. Okay?"

"Okay." I took a gulp of coffee.

"Have you and Shaun ever had sex?"

I spat the coffee across the table. "No! Of course not! Absolutely not."

Linzi's voice was sceptical, "Never? Not even a rebound-shag when he was heartbroken over me?"

I shook my head. "No! I've never even thought about Shaun in that... in that sort of way." An image of a t-shirt being tugged over a man's head flashed into my mind and I felt a guilty blush spread up my neck. "Never," I repeated.

"Well, I don't know why I was expecting you to tell me the truth."

"Now hang on a minute Linzi–" I began, but once again she interrupted me.

"Has Shaun ever come on to you? Tried to kiss you? Told you he thinks he loves you?"

I didn't really know how to respond and I suppose Linzi took my pause as some kind of admission because she yelled, "I knew it. I knew it. Bastard."

I was actually a little alarmed by the venom in her voice.

"Linzi, calm down. I categorically deny that allegation," I said, sounding like some foolish politician lying to save his career. But I got the feeling Linzi wasn't even listening.

"You see he talks about you all the time. Katy this, Katy that." She put on a whiny voice, "But what about Katy if I go back to Melbourne? He even talks about you in his sleep. And, my God, I don't know how I coped with all his pious hand-wringing when you claimed someone had tried to blow you up with a bomb–"

My anger ignited. "Now look here, Linzi, if it hadn't been for Jack–"

"Oh yes. Jack," she sneered. "Your fantasy man. If he even really exists." She paused as if she was trying to control her temper because when she next spoke, her voice was back to being hard and cold. "So, Shaun definitely isn't with you?"

I was just about to say he'd already left for our dinner date then decided that under the circumstances telling her Shaun and I were going out together for the evening wasn't the best tactic.

"No. He isn't. Look Linzi, I'll get him to call you. Okay?"

"Oh how terribly kind," she spat. "Well, do have a lovely time at the squash club tonight."

I frowned. "Squash club?"

"The squash club awards ceremony dinner. We were going to go together, our first engagement as man and wife. After I had to fly home, he told me he wasn't going to go, that he'd just have a quiet night in, but I knew he was really planning to take you." Linzi sounded as if she was on the brink of tears.

A diesel engine rumbled in the car park. I stood and peered through the gap in the fence. It looked like the same taxi that had just taken Shaun to the Bay View Hotel. "Listen Linzi, I know you're upset, but I have to go–"

"Oh yes, run along to meet my fiancé. But let me tell you this. Soon he'll be back here with me where he belongs. And tell him to call me. Right now." Then she hung up.

For several seconds I stared at my phone. My hands tingled as if I had pins and needles. What a complete bitch.

But I couldn't ignore a strange sensation that was curling up from the pit of my stomach. I tried to analyse it; nail it down, and after a while decided it was fear. Why had Shaun lied to Linzi about where he was going tonight? Why hadn't he told her the truth about my cheer-up surprise? I mean, going out for a drink with a mate was an innocent-enough thing to be doing. Wasn't it?

But Shaun, all dressed up, wearing in a suit for the first time since I'd known him? Lying to his fiancée? Ignoring her phone calls? Not even telling her about his new phone? And he'd never explained why he hadn't flown back to Australia with Linzi and her parents after her mum had been discharged from hospital.

All of a sudden, I wasn't looking forward to tonight. I caught a glimpse of my reflection in the patio door and my heart sank. What had seemed a perfectly suitable outfit half-an-hour ago, now seemed way too flirty. It looked like the sort of thing I'd wear on a date. I tried to think if I'd ever worn a dress when I'd been on a night out with Shaun and decided I never had. Right, time for a very quick change.

I ran into the bedroom, pulled the shirt-dress over my head, kicked off the gold stilettos and pulled on a pair of denim leggings and a stripy red t-shirt. I stuffed my feet into a pair of flip-flops, rubbed off most of the glittery eye make-up and tied my hair back in a quick French plait. I surveyed my appearance in the mirror. Okay, my outfit was now more quick trip to B&Q than dinner/drinks at the Bay View Hotel but at least it gave out the right message: you are engaged to Linzi and we are just good mates. Then I sent a quick text to Shaun: *Phone Linzi. Now.*

In the car park, the taxi gave an impatient toot.

*

It was only a five-minute ride to the Bay View Hotel. As I paid the taxi driver and got out, I mulled over the conversation I'd had with Linzi. I couldn't believe how horrible she'd sounded on the phone. I began to realise how miserable she must have made Shaun before they broke up the first time. I really hoped it wasn't going to happen all over again because it would totally destroy him.

I chewed my lips. Or would it? Now I thought about it, I realised he'd hardly mentioned her since coming back from London. Was he getting fed up with her bossiness? Was she pressuring him into a move back to Australia when he'd rather stay here? Did Shaun have an ulterior motive for wanting to meet tonight, that he was going to tell me he was about to call time on his relationship with Linzi? And if so, where did I fit into all that?

I pushed open the revolving door that led into the Bay View's reception with its pale wood floor, white wicker armchairs and huge leafy palms in terracotta pots, and I had to pause and catch my breath because suddenly my chest felt tight and a strange wave of dizziness rippled through me. It was as if time had re-wound and it was the evening I'd first met Jack all over again.

Come on Katy, get a grip, I told myself. It's just a few innocent drinks with Shaun. Maybe a meal as well. That's all. Just like old times. Two mates having a laugh. But my mind was racing as I speculated how the evening would end.

"Listen Katy. I think I've made a huge mistake about Linzi and there's something I need to say to you…"

And this time, would I kiss him back?

I wiped my damp palms against my t-shirt, strode down the narrow corridor to the hotel bar then hesitated outside the frosted glass door. Actually, I could turn around and go home. I could always tell Shaun I hadn't realised the text had been from him; that I'd thought it was a wrong number or someone messing around.

But then I thought of him sitting on a bar stool wearing his best suit, nervously shovelling peanuts in his mouth. Then in an hour, maybe more, the barman telling him with world-weary confidence, "Sorry mate, but I reckon she's stood you up."

And anyway, I couldn't avoid Shaun forever. Maybe we did need to talk; to clear the air, find out where we stood.

"Right. Okay. Let's get it over with," I muttered. I took a deep breath and pushed open the door to the bar. I looked around at the olive green walls, the framed pictures of boxing hares and the burnt-orange armchairs, the velvet curtains drawn back to let in the evening sunshine. My throat tightened as too many recent memories rushed into my mind. But I could already feel the anti-climax. The room was empty apart from the same skinny barman polishing glasses behind the bar.

He plastered a big smile of welcome onto his face. "Hello! What can I get you on this lovely evening?"

My eyes gave the empty room another pointless sweep and I glanced at my watch. It was bang on six o'clock. Maybe Shaun had nipped to the loo.

"I think I'm meeting someone," I said, instantly realising how silly that sounded.

"Might I suggest the sun terrace?" the barman said, placing a fresh bowl of peanuts on the bar. He nodded towards the French doors. "There's a splendid view across the bay."

My mouth was dry. Suddenly I wanted a glass of wine more than anything in the world. A big glass. Very big. Giant.

The barman must have read my mind. "I think you'll find your companion has a drink waiting for you." He gave me a knowing wink.

I stared at the French doors, felt a trickle of perspiration run down my ribs.

"Right." I pulled myself up straight, eyes wide, forcing a big smile of surprise on to my face. "*How lovely! It was you who sent that text! Wow, clever old you with the No Caller ID trick!*" Big friendly smile. We are just good friends. "*So, Linzi tells me you're moving back to Australia? How exciting! I am so pleased for you!*"

I sneaked a look through the French doors. I saw an ice bucket propped on a stand next to a table. A white linen napkin was draped over the neck of a bottle. My heart sank to my knees. A suit *and* some kind of fancy wine...

And in that split second I felt a hot rush of panic. Okay, Linzi was undoubtedly bitch of the world. She wouldn't make Shaun happy in a million years and she certainly didn't deserve someone as nice as him. But did that mean I was the alternative? Did I even want to be the alternative?

And yet I also knew that if I turned Shaun down, his hurt would be more than I could bear. What on earth was I going to do?

CHAPTER TWENTY-ONE

I shoved my sunglasses onto my face, pushed open the French doors and strode out into the evening sunshine.

There was only one person on the terrace. He sat with his back to the hotel, his fingers drumming gently on the white metal tabletop. I hadn't taken more than two steps towards him when he stood and turned to face me. And as usual, my breath caught in my chest and my legs turned to jelly. He wore a grey t-shirt over faded denim jeans. The t-shirt emphasised his broad shoulders and flat stomach. His bare arms looked muscular without being freakish. One of them rested in a sling.

"Hello Katy. Glad you could come."

For several seconds I thought I was hallucinating. I actually looked around the terrace, expecting to see Shaun wave and grin from another table. But the terrace was empty apart from Jack and me.

He frowned. "Your text promised a top hat and some kind of flower?"

I felt my cheeks flush. "Actually, I thought I was replying to someone else." *As usual.*

Jack smiled his heart-stopping smile. There were two wine glasses on the tabletop. He reached into the ice bucket and removed the bottle.

"Cloudy Bay Sauvignon." He said, pouring me a glass. "I hope that's okay."

"Lovely," I managed as he handed it to me. The tips of our fingers touched. Electricity seemed to fizz through me. He indicated the seat opposite. "Please."

I sat. My handbag was clutched hard against my chest. I dumped it on the ground next to my chair and gazed across the table. Why did he have to be so disconcertingly gorgeous?

Jack picked up his glass. "Your good health."

I grabbed my glass and took a gulp. "Yours too."

The wine was icy cold. The flavours danced across my tongue. Suddenly it was hard to know what to say. I ought to tell him something like, *"Thank you Jack, for saving my life again..."* But that line had more schmaltz than one of my romance novels. Instead, I found myself nodding towards his sling. "I thought it was your chest not your arm. How is it?"

He smiled and took another sip of wine. "Shoulder. Not bad. Stings a bit in the shower."

An image of Jack's naked, soap-sudded torso flashed into my mind. I blushed and looked away in case he could read my thoughts. "Um. Thank you for... you know... Um... being there when Butcher.... And for the bomb too..." My voice trailed off.

Jack shrugged. "No problem."

"So, why are you here?" I asked, a little more gruffly than I'd intended.

"We never got to have our chat in my car the night of your school reunion. I said I owed you a proper explanation. You had plenty of questions back then if I remember rightly. I'll do my best to answer them now."

"On the record?"

"Off the record. If you don't mind."

I wasn't surprised. I hadn't for one moment thought he might tell me something I could publish. I nodded. It was time to fill in some of the last empty blanks in the story.

A gentle breeze rippled off the sea, bringing with it the smell of Sands End in summer: fried food, candyfloss and donkey droppings. Beyond the hotel's car park and immaculate lawn, I could see people ambling along the promenade as another day of their holiday drew to an end.

I hadn't planned to be confrontational but suddenly I couldn't help it. Perhaps it was because he had wrong-footed me again. Perhaps because I had been so desperately worried about him after the shooting but he hadn't even got a message to me saying he was all right. Or perhaps it was the secret fear that had been rolling around my head ever since I'd got home from that dreadful afternoon up on the Mendip Hills.

I tilted my glass at him. "Okay. After Operation Sweetheart, the judge described you as morally bankrupt. That was a pretty damning statement. And Monica Fullegar was pretty damning about you too. It was you she wrote about in her diary, how after you'd tricked her into giving evidence, you'd as good as killed her. That's why Patrick was so sure you were the killer." I paused, "Do you regret your part in the operation?"

Jack's expression didn't change but his shoulders seemed to harden under his t-shirt. "Monica Fullegar was our best chance of getting Ray Butcher. But yes, I wish there could have been another way of doing it."

"You mean seducing her in the honey-trap?"

He nodded. "Yes."

"And I guess the honey-trap was doubly immoral, given you were a married man."

He shook his head. "I wasn't married."

I held his gaze. "But you are married now, aren't you?"

Jack returned my stare but said nothing.

I looked away. "You don't have to answer that. I know you're married because your wife came to pick you up from hospital after the bomb. The Porsche you were driving yesterday. That's hers, isn't it?"

Jack took a sip of wine. "Well, technically it's my car. But yes. Francesca drives it."

Brilliant. I just knew she'd be called something like Francesca.

I felt the ghost of his fingers stroking my face. "*We can talk all night if you like. Or we don't have to talk at all...*" My voice was icy, "So how does Francesca feel about you coming on to other women?" *Like you did with me in my kitchen that night.*

Jack frowned. "I'm sure it doesn't bother her at all."

My anger rose. "Why? Because it doesn't mean anything? Just like it didn't mean anything when you seduced Monica Fullegar? Just a means to an end?"

I gulped at my wine. I wanted to ask, *If Shaun hadn't interrupted us with the frying pan, and we'd ended up in bed, would that have meant anything? Or would that too just have been a means to an end? A way to win my trust, to seduce me into telling you what you thought I knew?*

But I didn't say any of that. Instead, I looked away and made another swift attack on my drink. Why did his deception hurt so much? I hardly knew the man. As I looked over at him, so perfect and so gorgeous, the breeze ruffling his hair, his t-shirt accentuating every muscle in his chest, I felt an absolute fool. How could I ever have seriously thought he'd been attracted to me? I saw myself as he was seeing me now: scruffy leggings, a shapeless t-shirt with a frayed hem, flip-flops showing the chipped orange nail varnish on my toes. Good grief... Why had I changed my clothes? Half an hour ago, I'd actually looked reasonably decent. Tears pricked my eyes. Furious with myself, I blinked them away. Every time I'd seen Jack, I'd ended up crying and it wasn't going to happen this time.

"Francesca is not my wife," Jack said at last.

"But you sleep with her, don't you?" As soon as the words were out of my mouth, I regretted them. I sounded exactly like jealous, possessive Linzi, and at least Linzi had some justification for feeling that way. I had none at all. Jack hadn't promised me anything. But he had been sly and he had not been honest with me, and that hurt.

I waved a hand at him. "Forget it. I don't want to know."

Jack leaned across the table, his grey eyes serious. "Katy, this isn't really about whether or not I'm married. Whether or not I misled you. It's about truth and trust. You realise now you should have trusted Patrick – believed he was telling you the truth, helped him to clear his name."

My cheeks grew warm then hot.

"You're conveniently forgetting something vital," I snapped. "Patrick didn't actually want to clear his name. The only reason he wanted me to find you, was so he could kill you, because he thought you were Kelly-Anne's killer."

Jack's voice was low, barely above a murmur, "But Patrick *was* innocent of the murder."

A hollow pit opened up in my stomach. Sharp tears pricked my eyes. My vision misted.

"You… you think I should have helped him thirteen years ago. Don't you?" My voice sounded brittle with anger. "You think I should have taken that message to her up at the club. You're saying all this *was* my fault–"

Jack's eyes grew hard. "No, I'm not saying any of that." He sat back in his chair. "Look, Katy, you can't re-write the past. All you can to do is try to put things right in the future, which is what you've done by figuring out who was the real killer."

I emptied my glass in two quick gulps. "And that's what you've done is it? Put things right by killing Ray Butcher?"

Jack shrugged. "He was about to put a bullet in each of our heads. Maybe you think I should have let him?"

I felt my face flush again. "No, of course not. But, I think this was personal for you too. The police – namely you – totally stitched up Monica Fullegar. She had absolutely no choice about grassing on Butcher. You knew that would be a death sentence for her. Police protection was no protection, given the number of serving officers in Butcher's back pocket. It was only a matter of time before one of them snitched on her. In the end, she felt so vulnerable, she fled police protection and disappeared. Ended up here in Sands End, penniless and terrified. I think you could have done more to keep Monica Fullegar safe, that's why this was personal for you too. Butcher was responsible for her murder. Butcher got away with that murder. And now he's dead." I saw Butcher walking through the flood, raising the rifle, heard my voice scream, *Jack! Oh God. Jack!*

Jack gave a heavy sigh, "Butcher was behind dozens of murders. Is the world a better place without him? Yes. I think so." He sipped his drink.

The breeze changed direction and I caught a whiff of his amazing aftershave. A random image of him, bare-chested, damp-haired, standing in front of a bathroom mirror, splashing his face with water popped into my mind. I sat back in my chair and waited for the image to go away. It seemed to take a long time. "Okay. You knew, right from the time of the murder, that Kelly-Anne was Monica."

Jack leant across the table and poured me another glass. He nodded, "I went to my boss and told him it was likely Butcher had been behind the murder. My boss didn't want to know. He said, the boyfriend's confessed, what's your problem."

"Did you believe Patrick had killed her?"

"No."

"Why not?"

"It was too neat."

"So why did your boss warn you off?"

"Because he was in Butcher's pocket."

"So why didn't you do something? Go over your boss's head? Tell someone higher up that your boss was corrupt and trying to protect Ray Butcher?"

Jack's gaze drifted towards the sea. His eyes became hard. He was even more good looking when he was angry. And then I remembered the calm – precise – way he'd shot Ray Butcher twice in the forehead. Despite the warm evening sunshine, I shivered.

"Because it wasn't as simple as that," Jack said at last.

I felt my throat tighten. "So you did nothing. The transfer from SO10 to SO1, was that a reward for keeping your mouth shut?"

He shook his head. "It was to get me out of the way. To stop me going after Butcher."

"But actually you didn't stop. Not right away. That's why someone in the police deliberately released your real name. It was a warning: back off. So you did."

I took a quick swig of my drink. "Do you think now, looking back, you should have pushed harder to get someone in the Met to look into Kelly-Anne's murder?"

For what felt like a long time, Jack's eyes continued to fix on the horizon then he nodded. "Of course I do."

I gave him a moment then I said, "Okay, so it's thirteen years later. I leave you a message saying I want to talk to you about the Kelly-Anne Davis murder. You think a journalist has finally figured out the truth and is writing a story saying Kelly-Anne was Monica, and that Ray Butcher ordered her murder. You already know all that. But what you don't know is who actually killed her and you think I do. You thought Patrick had told me who it was. Correct?"

"Correct."

I waited for him to elaborate but he didn't. So I said, "But when we met, it must have been obvious that I didn't know anything. I told you that I didn't even believe Patrick was telling the truth about being innocent."

I took a deep breath, steeling myself to ask one of the questions that had been bothering me since the previous night. "So, why did you stick around?"

For while I didn't think he was going to answer, then he said, "Because I didn't believe you. I thought you were hiding something."

We both reached for our drinks at the same time, took a sip in unison.

I said, "I wasn't hiding anything. But you were. You knew Ray Butcher would silence anyone who could prove his part in the murder."

A lump the size of a golf ball seemed lodged in my throat. "You thought Ray Butcher was going to try to kill me at my school reunion. That's why you kept asking me if there was anyone there I didn't recognise. That's why you went back inside the club. You were looking for Butcher. Am I right?"

I couldn't bring myself to look at Jack but I heard him exhale then he said, "Yes."

Again I waited for him to continue, but again he didn't.

"And the reason you kept quiet about that was because if I knew Butcher might want me dead, I'd drop the story and go straight to the police. You thought I'd tell the police who had really murdered Kelly-Anne and the police would arrest him. And you didn't want her killer arrested. Did you? Why was that?"

He didn't respond.

"You used me."

"Look Katy–"

My anger flashed. "You used me and you put my life in danger. The joke of it is, I didn't have the faintest idea who really killed her until yesterday. And even then I didn't know for sure it was Padovani until I'd been to his restaurant and stirred things up."

Jack's brow creased in what looked like frustration. "What were you thinking, going to confront Padovani? If you thought you'd figured out he was the murderer, why didn't you just call me?"

"Because I didn't have your mobile phone number. It was in my phone, and Patrick stole my phone, remember? And now the police have it, and when I called your office number you had changed it. Again. And I definitely wouldn't have confronted Nick Padovani if I'd known it would put me on Ray Butcher's kill list."

I noticed my hands were shaking. "By not telling me about Butcher you put my life in danger."

Jack leaned back in his seat, looked away. "Okay, maybe I should have levelled with you about that but–"

I cut him off. "I expect you're going to say something trite now like, but you can't make an omelette without breaking some eggs."

His eyes returned to mine. "For what it's worth, I was going to say, but I didn't and I'm sorry. Truly, I'm sorry."

I picked up my glass and rotated the stem, making the sunlight dance and glitter through the wine. "So, all this has been about you wanting to avenge Monica's murder. Wanting to find her real killer. You've gone to a lot of trouble with this, Jack. You've put your life on the line too. A few inches further down and Ray Butcher's rifle shot would have killed you."

I rotated my wine glass back the other way. "I think this was about more than you feeling guilty for Monica's murder. I think during the honey-pot sting she got under your skin. I think she ended up meaning something to you. Meaning quite a lot to you–"

The sound of a high-performance engine made me look down into the car park. A black Porsche pulled up in a shower of gravel.

"Looks like your lift home has arrived," I said bitchily. "Guess you'll be relying on your girlfriend a lot now until your shoulder heals."

I necked the rest of my drink, picked up my handbag and flashed Jack an insincere smile, "Well, you got what you wanted. You know who really killed Monica. Butcher's dead and Nick Padovani's killed himself. 'Justice' has been done." My fingers made sarcastic inverted commas in the air. "Oh, and I believe this is yours."

I reached inside my handbag and took out the little white cube I'd found inside my bag the night of the school reunion party. I'd assumed it was something techy belonging to Shaun but I now knew it was a GPS tracking device. Jack had dropped it into my handbag, perhaps that very first evening at the Bay View Hotel, or maybe when he'd left my flat later that same night after the near-miss in my kitchen. Either way that was how he'd magically turned up each time my life had been in danger, although that last

318

time, when Butcher had been about to shoot me dead, he'd only just arrived in time. Why was that?

I placed the cube on the table.

Up in the turquoise sky, white gulls keened and drifted on the evening air. The wind changed direction and a shiver ran across my shoulders. It was time to ask the question that had been really bothering me since the previous night.

"There is one last thing I can't figure out. As I said just now, you didn't tell me about Ray Butcher because you thought I'd drop the story, tell the police everything, and the real killer would be arrested, and you didn't want him arrested." I paused. "Why didn't you want the police to arrest him, Jack?"

He didn't reply.

"Was it because you wanted to bring him in yourself?"

Still he said nothing.

"Or was there another reason?" I shifted forward in my chair.

"Jack, was Nick Padovani's death really suicide, or did someone make it look like suicide? You see, when I watched Padovani leave Mario's in the taxi, I could have sworn there was someone in the back with him."

I held Jack's gaze and for the first time ever I didn't look away. We sat there, eyes locked, while my chest fizzed like an Alka-Seltzer in water.

He leaned across the table until our heads were just inches apart. His voice was so quiet his words seemed to be inside my head, "Are you worried that was me?"

I sprang back as heat rushed up to my face.

Down in the car park the Porsche revved its engine. Jack picked up his glass and swallowed the rest of his drink. With his good hand, he reached into the pocket of his jeans and took out a business card. He handed it across the table. "Next time you feel like stirring things up, give me a call first."

There was no name on the card, just a mobile phone number. I shook my head. "Trust me, there definitely isn't going to be a next time."

The sun was setting now. It had slipped behind a band of indigo clouds that were sitting on the horizon like a spit of land. Summer was coming to an end. In a couple of weeks, the crowds would disappear and the cafés and gift shops on the prom would close for another season. For countless holidaymakers, Sands End would just be a memory of sunburnt noses and sandy beach towels. But I probably wouldn't forget this summer in a hurry.

Jack stood and smiled. His eyes seemed darker. Despite everything, those pesky butterflies were back in my stomach.

"By the way," he said, "the answer is, yes. It would have meant something."

I frowned at him. "Sorry?"

"The question you wanted to ask me earlier, about the night I came to your flat."

I felt my face flush scarlet.

"And no, I don't sleep with Francesca. She's my business partner."

He extended his hand across the table. His grip was firm and his skin was warm. "Until the next time, Katy."

*

My taxi picked me up outside the hotel's pillared entrance. As I slid into the back seat, the driver asked, "Where to, love?"

I started to say, "Bluebell Meadow–" then stopped and shook my head. "Actually, can you drop me at the Esso Garage on the seafront, please?"

The forecourt was busy with holidaymakers filling up before they began their long journeys home. From a bucket outside the kiosk, I grabbed a soggy bunch of yellow chrysanthemums wrapped in cellophane. When I handed them to the cashier she asked in a suspicious voice, "Petrol?"

I shook my head. "Just the flowers. Thanks."

After I'd paid, I walked along the seafront and pushed open the kissing gate that led into the graveyard of St Cuthbert's Church.

The churchyard was bathed in yellow evening sunlight. Long shadows from the headstones stretched across the sun-bleached grass. Crows were caw-cawing loudly in the branches of a yew tree. As I approached they flapped into awkward flight and wheeled away.

After the birds had gone a heavy peace settled. The breeze swished through the longer grass the mower had missed and rustled through the spiky leaves of the yew. The sun was warm against my shoulders. A gull drifted over, silent as a ghost, the underside of its wings turned crimson by the setting sun, its yellow eyes fixed on me as if I was intruding. Rain clouds were coming in from the sea, a solid, muddy slab of grey streaked with gold.

I stood on the gravelled path, recreating the scene of her funeral from the photograph in the *Gazette*, the white-frocked vicar leading the small rag-tag procession of unwilling mourners through the rain. Among them the man who had murdered her. I took a deep breath, pulling the salty sea air into my lungs. Then I set off across the grass.

I found her grave almost at once. The headstone was a simple oblong of grey marble speckled with black. I glanced at the gravestone next to hers. The inscription on that read: *The song has ended but the melody lingers on.* There were no such words of comfort over Kelly-Anne's grave. All it said was her name, her date of birth and the date of her death twenty-five years later.

Resting in the grass on her grave was an empty Pepsi can into which had been shoved a spindly bunch of pale pink carnations, their petals tatty and edged with brown, their dying heads bowed. My throat tightened with the effort of stopping my tears. Those were the flowers Patrick said he had left for her a few days ago. It felt like a lifetime.

I crouched down and placed my bunch of chrysanthemums on her grave. The breeze picked up and they tumbled off into the long grass. To stop the flowers blowing away, I decided to wedge them between the drinks can and the headstone. But as I picked up the can I noticed a small rolled-up piece of paper tucked in with the carnations. For a moment I hesitated, then curiosity got the better of me. I pulled it out. In blue biro, written in careful awkward capitals, as if it had been copied down letter by letter, were the words:

GOD GIVES US LOVE. SOMETHING TO LOVE HE LENDS US.
Rest In Peace Kelly-Anne
Love Patrick

I rocked back on my heels. Tears flooded my eyes. In my mind, I saw her, sitting in the police interview room as the officers played the surveillance tapes, her mounting horror as she'd listened to her voice incriminating Ray Butcher in Lucas Brennan's murder. I imagined her growing shame as she'd stared at the covert photographs showing her with Jack; the awful realisation that she'd been tricked by an undercover police officer, a man she thought

322

had loved her. Then I saw the police, calmly outlining what would happen if she refused to play ball. She'd been left with no option but to testify against Butcher. One way or another in that room, her death warrant had been sealed.

I imagined her after the trial, under police witness protection. She'd probably been stuck in some dingy, inner-city safe-house, a far cry from the opulence of her old life, hating Jack but despising herself for her vain stupidity in believing he had ever loved her. And during those long, empty days had come the creeping, insidious fear, knowing that each night could be her last; that it was only a matter of time before someone in the police sold her out and told Butcher where she was.

The answer must have seemed obvious. One spring day, she'd packed a suitcase, got on a train and hadn't got off again until she reached Sands End, a seaside backwater so dull and small she'd believed it would be the last place Butcher would ever find her. A few months later another man she might have loved had also betrayed her: Nick Padovani.

"Maybe you'd have been better off staying with Patrick," I mumbled, and the cruel irony of that thought made my tears fall even faster.

Behind me I heard a soft cough. I scrambled to my feet, wiping at my eyes with the back of my hand. An elderly white-frocked vicar was standing a few feet away.

"I'm so sorry," he said, a frown creasing his eyes. "I didn't mean to interrupt. I was simply curious to see who was visiting her grave. No one ever does, you see."

"No need to apologise," I managed at last. "I was just leaving."

The vicar's eyes rested on my flowers. "You knew her?"

The breeze ruffled the yellow petals. I started to shake my head then I paused and nodded. "Actually, yes. I did know her. In a way."

The vicar seemed to notice the Pepsi can for the first time. His mouth turned down in a scowl. "Oh dear. That's not very picturesque. I'll remove it."

I put up a hand. "No. I'll do it."

He smiled. "Thank you. God bless." He turned to walk back to the church.

I bent down and dug into the sandy soil at the base of the headstone then I carefully pushed the stems of Patrick's carnations and my chrysanthemums into it. I dug deeper then buried his rolled-up message.

A lump was wedged in my throat. "Patrick, I'm so sorry," I croaked. "I know this is thirteen years too late, but I'm truly so very sorry."

Standing again, I watched as the vicar continued to walk away between the graves, his feet kicking up dry white dust from the path that led through the churchyard. At the door to the church he paused and turned back towards me. Then he disappeared inside.

And suddenly, in my mind's eye, I saw the funeral photo again, the lone bystander watching the service from the path, a tall man with broad shoulders and fair hair.

Jack.

*

It was half-past three in the morning when something woke me up. I lay on my back, squinting into the darkness, trying to figure out what it had been. And then I heard it again: the sound of metal scraping against metal followed by a low rhythmic thudding. The hairs on the back of my neck seemed to stand on end. It sounded as if someone was trying to break in through my front door.

Ever since the van-man attack, I'd got into the habit of putting the door chain on at night. It had made me feel safer. But now I imagined a pair of bolt cutters poke through the gap and chomp easily through the metal links.

Heart pounding, I sprang out of bed, pulled on my dressing gown then tiptoed across the dark sitting room. The thudding from the hall became more urgent. Someone *was* trying to break in.

I ran silently into the kitchen and grabbed the first thing I could find, a frying pan from the draining board. Then I went back into the dark hall. From the lobby, I heard a man's angry voice muttering but I couldn't make out the words, followed by more dull thudding as the door strained against the chain.

Right. I'd had enough of people trying to scare me or hurt me. Holding the frying pan at shoulder height, I silently slid off the chain with my other hand.

The door flew open, a tall man stumbled into my hall and I swung the pan down as hard as I could.

The pan missed his head, bounced off the doorframe, flew out of my grip, and shot over my shoulder. The large figure slapped at the wall and after a few attempts, found the light switch.

I shouted, "For heaven's sake Shaun, you nearly gave me a heart attack!"

His eyes squinted against the brightness and tried to focus. "Something wrong with my key..." he slurred. Then a wonky grin spread across his face. "Ah. Good. You're still up."

"Presumably you've had a fun time at the squash club dinner?" I said in an icy voice.

He nodded and swayed back on his heels. He was carrying a yellow carrier bag in one hand and a half-empty bottle of wine in the other. He was no longer wearing his suit jacket. His white shirt was soaked with sweat and his face was bright red. "Bloody brilliant night. Bloody, bloody brilliant."

He leant towards me, "I won't come in. I know I don't seem it, but I'm a little bit drunk." He thrust the wine bottle at me. "Surprise!"

I peered at the label. "Ooh, leftover Wolf Blass chardonnay. How nice."

Shaun tried to focus. "Ah. Wrong hand." This time he handed me the carrier bag, grinning like a maniac. "Surprise!" he bellowed again.

I reached inside and pulled out a car stereo. "Oh! Wow!"

Shaun wagged a finger. "See, I couldn't get it until I saw Ron at the dinner tonight. He got a whole load of them for absolute peanuts from a kank-rupt lale... a tank-trupt pale..." He pointed proudly at the manufacturer's logo on the front. "That's a really decent bit of kit."

"Oh Shaun, you didn't have to... Thank you. That's really, really thoughtful." I paused. "Um. Did you get my message earlier? About calling Linzi? She's been trying to get hold of you."

He slapped a big hand up to his head. "That's what I meant to tell you earlier. The phone company messed up transferring my phone number. It's all gone crook so I'm still on the temporary number." He paused and scratched at his damp hair. It was standing up in tufts all over his head. "Yeah, probably should've told Linzi that too..."

I nodded. "She sounded a bit... upset."

Shaun blinked through his haze of alcohol then he seemed to understand what I was trying to say. "Aw. Don't worry about her. She just gets like that now and again."

He must have the patience of a saint to put up with that sort of behaviour on a regular basis. I thought I might as well get the bad news over with too. "So, I hear you're moving back to Australia soon?"

Shaun's eyes widened in alarm, "Am I?"

"Well, Linzi mentioned something about an offer on a house."

He scratched his chest and turned to stagger up the stairs. "Nah. Why would I be moving back to Oz? I'm happy right here." He jabbed a finger unsteadily at the floor. "Right here."

Hmm. Not for much longer if Linzi had anything to do with it. I stared up at him, imagining his future. I saw Linzi dressed as a circus ringmaster, cracking her whip, Shaun as the Cowardly Lion, flinching away. And something tugged at me.

"Um. Shaun? When Linzi rang earlier... Look, she said some things..." I took a deep breath. "Um. I just wondered if you're really sure about... What I mean is, if you're not really sure... Maybe we could ... Maybe we could..." My voice petered out.

Shaun scratched at his chest and looked baffled. "Maybe we could what?"

I stared up at his pink shiny face, the beads of perspiration on his forehead, his damp shirt clinging to his chest. I saw him in a smart suit and tie, me in a frothy wedding dress, as everyone we'd ever known beamed and raised their glasses.

And then I saw the same scene, except Jack was by my side.

I shook my head. "Nothing."

Shaun grinned and flapped a big hand back at me. "Ya daft wallaby. Well, better hit the sack before it hits me." His big feet trudged unsteadily up the stairs. "G'night, Katy."

I smiled, "Goodnight, Shaun."

Read on for a taste of the next Katy Bennett Mystery

THE LAUGHING MINOTAUR

By Alex Brook

In her next adventure Katy gets much more than she bargains for when she chases down a strange story about skulduggery between two rival Somerset carnival clubs.

Meanwhile she has plenty of other important things on her mind. When will her friend Shaun stop cooking everything on the barbecue? Why does her elderly neighbour pretend to play the maracas when she's riding her tandem? What is making her mother even more prickly than usual? Who spray-painted BITCH on her bedroom wall? Why does the Hunky Dory carnival club captain hate her so much? What – if anything – has all this got to do with her mysterious Great Uncle Frank? And – more importantly – where is Jack when you really need him?

CHAPTER ONE

It was early November and Sands End was cold. I pushed back my chair and stared through the kitchen window. The frosty front garden was bathed in golden morning sunlight and looked as if it should smell of wood smoke and damp leaves. Spider webs strung between the legs of the metal patio table sparkled as if decorated by Swarovski crystals. Tendrils of pink fog curled around the Torbay palm and the high wooden fence around the lawn seemed sprinkled with fairy dust.

I returned my attention to the white envelope lying on the breakfast bar and thought, decisions, I hate making decisions. Once again, it felt as if everything was changing in my life. I didn't like it. It unsettled me.

I re-read the letter I'd received in the morning post. During a low point back in August, I'd applied for a cushy public relations job in Lincolnshire. In September, they'd invited me up for an interview and I'd had a second interview a month later. This morning, the postman had delivered a letter offering me the job.

On the plus side, Proactive PR seemed like nice people and the salary was higher than the one I'd received when I was a news reporter on the *South West Gazette*. On the minus side, I'd be working in public relations, the client I would be promoting sold nappies and I'd need to relocate to Lincoln. Not that I had anything against Lincoln. It had seemed a pleasant enough place on my two visits there. My problem was that since the summer I'd been nursing a forlorn hope that the *Gazette*'s editor – universally known as the Chief – would offer me my old job back as a staff reporter, meaning I could afford to move back to the bright lights of Bristol again. That was what I really wanted. Sands End had its charms but it was awfully small – only four restaurants, three of which were Indian – no decent shops, and since Glitz had closed back in the summer, not even one nightclub. So far, there had been no offer of a job back on the staff. Martin said the reason was financial. I felt the Chief wasn't quite ready to forgive and forget Secret Santagate. All I had got out of the *Gazette* since the summer was freelance work reporting Sands End stories deemed too unimportant to warrant wasting a staffer's time. The Chief might offer me a job back on the staff tomorrow or he might never have me back. There was no way of telling and therefore no financial stability in my life. Unless I took the dull job in Lincoln.

I glanced back at the letter. The HR department wanted my acceptance by return. In Lincoln I'd make new friends, earn regular money, maybe even find the love of my life.

Trouble was, I was fairly sure I'd already found him.

I opened the other envelope that had come in the morning post. It was a letter from the letting agency that managed my rented flat, notifying me that the landlord wished to make some "landscaping improvements" to my front garden. It was probably just a fancy way of saying my fence needed painting. Workmen would be turning up within the next few days.

Shaun, my upstairs neighbour and best friend, had also left me a note, having let himself into my flat while I'd been in the shower. As usual he'd used the key I'd given him for emergencies only. I'd long since stopped having a go at him about it because it made not a jot of difference.

His note said he would be out all day meeting website clients so could I pay a couple of cheques in for him at the bank? The cheques were with the note. One was for just under two thousand pounds, the other was for almost three thousand pounds. I stared at the cheques thinking, maybe I should retrain as a website designer. It certainly seemed to pay a lot better than the gooey romance novels I wrote for Rose Petal Publishing, or the freelance reporting I'd been doing for the *Gazette*. But if I accepted the PR job, I'd be solvent again for the first time in almost a year.

With a heavy sigh, I pulled my laptop towards me and clicked on the email I'd received the previous evening from Martin Sadler, my old news editor on the *Gazette,* giving me the go ahead to proceed with my next thrilling assignment. The *South West Gazette* covered four counties, Somerset, Gloucestershire, Wiltshire and parts of Dorset. Sand End was a very small seaside town within its vast circulation area and Martin couldn't always spare a reporter to cover stories here. That was where I came in.

Since the summer none of the stories I'd touted to Martin had been particularly thrilling but the latest wasn't too dull: with less than a week to go before the start of the Somerset Illuminated Carnival season, Hunky Dory Carnival Club in Sands End had had its float vandalised. The carnival was taken very seriously in this neck of the woods. Each November, hundreds of illuminated floats joined processions in towns across the South West raising money for charity. Every few years there were accusations of skulduggery between rival clubs. Sometimes there were claims that ideas had been stolen. Sometimes there were reports of entries being sabotaged.

So far I'd failed to persuade the Hunky Dory club's captain, Grant Tozer, to allow the *Gazette* to take pictures of the damaged float and I wasn't hopeful he'd change his mind. Carnival clubs were famously secretive about their floats – or carts – as they were also known. Some floats from the big clubs like Hunky Dory cost more to build than a large family car. But I had finally persuaded Mr Tozer to give me an interview. It was in an hour's time at Hailstones Farm.

*

At half-past ten I was behind the wheel of my ancient, racing green MX-5. I put the farm's postcode into my Sat-Nav and wasn't surprised to see it was in the middle of nowhere about five miles east of Sands End. Carnival floats were almost always constructed on isolated farms.

To convey a professional appearance, I had dressed smartly for the interview. My usually flyaway shoulder-length fair hair was tied back in a neat ponytail. I wore a white shirt under a black lambswool cardigan, a short black knitted skirt, opaque black tights and black knee-high boots. Despite the autumn sunshine, it was bitterly cold so my black quilted coat was next to me on the passenger seat.

As I drove along Sand End's seafront, now pleasantly deserted because the holiday season was over, I reminded myself of the laughable email I'd received from Grant Tozer, when I'd firmed up our interview. You'd have thought I was dealing with MI5 not a carnival club. My instructions were to drive to the entrance of his farm then phone to say I was there. I must not proceed through the gate until given the go ahead. I couldn't reveal the name of the farm in the story. I wouldn't be able to see the float or view the damage, and pictures were still out of the question. It was a bit of a pointless exercise even going there. I could easily have done the interview over the phone. But Martin had agreed to pay mileage and I had to at least try to persuade Tozer into letting me take a photo because without one, the story would have far less impact.

I headed out of town and onto the Somerset Levels, a flat area of lonely moorland criss-crossed by a maze of bumpy narrow roads flanked with willow trees and water-filled ditches known locally as rhynes.

When I arrived at the entrance of Hailstones Farm, I dutifully phoned Mr Tozer and told him I was outside. He sent a frumpy looking woman on foot to meet me at the gate. She wore muddy Wellington boots, a long corduroy skirt and a scruffy waxed jacket. Her mousy-brown hair was cut into a shapeless bob and the fringe was so wonky it looked as if she cut it herself.

At first glance she looked in her fifties but when she opened the gate and came closer to talk to me through the car window, I realised she was only in her early thirties, probably just a year or two older than me. Her face was anxious and her plump cheeks were red from the biting cold.

"I'm Jenny Elwood, the club's publicity assistant," she said in a timid West Country accent. "Grant says you're to follow me in your car as I walk up the track to the farm."

I frowned. "Follow you? Don't you want a lift? It's freezing."

Jenny's eyes widened in alarm, "Oh no! Grant's instructions were very strict. I'm to walk back to the farm, you must follow in your car."

And so, to my amazement, Jenny Elwood set off on foot in the cold, while my car crawled along the muddy track after her. By the time I'd parked in the frosty farmyard and pulled on my coat, Jenny was standing to attention nearby, a large hardback notebook clasped to her chest as if she was afraid someone would steal it.

Almost as soon as I'd got out of the car, a tall, well-built man with fair hair and a floppy fringe strode out of the large redbrick farmhouse, scowling and smoking a cigarette. He took a final quick drag of his fag then ground the butt under the toe of his sturdy leather boots.

"Better later than never," he snapped in a very posh voice. "I am extremely busy this morning and do not appreciate being kept hanging around." He thrust out his hand. "Grant Tozer."

I thrust my hand back at his. "Katy Bennett. Actually, Mr Tozer, I'm exactly on time." I was never late for appointments. My mother had drilled punctuality into me since birth. If I was even so much as a minute late for a family lunch, it was seen as a hanging offence.

Grant Tozer glared at me and rocked back on his heels. Even though it was freezing cold in the farmyard, he was wearing a short-sleeved red t-shirt over his denim jeans. His upper arms bulged with the sort of freakish muscles that could only be acquired after hours of obsessive workouts at the gym and possibly a side order of steroids. He probably thought they looked sexy.

"I can spare you five minutes," he barked.

I took an instant dislike to Grant Tozer. His type of 'in your face' machismo did nothing for me. In the distance behind him, I could see a large barn, which probably housed the damaged carnival float. Lying on the path that led to the barn were two tan and black Dobermans, their long snouts resting on the ground. I hoped the dogs were on chains. As I watched, they lifted their heads and glared at me.

Jenny Elwood trotted over and shook my hand. In her timid voice she said, "I do hope you don't mind me being here for the interview, Katy. I thought, under the circumstances, you know... under the circumstances..."

"Under what circumstances?" I asked, pulling my notebook out of my handbag.

Grant Tozer glared at her. She flinched and her cheeks became even rosier. "Um... nothing..." she stammered.

Tozer jerked his head towards Jenny. "Miss Elwood's role is to make a record of our interview in order to ensure you do not put false words into my mouth. She will play no other part." He turned to her. "Jenny, commence your note taking."

What a pompous cock. I took the top off my biro.

Jenny fumbled a pen out of her coat pocket and opened her notebook.

I decided to cut straight to the chase. "Mr Tozer, the *Gazette* would really like to publish a photo of the damage that's been caused to the Hunky Dory float."

Grant shook his head. "Uh-uh. No way José." He stood, feet apart, hands on his hips, trying to block my view of the barn. "And anyway it's been repaired now. There's nothing to see."

I felt a flash of annoyance that he hadn't mentioned that on the phone. The float had been damaged late on Friday night. Today was Monday and irritatingly, the police had only put the crime on its press voice-bank message service the previous afternoon.

"How about a photo that just shows the repaired area, not the whole float?" I asked without much hope.

Grant sneered. "Not a chance. I know what you press people are like. Give you an inch and you'll take a mile. Next thing I know, pictures of our float will be splashed all over the Internet."

I only just managed to stop myself from rolling my eyes. "Mr Tozer," I began, trying to keep the irritation out of my voice. "The carnival is in a week's time. Even if photos of your float are printed in the *Gazette*, there isn't time for another club to suddenly steal your idea because, as you know, floats take a whole year to build."

He shook his head. "Uh-uh. Still no way."

"Can I at least see the float? See the repairs?" I asked.

"You must think I was born yesterday," he sneered. "You'll have a secret spy camera in your bag."

That time I did roll my eyes. Good grief. A total cock.

Jenny stopped writing and her anxious eyes darted around the farmyard as if she thought we could be surrounded by hidden journalists. "Grant, perhaps we should do the interview inside your house?" she said in a tremulous voice.

Grant shook his head. "No. We'll do it here. Keep writing." He turned to me, his eyes hard. "And you, Missy Reporter, will only write what I tell you to write. I only agreed to this interview because if I didn't, your scummy, gutter-press paper would make up a story anyway."

I felt my anger rise. That way way out of line. You could say a lot of things about the *Gazette* but it wasn't gutter-press, nor were any of the journalists who worked on it. Somehow I managed to stop myself from telling him that.

"Shall we start?" I said through gritted teeth. "The police say someone set your float on fire—"

"That is a huge exaggeration," Grant interrupted.

Jenny stopped writing, went to put her hand on Grant's arm then seemed to change her mind. "If it hadn't been for Grant's quick thinking, it could have been a disaster." She turned to me, her eyes anxious. "We found jerry cans full of petrol in the barn."

338

My eyes widened, "Jerry cans of petrol? That actually sounds very serious—"

"No we didn't!" Grant snapped, shooting Jenny another furious glare.

My pen hovered over the page. "So, were there cans of petrol or not?"

"Not." Grant jutted out his chin and glared at Jenny. "No jerry cans. No petrol." He shook his head. "I have no idea where Jenny got that from. No idea."

Once again Jenny seemed to wither under his glare. "Sorry," she muttered, staring down at her feet. Her Wellington boots made a scuffing sound on the concrete yard. "I... I got confused..." She gave an odd high-pitched giggle, "I don't even know what a jerry can is! What is a jerry can, Grant?"

Grant ignored her.

What an odd woman. And what a vile man.

"The police say the float was attacked on Friday night?" I continued.

"It wasn't an attack," Grant snapped. "I don't want you putting it was an attack. That makes it sound much more serious."

I took a deep breath. "So, what would you call it, Mr Tozer?"

He shrugged. "It was... it was..." He jabbed a finger towards my notebook. "Put it was an incident. A very minor incident."

Good grief. Maybe he'd like to write the story for me. "Okay, when did the *incident* take place, Mr Tozer?"

"Ten o'clock Friday night."

I frowned and tapped my biro against my notepad. "And it happened inside the barn here on the farm?"

He gave a curt nod. "Yes."

339

"And, just to double-check, Hailstones Farm is your farm? You live here?"

Another nod. "Yes. But like I said earlier, you can't put the name of the farm in the story. In fact, don't name me either. Just call me... call me a spokesperson for the carnival club."

I fought to keep my patience. "Why don't you talk me through what happened?"

Grant jammed his hands into the front pockets of his jeans and again rocked back on his heels. "Like I told the police, it was ten o'clock. Pitch dark. The dogs were in but they'd been making a lot of noise. Wouldn't settle. I thought I'd have a quick look around. I let the dogs out and they went haring off across the fields. As I walked across the yard I thought I could smell smoke and when I entered the barn I saw a very small – tiny – area of the float's floor was smouldering. I grabbed a bucket of sand and doused it." He shrugged as if it had been nothing. "Fire went out. Job done. Drama over."

As I scribbled Grant's words in shorthand into my notebook, I thought his speech sounded a little too well rehearsed, as if he'd written it down and memorised it before I'd arrived. "And you were here alone at the farm that night?"

"Correct."

Jenny paused her biro and lowered her voice, "As soon as I heard about it the next day, I reported it to the police. Grant wasn't going to, but I said we had to get a crime number in case we had to make an insurance claim."

Grant rolled his eyes and looked as if he would like to throttle Jenny.

"And did you have to make an insurance claim?" I asked.

"No," Grant snapped.

"Could the fire have started by accident?"

Grant shook his head. "No."

I tried to keep my voice neutral, "A discarded cigarette perhaps?"

Now Grant looked as if he'd like to throttle me. His hands balled into fists. "No one is allowed to smoke inside the barn."

"Grant saw them off," Jenny said her eyes wide with admiration. "He bravely chased the vandals away."

I turned to him. "Did you? Do you know who they were?"

Grant gave a smug smile. "Yes, I chased them off. But no, I couldn't identify the culprits. I only saw their hastily retreating backs in the distance. I think there were three of them, or possibly more. Local kids most likely. They must have scarpered when they heard the dogs." He flashed me an unpleasant smirk. "I wouldn't hang around if I saw two Doberman Pinschers heading towards me out of the dark. Would you?"

I matched his smirk. "Oh... so it was the dogs that chased off the vandals rather than you? Or would you rather I didn't put that in the story either?"

A deep blush spread up Grant's cheeks and he looked away.

I turned to Jenny, "The police said there was some other damage to the float, apart from the fire?"

Once again Grant butted in before Jenny could speak, "There *was* no fire, just a tiny bit of scorched wood. The other damage was tiny... irrelevant."

"What other damage was caused?" I persisted.

He shrugged. "A few scratches, some light bulbs broken. Nothing serious."

"Has it spoiled your chances of winning a prize in the carnival?"

341

Grant gave me a disparaging sneer. "Not in the least. Hunky Dory is one hundred per cent confident of securing the top prize again in this year's parade."

I asked, "What makes you think local kids were behind the damage?"

Grant shrugged. "Sort of thing kids do, isn't it?"

"And the laughter," Jenny said in a helpful voice. "You said you heard laughter, Grant, as they ran away."

Again he gave a shrug. "Well, kids laugh, don't they?"

I kept my eyes fixed on Grant. "Your farm, it's in a very isolated spot, nowhere near any other houses... it seems odd that kids would be messing around out here..."

Again Tozer jutted out his chin. "So?"

"I'm just wondering if the damage was caused by members of a rival carnival club?"

He gave a short laugh like a bark. "Ha! You're not being serious?"

Out of the corner of my eye, I saw Jenny chewing her lips and wringing her hands.

I tapped my biro against my notepad. "Your biggest local rival is Minotaur CC. Do you think they might have been behind the damage?"

Jenny's hands twisted around each other, "Listen, if Minotaur wanted to destroy our cart, they'd have done a proper job. Grant's whole farm would've gone up in flames... probably..." Her voice trailed off under Grant's furious glare.

I raised my eyebrows. "Seriously? The rivalry between the two clubs is that bad?"

Grant gave me an oily smile. He put up his hands in a placatory gesture. "Katy, of course there is a healthy rivalry between our two great clubs. But Hunky Dory has been around for fifty years, whereas Minotaur is only a very recent addition to the carnival circuit. The top prize in the Feature Cart Open category has always gone to us, Hunky Dory, so of course there is rivalry–"

Jenny nodded, "And jealousy–"

Again Grant gave her his death-ray stare.

"But," he continued in the same oily tone, "to suggest that *anyone* from *any* club would stoop so slow as to deliberately sabotage another club's hard work…" He tried to make his face look suitably appalled.

"But it does happen," I said. "It has happened in the past. Not at this club, but at other clubs in the West."

Grant spread his hands. "I have heard stories that once in a blue moon at other clubs some of the more junior members' enthusiasm and competitiveness has got the better of them. But this wasn't – I stress wasn't – carnival rivalry. Like I said, it was just local kids messing about. And the damage was minor. Hardly worth bothering with."

After a pause Jenny said, "We should just be grateful that the damage wasn't worse." She turned me, "Poor *Pete* would have been heartbroken if anything too terrible had happened after all his hard work."

I noticed she'd put an odd emphasis on the man's name. I paused my shorthand. "Pete?"

Jenny nodded, "Pete *Alder*." Once again she seemed to stress his name. "He's the technical genius behind all our carts."

I raised my pen. "Is that spelt A L D E R?"

Grant Tozer put his hand on my wrist. His fingers were surprisingly warm. "I don't think we need mention Pete in the story," he murmured.

I ignored him and turned to Jenny. "Would it be possible to have a few words with Pete Alder? Just to ask him how he feels about the damage?"

Jenny's eyes widened. "Oh… well–"

"Not possible, I'm afraid," Grant cut in. "Pete's away on holiday."

I frowned. "Holiday? This close to the carnival?" I might not be a world expert on the West Country carnivals, but one thing I did know was that no one involved in a club would even think about going on holiday with the carnival just a week away.

Grant looked towards the barn. He put two fingers to his mouth and gave a sharp whistle. The Dobermans immediately got to their paws and started snarling and straining against long, silver chains.

I could tell the dogs were supposed to intimidate me so I tried to ignore them. "Are you worried about another attack on the float?" I asked.

Grant glanced towards the dogs. "What do you think? Now, I'm going to need to approve every word of your story before its printed–"

"Sorry. We don't do that." I flipped my notebook shut. I'd had enough of Grant and Jenny's ridiculous cloak and dagger secrecy. The police could give me a more detailed description of the damage and I'd also ask them about the petrol cans. I flashed Grant a quick and very insincere smile. "Thanks for your time."

"Jenny, the interview is over," he barked. "Stop writing. Go into the kitchen, write up your transcript and make me a coffee."

Poor woman. I watched Jenny trudge away, her notebook again clasped to her chest.

As I turned to walk back to my car, Grant Tozer touched my arm. He leaned his face towards mine and murmured, "You'll regret saying that, Missy."

Mystified, I jerked my head away, "Saying what?"

"The bit about the dogs chasing them off rather than me. You'll live to regret that." Then he turned on his heel and stalked away.

A shiver rippled across my shoulders. I shrugged it off and hurried back towards my car, thinking what a hideous man. Behind me, the Dobermans continued to bay for my blood. Grant strode towards them, calling "Good boys. Good boys."

I hadn't gone very far across the farmyard when I heard quick footsteps behind me. Thinking it might be Tozer coming back for another go at me, I spun around, my fingers clenched into fists. But it was Jenny, her cheeks still bright red. She didn't say a word, just tore a page from her notebook, folded it into four and quickly pressed it into my hand.

From the path, I heard Grant shout, "Jenny! What are you doing? Come here! Now!"

The barking Dobermans were now clipped to flimsy-looking red leads. Their teeth were bared and their jaws were flecked with white foam. Grant and the dogs began to walk towards us.

Jenny's eyes were wide. She gave the smallest shake of her head then turned and trotted towards him. "I was just reminding Katy to go left not right at the junction," I heard her call. "Vole Lane's still got those temporary traffic lights. She'll be stuck for ages if she goes that way."

The Dobermans were looking at me as if I was lunch. I yanked open the car door and threw myself inside.

Once I was a safe distance away from Hailstones Farm I pulled over and unfolded the piece of paper Jenny had given to me. In shaky block capitals it said:

PETE ALDER ISN'T ON HOLIDAY. HE HAS DISAPPEARED.

35672606R00202

Printed in Great Britain
by Amazon